Hartford Ordinances, Connecticut Laws

The Charter and Revised Ordinances of the City of Hartford

with the amendments and other acts relating to the charter, in force January 1,

1884

Hartford Ordinances, Connecticut Laws

The Charter and Revised Ordinances of the City of Hartford
with the amendments and other acts relating to the charter, in force January 1, 1884

ISBN/EAN: 9783337399702

Printed in Europe, USA, Canada, Australia, Japan

Cover: Foto ©Andreas Hilbeck / pixelio.de

More available books at **www.hansebooks.com**

THE

CHARTER

— AND —

REVISED ORDINANCES

— OF THE —

CITY OF HARTFORD,

WITH THE AMENDMENTS AND OTHER ACTS RELATING
TO THE CHARTER. IN FORCE JANUARY 1, 1884.

PUBLISHED BY AUTHORITY OF THE CITY GOVERNMENT,

FEBRUARY. 1884.

HARTFORD:
PRESS OF THE FOWLER & MILLER CO., 341 MAIN STREET.
1884.

PREFACE.

May 23, 1881, a committee, consisting of His Honor the Mayor (Hon. Morgan G. Bulkeley), the City Attorney (S. C. Dunham, Esq.), Messrs. Henry E. Taintor and George W. Fowler from the Board of Aldermen, and Messrs. John H. Brocklesby and Nelson G. Hinckley from the Council Board, were duly appointed to prepare for publication a new edition of the Charter and Ordinances, and to take into consideration that portion of the Mayor's message having reference to consolidation of town and city governments, and report what proceedings were necessary for the completion of the project. Acting under subsequent instructions, said committee prepared and submitted to the General Assembly a draft of a new Charter containing provisions for the consolidation of town and city governments. This Charter, with some amendments and alterations, was passed by the General Assembly at its January session, 1882, but was not adopted when submitted to the people for approval in June, 1882.

After this result was reached, the committee, through a sub-committee, Messrs. Taintor and Brocklesby, and the then City Attorney, Samuel O. Prentice, Esq., directed their attention to the publication of the new edition of the Charter and Ordinances. In doing this, it has been their endeavor to collect and arrange in form for convenient reference all amendments to the Charter, and all general and special laws having reference to the powers and duties of cities and their officers; also, to revise the ordinances, incorporating in the proper place those passed since last revision, and omitting such as have been repealed; and they have also prepared a new index to the volume.

The decisions of our Supreme Court have been extensively consulted, and very many cases bearing upon municipal rights and responsibilities will be found in the foot-notes, under their appropriate heads.

Believing it was not their province to legislate, they have carefully refrained from changing or modifying existing ordinances, seeking rather to give, in compact form, the law as it has been enacted by the present and previous councils. They have aimed to prepare a book that shall be accurate, convenient for use, and with an index furnishing ready means of reference to the topics included in the volume.

In the references, in side and foot notes, the General Statutes of Connecticut have been indicated by the letters R. S.; public laws by the letters P. A.; and private laws by the letters S. A. Except when otherwise noted, the reference to the General Statutes has been to the revision of 1875.

An extract from the preface to the Revision of Charter and Ordinances of 1873, containing facts of historical interest, has been reproduced.

In a work involving a compilation from so many different sources, some errors and omissions have been unavoidable, but the committee submit the result of their labors in the hope that reasonable completeness and accuracy have been attained.

For the committee,

MORGAN G. BULKELEY,

Chairman.

The territory now contained within the limits of the City of Hartford was first settled in the year 1635 by a party of English settlers from Massachusetts, which, forming a nucleus at Hartford and passing through the various stages of growth, in the seventeenth century had become the Town of Hartford. In the year 1784, by a vote of the town, a committee was appointed to draft a memorial to the General Assembly asking for incorporate powers, and on the 29th of May, 1784, a charter was granted, incorporating as the City of Hartford, the territory which is now the center of the city. The original bounds were determined chiefly by the residences of citizens, now changed or lost from sight in the progress of the last century. In the year 1810, the earliest available record of the population of the city, it is stated to be 3,955. Later, in the year 1821, a new charter, combining the various powers added up to this time, was granted by the General Assembly, preserving nearly the former limits.

In 1853 the city limits were enlarged, and in 1859 the present city charter was granted, embodying in substance all powers before possessed, and later, in 1871, the city limits were extended on the south so as to be co-extensive with the southern limits of the Town of Hartford. The powers granted in the original charter were few and exceedingly guarded, and all ordinances permitted to be passed were, as late as the charter of 1859, made repealable by the Superior Court, if, upon a hearing, the same should be found unreasonable. By the charter of 1784 the present City Court was created, and the mayor and the two senior aldermen were constituted its judges, and so remained until the year 1836, when the office of recorder was created. By the charter of 1821, equity jurisdiction was first conferred upon the City Court, and has since been extended so as to embrace (except relief from judgments of the Superior Court) all causes in equity arising within the limits of the city. The state constitution adopted in 1818 preserved the rights before vested in corporations, thus leaving the ancient rights vested in this tribunal at least, until a new amendment beyond the reach of legislative enactment.

The mayor was originally chosen by the freemen of the city, and held his office during the pleasure of the General Assembly, until 1825, when the office of mayor was fixed for the term of two years, and has since so remained. The criminal jurisdiction of the city remained in justices of the peace in the town until the year 1851, when the present Police Court was established, taking to itself exclusive jurisdiction within the limits of the city. Before the adoption of the charter of 1859, certain water debts and other obligations of the city had been created, and were by the charter confirmed and left obligatory on the city, some of which are now outstanding.

CHARTER

OF THE

CITY OF HARTFORD,

ACCEPTED SEPTEMBER 3D, 1859.

AN ACT TO ALTER THE CHARTER OF THE CITY OF HARTFORD, AND TO COMBINE SUNDRY PUBLIC STATUTES RELATING THERETO.

SECTION I.

| Territorial limits. | Corporate name. |
| Property exempt from full taxation. | Jurisdiction and Powers. |

SECTION 1.   The territorial limits of the body politic and *Territorial limits.* corporate heretofore existing under the name of "The Mayor, Aldermen and Common Council, and Freemen, of the City of Hartford," shall hereafter be the following:[1] the north line of said city shall commence at a point on the east bank of the north fork of Park river, seven hundred feet due north of the north line of Albany turnpike road; thence run due east to Connecticut river; the west line of said city shall commence at the first named point, and run thence southward along said bank of said north fork, inclosing a small island formed by a division of said fork, to the westerly line of the Hartford and New Haven railroad;

---

[1] Amended, 1871. See page 39; 1873, page 40; 1881, page 41.

thence continuing due south, across said Park river, to the east bank of the south fork thereof; thence along said east bank and the east bank of the east branch of said south fork to a point two hundred and fifty feet due south of the south line of the New Britain road (so called); the south line of the said city shall run from the point last described, east to Connecticut river; and said river shall be the east boundary

of said city: *provided always*, that no city tax[2] exceeding two cents on a dollar of the grand list, shall be assessed or levied upon any land or lands within the territory added to said city by virtue of this act, so long as said land is or shall be used exclusively for farming purposes, or is vacant and unoccupied land; and that all farming produce, and all stock used in farming, and all implements of husbandry, belonging to persons residing on said territory so annexed, shall be exempt in the same manner and to the same extent from such city

taxation: *and, provided also*, that the persons now and hereafter residing on said territory so added to said city, and the estate of such persons, both real and personal, shall not be liable by taxation or in any other mode, for any bonded debt of said city, or for interest on the same, or for any part of the present indebtedness of said city on account of the city park, provided that this act shall not be so construed as to exempt from liability any property invested in business in said city and now liable to taxation for said city debt. All the inhabitants of the State of Connecticut, being electors thereof, dwelling within said limits, shall continue forever hereafter, to be a body politic and corporate, in fact and in

name, by the name of "THE CITY OF HARTFORD;" and that by that name they and their successors shall and may have

perpetual succession, and be persons in law, capable of suing and being sued, pleading and being impleaded, in all suits of what nature soever; and also to purchase, hold, and convey any estate, real and personal; and may have a common seal, and may change and alter the same at pleasure; and shall be electors of said city; and by virtue of this act, shall become

---

[2] Amended, 1860. See page 166; 1867, page 167; 1871, page 39; 1873, page 40; 1881, page 41.

and be absolutely vested with, possess, and enjoy, all the lands, tenements, hereditaments, property and rights, choses in action, and estate whatsoever, which since the time of the original incorporation of said city have become vested in the inhabitants of said city in their corporate capacity, and which in that capacity are still vested in and belong to said inhabitants, that is to say, in the said city; and said city shall have jurisdiction in civil and commercial matters on the Connecticut river opposite the town of Hartford; and the marshal and deputy marshals of said city shall have authority to execute legal process on said river opposite said town; *it being provided*, that said city shall in no manner regulate[3] or interfere with the navigation thereof, or impose any tax, toll, or duty, on the commerce upon said river.

(margin: Connecticut river jurisdiction.)

SECTION II.

Annual meetings; when and where held.	Water Commissioners; when and how
Number of Wards.	chosen and term of office.
Mayor; when and how chosen.	City Collector; when and how chosen
Powers and terms of office.	and duties.
City Marshal; when and how chosen	City Auditor; when and how chosen.
and powers.	Aldermen and Common Councilmen;
City Clerk, when and how chosen and	when chosen, and term of office.
duties.	Vacancy on tie vote; how filled.
City Treasurer; when and how chosen	
and powers.	

Annual meetings of said city (except the first) shall be held at such times and places as the ordinances thereof shall direct; and shall be held in wards into which said city shall be divided by its ordinances; the number of which wards shall not exceed seven.[1] And at such annual meetings there shall be chosen by said city, by a plurality of ballots, a mayor, who shall be the chief executive officer of said city, and conservator of the peace therein, and have for that purpose,

(margin: Annual city meetings.)

(margin: Wards, number of.)

(margin: Mayor; duties and powers.)

---

[3] Amended. See page 55.
[1] Amended, 1869. See page 42; 1871, page 39; 1873, page 40; 1876, page 45; 1881, page 42.

and especially for the suppression of riots and tumults within the limits of said city, all the powers of a sheriff of the county of Hartford, including due authority to raise the power of the county and the militia thereof, which authority shall be obeyed in the same manner and under the same penalties as that of sheriffs in like cases; and the mayor shall also have all the power necessary to the due execution of the ordinances of said city, when in such ordinance he shall be directed to execute the same; and he shall hold
Term of office. his office for two years, and until his successor shall be
City marshal; and powers of. chosen; a city marshal,[a] who shall have within the limits of said city the same power and authority as sheriffs of counties, and be liable for neglect of duty in the same manner; and shall in case of riots within said city, be subject to the direction of the mayor; and said marshal shall be empowered
Deputy marshals. to appoint deputy marshals, with like power, not exceeding
City clerk. two in number; a clerk,[2] who shall record all the votes and proceedings of said city, and whose records shall have like validity,[b] as evidence and otherwise, with those of town
City treasurer. clerks; a treasurer, who shall have the same power and authority as town treasurers, and shall be accountable to said
Water commissioner. city; a water commissioner,[3] who shall hold his office for four
Collector. years from the time of his election; a collector,[4] who shall col-
Auditor. lect all taxes imposed by said city; and an auditor of city accounts. At the annual meeting of said city, holden next after this act shall take effect, to wit, on the second Monday of April, A. D. 1860, for the choice of the aforesaid officers, there shall be chosen, by plurality vote in each ward,
Aldermen and common councilmen; how chosen; term of office. from among the electors entitled to vote therein, two aldermen and four common councilmen; and one of said aldermen

---

[a] Marshal may serve within the city processes returnable to other courts. Dow v. Kelley, 1 Root, 552.

[2] Clerk *pro tempore.* See page 47.

[b] Clerk may at any time while in office correct his record. Boston Turnpike Co. v. Pomfret, 20 Conn., 590.

Record can not be affected by parol evidence in collateral proceeding. Gilbert v. New Haven, 40 Conn., 102.

Records amended only by Clerk in office or by Court upon mandamus. Samis v. King, 40 Conn., 298.

[3] See *post*, Section XXIV, page 27. Amended, 1865. See page 52; 1872, page 53.

[4] Amended, 1878. See page 170: see page 171.

chosen in each ward shall hold office for one year, and the other for two years, and until their successors are chosen and qualified; and in case of a tie vote, the vacancy in the office Vacancy on tie vote; how filled. of alderman or common councilman, shall be filled at a new election to be held on the next day, for the special purpose of filling such vacancy; and at all subsequent annual meetings held for the choice of the aforesaid officers, there shall be chosen, as aforesaid, in each ward, one alderman and four common councilmen; and such alderman shall hold his office Terms of office. for two years, and until his successor shall be chosen and qualified. And all the aforesaid officers, whose term is not hereinbefore prescribed, shall hold office for one year, and until others are chosen and qualified in their stead.

SECTION III.

Qualifications of Voters.

Every elector of the State, residing in said city, at the time Electors must reside in the city four months. of any city meeting, and who shall have resided in said city four months next preceding the day of said meeting, may vote in such meeting: *provided always*, that no person not legally settled in the town of Hartford, shall vote in city Unless resident of town, must reside one year in city. meeting until he shall have resided in said city one year next preceding the day of said meeting: *and provided further*, that no person shall vote in any ward meeting, held for the choice of city officers, unless he shall have resided in such ward Must reside in ward sixty days. sixty days next preceding the day of said ward meeting. If any person, otherwise qualified to vote in said city meeting, shall have removed from one ward to another within said Removal within sixty days; where to vote. sixty days, he shall be entitled to vote in the ward in which he last resided before his removal.[1]

---

[1] Amended, 1877. See page 75.

SECTION IV.

Duties of City Clerk.   Penalty for false swearing.
Duties of Presiding Officer of Ward meet-
ings.

*City clerk to pre-
pare a list of city
voters.*
The clerk of the City of Hartford shall, during the week
next preceding the time of holding any annual city meeting
for the choice of city officers of said city, prepare a list, as
nearly perfect as is practicable, of the names of all persons
entitled to vote in each and every ward in said city, at the
said city meeting, and of the street in which each such
person resides, and the number of location of his residence in
such street, which names shall be duly arranged in alphabeti-
cal order; for which service said city clerk shall be paid a
*Compensation of
clerk.*
reasonable compensation from the city treasury; and any
elector of such city shall be entitled to demand and receive
of such city clerk a copy of any list so made as aforesaid, on
paying therefor the same fees as town clerks are by law entitled to receive for copies of records.   The presiding officer of
*Ward meetings, and
duties of presiding
officer.*
every ward meeting may receive the votes of all persons
whose names are on the ward list prepared as aforesaid, unless the right of any such person to vote at said ward
meeting is challenged; and if any person whose name is not
on said list shall offer to vote at said meeting, such person
*Persons not allowed
to vote in certain
cases.*
shall thereupon be required to inform the presiding officer of
said ward meeting of the street in which he resides, and the
number or location of his residence in such street, and the
said presiding officer, if of the opinion that the person so
offering to vote is legally entitled so to do, shall thereupon
see that the name of such person, and of said street, and said
number or location is entered upon said list, and may then
receive his vote, unless the right of such person so to vote is
challenged.   In case any person offering to vote at any such
ward meeting, shall have willfully refused to furnish to the
city clerk, or to the proper presiding officer, full and satisfactory information of his name, the street in which he resides,
and the number or location of his residence, said presiding

officer shall not allow such person to cast his vote at such meeting. If the vote of any person shall be challenged as aforesaid, it shall be the duty of the presiding officer, before receiving such vote, if thereto requested by the challenger, to administer an oath to the person offering to vote, and to make due inquiry into the right of such person to vote, and to hear and determine such challenge; and if of the opinion that such person is entitled to vote at such ward meeting, to cause his name and residence to be registered as aforesaid, and to receive his vote. Any person who shall be guilty of willful false swearing, when examined as aforesaid, by any presiding officer, shall be liable to the penalties of perjury; and if any person not under oath shall willfully give a false statement when so examined by the presiding officer, relative to the right of himself or any other person to vote, he shall forfeit the sum of fifty dollars to the treasury of the State.[1]

Presiding officer may administer oath.

False swearing and false statement; penalties for.

SECTION V.

Duties of Presiding Officer of Ward Meetings.

Such presiding officer shall check or cause to be checked the name of each person voting at such ward meeting, at the time his vote shall be received, and shall erase or cause to be erased from said list the name of every person who shall be found not entitled to vote at such ward meeting, in manner aforesaid; and within twenty-four hours after the final adjournment of said meeting, the said list, with the marks and checks thereon, shall, by such presiding officer, be lodged in the office of the city clerk, where the same shall be kept on file, and carefully preserved.[1]

List to be checked and returned to the city clerk's office.

---

[1] Amended, 1877. See page 79.
[1] Amended, 1877. See page 76.

SECTION VI.

Court of Common Council; how com- | Vote appropriating more than ten thou-
posed; powers of. | sand dollars invalid.
Vote of; subject to approval by Mayor. |

What Court of Common Council shall consist of.

There shall be a court of common council of said city, which shall consist of two separate branches, a board of aldermen and the common council board, who shall convene separately, except in the cases hereinafter specified, and in

Powers of.

whom shall be vested the government, control, and management of said city, its property and its affairs, subject to the exceptions hereinafter set forth. The board of aldermen shall be composed of all the aldermen of said city, and the common council board of all the common councilmen of said

Each board judges of election of its members.

city; and each branch of said court shall be final judge of the election returns, and validity of elections and qualifications of its own members. Every vote, resolution, ordi-

Mayor's approval of votes, etc.

nance, or by-law in the passage of which both the branches of said court shall have concurred by a majority of each, shall be submitted to the mayor for his approval; and if not by him disapproved, the same shall become valid and effectual

After disapproval, how passed.

as a corporate act of said city; if disapproved, the same shall be by him returned to the next court of common council, each board of which shall thereupon reconsider the vote, resolution, ordinance, or by-law, and if a majority of each board shall thereupon concur in again adopting or enacting the same, it shall thereupon become a valid, corporate act; it

Expenditure limited to $10,000,

being expressly provided, that no vote or resolution of said common council, ordering a public work or improvement which shall require an expenditure of more than ten thou-

Unless same be approved by city vote by ballot.

sand dollars, shall be obligatory on said city, unless approved by a majority vote of a city meeting, duly warned and holden for that purpose; which vote shall be by ballot.[*]

---

[*] Applies only to improvements which affect the public at large and are paid for by the city. Park Ecclesiastical Society *et al.* v. Hartford, 47 Conn., 89.

SECTION VII.

REPEALED.

See substitute act, page 96.[1]

SECTION VIII.

| What ordinances Common Council may make and repeal. | Violation of ordinances; what are misdemeanors, and penalties for the same. |

The Court of Common Council shall have power,[a] by a majority of the members of each branch, present and absent, subject to the approval or disapproval of the mayor, as aforesaid, to make, alter, and repeal ordinances for the following purposes:[2]

Court of Common Council have power to make, alter and repeal ordinances for certain purposes.

To regulate trade, markets, and commerce, and to regulate weights and measures, in conformity with the lawful standards thereof, within the limits of said city:

Trade, markets and measures.

To manage, regulate, and control the finances and property, real and personal, of the city, and regulate the borrowing of money by the city for any purpose for which said court are authorized to lay taxes under the restrictions of this act;[3] to provide for the due authentication, execution, and delivery of deeds, grants, and releases of city property, and evidences of debt issued by said city; to prevent and secure the removal of all nuisances injurious to health, or offensive to the public, at the expense of the owner of the premises where such nuisance exists, or otherwise; for the laying out, altering, establishing and making highways, streets, parks, public grounds and walks, openings for the circulation of air, building lines, drains and sewers; to drain

Finances, property, and loans.

Execution of instruments.

Nuisances.

Highways, etc.

---

[1] See also page 50.

[2] See pages 51, 99, 100, 128, 133, 134, 148, 156, 174.

[3] Amended, 1863, page 85: 1870, page 86.

[a] Whenever the performance of a public duty is imposed the powers necessary for its full performance are impliedly given. New Haven v. Sargent, 38 Conn., 50.

and raise low lands; to make, repair, purify, light and keep
open and safe for public use and travel, and free from
encroachment or obstruction, the streets, highways,[b] pass-
ways and public grounds and places in said city, which is
hereby constituted a highway district by itself; to secure the
safety of persons passing through or in the same, by regulat-

Fireworks, shows, etc.

---

[b] No obligation rests upon the city at common law to repair highways. This
obligation is wholly statutory. Chidsey v. Canton, 17 Conn., 475; Stonington v.
States, 31 Conn., 213.

The city is bound to keep in repair all the highways within its limits. Manchester v. Hartford, 30 Conn., 118.

The duty to repair involves the duty of reasonable supervision. Manchester v.
Hartford, 30 Conn., 118; Cusick v. Norwich, 40 Conn., 274.

City bound to remove obstructions. Hawley v. Harrall, 19 Conn., 142.

What are defects. Hewison v. New Haven, 34 Conn., 136; Lee v. Barkhamsted, 46
Conn., 213; Wilson v. Granby, 47 Conn., 59; Burr v. Plymouth, 48 Conn., 460.

Objects in or near highway, calculated to frighten horses of ordinary gentleness
are defects. Dimock v. Suffield, 30 Conn., 129; Ayer v. Norwich, 39 Conn., 376;
Young v. New Haven, 39 Conn., 435.

An erection in the highway, though not in the traveled path, may be a nuisance.
State v. Merrit, 35 Conn., 314.

City liable for defective sidewalk. Manchester v. Hartford, 30 Conn., 118.

Liability for snow and ice on sidewalk. Congdon v. Norwich, 37 Conn., 414;
Landolt v. Norwich, 37 Conn., 615; Boucher v. New Haven, 40 Conn., 456; Dooley v.
Meriden, 44 Conn., 117.

Adjoining proprietor not liable to city when snow and ice accumulates from natural causes. Hartford v. Talcott *et al.*, 48 Conn., 525.

Iron grating in sidewalk, when and when not a defect. Littlefield v. Norwich, 40
Conn., 406.

Discontinued highway to be guarded. Munson v. Derby, 37 Conn., 298.

Liability for defective bridges and railings. Eldridge v. Pomfret, 1 Root, 270;
Swift v. Kent, 1 Root, 448; Lewis v. Litchfield, 2 Root, 436; Daniels v. Saybrook, 34
Conn., 377; Thorp v. Brookfield, 36 Conn., 320; Bronson v. Southbury, 37 Conn., 199;
Ward v. North Haven, 43 Conn., 148.

What evidence admissible on question of defect. Calkins v. Hartford, 33 Conn., 57.

Secret defect in carriage or harness contributing to the injury will not preclude
recovery. Baldwin v. Greenwoods Turnpike Company, 40 Conn., 238.

City liable for negligent performance or non-performance of a private duty.
Jones v. New Haven, 34 Conn., 1.

Not liable if it is a public governmental duty. Hewison v. New Haven, 37 Conn.,
475.

City liable for nuisance created by performing lawful act in unlawful manner.
Mootry v. Danbury, 45 Conn., 550; Healey v. New Haven, 47 Conn., 305; Morse
v. Fair Haven, 48 Conn., 220.

As to what constitutes notice of a defect. Manchester v. Hartford, 30 Conn., 118;
Boucher v. New Haven, 40 Conn., 456; Cusick v. Norwich, 40 Conn., 375; Littlefield
v. Norwich, 40 Conn., 406.

Notice to a citizen is not notice to the city. Bill v. Norwich, 39 Conn., 222.

The written notice of injury required by statute cannot be waived by town agent.
Hoyle v. Putnam, 46 Conn., 56.

As to requisites of notice, see Shaw v. Waterbury, 46 Conn., 263.

Macadamizing a street is not a public improvement. New Haven v. Whitney *et
al.*, 36 Conn., 373.

Liability for obstructions without highway limits. Beardsley v. Hartford, 50
Conn., —.

ing fireworks, shows, parades and rendezvous, processions and music, the speed of animals, vehicles and cars, the run- *Speed of animals.* ning at large of animals through or in any part of said city, and the impounding of the same; to protect and preserve trees and other ornaments of public places; to regulate or *Excavation of streets, removal of buildings, etc.* prohibit the excavation or opening of streets, highways, and public grounds for public or private purposes, and the location of any work or thing therein, whether temporary or permanent, upon or under the surface thereof, and the removal of buildings upon or through the same; to keep the same quiet and orderly, and free from undue noise upon the *Lord's day.* Lord's day, and regulate and prohibit the ringing of bells, and crying of goods in said city; and to protect the state *State House yard.* house yard in said city, and all things appertaining thereto; to restrain cruelty to animals, and inhuman sports; to pre- *Cruelty to animals.* scribe the forms of proceeding in all cases of taking land *Taking lands.* for public use within said city, not specially prescribed in this act; to prevent vice and immorality, preserve public *Peace, good order and morals.* peace and good order; prevent and quell riots and disorderly assemblages, suppress gambling houses, and houses of ill fame, and disorderly houses; and to confer upon the mayor and police officers of the city all powers necessary for such purposes; to prohibit, restrain, license and regulate all sports, *Amusements, billiard saloons, etc.* exhibitions, public amusements and performances, and billiard and bowling saloons within said city:[*]

To regulate or prohibit swimming or bathing in public or *Swimming or bathing.* exposed places within said city; to prevent and punish trespasses in gardens, cemeteries, and enclosures, and public *Trespasses.* buildings:

To regulate the burial of the dead, and provide for the *Burial of the dead, and returns of.* registration and return of the deaths and burials in said city:

To regulate the mode of taxation for city purposes: *Taxation.*

To provide and regulate and prescribe the duties of a city *Police force.* watch, and police force; and to confer upon city watchmen and policemen the ordinary powers of constables of towns, within the limits of said city; and to punish the resistance,

---

[*] When a corporation is authorized to grant licenses, the power to charge a reasonable sum therefor is implied. Welch v. Hotchkiss, 39 Conn., 140.

or obstruction of public officers in the discharge of their duty:

Fire department and fires. To organize and regulate a fire department and fire apparatus; to protect said city from exposure to fire, regulate the mode of building, and the materials used for building, or altering buildings within said city, or any part thereof, and the mode of using any buildings therein, when such regulations seem expedient for the purpose of preserving said city from the dangers of fire:[d]

Public hacks. To license and regulate public hacks or carriages, the charges of hackmen and public drivers, cartmen, and truckmen:

Gunpowder. To prohibit and regulate the bringing in, carrying out or through, or storing gunpowder in said city:

Oaths. To provide forms of oaths for all officers of said city elected by city meeting, or appointed by the court of the common council:

Width of streets, etc. To regulate the width of streets, highways, and alleys:

Warning of city meetings. To provide for the manner of warning city meetings, and meetings of the court of common council, and times and places of holding the same:

Vacancies. To provide for the filling of vacancies[f] which may occur in any office appertaining to said city, or may exist in consequence of a tie vote at any city election, for the unexpired term of such office:

Bonds and penalties. To provide for bonds[e] and sureties of any officer chosen by said city, or by said court of common council, and penalties for the refusal of any such officer, or of any juror of the city **Election and duties of certain officers.** court to serve: to provide for the election and prescribe the

---

[d] The fire department, when engaged in extinguishing fires, is performing a public governmental duty, and the city is not responsible for the acts of its members. Jewett v. New Haven, 38 Conn., 368.

Same principle applied to volunteer company. Torbush v. Norwich, 38 Conn., 225.

An ordinance forbidding the erection of wooden buildings within fire limits, without a license therefor, and providing for their removal, held to be authorized by charter and reasonable. Hine *et al.* v. New Haven, 40 Conn., 478.

[f] Amended, 1872. See page 53.

[e] As to liability of bondsmen of public officers, see Hartford v. Franey *et al.*, 47 Conn., 76.

duties of city surveyors, port wardens, coroners,[5] street commissioners, public weighers, officers of the fire department, sealers of weights and measures, health officers, inspectors of any kind of produce of the United States, brought to said city for sale or exhibition, and such other functionaries[6][f] as are proper for the administration of the affairs of said city, *Trade and commerce.* and the proper regulation of trade and commerce thereof:

To provide for the election and prescribe the duties of offi- *Officers of Court of Common Council.* cers of said court, including the clerks of each board:

To provide for the mode of keeping of the accounts of said *Keeping of accounts.* city:

To prescribe the place and manner of holding the annual *Elections.* election of said city in the wards thereof: to designate the persons who shall preside at said election, and who may examine persons offering to vote, under oath; the mode of balloting and conducting such elections, and all the incidents thereof, except in matters expressly regulated by this act:[7] to provide for or continue the division of said city into wards[8] *Wards.* for the election of all city officers: to prevent illegal voting *Illegal voting.* at city meetings: to regulate the duties of the collector of *Taxes.* city taxes, and to provide the mode of collecting the same:[9]

To confer the freedom of the city on persons living out of *Freedom of the city.* the limits of the same:

To regulate the location of stationary steam boilers, barns, *Steam boilers, etc.* and out-houses, sinks, and drains, in said city:

To prescribe the salaries and compensation of all officers *Salaries and compensation.* of said city,[10] and the duties of such officers, not expressly defined by the provisions of this act:[11][g]

---

[5] Amended, 1883, see page 57.
[6] Amended, 1872. See page 53; see page 147.
[f] Certain officers held to be public officers and the city not liable for their acts performed while engaged in their official duties. Judge v. City of Meriden, 38 Conn., 90; Jewett v. New Haven, 38 Conn., 368; Mead v. New Haven, 40 Conn., 72.
[7] Amended, 1877. See page 74.
[8] Amended, 1869. See page 42; 1876, see page 45.
[9] Amended, 1866. See page 167.
[10] Amended, 1866. See page 169; 1881, see page 65; see, also, page 67.
[11] Amended, 1869. See page 48; 1861, see page 175.
[g] City may indemnity a public officer for loss sustained by him in the performance of his official duty, but the duty must have been authorized or imposed by law and the matter one in which the city had an interest. Gregory v. Bridgeport, 41 Conn., 76.

Highways, etc.

To carry out all the powers conferred and duties imposed on said court by the seventh section of this act:

Dead bodies.

To prevent illegal practices with dead bodies in medical institutions or elsewhere in said city:

Coroner and juries of inquest.

To prescribe the mode of appointing a coroner,[12] his duties and compensation, and the duties and compensation of other persons engaged in proceedings by or before such coroner, including juries of inquest: which said coroner, for the purpose of arresting persons suspected of being the cause of the death of another, and summoning juries of inquest, shall have all the power of justices of the peace: and his process shall be returnable to the police court of said city, in which court he shall have, relative to such suspected persons, all the powers of a grand juror:

Assessment lien on land.

To provide that assessments of benefits[h] for any public work shall be a lien[13] upon the land or real estate, on account of which said assessment is made: which lien may be foreclosed at the suit of the city, in the same manner as a mortgaged incumbrance:

Removal of officers.

To provide for the removal or expulsion of any officer on account of corruption or misfeasance in office:

Oaths.

To prescribe oaths of city officers, and to authorize the mayor[14] to administer oaths in all courts:

Courts.

To prescribe the time and place of holding the courts of said city, where no express provision is made concerning the same in this act.

Penalties and forfeitures.

And said court of common council may impose and inflict penalties and forfeitures of goods and chattels, for the violations of such ordinance;[1] which penalties and forfeitures shall be recoverable by the attorney of the city before the city

---

[12] Amended, 1883. See page 57.

[h] Mortgagee's interest liable to pay city lien for improvement. Norwich v. Hubbard *et al.*, 22 Conn., 587.

Assessment for local improvements is not a tax. Bridgeport v. N. Y. and N. H. R. R. Co., 36 Conn., 255.

[13] Amended, 1877. See page 110; 1883, page 111.

[14] Amended, 1863. See page 37.

[1] Penalty for violation of city-law, how affected when same ground is covered by general statute. State v. Welch, 36 Conn., 215.

Several penalties incurred by a single act may be sued for in one action. Barkhamsted v. Parsons, 3 Conn., 1.

court in an action of debt, brought in the name of the city of Hartford, for the use of the city treasury; and in such action no appeal shall be allowed. The violation of any ordinance or by-law relative to nuisances injurious to health, *Misdemeanors.* illegal voting, obstructions of highways, if malicious, illegal charges of hackmen, and weights and measures, or any by-law or ordinance designed to prevent vice, immorality, or disorder, or the obstruction and resistance of officers, shall be a misdemeanor,[15] and may be prosecuted as such before the city police court, like other offences, which court may inflict therefor the penalty named in such by-law, and enforce the same in the same manner as other judgments of said city police court are enforced;[j] provided that no penalty, or forfeit- *Limitation of forfeiture.* ure of goods, other than such forfeiture as shall indirectly accrue by the abatement of nuisances, shall exceed the sum of fifty dollars for a single offence; except in the case of the illegal sale and transportation of gunpowder, for which, when the quantity of the same sold or transported exceeds twenty-five pounds, a penalty at the rate of one dollar per pound for the excess may be imposed. In addition to said penalty, said court may by their ordinances, subject to four-fold city *Four-fold city taxation.* taxation any building erected or added to, or removed, or located, in violation of any by-law or ordinance designed to save said city from the perils of fire, or to keep streets and public places free from encroachment and obstructions.

SECTION IX.

Publication of Ordinances.

Every ordinance[1] of said city shall be published ten days *Ordinances, how published.* at least in two or more daily papers issued within the City of Hartford, before it shall take effect; and the certificate of the city clerk upon the record of such ordinance, that the same has been so published, shall be *prima facie* evidence

---

[15] Amended, 1862. See page 128; see also page 134.

[j] This provision not unconstitutional. State v. Tryon, 39 Conn., 183.

[1] Amended, 1860. See page 135; 1872, see page 135.

thereof, in any suit or proceeding; and no ordinance shall be
valid if repugnant to the laws of the State.

SECTION X.

Certain duties of Mayor, City Clerk, and | Quorum of Common Council.
    Board of Aldermen.

Mayor the presiding officer.

May give casting vote, when.

Clerks of Common Council.

Acting president, and powers of.

Quorum.

The mayor shall be the presiding officer of the board of
aldermen, and of all joint conventions of the court of common council, and be empowered to give a casting vote in all
cases where the action of either said board or convention
shall result in a tie.* The city clerk shall be *ex officio* clerk
of the board of aldermen; and the common council board
may choose a clerk who shall not be a member of said board.
It shall be the duty of the board of aldermen to choose one
of their own number as acting president of said board, who
shall have all the powers and discharge all the duties of the
mayor during the absence of the mayor or any temporary
vacancy in the office of mayor.   One-half of either board of
the court of common council shall constitute a quorum thereof.   The six aldermen, among those chosen at the first annual
meeting, who shall hold office for two years, shall be designated by lot within ten days after said meeting; and lots
shall be drawn under the superintendence of the mayor,
who shall certify the result of said drawing in some public
manner.

SECTION XI.

Jurisdiction and Powers of City Court.

City Court to be holden when.

Jurisdiction.

A city court of said city shall continue to be holden in
said city on the first Monday of each month; and to have
power to adjourn from time to time; and shall continue to
have cognizance of the cases of which it now has jurisdiction
by virtue of the original charter of said city and of subsequent amendments thereof; and its jurisdiction[1] is hereby

---

* As to what constitutes tie vote see State *ex rel.* Cole v. Chapman, 44 Conn., 595.
[1] Amended. See page 58.

declared to embrace all cases either at law or in equity, whenever the cause of action shall arise or have arisen within the limits of said city,[a] or concerns land within said limits, and one or both parties live within the same,[b] and any suit or action that may be commenced in favor of any bank, located in said city, upon any writing obligatory, payable by the terms of it at said bank, or endorsed to said bank. Said city court shall continue to have power to proceed to try, decide, and enforce judgment and execution, in cases within its jurisdiction, in the same manner as the superior court; and its executions shall be served and returned in the same manner as superior court executions. An appeal[c] shall be *Appeals.* allowed and certified in due form of law at the first term to which any suit at law is returnable, and before trial to the jury, from the judgment or determination of said city court in such suit, when the matter in demand exceeds one hundred dollars, to the next superior court to be holden in Hartford county; but if it shall appear to the court that such appeal is taken for delay only, then such court may at their discretion, upon application of the plaintiff at the term when such judgment is rendered, grant execution for the amount of such judgment, notwithstanding the appeal, and the same may be enforced according to law: *provided*, that the plaintiff *Execution to issue upon bond.* before taking out execution, shall enter into a recognizance

---

[a] Declaration must show that cause of action arose within the city. Strong v. Avery, 1 Root, 260; Maples v. Wightman, 4 Conn., 376; Hart v. Stevenson, 25 Conn., 499.

A note delivered within the city, though executed elsewhere, is within the jurisdiction of the City Court. Champion v. Mumford, Kirby, 172.

An action on a letter of guaranty written and directed out of the city, but delivered to the plaintiff within the city, is not within the jurisdiction of City Court. Austin v. Fitch, 1 Root, 289.

A judgment of the City Court for a cause of action that arose without the city is wholly void. Austin v. Fitch, 1 Root, 290.

[b] Not necessary to appear that either party lived within the limits of city when cause of action arose. Richards v. Steward, 2 Day, 328.

It must be alleged that one of the parties resides in the city. Nichols v. Shaw, 1 Root, 318.

What constitutes "residence." Charter Oak Bank v. Reed, 45 Conn., 391.

City Court has jurisdiction in *scire facias* where original judgment was rendered in said court, irrespective of residence of parties. Sherwood v. Stevenson, 25 Conn., 431.

As to necessary allegations in such case. *ib.*

[c] *Scire facias* upon foreign attachment is a "suit at law" which may be appealed to the Superior Court. White v. Washington School District, 45 Conn., 59.

before said court, with two sufficient sureties, in double the value of the property or sum recovered by said judgment, that he will, within one week after final judgment in the appellate court, fully restore the property taken and repay the sum collected by virtue of said execution, (including fees for levying the same,) with interest on such entire sums, to the full extent to which such judgment shall be reversed and reduced upon such final judgment; and no appeal shall be allowed on any suit commenced on said recognizance.

SECTION XII.

| City Court; how composed. Judges; how appointed. | City Attorney; how appointed and duties. |

City Court, how composed.

Judges; how appointed. Term of office.

Said court shall continue to be composed of a recorder, who shall be chief judge, and two associate judges of said court;[1] and after the expiration of the term of the present recorder and judges, the recorder shall·hold office for two years, and until his successor shall be appointed; and the associate judges for one year, and until their successors shall be appointed; and they shall be appointed by a major vote[a] of the entire court of common council in joint convention assembled, at such time as the by-laws or ordinances of said city shall prescribe. And said court shall appoint and swear

Clerk of; duties and authority.

a clerk of such court, who shall continue in office during pleasure, and shall be sworn in to a faithful discharge of his duties, and shall give bonds therefor, if required to do so by the by-laws or ordinances of said city; and the said clerk shall have, in matters pertaining to said court, the same

City attorney; how appointed.

authority as clerks of the superior court. And an attorney of the city, who shall be counsel to the corporation, and

Duties and compensation of, how prescribed.

whose duties and compensation shall be fixed by a by-law or

---

[1] Amended, 1872. See page 61.

[a] What constitutes a "major vote." State ex rel. Cole v. Chapman, 44 Conn., 595. Blank ballot should be counted. ib.

Where each of two candidates received an equal number of votes and there was also a blank ballot, held that mayor could not give casting vote. ib.

ordinance of said city, shall be appointed in the same manner as the recorder at such time as said ordinance shall prescribe, and shall hold office for one year, and until his successor shall be appointed and qualified.

SECTION XIII.

Vacancies in City Court; how filled. Fees and Appeals in same.

If any member of said court shall be absent or disqualified, the remaining judges, whenever such absence or disqualification is not waived by the parties to the suit on trial, may fill the vacancy or vacancies by calling in place of each absent judge a justice of the peace residing in the county of Hartford; and the court so constituted shall be, for the time being, the city court.[1] If all the judges shall be absent or disqualified at any time when said court should be holden according to law, the mayor shall designate three justices of the peace of the county of Hartford to hold said court, who shall for the time being, constitute such court. Vacancies for the unexpired term of any judge shall be filled in the same manner as said judges are to be appointed. Continuances and defaults of cases may be ordered and caused to be entered, by any one judge, or two judges of said court if no more are present. The taxable fees of the city court shall be prescribed by a by-law or ordinance of said city.[2] All appeals from judgments rendered by justices of the peace residing within the said city shall continue to be taken and allowed, as by law provided, to the city court.[3]

Temporary vacancy provided for.

Provision for the absence of all the judges.

Vacancies; how filled.

Continuances and defaults.

Taxable fees.

Appeals.

SECTION XIV.

City Court; motion in Error.

Whenever final judgment or decree is rendered in said court in any cause in which a party may be entitled to a

---

[1] Amended, 1871. See page 69.
[2] Amended, 1881. See page 66; 1881, see page 73,
[3] Amended, 1869. See page 59.

Motion in error.

writ of error[1] to the superior court, such party may, in the same term and within twenty-four hours after final judgment or decree, file his motion[2] that the record in such cause may

Transmission of records.

be transmitted to the next superior court in Hartford county; and thereupon such city court shall have the same powers with reference to such motions as are given to the superior court upon similar motions in the superior court for the transmission of records to the supreme court of errors, and

Copy of record; where entered.

upon the allowance of such a motion, a copy of the record shall be entered on file in the next superior court for said county, which shall proceed therein as on a writ of error,

Stay of execution.

and said city court may, upon allowing said motion, stay execution whenever it shall think proper so to do.

SECTION XV.

City Court; service of process.

Service.

When the defendant who is sued to said city court at law or in equity lives within the limits of said city, the writ shall be served upon him at least six days before the sitting of the court to which the same is returnable; but if the defendant lives without the limits of said city, the writ shall be served at least twelve days before the sitting of the court; and all

Return.

writs returnable to the city court shall be returned to said court before the first opening thereof.

SECTION XVI.

City Court: Neglect to serve writ to, how punished.

Neglect of officer to serve writ.

In case any sheriff, deputy sheriff or constable shall not serve a writ directed to and received by him, that is returnable to the city court, or shall neglect to make return of said writ, or shall make a false return thereof, and a suit for such default be brought against him to such city court by the

---

[1] Amended, 1882. See page 70; 1881, see page 70.
[2] Amended, 1874. See page 69; 1882, see page 70.

person, his executor or administrator, in whose favor the suit issued, and the defendant be found in default, the court over and above awarding just damages to the party, shall, on said suit, set a suitable fine on the defendant, according to the *Penalty.* nature of the case, and may issue execution for the same, which fine shall be to the treasury of the city.*

SECTION XVII.

Jurors of City Court; how appointed. | Issues of fact; how tried by agreement.

The board of aldermen shall hold a special meeting at *Jurors of City Court.* such time and place as the by-laws or ordinances of said city shall prescribe, for the choice of not less than seventy nor more than one hundred and fifty electors of said city to serve as jurors at said city court: *provided*, that the judges thereof may try and decide all issues of fact which come before *Issues of fact; how tried.* them, by themselves, or by a jury of six when the parties shall agree to it. The mode of returning the names of the city jurors, and of putting the same in a box for the purpose of drawing the same, and of summoning said jurors, and the *City jurors; how returned and drawn.* form of the oath by them to be taken, shall be fixed by ordinance of said city.

SECTION XVIII.

Police Court; how constituted; jurisdiction of.

There shall continue to be a city police court established *Judge; how appointed.* and holden within and for said city, the judge of which shall be appointed in the same manner as the recorder of said city,[1] and hold his office for the term of one year[2] and until his successor shall be chosen and sworn.[3] He shall con-

---

* City marshal liable for neglect of duty in the same manner as sheriff. See *ante*, · page 4.

[1] Amended, 1871. See page 62.

[2] Amended. See Constitutional Amendment, Article XX, page 35.

[3] Associate judge, how appointed, 1872, see page 63. Term of office, see Constitutional Amendment, Article XX, page 35. Substitute judge, see page 63.

Jurisdiction.

tinue to have and exercise the jurisdiction and powers relative to and over criminal cases, (including cases where sureties of the person and good behavior are required,) arising within incorporated limits of the city and on Connecticut river opposite said city,[4] now vested by law in justices of the peace within towns, which jurisdiction and powers shall continue to be exclusive:[5] *provided,* that no magistrate shall be prohibited hereby from issuing warrants for the arrest of offenders, or from exercising jurisdiction in all prosecutions under the act for the suppression of intemperance, or from discharging any ministerial duty or office now by law imposed upon him; but all warrants on account of any offence within the jurisdiction of said police court, except under said act, shall require the offender to be brought before the said police court, there to be dealt with according to law. Said court shall have authority, subject to the provisions of this act, to hear and determine charges for crimes and misdemeanors committed within the limits of the City of Hartford, the punishment of which, as prescribed by law, does not exceed a fine of two hundred dollars, or six months imprisonment in a common jail, work-house or city penitentiary, or such fine and imprisonment both;[6] and in all such cases said court may proceed to trial, render final judgment thereon, and grant a warrant for the execution thereof, according to law.   But in all cases the person convicted may

Appeals.

appeal from the judgment of said police court to the superior court next to be holden in the county of Hartford, except when the convictions shall be for the crimes of profane cursing and swearing, and Sabbath breaking: *provided,* that he give such bond on the appeal as said court shall order, payable to the treasurer of the county of Hartford, conditioned for the appearance of the person so convicted, before the superior court, to answer concerning the offence whereof he stands charged, and to abide the judgment that

---

[4] Amended, 1875. See page 60; 1879, see page 60.
[5] Powers *de* truants. See page 142; *de* commitment to Reform School, 1881. See page 143: *de* commitment to Industrial School. See page 145; *de* breach of by-laws of water commissioners, 1861. See page 175.
[6] Amended. See pages 60 and 61.

may be rendered by the court last aforesaid. If the crime charged against the accused shall in any case be of so aggravated a nature as to require a greater punishment than is above specified, the accused shall be by said police court bound over to the next superior court having cognizance of **Binding over.** such offence, in the same manner as is provided in cases of binding over by justices of the peace in and by the one hundred and forty-eighth section of the sixth title of the revised statutes of this state. Said court shall have and appoint a **Clerk of Police Court, and his** clerk, who shall keep a record of the same, and certify its **duties.** proceedings, whose duties, compensation, bond, (including his duties relative to the payment of prosecuting officers,) shall be regulated by city ordinance.

SECTION XIX.

Complaints to police court; how made. | May arrest without warrant; when.
Bench warrant; when to issue.

Presentments or complaints in any criminal matter cog- **Complaints; who may make.** nizable by said police court, may be made to the same by any grand juror of the town of Hartford,[1] or the attorney for the city of Hartford; and said court shall exercise the same powers in relation to the issuing of process against per- **Summons and capias.** sons so complained of, and the granting of a summons or capias for witnesses, as are conferred upon justices of the peace, in and by the one hundred and fifty-seventh section of the sixth title of the revised statutes of this state. Process issued by or returnable to said police court, may be served by the sheriff or deputy sheriff of Hartford county, or the **Service.** marshal or deputy marshals of said city, or any constable of the town of Hartford, or any policeman or watchman of said city, who shall severally receive therefor the fees now prescribed by law for like services by constables of towns. Whenever information shall be given to the judge of the city police court of the city of Hartford, of the commission

---

[1] Amended, 1875. See page 64.

of any criminal offence within the jurisdiction of said court, said court may inquire into the truth of the same, and issue *Bench warrant.* a warrant or bench warrant for the arrest of the person or persons complained of and proceed to trial and render judgment concerning said person or persons, without any previous presentment by an informing officer.

Arrest without complaint or warrant. It shall be lawful for all officers by law authorized to serve process issued by and returnable to the city police court, and it shall be their duty to arrest, without previous complaint and warrant, all such persons as are guilty of drunkenness, vagrancy, disorderly conduct, breaches of the peace, and common assaults, and other offences, when such offences shall be committed within the jurisdiction of said court, and such offenders shall be taken and apprehended in the act, or on speedy information of others; and it shall be lawful for said *Trial without complaint or warrant.* court to proceed to trial and render judgment, without previous complaint and warrant, upon persons so arrested, in the same manner as if they had been arrested upon process issued by said court.

SECTION XX.

Police court; may suspend judgment, when.

Judgment may be suspended. Whenever any person shall be arraigned before said city police court, for drunkenness, vagrancy, disorderly conduct, or a breach of the peace, said court may indefinitely suspend the rendition of judgment concerning him, whenever such forbearance shall seem to the court required by the age of the accused, or the circumstances under which the offence was committed.

SECTION XXI.

Adjournment of cases in the police court. | Bail; extent of; how taken.

May adjourn cases not to exceed ninety days. Before entering upon the trial of any criminal cause, the said police court may adjourn the hearing or trial thereof from time to time, not exceeding fifteen days, unless said court, upon good cause shown, may deem a longer time necessary for the purpose of procuring material testimony, which time shall not exceed ninety days. And said court, if the offence charged shall be bailable, and good and sufficient *Ball; when taken.* bail is at the time of any adjournment, or during the period of adjournment, offered, shall take the same, conditioned that the person charged shall appear before said court at the day to which the hearing or trial is adjourned, and then, and at all times thereafter, abide the final order or judgment of said court. If the case is within the final jurisdiction of said police court, the bond of recognizance shall be payable to *Bond; to whom payable.* the city treasurer, otherwise to the county or state treasurer, as the nature of the offence shall require.[1]

SECTION XXII.

Police court: taxable costs in.

Said police court is hereby required to charge and tax, for *What fees Police Court may tax.* the use of the city of Hartford, in any criminal proceedings, such clerk fees as are allowed by law to the clerks of the city court, and also one dollar for the trial of each cause, and one dollar duty on each appeal; and the fee of the prosecuting officer, who shall make any complaint or presentment, shall be the same as those provided by law for grand jurors of *Fees; how paid.* towns, and payable from the city treasury; and all such fees of the prosecuting officer shall be taxed and received by the clerk in favor of the city of Hartford. Said police court may establish rules of practice concerning the reduction or *Taxable costs; disallowed when.* disallowance of fees now taxable by said court in cases where the negligence of any ministerial or informing officer, or the discharge of the accused for want of evidence, or the insufficiency of the service rendered, or other circumstances, shall render such reduction or disallowance expedient in the view of said court in the exercise of its sound discretion.

---

[1] Amended. See page 72.

All moneys collected by the clerks of the police court, and city court, shall be paid into the city treasury; all fines paid after commitment shall be received by the keeper of the jail, workhouse, or penitentiary, where the offender shall be confined, and by such keeper be paid to the city treasurer within thirty days after the receipt thereof.

SECTION XXIII.

Police court; persons sentenced by, where and how conveyed.
May commit to reform school; when.

City of Hartford may establish penitentiary.
Rules and regulations of; how made.

Whenever any person shall be sentenced to confinement in the common jail of said county, or in any workhouse therein, it shall be the duty of the sheriff of Hartford county, and his deputies, of the city marshals, and of any constable or city watchman, or policeman resident within the town of Hartford, to convey all persons, so sentenced, without delay, to the appointed place of confinement, and deliver them to the keeper thereof, who shall receive and imprison such persons, and employ them according to the rules, regulations, and discipline of such place of confinement, during the term for which they shall severally be sentenced and committed, or until they are discharged according to law.[1]

It shall be lawful for said police court, at its discretion, to order any person brought before said court on any criminal presentment, to be committed to any reform school or other institution now or hereafter to be established within this state for juvenile offenders; and the proper officer of such institution shall receive and keep such persons, according to the rules and discipline of the same. It shall be lawful for the city of Hartford to authorize and establish a city penitentiary, for the confinement of persons sentenced to be committed by said police court; the rules, regulations, and discipline of which said city penitentiary, when erected, may

May commit to reform school.

City penitentiary.

----

[1] Amended. See page 72.

be ordered and established in and by any city ordinances relating thereto, which shall thereafter be enacted in due form of law.

SECTION XXIV.

Water commissioners; how chosen; their | Corporate name.
  powers and duties.

There shall continue to be a board of five[1] water commis- Board of water commissioners.
sioners of said city; and the present commissioners shall hold office until the expiration of the terms for which they were chosen, and until their respective successors shall be elected and qualified. One commissioner shall be chosen Term of office.
annually by the court of common council, from among the members thereof, at such time as the ordinances of said city shall prescribe. The water commissioners that shall be hereafter chosen by city meeting shall hold office for the term of four years, and succeed the commissioners whose terms shall then have expired.[2] Said board shall continue to Powers and duties.
be empowered[3] to take and convey for and in behalf of said city, from the Connecticut river at some point near or within the city of Hartford, such supply of water as the conven- ience and necessity of the inhabitants of said city may require; and to take and hold for and in behalf of said city, May take lands and estate for water purposes.
lands or other estate necessary for the construction of any canals, aqueducts, reservoirs, or other works for conveying or containing water, or for the erection and construction of any buildings or machinery, or for laying any pipes or con- ductors for conveying water into or through said city; or to secure and maintain any portion of the water works; and in general to do any other act necessary or convenient for accomplishing the purposes of supplying said city with water, and to distribute said water through said city;[4] to establish public hydrants;[5] to prosecute or defend any action May prosecute and defend actions in name of board.

---

[1] See pages 86–93. Amended, 1865. See page 52.
[2] Amended, 1872. See page 53.
[3] Amended, 1865. See page 177; 1875, page 178.
[4] Amended, 1869. See page 176; 1865, page 177,
[5] Amended, 1874. See page 179.

or process at law or in equity, by the name of the "Board of Water Commissioners of the City of Hartford," against any person or persons or corporation for the breach of any contract, express or implied, relating to the performance of any work or labor upon said water works, or the management of the same, or the distribution of the water, or for money due for the use of the water, or for any injury, or trespass, or nuisance affecting the water, machinery, pipes, buildings, apparatus or other things under their superintendence, or for any improper use of the water, or any wasting thereof, or upon any contract or promise made with and to them as water commissioners, or with their predecessors or successors in office; and said board shall be regarded as a corporation for the purpose of suing and being sued. Said board are

Power to bargain for land. hereby authorized to enter in and upon any land or water for the purpose of making surveys, and to agree with the owner or owners of any property or franchise which may be required for the purposes of this act, as to the amount of compensation to be paid to such owner or owners for the same. And in case of disagreement between said board and any owner or owners as to such compensation, or as to the

Power to condemn land. amount of damages which ought to be awarded to any person claiming to be injured in his estate by the doings of said commissioners, or in case any such owner shall be an infant, or married woman, or insane, or absent from this state, or unknown, or the owner of a contingent or uncertain interest, either judge of the supreme court of errors may, on the application of either party, cause such notice to be given of said application as said judge shall see fit to prescribe, and after proof thereof may nominate and appoint three disinterested persons to examine such property as is to be taken for or damaged by the doings of said commissioners, and they being duly sworn to a faithful and impartial discharge of their duty, shall estimate the amount of compensation which said owners shall receive, and report the same in writing to the clerk of the superior court for Hartford county, to be by him recorded. Said judge of the supreme court of errors may thereupon confirm the doings of said appraisers, and direct whether said commissioners shall pay the same, in such manner as said judge may prescribe, in full compensation for the property acquired or the injury done by said commissioners; and, on compliance with the order of said judge, said commissioners may proceed with the construction of their works without any liability to any further claim for compensation for damages.[6]

SECTION XXV.

Water Commissioners; powers of. Duties prescribed by ordinance.

Said commissioners shall also be empowered to make use of the ground or soil under any road, railroad, highway, street, private way, lane or alley, within this State, for the purpose of constructing the water works; but shall in all such cases, cause the surface of such road, railroad, highway, street, private way, lane or alley, to be restored to its usual condition, and all damages done thereto to be repaired, and all damages sustained by any person or corporation, in consequence of the interruption to travel, to be paid to such person or corporation.

It shall be the duty of the court of common council of said city to make ordinances prescribing the duties of the board of water commissioners not expressly prescribed by this act; their powers over the water fund of the city of Hartford and duties relative thereto; the officers of said board, and their compensation, and bonds, and oaths, and the powers of said board over the water works of said city; and the mode in which water rents or taxes shall be secured by lien on lots, houses, tenements, or otherwise, or shall be collected; also, relative to the proper number of said commissioners to constitute a quorum.

Commissioners empowered to use certain grounds.

Damages; how paid.

Ordinances to be made prescribing duties.

Compensation of; how determined.

Quorum.

---

[6] Amended, 1883. See page 180.

SECTION XXVI.

Offences against water property; how punished.

Malicious corrupting of water. If any person shall maliciously and wilfully corrupt the water collected or conducted in or into any reservoir, cistern, hydrant, conductor, engine, pipe, or any portion of the water works of the city of Hartford, or destroy or injure any work, machinery, materials, or property erected, constructed, used, or designed to be used within the city of Hartford, or elsewhere, for the purpose of procuring and keeping a supply of water, the city police court of said city shall have juris-**Penalty.** diction of said offence, and may punish the offender by a fine not exceeding five hundred dollars, or by imprisonment not exceeding one year, or by both fine and imprisonment. And **Treble damages.** said offender shall also be liable to treble damages in an action of trespass brought by said commissioners.

SECTION XXVII.

The inhabitants living within the limits of said city shall be and remain a part of the town of Hartford.

SECTION XXVIII.

Obligations of city not impaired. This act shall in no manner impair or qualify the obligation of any bond, liability, note, contract, or debt of said city, or the evidences thereof, and said city shall be liable thereon under the name conferred by this act.

SECTION XXIX.

Original charter and all acts inconsistent herewith hereby repealed.

Provisions not herein re-enacted repealed. All those parts of the charter of the city of Hartford, and acts amending the same not re-enacted in this act, and all laws relating to the city of Hartford, inconsistent with or superseded by the provisions of this act, are hereby repealed.

SECTION XXX.

Charter; how ratified.

This act may be altered or amended by the General Assembly; and shall not take effect until the same shall have been accepted in the manner following, viz.: the mayor of said city shall notify the citizens residing within the present and proposed boundaries of the same, to meet in the several wards of said city, at any time not less than six days from the date of said notice; and shall then and there cause the votes of said citizens to be received on the acceptance of this act; which votes shall be by ballot, those in favor of the same voting *Yes*, and those opposed voting *No;* and said ballots shall be received and counted in the manner now by law provided for the reception of votes for the choice of city officers; and if, on counting the same it shall appear that a majority of all the votes are in the affirmative, then this act shall be deemed to be accepted, and shall take effect at such time thereafter as the mayor of said city shall make proclamation of said acceptance.* And all the present officers of the city of Hartford elected in city meeting, shall retain their offices until new officers, with like functions, are chosen under this act; and all officers of said city appointed by the court of common council, or by the courts of said city shall retain their offices until other officers, with like functions, are appointed or chosen under the provisions of this act; and all by-laws of said city shall remain in full force and operation, in the same manner as if this act had not been passed, until such time as the court of common council, elected under the provisions of this act, shall appoint to be the time when the same shall become inoperative and void.

Acceptance of this act.

Present appointees, retained until new election.

Existing ordinances.

Approved, June 24, 1859.

---

* Subsequent meeting may be held in case the first fails to ratify, when. Society for Savings v. City of New London, 29 Conn., 174.

CONSTITUTIONAL AMENDMENTS,

AMENDMENTS TO THE CHARTER

OF THE

CITY OF HARTFORD,

And Other Acts and General Statutes in Force
Relating Thereto, September 1, 1883.

CONSTITUTIONAL AMENDMENTS.

ARTICLE XX.

[Adopted October, 1876.]

Judges of the Courts of Common Pleas, and of the District Courts, shall be appointed for terms of four years. Judges of the City Courts and Police Courts shall be appointed for terms of two years.

ARTICLE XXIV.

[Adopted October, 1877.]

Neither the General Assembly, nor any county, city, borough, town, or school district, shall have power to pay or grant any extra compensation to any public officer, employee, agent, or servant, or increase the compensation of any public officer or employee, to take effect during the continuance in office of any person whose salary might be increased thereby, or increase the pay or compensation of any public contractor above the amount specified in the contract.

ARTICLE XXV.

[Adopted October, 1877.]

No county, city, town, borough, or other municipality, shall ever subscribe to the capital stock of any railroad corporation, or become a purchaser of the bonds, or make donation to, or loan its credit, directly or indirectly, in aid of any such corporation; but nothing herein contained shall affect the validity of any bonds or debts incurred under existing laws, nor be construed to prohibit the General Assembly from authorizing any town or city to protect by additional appropriations of money or credit, any railroad debt contracted prior to the adoption of this amendment.

AMENDMENTS TO CHARTER

ACTS RELATING THERETO.

APPROPRIATIONS.

I. For public celebrations.
II. For improvement of navigation of Connecticut river.

III. Annual estimates to be made, and not to be exceeded.
IV. For public library.

I.

SECTION 1. That the Court of Common Council of the *How made. S. A., vol. 5, p. 535.* City of Hartford be, and hereby is, authorized and empowered by concurrent vote, to appropriate at its discretion from time to time, sums of money for the purpose of defraying the expenses of public celebrations and receptions within said city; said sums of money so appropriated not to exceed the *Limitation.* amount of five hundred dollars for any one public celebration or reception.

SEC. 2. The mayor of said City of Hartford is hereby *Mayor may administer oaths.* authorized and empowered to administer oaths within said city.

Approved, June 10, 1863.

II.

Connecticut river.
S. A., vol. 6, p. 317.
That the City of Hartford be, and is hereby, authorized to expend a sum not exceeding five thousand dollars annually in improving the navigation of the Connecticut river, provided the same be voted and authorized by a majority of the Board of Aldermen and Common Council of said city.

Approved, July 27, 1867.

III.

Estimates of ex-
penditure to be
made, and not ex-
ceeded.
S. A., vol. 8, p. 264.
It shall be the duty of the Court of Common Council of the City of Hartford at their last meeting in each fiscal year, to make an estimate of the sums necessary to defray the expenses of the several departments of said city for the ensuing year, and the Court of Common Council of said city for the year ensuing shall not make any appropriation or authorize the expenditure of any sum in excess of the estimates made as aforesaid, excepting upon a two-thirds vote of said Court of Common Council; nor shall any of the departments of said city expend any sum in excess of said estimates, except the same be authorized by a two-thirds vote of said Court of Common Council.

Approved, March 21, 1879.

IV.

Appropriation for
free public library.
S. A., 1883, p. 726.
That the City of Hartford be, and it hereby is, authorized and empowered to appropriate by concurrent vote of the Court of Common Council of said city, and to expend annually, a sum not exceeding one-fifth of one mill upon the grand list of said city last made and perfected, for the purpose of supporting and maintaining a free public library and art gallery, with their appurtenances, and of furnishing needed accommodations therefor.

Approved March 14, 1883.

BOUNDARIES.

I.

SECTION 1. That the territorial limits of the body politic and corporate existing under the name of the City of Hartford shall hereafter consist of the land and territory included in the present territorial limits, and in addition thereto the land and territory in this resolution hereinafter described, viz.: all the land included in the following limits and bounds: beginning at a certain brook where it crosses New Britain avenue, in the town of Hartford, and in the line of the present southwestern territorial limit of the City of Hartford and between the lands of Michael L. Seymour and J. S. Rood; thence running southerly along the present western bank of said brook to the division line between the towns of Wethersfield and Hartford; thence running easterly upon said division line to the Connecticut river; thence northerly along said river to the present southeasterly territorial limit of the City of Hartford; thence from said point westerly along the present southerly line of said city limits to place of beginning; and all the land included in said bounds is hereby annexed and added to the corporate territory of the City of Hartford; and shall be included for purposes of suffrage, and for all other proper purposes in the fourth ward of said city. In making assessments for benefits in building sewers through said territory hereby added to the city, the proper boards of assessment may make proportional assessment upon all persons whose land in their judgment is specially benefited by such sewers, whether their land abuts upon said proposed sewers or not.

Southern limits of city extended.
S. A., vol. 7, p. 136.

Sewers.

SEC. 2. No city tax exceeding six-tenths of one mill on a dollar of the grand list shall be laid or levied upon any land or lands hereby added to said city, so long as said land is or

Taxation.

shall be exclusively used for farming purposes, and has a
market value not exceeding one thousand dollars an acre.

Exemption.

And no city tax shall be imposed upon those meadow lands
included in this addition lying upon the east of Wethersfield
avenue and not protected by a dyke.

Approved, July 26, 1871.

II.

**Western limits of
city extended.
S. A., vol. 7, p. 620.**

SECTION 1. The territorial limits of the body politic and
corporate existing under the name of the City of Hartford
shall hereafter consist of the land and territory included in
the present territorial limits thereof, and in addition thereto
of all the land now lying within the town of Hartford,
except that portion thereof lying northerly of the present
north line of said city, and of the same line produced westerly until it intersects the present boundary line between the
towns of Hartford and West Hartford; and all the land and
territory within the town of Hartford, except as aforesaid, is
hereby annexed and added to the corporate territory of the
City of Hartford, and so much of the same as lies within the

Division by wards.

first voting district of the town of Hartford shall be included
in the first ward of said City of Hartford; so much of the
same as lies within the second voting district of said town
shall be included in the second ward of said city; so much
thereof as lies within the third voting district of said town
shall be included in the third ward of said city; so much
thereof as lies within the fourth voting district of said town
shall be included in the fourth ward of said city, and so much
thereof as lies within the seventh voting district of said town
shall be included in the seventh ward of said city: *provided,*

Taxation.

always, that no city tax exceeding six-tenths of one mill on a
dollar of the grand list shall be laid or levied upon any land
or lands within the territory added to the said city by virtue
of this act, so long as said land is or shall be used exclusively
for farming purposes, or is vacant or unoccupied land, and
has an assessed value not exceeding six hundred dollars an
acre, and that all farming produce and all stock used in farming, and all implements of husbandry belonging to persons

residing on said territory, so annexed, shall be exempt in the
same manner and to the same extent from such city taxation:
and provided, also, that the persons now and hereafter residing on said territory hereby added to said city, and the estate
of such persons, both real and personal, within said added
territory, and the real estate lying within said added territory, and owned by persons residing outside of the same,
shall not be liable to taxation, or in any other mode for any
now outstanding, funded or bonded debt of said city, or for
interest on the same, excepting "capitol bonds" and the
interest thereon: *provided,* that this act shall not be so construed as to exempt from liability any property invested in
business within the present city limits and now liable to
taxation for said city debt.

Approved, July 9, 1873.

III.

SECTION 1. That the territorial limits of the body politic *Northern limits of city extended. S. A., 1881, p. 245.*
and corporate existing under the name of the City of Hart-
ford shall hereafter consist of all the land and territory
situate within the present limits of the town of Hartford, so
that hereafter the limits of said city and town shall be the
same.

SEC. 2. No city tax, exceeding six-tenths of one mill on a *Taxation.*
dollar of the grand list, shall be laid or levied upon any land
or the buildings on the same which are added to the territorial limits of the City of Hartford by the foregoing section,
so long as said land has an assessed value not exceeding six
hundred dollars per acre, exclusive of the buildings thereon,
and all farming produce and all stock used in farming, and
all implements of husbandry belonging to persons residing
on said territory so annexed, and all personal property
belonging to persons now residing on said territory so
annexed, so long as they shall continue to reside thereon,
shall be exempt in the same manner and to the same extent
from such city taxation. And the persons now and hereafter
residing on said territory hereby added to said city, and the
estate of such persons, both real and personal, within said

added territory, and the real estate lying within said added territory and owned by persons residing outside of the same shall not be liable to taxation or in any other mode for any now outstanding funded or bonded debt of said city or for interest thereon, excepting capitol bonds and the interest thereon: *provided*, that this act shall not be so construed as to exempt from liability any property invested in business within the present limits of said city, and now liable for taxation for said city debt.

Public improvements.

SEC. 3. The said City of Hartford shall not have power to order to be made any new street, sewer, curb, gutter, sidewalk, or other public improvement of any kind, within or upon the territory added to the limits of said city by this resolution, except upon the written application of not less than twenty-five real estate owners residing and owning land within the territory so added to the limits of said city.

Voting place.

SEC. 4. The said land and territory hereby added to said city shall be included in and be a part of the seventh ward of said city.

Building line.

SEC. 5. The ordinance of said city relating to building lines and to building permits shall not be applicable to the territory so added to said city while said territory shall be used for farming purposes.

Taxation.

SEC. 6. No city tax of any kind shall be laid or levied upon that tract of land known as the Hartford North Meadows, the boundaries of which were established by a decree of the superior court for Hartford county, passed at its March term, A. D. 1868, upon the petition of Henry Drake and Samuel Mather, so long as the same shall remain a common field, and the roads therein shall be kept and maintained by the proprietors of said meadows.

Approved, April 14, 1881.

IV.

City divided into seven wards. P. A., 1881, p. 324.

That said City of Hartford shall be, and hereby is, divided into seven wards, as follows, viz.:

First ward.

First Ward. Beginning at the intersection of the center lines of Main and Church streets, and running thence northerly and westerly through the center line of Main street to its intersection with the center line of Albany avenue; thence westerly through the center line of Albany avenue and Albany road, so called, to the western boundary line of said city; thence southerly on said western boundary line to its intersection with the center line (produced) of Collins street; thence on said line through the center line of said Collins street to its intersection with Garden street; thence through the center line of said Garden street to Myrtle street; thence through the center of Myrtle street to its intersection with Spring street; thence through the center of Spring street to its intersection with the road and alley leading from Spring street to Church street; thence through the center of said road and alley and Church street to the place of beginning.

Second Ward. Beginning at the point of intersection of Second ward. Main and Church streets, and running thence westerly through the center of Church street to its termination; thence through the center of a road and alley to Spring street; thence through the center of Spring street to Myrtle street; thence through the center of Myrtle street to Garden street; thence northwesterly through the center of Garden street to the center line of Collins street; thence westerly through the center line of Collins street, and said line produced to the western boundary of said city; thence southerly along the said western boundary to the south fork of Park river, so called; thence easterly through the center of said river to its intersection with Main street; thence northerly through the center of Main street to the place of beginning.

Third Ward. Beginning at the point of intersection of the Third ward. eastern line of said city, and the center line of Park river, and running thence westerly through the center of said river, and the south fork thereof, to its intersection with the center line of a road in continuation of Park street; thence easterly through the center of said road to Washington street; thence northerly on the center line of Washington street to Buckingham street; thence easterly through the center of Buckingham street to its intersection with Main street; thence southerly through the center of Main street to its intersection with Charter Oak avenue; thence on the center line of Charter Oak avenue, and the same line continued, to its intersection with the eastern boundary line of said city; thence on said eastern boundary line to place of beginning.

Fourth ward. *Fourth Ward.* Beginning at a point on the eastern line of said city at its intersection with the center line of Charter Oak avenue continued, and running thence westerly to the center line of Charter Oak avenue, and thence through the center of Charter Oak avenue to its intersection with Main street; thence through the center of Main street to its intersection with Buckingham street; thence through the center of Buckingham street to its intersection with Washington street; thence southerly through the center of Washington street to its intersection with Park street; thence westerly through the center of Park street and the road in continuation of it, to the western boundary line of the city; thence southerly on said boundary line to the southern boundary line of the city; thence easterly on said southern boundary line to the eastern boundary line of the city, and thence northerly on said eastern boundary line to the place of beginning.

Fifth ward. *Fifth Ward.* Beginning at the point of intersection of the east line of the city and the center line of Kilbourn street, and running thence westerly on said center line to its intersection with the center line of Front street; thence northerly through the center of Front street to its intersection with Temple street; thence westerly through the center of Temple street to its intersection with Main street; thence southerly through the center of Main street to its intersection with the center line of Park river; thence easterly on the center line of said river to the eastern boundary line of the city; and thence northerly on said eastern boundary line to the place of beginning.

Sixth ward. *Sixth Ward.* Beginning at the point of intersection of the center line of Kilbourn street and the eastern boundary line of the city; and running thence northerly on said boundary line to its intersection with the northern boundary line of the city; thence westerly on said northern boundary line to its intersection with the center line of the railroad of the Hartford and New Haven Railroad Company; thence southwesterly on the center line of said railroad to its intersection with the center of Windsor street; thence southerly through the center of Windsor street to its intersection with Main street; thence southerly through the center of Main street to Temple street; thence easterly through the center of Temple street to Front street; thence southerly through the center of Front street to Kilbourn street; thence easterly through the center of Kilbourn street to the place of beginning.

Seventh Ward. Beginning at the intersection of Main and Windsor streets and running thence northwesterly through the center of Main street to Albany avenue; thence westerly through the center of Albany avenue and Albany road, so called, to the western boundary line of said city; thence northerly, on said western boundary line to the northern boundary line of said city; thence easterly on said northern boundary line to the center line of the railroad of the Hartford and New Haven Railroad Company; thence southerly on the center line of said railroad to the center line of Windsor street; thence southerly on the center line of Windsor street to the place of beginning.

Approved, July 9, 1869.

V.

SECTION 1. That that portion of the fourth ward of the City of Hartford, as is included within the following boundaries, to wit: beginning at a point on the southern line of said city at its intersection with the center line of Maple avenue, and running thence northerly, through the center of said Maple avenue to its intersection with Webster street; thence through the center of Webster street to its intersection with Washington street; thence through the center of Washington street to its intersection with Park street; thence westerly through the center of Park street, and the road in continuation of it to the western boundary line of the city; thence southerly along said boundary line to the southern boundary line of the city; thence easterly along said southern boundary line to place of beginning, shall constitute and be the eighth ward of said City of Hartford.

SEC. 2.   At the annual meeting of said City of Hartford, holden next after this act shall take effect, to wit: on the first Monday of April, A. D. 1877, there shall be chosen in said eighth ward two aldermen and four councilmen; and one of said aldermen shall hold office for one year and the other for two years, their respective terms of office to be designated on the ballot of the electors; and at all subsequent annual meetings there shall be chosen as aforesaid one alderman and four councilmen, who shall hold office as in the other wards of said city.

SEC. 3.   All acts and parts of acts inconsistent herewith are hereby repealed.

Approved, June 27, 1875.

CHARTER: HOW AMENDED.

1838. 1858. 1866.
Notice of petition
for alteration of
charter.
R. S., p. 79, § 7.

No petition for the incorporation of any bank, or savings bank, or for the alteration of the charter of any city or borough, shall be heard by the General Assembly, unless public notice shall have been given by advertisement in some newspaper published in the town where such bank, or savings bank is intended to be, or where such city or borough is located, if any, otherwise in some newspaper published in the same county, at least three weeks before the first day of the session to which it is preferred, stating the proposed capital and location of such bank, the proposed location of such savings bank, or the proposed alteration of such charter; but such publication shall not dispense with any other notice required by law.

CITY CLERK.

WHEREAS, Owing to the temporary absence of the city S. A., vol. 5, p. 436. clerk of the City of Hartford, a city clerk *pro tempore* has been appointed by the Court of Common Council of said city.

SECTION 1. That the said appointment of said city clerk Appointment validated. *pro tempore* is hereby validated and confirmed, and all official acts heretofore done by him while acting in said capacity, are hereby legalized, and said city clerk *pro tempore* is hereby Powers of city clerk *pro tempore*. authorized to perform all the duties, and is hereby clothed with all the legal authority of the city clerk of said city while he continues to act in said capacity.

SEC. 2. The Court of Common Council of said city are Common Council empowered to appoint city clerk *pro tempore*. hereby empowered, in case of the temporary absence or inability of any city clerk of said city, by concurrent vote to appoint a city clerk *pro tempore*, whose official acts, while he continues in said capacity, shall be of the same binding Powers. authority as the official acts of said city clerk.

Approved, June 25, 1861.

CITY MAP.

SECTION 1. The Court of Common Council of the City of Council authorized to establish street and building lines as on map of 1866. P. A., 1869, p. 311. Hartford shall have power, by a majority of the members of each branch, present and absent, subject to the approval of the mayor of said city, to make, alter, and repeal ordinances, for the purpose of making the map of said city, made in 1866, by the city government, operative and binding, relative to the lines of streets projected and laid out on the same, and also for the purpose of making such street and building lines as may hereafter be mapped out or projected by authority of the city government, operative and binding on said city, and on all parties whose property is affected thereby: *provided* that the Court of Common Council of said city shall have the power, at any time, to lay out and adopt streets in said city, and to change the lines of the streets as now projected and laid out on said map.

Approved, July 9, 1869.

COMMISSIONERS.

1.

Board of street commissioners created. P. A., 1869, p. 292.

How appointed.

Terms of office.

SECTION 1. There shall be a board of street commissioners of the City of Hartford, consisting of six freeholders of said city who shall not be members of the Court of Common Council. At the first meeting of the Court of Common Council, held after the ratification of this act by said court as hereinafter provided, said Common Council by concurrent vote shall choose six persons, who shall constitute the board of street commissioners, and, in voting for such commissioners, each member of the council shall vote for three persons and no more, whose names shall all be written or printed upon one piece of paper; and the six persons who shall receive the highest number of votes shall be declared elected, whether they receive a majority of all the votes cast or not. The persons so elected shall hold their office, two for the term of one year, two for the term of two years, and two for the term of three years, from and after the second Monday of April, previous to the time when said board is so chosen, which term shall be decided by lot, to be drawn in the presence of the mayor of the city and the city clerk; and in drawing said lots, the persons so elected shall be divided into two classes: the first class to consist of the three persons who *Classes, and how determined.* receive the highest number of votes, and the second class of those who received the lowest number of votes, and were elected by said council. Each class shall draw by themselves, one person only in each class shall hold office for each of the terms above mentioned. At the annual city election *Second board; how chosen, and terms of office.* of said city, first held after the ratification and acceptance of this act by the Court of Common Council, as hereinafter provided, and at each annual city election thereafter, there shall be chosen by ballot from among the freeholders of said city two members of said board, who shall hold office for the term of three years from the second Monday of April of the year in which they are so elected, and until their respective successors shall be chosen and qualified, and in voting for such members of such board, each elector may vote for one person and no more; and the two persons having the highest number of votes shall be declared elected, and in case of vacancy *Vacancies; how filled.* in said board by death, resignation, or otherwise, the members of the Court of Common Council of said city, elected to said court by the same political party which elected the member of said board whose place shall so become vacant, shall nominate some freeholder of said city as a member of said board for the unexpired term, to fill such vacancy; and the. person so nominated shall be appointed to fill such vacancy by the mayor of said city, and shall hold said office for said unexpired term. The members of said board may be paid *Compensation of members; how paid.* from the city treasury such sums as shall be fixed by the Court of Common Council.

SEC. 2. Said board shall keep a record of all their acts and *Record of proceedings, etc.* proceedings, and an account of expenditures and receipts, which shall be open to the inspection of any member of the Court of Common Council. Said board may, if they see fit, appoint a clerk to keep such record and accounts, and shall *Clerk.* appoint a superintendent of streets, to hold office during the *Superintendent.* pleasure of said board, and to act under the instructions thereof, in the immediate care and management of such works as may be under the charge of said board; and said

Compensation of clerk and superintendent.

clerk and superintendent of streets shall receive such compensation for their services as the Court of Common Council may grant.

Powers of board.

SEC. 3. Said board shall have power, and it shall be their duty, to cause to be executed all orders of the Court of Common Council, for the construction or alteration of highways,

Construction of highways, etc.

streets, sewers, gutters, sidewalks, and crosswalks, the exchange or sale of highways, the establishment of building lines, the erection of street lamps, the raising, filling up, or draining of low grounds, and all other orders of said court for the construction, alteration, or repair of other public works not expressly ordered to be executed or superintended by other officers or persons. Said board shall also cause the

Repairs of highways, etc.

prompt completion of all necessary repairs of streets, highways, sewers, and public works within the limits of the streets, highways, and thoroughfares of the city, other than public buildings; shall keep all public places, streets, and

Obstructions and nuisances.

highways, clear of obstructions and nuisances; shall cause the prompt removal of all filth, encroachments, incumbrances, and obstructions, and shall require all persons to conform to the city ordinances in the use of such streets, highways, and public places; shall superintend and provide for the lighting

Street lamps.

of the street lamps, and the repair of the same, and, in general, may do all acts necessary or proper in the execution of

Legal counsel.

the powers and duties aforesaid.* Said board shall have power, in behalf of said city, to employ the city attorney to prosecute or defend any action at law or in equity, civil or criminal in its nature, whenever, in their judgment, it may be necessary in carrying out the powers and duties of their office.

Common Council shall pass no vote establishing street, sidewalk, or sewer, until after reference to board.

SEC. 4. The Court of Common Council shall pass no vote laying out, establishing, or ordering to be constructed, any new street, sidewalk, or sewer, or any alteration or improvement, relating to streets and sewers, until such vote, or the

---

*City is not liable for the acts of its officers whose duty it is to repair highways, and who, in the performance of this public duty, occasion damage to individuals. Judge v. Meriden, 38 Conn., 90.

petition asking for the passage of such vote, shall have been referred to said board of street commissioners for investigation.

SEC. 5. Said board shall act as a court for the assessment of betterments and appraisals of damages, and all powers now vested by the charter in the Court of Common Council in reference to the appraisal of damages and assessment of betterments, shall hereafter be exercised by said board. *Provided,* That the Court of Common Council shall continue to have power to prescribe, by ordinance, the manner of proceeding in such assessment and appraisal, and that an appeal shall be allowed to any person aggrieved by any appraisal of damage or assessment of betterments to the tribunal, and in the time and manner which may be by law provided. *Assessments of betterments and appraisal of damages vested in board.* *Common Council to prescribe manner of assessment and appraisals.* *Appeal from al lowed.*

SEC. 6. Said board shall, on the first day of January, in each year, make a report to the Court of Common Council of said city of all receipts, and from what sources, and of all expenditures, and for what purposes, which have been received and expended during the previous year, and shall also specify what orders of said court have been complied with, and what orders have not been carried out, and the reasons for the same; and shall present said report, with such recommendations as they may deem best, concerning the management of their department, to said Court of Common Council, at its first regular meeting after said first day of January. *Reports of receipts and expenditures.*

SEC. 7. This act shall take effect whenever the Court of Common Council, by concurrent action shall vote to ratify and accept the same; and whenever said court shall vote so to ratify, this act shall be and become a part of the charter of said city, and thereupon all acts, and parts of acts, inconsistent herewith are repealed; and upon said ratification, the office, duties and emoluments of street commissioner, shall thereupon cease and be at an end. *Ratification of act.* *Office of street commissioner abolished.*

Approved, July 9, 1869.

II.

Whenever two or more members of the board of street commissioners of the City of Hartford shall be disqualified by reason of interest or other cause from acting upon any *Members of board temporarily appointed in event of disqualification. S. A., vol. 7, p. 673.*

assessment or other matter pending before said board requiring the action of a majority of the whole of said board, the
mayor of said city may appoint two or more freeholders of
said city, not members of the Court of Common Council, to
serve in the places of said members while so temporarily disqualified; and the persons so appointed by the mayor shall
have, while acting as temporary members of said board, the
same powers and duties as are by law conferred upon the
regularly appointed members thereof.

Approved, June 24, 1874.

III.

Water board, how
constituted.
S. A., vol. 5, p. 770. **SECTION 1.** The board of water commissioners of the City
of Hartford shall, after the second Monday in April, A. D.
1867, consist of six persons, who shall be chosen as follows,
and shall hold office until their respective successors shall be
elected and qualified. Said city shall annually, at the annual
city meetings for the choice of city officers, choose two persons by ballot to be members of said board, who shall hold
their offices for the term of three years; and in voting for
said officers each person shall vote for one person for water
commissioner and no more; the two persons who shall have
the highest number of votes shall be deemed to be elected.

SEC. 2.   The board of commissioners chosen under the provisions of this act, shall, until the second Monday in April,
A. D. 1868, act in concert with those heretofore elected during
their several terms as the board of water commissioners of
the City of Hartford: and after said second Monday of April,
1868, the six commissioners who shall then have been chosen
under the foregoing provisions shall constitute the board of
water commissioners of the City of Hartford, and shall discharge the duties and possess all the powers and privileges of
the present board.

SEC. 3.   All acts and parts of acts inconsistent with this act
are hereby repealed.

Approved, July 21, 1865.

IV.

SECTION 1.   That the mayor of said City of Hartford shall, by and with the advice and consent of the board of aldermen of said city appoint the members of the several boards of water commissioners, street commissioners, police commissioners, fire commissioners, and park commissioners, of said city, and when members of any of said boards of commissioners are to be appointed for different terms, the term for which each member is to serve shall be designated by the mayor at the time of making the appointments as aforesaid.

SEC. 2.   The appointment of the members of the said several boards of commissioners as aforesaid shall be made in such a manner as to divide the membership of each of said boards as nearly as may be equally between the two leading political parties for the time being.

SEC. 3.   Whenever a vacancy shall occur in any of said several boards of commissioners it shall be filled in the manner provided aforesaid for the appointment of members.

SEC. 4.   The mayor of said City of Hartford, by and with the advice and consent of any four members of the board of aldermen, may remove any member of either of said boards of commissioners for cause.

SEC. 5.   The members of either of said boards of commissioners now in office shall retain their positions during the term for which they were elected, subject to removal in the manner provided for in the fourth section of this act.

SEC. 6.   So much of the charter and ordinances of said City of Hartford as is inconsistent herewith is hereby repealed.

SEC. 7.   This act shall take effect from and after its passage.

Approved, May 23, 1872.

CHARTER AND AMENDMENTS CONFIRMED.

Charter and various
amendments con-
firmed and re-en-
acted.
S. A., vol. 6, p. 441.

SECTION 1. The charter of the City of Hartford as contained in the resolution of the General Assembly, entitled "An Act to alter the Charter of the City of Hartford and to combine sundry public statutes relating thereto;" approved June 24, A. D. 1859, and in the supplement to said resolution. approved June 23, A. D. 1859, and in the several resolutions in amendment and addition to said resolutions, to wit: The resolution approved July 3, A. D. 1861; the resolution approved July 1, A. D. 1863; the resolution approved July 21, A. D. 1865; the resolution approved June 20, A. D. 1860; the resolutions approved July 3, A. D. 1861; the resolution approved June 25, A. D. 1861; the resolution approved June 29, A. D. 1862; the resolution approved June 24, A. D. 1863; the resolution approved June 10, A. D. 1863; the resolution approved July 1, A. D. 1863; the resolution approved July 7, A. D. 1865; the resolution approved June 20, A. D. 1866; the resolution approved July 24, A. D. 1867; the resolution approved July 12, A. D. 1867; and the resolution approved July 26, A. D. 1867, is hereby confirmed and enacted word for word as contained in said several resolutions.

Ordinances and
votes confirmed.

SEC. 2. All ordinances and votes passed, and all acts of every kind whatsoever, done in pursuance of and under the authority of said resolutions are hereby confirmed and ratified, and declared to be lawful as fully and to the same extent as if each of said resolutions had been enacted under the style of this act. And the duties, powers and authority and all other matters prescribed and contained in said resolutions confirmed and enacted in the preceding section are to be construed in the same manner as if each of said resolutions had been originally passed under the style of this act. *Provided*,

To affect no suits
pending.

that nothing herein contained shall affect any suit or proceeding in law now pending, in which the validity of any of said resolutions or matters therein contained, has been questioned.

Approved, July 24, 1868.

CONNECTICUT RIVER.

I.

If any steamboat or other vessel propelled by steam shall approach at a greater rate of speed than six miles an hour any wharf, pier or dock in the City of Hartford between the bridge over Connecticut river and the southern limits of said city, or the Long wharf and pier in New Haven harbor when any vessel shall be lying thereat at any berth below the north end of the platform on the east side of the wharf, or the wharf or pier in Bridgeport harbor, known as "Mather's Dock," or any dock, pier, or wharf in New London harbor within two hundred feet of the same, or any wharf on either side of the Mystic river between Mystic bridge and a point two hundred yards south of the wharf of Joseph S. Avery, or any wharf, pier or marine railway in Norwalk harbor, or any wharf in the city of Middletown when covered with water, the person in command of such vessel shall forfeit one hundred dollars, half to him who shall prosecute and half to the treasury of the county in which the offence is committed, and shall also be liable to pay three-fold damages to him whose property shall be injured thereby.

Speed of steam vessels regulated. R. S., p. 252, § 16.

II.

SECTION 1. The person in charge of every vessel of a draft of more than six feet, and of over fifty tons burden, carrying cargoes to the City of Hartford from any port or place beyond the mouth of Connecticut river, and of every steamer engaged in towing on said river, shall report to the port warden of the City of Hartford within twenty-four hours after every arrival at said city, stating the name and registered tonnage of the same, and pay to him for every vessel carrying cargoes, and for every steamer engaged in towing, a toll of two cents a ton upon its registered tonnage, except that where the actual weight of cargo can be determined by

Vessels arriving at Hartford to pay tolls to the port warden. R. S., p. 251, § 11-15.

its bills of lading, said toll shall be imposed on said actual tonnage, at the rate of one cent a ton; and the Hartford and New York Steamboat Company shall, on the first day of June in each year, pay to said port warden one thousand dollars, in lieu of all tolls imposed by this section.

Person in charge liable for toll.

SEC. 2.   The person in charge of any such vessel, and the owner, shall be jointly and severally liable for such toll; and if the person in charge of any such vessel shall neglect so to report, and to pay toll, after demand by said port warden, he and the owner of such vessel shall be jointly and severally liable to pay double the amount of toll hereby imposed, to the City of Hartford; and the City Court of said city shall have jurisdiction of all suits instituted for the recovery thereof.

Port warden to keep a record and account monthly with city treasurer.

SEC. 3.   The port warden shall keep a record of all vessels, paying or liable to pay such toll, and the amount of toll collected from each, and render an account monthly to the treasurer of the City of Hartford, of all moneys received by him for toll, and pay over the same to said treasurer; and the Court of Common Council of said city shall cause all moneys so received, and any other moneys they may appropriate for

To be expended for improving channel of the river.

the purpose, except as hereinafter provided, to be expended for the improvement of the navigation of Connecticut river between Hartford and Middletown, under the direction of a committee to be appointed by said Court of Common Council; and said committee shall, from time to time, render accounts with vouchers for all moneys expended by them to said treasurer, which shall be audited and adjusted as other accounts

Annual report.

of said city, and annually report to the General Assembly, stating particularly the amount of money received from tolls, and expended by them, the purpose for which, and the manner in which, the same was expended, and the condition of the channel of said river between said towns.

Compensation of port warden.

SEC. 4.   Said port warden shall receive such compensation as said Court of Common Council may prescribe, not exceeding two hundred dollars a year, to be paid from said tolls; and, before entering upon the performance of said duties, he shall give a bond to said city with surety, to be approved by the mayor, of not less than one thousand dollars, conditioned for the faithful performance of the same.

SEC. 5. The four preceding sections shall not take effect, until accepted and approved by said Court of Common Council.

Common Council to approve these provisions.

CORONER.

All acts and parts of acts inconsistent herewith, including chapter twenty-three of title thirteen of the general statutes (page 181), and part one of chapter two, title sixteen of said statutes (page 205), and section thirty-one of chapter twelve, title twenty of said statutes (page 529), and chapter thirty-nine of the public acts of 1882 (page 139), and the provisions of all special acts giving authority to hold inquests on dead bodies, or perform any of the duties assigned to coroners and medical examiners by this act, are hereby repealed.

Repeal of coroner's powers,
P. A., 1883, p. 301.

Approved, May 1, 1883.

COURTS.

I.

Jurisdiction of City and Police Courts.
R. S., p. 62, § 18.

The several city and police courts, and, the officers thereof, shall have all the powers and jurisdiction which shall have been conferred upon them, and shall be subject to all the duties imposed upon them by law and the charters of their respective cities; and appeals from the judgments of said courts shall be taken and allowed in the manner provided by the laws in force on the thirty-first day of December, 1874.[1]

II.

Jurisdiction of City Court in equity.
R. S., 1866, p. 245, § 137.

The City Court of the City of Hartford shall have jurisdiction of all suits in equity, except for relief against any judgment rendered, or against any cause pending in the Superior Court, and may inquire into the facts, itself or by a

---

[1] City Court has jurisdiction of a *scire facias* on a judgment rendered by it in a suit of foreign attachment. Sherwood v. Stephenson, 25 Conn., 431.

committee, and may proceed to final judgment and decree, _{May appoint committee.} and enforce the same according to the rules of equity, provided the cause of action or proceeding in equity originated _{Proviso.} and one or both of the parties reside within the limits of said _{Residence of parties.} city, and the premises in question in cases of foreclosure or the proceedings relating to real estate shall be situated within _{Location of real estate.} said city limits.

III.

Any judge of any court of equity may, on motion, accord- _{Injunction. R. S., p. 477, § 1.} ing to the course of proceedings in equity, grant and enforce writs of injunction, in all actions in equity returnable to any court, when such court is not actually in session, whether in term-time or vacation; which writs shall be of force until the sitting of such court, and its further order thereon.

IV.

In all civil actions, except those of summary process, _{Appeals in Justices' suits. R. S., p. 415, § 15.} brought before a justice of the peace, an appeal from any judgment rendered therein, upon any issue, may be had and allowed to either party, to the next Court of Common Pleas in the county in which such judgment is rendered, or if there be no such court in said county, then to the Superior Court in said county, unless such judgment be rendered within the judicial district of Litchfield county, in which case such an appeal shall be taken to the next District Court in said district; but no appeal shall be allowed until the party appealing shall become bound to the adverse party, in such sum as the justice of the peace shall order, in a recognizance, with a sufficient surety, conditioned to prosecute such appeal to effect.[1]

All appeals hereafter made from justices of the peace in _{Appeals from justices, where taken. P. A., 1869, p. 341.} the town of Hartford, whether the cause of action may have arisen within the limits of the City of Hartford, or without the same, shall be taken to the Court of Common Pleas for the county of Hartford.

Approved, July 9, 1869.

---

[1] See Public Acts, 1880, p. 512.

V.

Limitation of Jurisdiction of Police Court. R. S., p. 533, § 8. No justice of the peace, or Police or City Court, shall have final jurisdiction of any prosecution for crime, the punishment for which may be imprisonment in the state prison.

VI.

Jurisdiction of Police Court over Charter Oak park. S. A., vol. 7, p. 959. SECTION 1. The Police Court of the City of Hartford shall have jurisdiction over all crimes, offences and misdemeanors, that shall be committed in that part of the town of West Hartford, in the county of Hartford, known as Charter Oak park, in the same manner as said court now has over crimes, offences and misdemeanors that are committed within the limits of the City of Hartford.

Authority of police over said park. SEC. 2. The officers and members of the police department of the City of Hartford, shall have the same authority and power to arrest any person or persons, on said premises known as Charter Oak park, that they now have to make arrests within the limits of the City of Hartford, and all persons so arrested by them, shall be brought forthwith before the Hartford City Police Court, which court shall thereupon proceed to trial and judgment, as in all other similar cases now within its jurisdiction.

Concurrent jurisdiction of justices of West Hartford. SEC. 3. Nothing in this act contained shall affect the jurisdiction of justices of the peace, in said town of West Hartford, in any complaint that may be brought before them.

SEC. 4. This act shall take effect from its passage.

Approved, July 8, 1875.

VII.

Policemen for Cedar Hill cemetery. S. A., vol. 8, p. 242. SECTION 1. The mayor of the City of Hartford may, from time to time, appoint one or more suitable persons, to be designated by the Cedar Hill Cemetery Association, to be and act as policemen, upon the grounds and at the expense of said association. Such policemen shall hold office during the pleasure of the mayor. They shall wear in plain sight a suitable shield, marked "Cemetery Police;" shall enforce the rules of the association, and may arrest any persons violating, or who shall have violated, said rules; and they shall have within said grounds the power of the police of the City of Hartford.

SEC. 2. Resistance to such policemen shall be punished in the same manner and to the extent as is now provided by law for resistance to constables. *Resistance of said policemen.*

SEC. 3. The Police Court of the City of Hartford shall have jurisdiction of all crimes committed upon the grounds of said association, and the breach of the reasonable rules and regulations of said association shall be held to be a breach of the public peace. *Police Court jurisdiction.*

Approved, March 11, 1879.

VIII.

SECTION 1. When any complaint shall be brought before any Police or City Court for the commission of any offence prohibited by section twelve, chapter eleven, title twenty, of the general statutes, such court may try the same, and if in the opinion of such court no greater punishment ought to be imposed, such court may render judgment therein for a fine of not more than fifty dollars, or imprisonment in a county jail for not more than six months, or both, and grant a warrant for the execution of the same, but if in the opinion of such court, such offence requires a greater punishment, the accused shall be bound to the next Superior Court, having criminal jurisdiction, to be holden in the county in which the offence is committed, and any person convicted by said court, shall have a right of appeal, in the manner now provided by law. *Obtaining goods under false pretences; jurisdiction of Police Court. P. A., 1876, p. 107.*

SEC. 2. All acts and parts of acts inconsistent herewith are hereby repealed. *Repeal.*

Approved, June 22, 1876.

IX.

That so much of the charter of said City of Hartford as provides that there shall be two associate judges of the City Court of said city, and for the manner of their election, be *Office of associate judge of City Court abolished. S. A., vol. 7, p. 276.*

and the same is hereby repealed, and the office of associate judge of said City Court shall be abolished from and after the first Monday of April, A. D. 1873.

Approved, June 26, 1872.

X.

Recorder may act as judge of Court of Common Pleas. R. S., p. 39, § 18.

When any judge of the Court of Common Pleas shall be disqualified or unable to act in any cause or matter pending before him or said court, which he may consider as improper to be tried or disposed of by him or by said court when held by him, he, or in his absence, the clerk thereof, may call in any other judge of said court, or the judge of the District Court of Litchfield county, or any judge, assistant judge, or recorder of any City Court in the county where such Court of Common Pleas is held, to hear and determine such cause; and the judge of the District Court may, for the same reason and purpose call in any judge of the Court of Common Pleas, or the judge of the City Court of the city of Waterbury.

XI.

Special terms of Court of Common Pleas. P. A., 1875, p. 22, § 4

Any person who is *ex-officio* authorized to hold a session of the Court of Common pleas in any county in the absence of the judge of such court, may hold a special term or session thereof at the request of the judge during the session of the regular term, and at such special sessions the person holding the same shall have all the powers of the judge of said court, and said court when so constituted and held shall be deemed the same as if such person were holding the regular term thereof in the absence of the judge.

XII.

Appointment of Police Court judge. P. A., 1871, p. 522.

SECTION 1. That the Legislature shall annually appoint a judge of the Police Court for the City of Hartford, to continue in office for one year,[1] and until his successor shall be appointed and sworn.

---

[1] Term changed to two years. See Constitutional Amendment, Article XX, p. 35. Term commences July 1. See P. A., 1876, p. 87.

Sec. 2. That so much of the charter of the City of Hart- Repeal. ford as provides for the election of the judge of the Police Court for said city, by the Common Council thereof, be and the same is hereby repealed.

Sec. 3. This act shall take effect from the day of its Take effect, when. passage.

Approved, June 6, 1871.

XIII.

Section 1. The General Assembly shall annually choose Associate judge of Police Court; how an associate judge of the Police Court of said city, who shall chosen, and term of office. hold his office for the term of one year[1] from the fourth day S. A., 1872, p. 300. of July of the year of his appointment and until his successor shall be chosen and sworn.

Sec. 2. The associate judge shall perform the duties and Duties and powers. be vested with all the powers and functions of the judge of said court whenever there shall be a vacancy in the office of said judge and in case of his absence or disability.

Sec. 3. The associate judge shall be paid for actual service Compensation. at the same rate as the judge of said court.

Sec. 4. This act shall take effect from its passage.

Approved, August 1, 1872.

XIV.

That in case the judge of the Police Court of the City of Police judge may designate substi- Hartford shall at any time be disqualified or unable to act in tute. S. A., vol. 5, p. 368. any cause, or in any case that the duties of the office shall be too great for him reasonably to perform, he may designate and request any justice of the peace resident within the City of Hartford, to act as his substitute, and such justice while acting under such request shall have the same powers as such judge would have in like causes.

Approved, June 20, 1860.

---

[1] Term changed to two years. See Constitutional Amendment, Article XX, p. 35. .

XV.

Pay of substitute judge holding Court of Common Pleas.
P. A., 1878, p. 309.

SECTION 1. The judges of City Courts and Police Courts, when holding Courts of Common Pleas, shall be paid eight dollars a day, to be taxed and paid as now provided by law.

Repeal.

SEC. 2. All acts and parts of acts inconsistent herewith are hereby repealed.

Approved, March 27, 1878.

XVI.

Prosecuting attorney; powers and duties
S. A., vol. 7, p. 917.

SECTION 1. The Court of Common Council of the City of Hartford, shall appoint a prosecuting attorney who shall have all the powers of a grand juror in presenting and prosecuting complaints and informations before the Police Court of said city; and it shall be his duty to prosecute before said court, all crimes and misdemeanors, and violations of city ordinances, committed within the limits of said city, and of which said court has jurisdiction; he shall be duly sworn to the faithful discharge of his duty, and shall receive such compensation as the Court of Common Council shall by ordinance direct.

Powers of grand jurors cease.

SEC. 2. After said prosecuting attorney shall be appointed and qualified, the powers of grand jurors of the town of Hartford within the limits of the City of Hartford, shall, after the first Monday of October, A. D. 1875, cease.

Special prosecuting attorney.

SEC. 3. Whenever said prosecuting attorney shall be absent from the City of Hartford, or unable or disqualified to act in any case before said Police Court, said court shall appoint a special attorney to act during such absence, disability or disqualification, who shall receive for his services the same fees provided by law for grand jurors, for like services.

How appointed.

SEC. 4. The prosecuting attorney first appointed under the provisions of this act, shall be chosen in joint convention of the Court of Common Council, at a meeting specially warned for that purpose, and he shall hold his office until the second Monday after the next annual city election, and until his successor shall be chosen and qualified; and thereafter said prosecuting attorney shall be chosen in joint convention of said Court of Common Council, at the same time and in the same manner as is provided in the ordinances of said city, for the election of such other officers as are to be chosen in joint convention of said Court of Common Council, and said prosecuting attorney shall hold his office for the term of one year, and until his successor shall be chosen and qualified.

Term of office.

Sec. 5. The same fees shall be taxed by said Police Court for the services of said prosecuting attorney as are by law taxable for the services of grand jurors; and the same when collected by the clerk of said court, shall be by him paid or accounted for to the treasurer of the City of Hartford.

Fees.

Sec. 6. This act shall take effect from and after its passage.

When to take effect.

Approved, June 24, 1875.

XVII.

Section 1. Clerks of courts shall receive the files, processes, and documents, returnable to their respective courts, make perfect records of all proceedings required to be recorded, have the custody of the files and records of the court, make and keep dockets of causes therein, issue executions on judgments, and perform all other duties imposed on them by law.

Duties of clerks. R. S., p. 61, § 11-14.

Sec. 2. The clerk of any court may, when so directed by such court, make up, amend and complete any record thereof which may have been omitted to be done by a former clerk, in such manner as the court may direct.

Clerks to complete records.

Sec. 3. The clerk of the court before which any civil action is pending may, in vacation, take bonds for its prosecution.

Clerks may take bonds in vacation.

Sec. 4. Each court having a clerk shall have its proper seal, which shall be kept by him.

Courts to have a seal.

XVIII.

Section 1. Clerks of courts, other than Probate Courts, shall receive for entering each civil cause three dollars; for recording each judgment in causes brought by appeal from justices of the peace, and for recording each judgment on

Fees of clerks of courts. P. A., 1841, p. 76.

default or non-suit where such judgment is rendered at the first term, three dollars; for recording each judgment in complaints for divorce, on default or non-suit at the second term, and in all actions where damages less than two hundred dollars are recovered, seven dollars; for recording judgments in all other cases, ten dollars.

Continuance fee abolished.

SEC. 2. The fees provided by section one of this act may be demanded by the clerk before the cause is entered, or the judgment is recorded. Clerks of courts shall not demand, charge, or collect any fees for any entry of any cause subsequent to the first term, nor for any continuance of any cause. Whenever, in any cause now pending in any court, the clerk thereof has collected entry fees equal to those chargeable by the provisions of this act, he shall not charge or demand any additional fees for the continuance or further entry of such cause upon the docket, and whenever in any cause now pending he has collected entry fees equal to those chargeable by the provisions of this act for the entry of the same, and the recording of the judgment in the same, he shall not charge or demand any fee for the record of the judgment when the same is obtained. All fees collected for the entry of causes now pending, under the provisions of statutes repealed by this act, shall be credited by the clerks of courts to the parties who have paid the same, against any additional fee such clerks may be entitled to demand under the provisions of this act for the further entry of such causes, or for the recording of the judgments rendered in the same.

Judgment file.

SEC. 3. The prevailing party in any civil action may recover for the judgment file the sum of one dollar, and the further sum of seventy-five cents for each additional page, when such judgment file exceeds one page; and the clerks of courts who draw such judgment files may demand and receive such fees from the prevailing party.

Fees due to be paid before entry of further proceedings.

SEC. 4. No clerk shall be required to continue any cause on the docket, or to enter or record any judgment therein, or to issue any execution on any such judgment until all court and clerk fees already due shall have been paid.

Repeal. General statutes, p. 175.

SEC. 5. The provisions of chapter seven, title thirteen, of the general statutes, providing for fees on continuances, and judgments on trials, defaults, and non-suits, and all acts and parts of acts inconsistent herewith are hereby repealed.

Approved, April 14, 1881.

XIX.

Clerks of city and police courts, in addition to their salary, may receive the same fees for copies upon appeals or binding over, as justices of the peace.

Fees for copies. R. S., p. 176.

XX.

Section 1. Whenever any complaint shall be brought to the City Police Court of the City of Hartford by the city attorney under authority of the charter of said city for any act made an offence by said charter and the amendments thereto, or by the ordinances of said city passed in pursuance thereof, and cognizable by said court, a form substantially like the following form may be used and shall be sufficient:

Complaint for offence against charter or ordinance. S. A., vol. 6, p. 313.

To the honorable City Police Court for the City of Hartford comes A. B. city attorney of said city, and on his oath of office complaint and information makes, that since the incorporation of said city, to wit, on the   day of   A. D. 18   and within the limits of said city,   of the town of
in the county of   with force and arms, [set forth the act complained of,] against the peace, contrary to the ordinance [or order as the case may be] of said city in such case provided, and contrary to the form of the statute in such case provided, therefore the said city attorney prays process, and that the said   may be arrested, held to answer to this complaint, and be thereon dealt with according to law.

Form for criminal process.

Dated at said Hartford, this   day of   A. D. 18
                          A. B., City Attorney.

Sec. 2. Whenever there shall be brought to the City Court of the City of Hartford, any action of debt, in the name of

Collection of fine or forfeiture.

said city, to collect any fine, penalty, or forfeiture due and payable under the authority and by virtue of the charter and ordinances of said city and collectible by action of debt in said court, a form substantially like the following form may be used and shall be sufficient:

To the Marshal of the City of Hartford, etc.:

Form for civil process.

By authority of the State of Connecticut, you are hereby commanded to summon A. B. of   to appear before the City Court of the City of Hartford, within said county, next to be holden at the city hall in said city, on the first Monday of   A. D. 18   then and there to answer unto the City of Hartford in a plea that to the plaintiff the defendant render the sum of   which to plaintiff the defendant owes and from them unjustly detains, whereupon the plaintiff declares and says: that heretofore, to wit, on the   day of   A. D. 18   the said A. B., [state the act or negligence which subjects the defendant to the fine, penalty, or forfeiture to be collected,] all which was contrary to the ordinance of said city, entitled [give the title to the ordinance imposing the fine, penalty, or forfeiture]. And the said defendant there became and still is liable to forfeit and pay to the plaintiff for the use of the city treasurer the sum of   recoverable in an action of debt on said ordinance, whereby an action hath accrued to the plaintiff to demand and recover of the defendant the sum of   .   which to the plaintiff the defendant hath never paid though often requested so to do. All which is to the damage of the plaintiff in the sum of   and therefore they bring their suit.

Hereof fail not, but due service and return make.

C D, of said Hartford, is recognized in the sum of to prosecute, etc.

Dated at Hartford, this   day of   A. D. 18

Other forms not invalidated.

SEC. 3. Nothing in this resolution shall be construed as prohibiting the use of other forms in reference to the same matters, or as invalidating any other forms. This resolution

shall go into effect from and after the date of its passage, but
shall not affect any suit now pending.

Approved, July 12, 1867.

XXI.

In all complaints or other processes for an offence against
a private act, or an ordinance, or by-law of any town, city,
or borough, it shall be sufficient to set forth the offence in the
same manner as in case of offences created by a public act.

XXII.

SECTION 1. The City Court of the City of Hartford, and
the judge thereof, shall have the same powers to grant
motions in error and for new trials, and grant bills of exceptions in all cases hereafter arising therein and now pending,
with all the rights and powers incident thereto, as is now
given by law to the Superior Court and the judges thereof in
similar cases.

SEC. 2. Said City Court may reserve questions of law
arising therein, and in cases now pending, for the advice of
the Supreme Court of Errors at its next regular term in the
first judicial district, in the same manner as now provided by
law in the Superior Court, and said City Court shall conform
to the advice of the Supreme Court in the judgment, decree,
or decision made or rendered in such cases.

SEC. 3. Motions in error, and for a new trial, in said City
Court may be joined and allowed at the same time, as is now
provided in the Superior Court; and all motions in error or
for a new trial heretofore granted by said court, or now
pending therein, or which shall hereafter be granted, shall be
taken to the next regular term of the Supreme Court of
Errors in said district: *provided*, that the Superior Court shall
try and decide all actions brought from said City Court and
now entered upon the docket of the Superior Court.

SEC. 4. Whenever, by reason of sickness, interest, disqualification, absence, or from any other cause, the recorder of
said City Court shall be rendered unable or disqualified to act

as judge therein, said recorder may designate some one justice of the peace resident within the City of Hartford to act as judge thereof, and such justice of the peace, so appointed and entered upon the record, shall, for the time of such disqualification, sickness, interest, absence, or other cause, have all the powers vested in the recorder of said court by law, except in case of a vacancy in said office.

To be a public act.

SEC. 5. This shall be deemed a public act, and all acts and parts of acts inconsistent herewith are hereby repealed.

When to take effect.

SEC. 6. This act shall take effect from the day of its passage.

Approved, July 24, 1874.

XXIII.

Appeals.
P. A., 1882, p. 144.

All questions of law arising on the trial of any cause or action, civil or criminal, before the Superior Court or any inferior court, which may now by law be carried to the Superior Court or to the Supreme Court of Errors for revision, by motion for a new trial either for errors of a judge or for verdict against evidence or for any other cause whatever, or by motion in error, shall hereafter be removed to such higher court by an appeal from the judgment of the court where such cause or action was tried, and no motions for new trials or motions in error shall hereafter be allowed; but this act shall not affect writs of error or petitions for new trials.

Approved, March 29, 1882.

XXIV.

Joinder of matters of law and of fact in writ of error.
P. A., 1881, p. 5.

Matters of fact and matters of law may be joined in any writ of error which is returnable to a court having jurisdiction of both error of fact and law.

Approved, March 1, 1881.

XXV.

Writs of error, how brought.
P. A., 1882, p. 214.

SECTION 1. Writs of errors from matters of fact, or in which matters of fact and matters of law shall be joined in the same writ, may be brought to the Superior Court from

the judgments or decrees of the Superior Court, Court of
Common Pleas, District Court, or any city court of the
county in which said courts are situated.

Sec. 2. Writs of error for matters of law only may be
brought to the Supreme Court of Errors of any judicial district or county from the judgment and decrees of any city
court in such judicial district or county.

Sec. 3. All acts inconsistent with this act are hereby
repealed.

Approved, April 26, 1882.

XXVI.

The Superior Court shall have sole jurisdiction of all *Jurisdiction of Superior Court in appeals. R. S., p. 536, § 1.* appeals from the police and city courts in cities, and from
justices of the peace, and of all offences except such as are by
law within the sole jurisdiction of said police or city courts,
or justices of the peace; and in all prosecutions for the violation of the provisions of any charter, or ordinance or by-law
of a city or borough, the defendant shall have a right of
appeal as in other cases.

XXVII.

When any police or city court, or justice of the peace, *Appeals to be transmitted within ten days. R. S., p. 535, § 12.* shall bind over or hold for trial, before the Superior Court,
any person charged with any criminal offence; or when such
court or justice shall not find probable cause to so bind him
over or hold him for trial; or when an appeal shall be taken
to the Superior Court from any judgment of a police or city
court, or justice of the peace, such court or justice shall,
within ten days thereafter, transmit to the clerk of such
Superior Court, or to the State's attorney for the county
where such prosecution shall have been had, copies of the
files and record in such cause, with the particulars of the
costs therein; and shall enter upon the same the names of all
persons who testified on the trial of such cause, with their
places of residence, so far as known to him, designating
therein the witnesses offered on behalf of the prosecution,

and those for the defence; and no costs shall be taxed or paid to any police or city court, or justice of the peace, failing to comply with the provisions of this section.

XXVIII.

Bonds before jus-
tice, Police, or City
Court.
R. S., p. 634, § 11.
Upon the adjournment of the hearing of any criminal cause by any justice of the peace, or police or city court, the accused shall be required to enter into a recognizance in a proper sum, with surety, conditioned that he shall appear at the time to which said hearing shall be adjourned, and abide the order of the court. If the cause is or may be within the final jurisdiction of the court, said recognizance shall be taken to the town wherein said hearing is had, if said cause is pending before a justice of the peace; and to the city wherein such police or city court is holden, if said cause is pending before such court, and is, or may be, within the final jurisdiction of said court; but, if said cause is not within the final jurisdiction of the court before which the same is pending, said recognizance shall be taken to the State.

XXIX.

Prisoners in Jail by
sentence of Police
Court.
R. S., 1866, p. 635,
§ 42.
All persons sentenced to any term of imprisonment by the Police Court of the City of Hartford, to the common jail of the county of Hartford, shall be delivered to the keeper thereof by any proper officer of said court, and said keeper shall receive and imprison such persons, and employ them according to the rules, regulations, and discipline of said jail, during the term for which they shall be severally sentenced and committed, or until they are discharged according to Cost of maintaining,
how defrayed. law, and the cost of maintaining said persons so committed to said jail shall be defrayed in the same manner as that of persons committed to said jail by sentence of the Superior Court, or of a justice of the peace for said county.

XXX.

SECTION 1. No attorney fees, or fees for travel to or at- tendance at court, shall hereafter be allowed as costs to parties in civil actions. Attorney fees, travel and attendance abolished.— P. A., 1881, p. 51.

SEC. 2. There may be allowed to the prevailing party in any civil action in the Superior Court, Court of Common Pleas, District Court, or City Court, by way of indemnity, the following sums: for all proceedings before trial, ten dol- lars; for the trial of an issue of law or fact, fifteen dollars; and if more than one issue of fact shall be tried at one time, only one trial fee shall be allowed. * * * Costs to parties.

SEC. 5. Nothing in this act contained shall be construed to interfere with the discretion of the court, in taxing costs in equity.

SEC. 6. So much of chapter thirteen, of title thirteen of the general statutes (pages 177, 178), as relates to fees for travel and attendance of parties in civil actions, and attorney fees, is hereby repealed. Repeal.

SEC. 7. Section fourteen, title nineteen, chapter five (page 418), of the general statutes is hereby amended by striking out, in the eleventh line thereof, the words "except for travel and attendance."

SEC. 8. No provisions in the statutes or rules of court for the taxation of costs, other than those specified in the two next preceding sections of this act, are repealed or annulled by this act.

SEC. 9. This act shall not affect any suit now pending.

Approved, April 12, 1881.

DYKE.

SECTION 1. The Court of Common Council of the City of Hartford shall have the exclusive power to lay out, make, and establish within the limits of said city, any dyke neces- Common Council empowered to lay out dyke. S. A., vol. 5, p. 717.

sary to prevent the water of the Connecticut, or Mill river, from inundating or overflowing said city, or any part thereof, which shall be considered and treated as a public work of said city.

How proceeded with.

SEC. 2. The powers conferred, and the duties imposed in said Court of Common Council, by the provisions of the seventh and eighth sections of the act to which this is an addition (approved June 24, 1859), are hereby extended to the work described in the preceding section, and the laying out and establishing the locality of said dyke, the building or making thereof, the taking of land or other private property for the same, the appraisal thereof and compensation therefor, the notice to persons interested therein, the assessment of a proportional sum of the expenses incident to the completion of said work upon any person specially benefited thereby, and the collection thereof, the appeal by the persons aggrieved, and the proceedings thereon, and the laying of taxes to defray the necessary expenses of said dyke, shall be regulated by the provisions of said seventh and eighth sections in the same manner, and to the same extent, as if the provisions of the first section of this act were incorporated in and made a part of said seventh and eighth sections.

Approved, July 7, 1865.

ELECTORS AND ELECTIONS.

I.

Conduct of city meetings.
R. S., p. 84. § 10.

Town and city meetings for the election of officers shall be holden and proceeded with, so far as may be, in the same manner as electors' meetings, unless when it is otherwise provided.　　*　　*　　*　　*　　*

II.

SECTION 24. The registrars of voters in the several towns, and in towns where there are different registrars for different voting districts, the registrars of voters in such districts shall appoint the moderators of the meetings of electors in their respective towns or districts. In case registrars shall fail to agree in the choice of a moderator, the choice shall be determined between them by lot, and in like manner they shall appoint the moderators to have charge of any vote by ballot in town meetings for the election of officers, and of any vote by ballot in any city meeting or ward meeting for the election of officers.

Moderators of electors' meetings. P. A., 1877, p. 240, § 24, 25, 26, 29, 32, 33, 34, 35, 38.

SEC. 25. At every electors' meeting and at every election of town, city, or ward officers by ballot, the registrars of each town or district. as the case may be, shall appoint a suitable elector, residing therein, for each ballot-box to be box-tender, and one or two others, as may be necessary, to be substitute box-tenders for each box, respectively. No person not so appointed shall have charge of any ballot-box during the taking of any vote, and no known candidate for any office shall be moderator, or be put in charge of any box in which votes are cast for said office, or take part in the count thereof; and any violation of this section by any such candidate shall render the votes cast for him void.

Box-tenders.

SEC. 26. In the town and City of Hartford, the moderator of the second voting district, and in every other town and city divided into voting districts, unless otherwise provided by special statute, the moderator of the first district shall be the presiding officer for the purpose of declaring the result of the ballot of the whole town or city, and of making returns to the secretary of state, and the moderators of the other districts shall be assistant presiding officers, and shall make returns of their polls as required by law.

Who to declare result of the ballot and to make the returns to the secretary.

SEC. 29. At any electors' meeting, and at any town or city meeting for the election of officers by ballot, those only shall vote who were registered on the revised registry list then last completed according to law, and each shall vote in the district

Who may vote at electors' and city meetings.

in which he was so registered: *provided, also*, that those persons may vote whose names are restored to the list under the provisions of section thirteen of this act, and those whose names are added on the day before electors' meeting under the provision of section fifteen of this act. Every person so registered shall be permitted to vote unless he shall have lost his right by removal from the town after such registration, or by conviction of some crime which disfranchises; and every person offering so to vote, and being challenged as to his identity, or residence, shall before he votes prove his identity with the person on whose name he offers to vote, or his continued residence in such town, since the completion of .such list, as the case may be, by the testimony, under oath, of at least one other elector.

Registrars to be present during the taking any vote at electors' meeting or city election. SEC. 32. Each registrar shall be present during the taking of any vote at any electors' meeting, or annual town meeting, or city election in his town or district. In Hartford, New Haven, Bridgeport, Waterbury, Norwich, Meriden, New Britain, and Middletown, the assistants in their respective districts shall, when requested by either registrar, be present at the taking of any such vote, and discharge the duties of registrars. The several registrars shall appoint some proper person to check the list in each district, who shall check the name of each voter thereon, when he offers his vote, and no box-tender shall suffer any vote to be deposited in the box until the name is so checked. Immediately after the close of the polls the said registrars, acting at the respective polls,

Check lists. shall write and sign with ink, on the list so used and checked, a certificate of the whole number of names registered thereon, the number of names checked as having voted, and the number not checked thereon, and deposit it in the town clerk's office of their town, on or before the following day, and such town clerk shall carefully preserve the same on file, with the marks on it without alteration, for public inspection, and shall immediately enter a certified copy of such certificates on the town records.

Counting the ballots. SEC. 33. At every election specified in the preceding sections, each registrar shall appoint from one to five persons.

as may be necessary, for each ballot-box in his district or town, who shall make the official count of the ballots in said box, and said counters shall be sworn before entering on their duties. Immediately after the ballot-boxes are closed at such meeting, and not before, the counters shall, in public meeting, sort and count the ballots found therein. In case of doubt or dispute as to the reading of a ballot, or whether a ballot should be rejected as double, or for any other cause, the moderator shall decide. All ballots rejected for being in the wrong box, for being double, or containing an excess of candidates, or for any other cause, shall, after being indorsed by the moderator with the cause of rejection, be preserved, in a separate parcel, securely tied or sealed, and returned to the box with the valid votes. The counters, immediately after the count is completed, shall, under their hands or the hands of a majority of them, deliver to the moderator a certificate in duplicate, stating the whole number of ballots found in their box, the number of ballots rejected because in the wrong box, the number rejected as double, the number rejected for any other reason, and the number of votes counted for each candidate and office respectively. · The moderator shall, before adjournment, publicly declare the result Declaration of the result. of the count. The moderator shall forthwith indorse on said certificates, in writing signed by him, that said certificates show the result of the official count for each box, respectively, in his town or district. One of said certificates he shall place in the ballot-box and seal up with the votes cast and returned to that box, the other, in towns not divided into voting districts, shall by the moderator, on or before the following day, be deposited in the office of the town clerk, and in towns divided into voting districts, shall by the assistant presiding officers forthwith be returned to the presiding officer, who shall, on or before the following day, deposit the same, with his own duplicate certificate, for his district, with the town clerk, who shall carefully preserve the same on file in his office. The presiding officer, after having ascertained the result of the ballots of the whole town, as given in the several districts, shall declare the same in open meeting, at the voting place where he presides; and such meeting shall not be adjourned until such vote is declared. The presiding

officer shall, with the certificate upon the result of the electors' meeting, which he is required by law to send by mail to the secretary of state, also send to the secretary of state his certificate of the whole number of names on the registry lists, the whole number checked as having voted at such elections, the whole number of names not checked, the number of ballots found in each box, viz.: "general" and "representative," and the number of ballots in each box not counted as in the wrong box, and the number not counted for being double, and the number rejected for other causes, which other causes shall be stated specifically in the certifi-

cate. The secretary of state shall enter said returns in tabular form, in books kept by him for that purpose, and annually report the same to the General Assembly.

SEC. 34. No double ballot for the same officer, nor any ballot found in any other box than the one designated therefor, shall be counted. No ballot shall be deemed a double ballot unless it shall consist of two or more pieces of paper upon which are duplicated or repeated the names of one or more candidates for the same office. If any ballot shall contain a greater number of names for any office than is provided by law, it shall not be counted for any person for such office.

SEC. 35. All the ballots cast at any electors' meeting, or at any town or city election by ballot, shall by the moderator immediately after they are counted, be returned to the box, which shall be locked and sealed up by him, so that the same cannot be opened without his knowledge, and deposited in the town clerk's office, and shall be by such clerk carefully preserved with the seal unbroken for six months after such meeting, to be opened and the ballots examined only by those authorized to make an official examination of them. If such boxes are opened under authority of a judge of Superior Court, charged with inquiring into an election, the said judge shall see that all the ballots and the accompanying certificates are returned to the box, and the same effectually sealed up again.

Sec. 38. The several moderators, box-tenders, and official checkers, provided for in this act, shall, before they enter on the discharge of their respective offices, be sworn to a faithful discharge of the duties of the same, and the several moderators and registrars shall have power to administer such oath. *Moderators, box-tenders, and checkers to be sworn, and who may administer oaths.*

III.

Section 1. The registrars of the town of Hartford shall, at least three weeks before any annual city meeting of the City of Hartford, prepare for each ward of said city a correct list of all persons entitled to vote in such ward at such meeting, under the provisions of the charter of said city. Said list shall contain all the matters of description required by law for lists made for the annual electors' meeting of the town of Hartford. Said lists shall be alphabetically arranged, certified by the registrars, and deposited in the office of the city clerk for public inspection, and a copy of the list for each ward, duly certified, shall be posted in some public place in such ward at least three weeks before the annual city meeting. *Registry lists for city meeting. S. A., vol. 8, p. 107.*

Sec. 2. The registrars shall give notice on said lists of the times and place at which they will hold two sessions, within the next twelve days, for the revision and correction of such lists, and shall also give notice of the.times and place of said sessions by publication in two newspapers published in said city, at least five days before the first of said sessions. *Notice of meeting for revision of lists.*

Sec. 3. Said registrars shall meet, pursuant to said notice, and shall correct said lists by the addition or erasure of names, as required; they shall complete said corrected lists and deposit them in the city clerk's office on or before the Monday preceding the annual city meeting, and shall furnish to the city clerk a sufficient number of copies of said lists, duly certified, to be used at said meeting. *Lists to be completed and furnished to city clerk.*

Sec. 4. The compensation of said registrars shall be fixed by the Court of Common Council and paid by said city, but shall not be regulated by the number of names registered. *Compensation of registrars.*

Sec. 5. For the first annual city election holden after the passage of this act, a preparation of the registry list two weeks before said election, and the posting of said list two weeks before said election, shall be sufficient.

When to take effect.

SEC. 6. This act shall take effect from its passage.

Approved, March 16, 1877.

IV.

Contested city elections, how determined.
P. A., 1878, p. 326.

SECTION 1. Any person claiming to have been elected selectman, clerk, treasurer, collector of taxes, assessor, grand juror, constable, registrar of voters, or registrar of births, deaths, and marriages of any town, or mayor, clerk, treasurer, auditor, collector of taxes, alderman, or councilman of any city, but not so declared, may, within sixty days after the time of holding the elections, bring his petition to any judge of the Superior Court, alleging the facts on which such claim is founded, which shall be served upon the party against whom the claim is made at least six days before the return day, and returnable not more than sixty-three days after the day of such election, and such judge shall thereupon hear and determine said petition, and his decision thereon shall be conclusive, and if in favor of the petitioner, his certificate to that effect, under the seal of the court, shall entitle the petitioner to hold and exercise the duties and powers of such office. And said judge may, if necessary, issue his writ of mandamus requiring the adverse party and those under him to deliver to the petitioner the appurtenances of such office, and shall cause his finding and decree to be entered in the records of said court, in the proper county.

Repeal acts 1877, chapter cxlvi, section 36, p. 244.

SEC. 2. Section thirty-six of chapter one hundred and forty-six of the public acts, passed January session, 1877, is hereby repealed.

Approved, March 27, 1878.

V.

City meetings; how warned.
R. S., p. 83, § 1.

The warning of every meeting of a town, city, borough, school society, school district, or other public community, or of an ecclesiastical society, or of proprietors of common fields shall specify the objects for which such meeting is to be held.

FINANCE AND LOANS.

I.

That for the purpose of defraying the expense of construct- *City authorized to issue bonds for construction of state house and purchase of land.* S. A., vol. 7, p. 99. ing a state house in the City of Hartford, and of purchasing the land upon which the same shall be erected, said City of Hartford be and hereby is authorized to issue its bonds with coupons attached, to an amount not exceeding the sum of one million of dollars, and bearing interest at no greater rate than six per cent. per annum, payable semi-annually; said bonds shall be called and known as capitol bonds of the City of *To be called capitol bonds, and to be free from taxation.* Hartford, and the same shall be free from taxation; said bonds shall be executed under the corporate name and seal of said city, by such person or persons as shall by the Court of *How executed.* Common Council of said city be appointed for such purpose, and said Court of Common Council shall prescribe the amount for which said bonds shall be severally issued, the form thereof, the rate of interest thereon, not greater than the rate herein mentioned, the time of paying the same, and the principal thereof.

This resolution shall not take effect unless the issue of said *Resolution to take effect when.* bonds shall be approved by a city meeting of said City of Hartford, specially warned and held for that purpose.

Approved, July 17, 1871.

II.

That the City of Hartford be and hereby is authorized to *Special city meeting, de capitol bonds.* S. A., vol. 7, p. 99. hold a special city meeting, to be warned in the manner provided by the charter and ordinances of said city for holding city meetings, for the purpose of authorizing said city, if said

meeting shall so direct, to issue its bonds in accordance with
a resolution heretofore passed by the General Assembly at its
present session, entitled a resolution relative to the issue of
capitol bonds of the City of Hartford; the vote of said meet-
Vote to be by ballot. ing shall be by ballot, and shall be cast by the freemen of said
city in their respective wards, and the ballot-boxes shall be
Polls open and close, when. opened at seven o'clock in the forenoon and closed at five
o'clock in the afternoon of the day of said meeting.
Ballots.   Upon each ballot shall be written or printed the word yes,
or the word no, and if a majority of the ballots cast at said
meeting shall have upon them the word yes, then the issue of
said bonds shall be deemed approved; otherwise not.

Approved, July 17, 1871.

III.

Additional capitol bonds.
S. A., vol. 7, p. 509.
Whereas, At the session of the General Assembly, holden at
Hartford on the first Wednesday of May, A. D. 1871, a
resolution was passed authorizing the City of Hartford to
issue its bonds to an amount not exceeding the sum of one
million dollars for the purpose of defraying the expense of
constructing a state house in said city, and of purchasing
the land upon which to erect the same, said bonds to be
known and called capitol bonds of the City of Hartford;
and

Whereas, The said City of Hartford has expended the sum
of six hundred thousand dollars for the purchase of said
land; therefore,

Resolved by this Assembly, That said City of Hartford be,
and hereby is authorized for the purpose of defraying said
additional expenditure, to issue its bonds with coupons
attached to an amount not exceeding the sum of one hundred
thousand dollars, and bearing interest at no greater rate than
six per cent. per annum, payable semi-annually; said bonds
shall be known and called additional capitol bonds of the
City of Hartford, and the same shall be free from taxation;
said bonds shall be executed under the corporate name and
seal of said city, by such person or persons as shall by the
Court of Common Council of said city be appointed for such

purpose; and said Court of Common Council shall prescribe
the amount for which said bonds shall be severally issued, the
form thereof, the rate of interest thereon, not greater than
the rate herein mentioned, the time of paying the same, and
the principal thereof.

Approved, June 27, 1873.

IV.

SECTION 1. That the mayor, aldermen, common council, *City empowered to issue notes, etc., in payment of park lands.*
and freemen of the City of Hartford, be and they are hereby *S. A., vol. 5, p. 65.*
authorized and empowered to issue notes, scrip, or certificates
of debt under the corporate name and seal of said city, bearing interest at no greater rate than six per cent. per annum,
to any amount not exceeding in the whole the sum of one
hundred thousand dollars; the principal of which said notes,
scrip, or certificates of debt, shall be payable at some certain
time or times within twenty-five years from the issuing of
the same; and said notes, scrip, or certificates of debt shall
be denominated "The Park Fund of the City of Hartford,"
and the avails thereof shall be applied and expended to and *Avails of notes, etc., to pay for park lands.*
for the purpose of the payment for lands heretofore pur-
chased or hereafter to be purchased by said city for a public
park, or for the payment of damages heretofore assessed, or
hereafter to be re-assessed, for lands to be taken by said city
for said park, and for no other purpose whatsoever; and said
notes, scrip, or certificates when issued and delivered by said
city, or its agents thereunto duly authorized, shall be obligatory upon said city and the inhabitants thereof according to
the tenor and purport of the same; and said city at a meeting
legally warned and holden for that purpose, may prescribe *City meeting to prescribe amount, etc.*
the amount for which said notes, scrip, or certificates shall be
issued, and direct concerning the form thereof, the rate of
interest, and the time of payment of the interest which shall
accrue thereon.

SEC. 2. The treasurer of said City of Hartford, shall be *City treasurer to be trustee.*
the trustee of the notes, scrip, or certificates of debt issued
by said city, to hold the same subject to the direction of the
Court of Common Council; and after the same or any part

of the same have been issued, said court may order and
Sale of notes; how
made.
require said treasurer to sell such notes, scrip, or certificates
of debt, at public or private sale, or hypothecate the same,
at their par value, or at such higher rates as the same may
command, at such time or times as the avails of the same
shall be needed to meet payments for lands purchased, or
damages assessed as aforesaid; and said court may make all
Record; how kept.
necessary orders for the security and safe keeping of said
notes, scrip, or certificates of debt and of the moneys accruing therefrom, not in conflict with this act. And a duplicate
record shall be kept by said treasurer of all notes, scrip, or
certificates of debt issued, sold or pledged in pursuance of the
provisions of this act, one copy of which shall be deposited
with the clerk of said city, which copy shall at all times
exhibit a true account of said notes and moneys; and the
Avails of notes, etc.,
to be deposited in
city banks.
avails of said notes, scrip, or certificates shall be deposited in
one or more of the banks of said city, and shall be drawn out
only on the order of the auditor of city accounts; and said
Compensation of
treasurer.
court may fix a reasonable compensation for any services rendered by said treasurer in conformity with this act.

Act; how confirmed.
SEC. 3. This act shall be, to all intents, a part of the charter of said City of Hartford, whenever said city shall vote in
pursuance of the provisions of the first section hereof, to
issue notes, scrip, or certificates of debt, as herein authorized.

Approved, June 19, 1857.

V.

Park bonds.
S. A., vol. 5, p. 316.
Upon the petition of the mayor, aldermen, common council, and freemen, of the City of Hartford, praying for authority to issue bonds in payment of lands purchased for the park
in said city, as per memorial on file, dated May 10, 1859, will
more fully appear:

Council authorized
to issue notes, etc.
Resolved by this Assembly: That the Court of Common
Council of the City of Hartford be, and they are hereby
authorized and empowered to issue notes, scrip, or certificates
of debt, under the corporate name and seal of said city, bear-
Six per cent.
ing interest at no greater rate than six per cent. per annum,
Not to exceed
$30,000.
to an amount not exceeding thirty thousand dollars, the prin-

cipal of which said notes, scrip, or certificates of debt shall be payable at some certain time or times, within twenty-five years from the issuing of the same, as the said Court of Common Council may direct; and said Court of Common Council may prescribe the amount for which said notes, scrip, or certificates shall be issued, and direct concerning the form thereof, the rate of interest, and the time of the payment of the interest which shall accrue thereon; and said notes, scrip, or certificates of debt, shall constitute a part of the "Park Fund of the City of Hartford," and the avails thereof shall be applied and expended for the payment of lands purchased by said city for a public park, and for no other purpose whatever; and said notes, scrip, or certificates, when issued and delivered, shall be obligatory upon said city and the inhabitants thereof, according to the tenor and purport of the same. The treasurer of said City of Hartford shall be the trustee of the notes, scrip, or certificates of debts, as hereby authorized, to hold, dispose of, and account for the same, subject to the orders and directions of the Court of Common Council, and the provisions of the charter of said city.

Payable within twenty-five years.

Council to prescribe amount, etc.

Also form of, interest, and payment.

Avails of notes to pay for park land.

Notes, etc., obligatory upon the city.

City treasurer trustee of notes.

Approved, May 27, 1859.

VI.

That, whenever the City of Hartford shall desire to borrow money for any purpose for which the Court of Common Council, of said city, are authorized to lay taxes, under the restrictions of the act to which this act is an addition, the said Court of Common Council be, and they hereby are, authorized and empowered to issue bonds, under the corporate name and seal of said city, bearing interest at no greater rate than six per cent. per annum; the principal of which said bonds shall be payable at some certain time or times within twenty-five years from the issuing of the same, as the said Court of Common Council may direct; and said Court of Common Council may prescribe the amount for which said bonds shall be issued, and direct concerning the form thereof, the rate of interest, and the time of payment of the interest which shall accrue thereon; and said bonds, when issued and

Council authorized to issue six per cent. bonds, when. S. A., vol. 5, p. 538.

delivered, shall be obligatory upon said city and the inhabitants thereof, according to the tenor and purport of the same.

City treasurer to be trustee of bonds. The treasurer of said City of Hartford shall be trustee of said bonds, to hold, dispose of, and account for the same, subject to the orders and directions of the Court of Common Council, and the provisions of the charter of said city.

Approved, July 1, 1863.

VII.

Cities may issue either registered or coupon bonds. S. A., vol. 6, p. 890. SECTION 1. The several towns, cities, and boroughs, of this state, authorized by law to issue bonds, may issue either registered or coupon bonds, and such towns, cities, and boroughs, as have heretofore issued coupon bonds by authority of law, are hereby empowered to issue registered bonds and exchange the same for the coupon bonds now issued by such towns, cities, or boroughs: *provided*, that no greater amount of bonds shall be issued than is now authorized by the laws of this state.

Exchanged bonds, canceled and recorded. SEC. 2. The coupon bonds received by the several towns, cities, and boroughs, in exchange for registered bonds, shall be canceled, and a full record made on the books of the town, city, or borough, of all such bonds so exchanged and canceled.

Approved, July 8, 1870.

VIII.

City authorized to supply water from Connecticut river. S. A., vol. 3, p. 386, § 1, 10, 15-18. SECTION 1. That the mayor, aldermen, common council, and freemen of the City of Hartford be and hereby are authorized and empowered in the manner hereinafter prescribed to take and convey from the Connecticut river, at some point within or near the City of Hartford, such supply of water as the necessities and convenience of the inhabitants of said city may require; and are also hereby authorized and **May issue bonds therefor.** empowered to issue notes, scrip, or certificates of debt under the corporate name and seal of the city, bearing interest at no greater rate than six per cent. per annum, to any amount not exceeding in the whole the sum of two hundred and fifty thousand dollars; the principal of which said notes, scrip, or

certificates shall be payable at some certain time or times
within twenty-five years from the issuing of the same, and
said notes, scrip, or certificates shall be denominated the
" Water Fund of the City of Hartford," and the avails thereof Avails of, how applied.
shall be applied and expended to and for the purpose of sup-
plying said city with pure and wholesome water, according
to the mode or plan adopted in pursuance of the provisions
of this act, and for no other purpose whatsoever; and said
notes, scrip, or certificates when issued and delivered by said
city or by its agent thereunto duly authorized, shall be obligatory upon said city and the inhabitants thereof according
to the purport and tenor of the same; and said city in a city City meeting may prescribe amount, etc.
meeting legally warned and holden for that purpose, may
prescribe the amount for which said notes, scrip, or certificates shall be issued, and direct concerning the form thereof,
the note of interest and the time of paying the interest which
shall accrue thereon.

SEC. 10. Said commissioners or board shall be the trustees Water commission-ers trustees of scrip.
of the notes, scrip, or certificates of debt issued by said City
of Hartford, and may be authorized by said city to superintend the issuing of the same and regulate the particular form
thereof, and after the same or any part of them shall be
issued, said commissioners may sell such notes or certificates Scrip, how dis-posed of.
at public or private sale for their par value, or at such higher
rate as said scrip shall command, or may pledge the same for
loans not usurious under the direction of the Court of Common Council at such times as the proceeds or avails of the
same shall be required to meet the appropriations made or
allowed for the surveying, preparing, constructing, and maintaining of water works by the Court of Common Council,
and the Court of Common Council shall direct what sum of
money shall be raised from and upon said scrip before they
shall permit the construction of water works to be commenced
and prosecuted, and a duplicate record shall be kept by said Record, how kept.
commissioners of all notes or certificates issued, disposed of,
or pledged in pursuance of the provisions of this act, one
copy thereof to be by them delivered to the city treasurer,
and all moneys received by said commissioners shall be de-

Monies received deposited in city banks.

posited in one or more of the banks in the City of Hartford,

Money, how drawn. and shall be drawn out only on the order of the city treasurer.

Commissioners, duties of.

SEC. 15. Said commissioners shall keep a register of all persons who use the water and of the prices by them payable therefor, and shall apply the avails of water rents to the payment of the ordinary and current expenses of said water works, such as repairs, the hire of clerks and agents, and of extending pipes into new localities (under the direction of the Court of Common Council) and shall pay any excess of such avails over the sum requisite for the last-mentioned purposes, to the city treasurer on the first Monday of each and every month on account of water rent received and expended

Account of water rents, how audited.

during the preceding month, having been first audited by the auditor of city accounts on the same day and by him approved. The account so presented shall be attested by the oath or affirmation of at least one member of the board.

SEC. 16. It shall be the duty of the city treasurer to apply

Avails of water rents, how expended.

any avails of water rents by him received to the payment of interest on the aforesaid scrip or certificates of debt; and if there be an excess to report the fact to the Court of Common

Council may direct concerning.

Council, who may direct whether the same shall be applied to the extinguishment of the principal debt incurred by the issuing of said scrip or to the enlargement of the water works.

SEC. 17. In case the avails of water rents in any year shall be inadequate to meet the current expenses of said water works and the interest on said scrip, the deficiency shall be

Tax authorized, when.

supplied by the laying of a tax on the grand list of all persons liable to city taxation, which said tax shall be estimated by the Court of Common Council and recommended to a city meeting especially called for the purpose of laying the same,

Tax, how laid.

and said meeting may then lay such tax as shall be necessary to meet the aforesaid deficiency. And said city at any city meeting specially called and holden for that purpose may lay taxes for the purpose of paying the principal debt aforesaid

Sinking fund.

or any part thereof, by the establishment of a sinking fund, or in any other proper manner.

SEC. 18. Taxes laid for the purposes mentioned in the preceding section may be collected in the same manner as other ^{Tax, how collected.} city taxes; and any claim of said commissioners for the use of water shall be a lien upon the house, tenement, or lot, wherein or in connection with which said water was used by the owner or occupier thereof. And said lien may be fore- ^{Lien created.} closed before the City Court of the City of Hartford in the same manner as a mortgage is now foreclosed according to the rules of equity.

Passed, 1853.

IX.

SECTION 1. That the mayor, aldermen, common council, ^{Additional water bonds.} and freemen of the City of Hartford be, and they are hereby ^{S. A., vol. 3, p. 398.} authorized and empowered to issue notes, scrip, or certificates of debt, under the corporate name and seal of the city, bearing interest at no greater rate than six per cent. per annum, to any amount not exceeding in the whole the sum of one hundred and twenty-five thousand dollars; the principal of ^{Amount not to exceed $25,000.} which said notes, scrip, or certificates, shall be payable at some certain time, or times, within twenty-five years from the issuing of the same; and said notes, scrip, or certificates shall be denominated the "Additional Water Fund of the City of Hartford," and the avails thereof shall be applied and ^{Avails to be expended for water purposes.} expended to and for the purpose of supplying said city with pure and wholesome water, according to the mode or plan adopted in pursuance of the act to which this is an addition, and for no other purpose whatsoever; and said notes, scrip, or certificates, when issued and delivered by said city or its agents thereunto duly authorized, shall be obligatory upon said city, and the inhabitants thereof, according to the tenor and purport of the same; and said city, in a meeting legally ^{City meeting to prescribe amount, etc.} warned and holden for that purpose, may prescribe the amount for which said notes, scrip, or certificates shall be issued, and direct concerning the form thereof, the rate of interest, and the time of paying the interest which shall accrue thereon.

SEC. 2. Said notes, scrip, or certificates, and all the moneys ^{Regulations de notes, etc.} accruing therefrom, shall be subject to all the provisions and regulations prescribed by the tenth section of the act to which this is an addition.

Act, when to take effect,

SEC. 3. This act shall go into effect whenever it shall be accepted by said city, as a part of its charter, at a special city meeting legally warned and holden for that purpose.

Passed, 1856.

X.

Additional water bonds.
S. A., vol. 5, p. 356.

That the Court of Common Council, of the City of Hartford, be, and they are hereby authorized and empowered to issue notes, scrip, or certificates of debt, under the corporate name and seal of said city, bearing interest at no greater rate than six per cent. per annum, to an amount not exceeding

Amount not to exceed $100,000,

one hundred thousand dollars, the principal of which said notes, scrip, or certificates of debt, shall be payable at some certain time or times within twenty-five years from the issuing of the same as the said Court of Common Council may direct; and said Court of Common Council may prescribe the amount for which said notes, scrip, or certificates shall be issued, and direct concerning the form thereof, the rate of interest, and the time of payment of the interest which shall accrue thereon; and said scrip, or certificates of debt, shall be denominated the "Supplementary Water Fund of the City

Avails to be expended for water purposes.

of Hartford;" and the avails thereof shall be applied and expended for water purposes and for no other purpose whatever; and said notes, scrip, or certificates, when issued and delivered, shall be obligatory upon said city and the inhabitants thereof, according to the tenor and purport of the same. The treasurer of said City of Hartford shall be trustee of the notes, scrip, or certificates of debt, as hereby authorized to hold, dispose of, and account for the same, subject to the orders and directions of the Court of Common Council, and the provisions of the charter of said city.

Approved, June 6, 1860.

XI.

Additional water bonds.
S. A., vol. 5, p. 510.

That the Court of Common Council of the City of Hartford be, and they hereby are, authorized and empowered to issue notes, scrip, or certificates of debt, under the corporate name and seal of said city, bearing interest at no greater rate than six per cent. per annum, to an amount, in addition to the amount which they are now authorized to issue, by virtue of the resolution to which this is an addition, not exceeding fifty thousand dollars, the principal of which said notes, scrip, _{Amount not to exceed $50,000.} or certificates of debt shall be payable at some certain time or times, within twenty-five years from the issuing of the same, as the said Court of Common Council may direct, and said Court of Common Council may prescribe the amount for which said notes, scrip, or certificates shall be issued, and direct concerning the form thereof, the rate of interest, and the time of payment of the interest which shall accrue thereon; and said scrip, or certificates of debt, shall be denominated the "Additional Supplementary Water Fund of the City of Hartford." And the avails thereof shall be _{Avails to be expended for water purposes.} applied and expended for water purposes, and for no other purpose whatever; and said notes, scrip, or certificates, when issued and delivered, shall be obligatory upon said city and the inhabitants thereof, according to the tenor and purport of the same.

The *treasurer* of said City of Hartford shall be trustee of _{City treasurer trustee of notes.} the notes, scrip, or certificates of debt, hereby authorized; to hold, dispose of, and account for the same, subject to the orders and directions of the Court of Common Council and the provisions of the charter of said city.

Approved, July 1, 1863.

XII.

SECTION 1. That the board of water commissioners of the _{New main and reservoir. S. A., vol. 7, p. 682.} City of Hartford, with the consent of the mayor and common council of said city, be and they are hereby authorized and empowered to extend and improve the water works of said city, by the construction of a new main from the reservoir in West Hartford to said city, and by the construction of a new reservoir or reservoirs in the town of West Hartford, and by such other improvements in and about said water works in the towns of Hartford or West Hartford, as they shall deem proper: *provided*, that the amount expended by authority of this act shall not exceed the sum of two hundred and fifty thousand dollars.

SEC. 2. That the Court of Common Council of said city, be and they hereby are authorized and empowered to issue notes, scrip or certificates of debt under the corporate name and seal of said city, bearing interest at no greater rate than six per cent. per annum, to an amount not exceeding two hundred and fifty thousand dollars, the principal of which said notes, scrip or certificates of debt, shall be payable at some certain time or times, within twenty-five years from the issuing of the same, as the said Court of Common Council may direct; and said Court of Common Council may prescribe the amount for which said notes, scrip, or certificates of debt shall be issued, and direct concerning the form thereof, the rate of interest, and the time of payment of the interest which shall accrue thereon; and said scrip or certificates of debt shall be denominated "Water works improvement fund of the City of Hartford." And the avails thereof shall be applied and expended for improving and extending the said water works in the manner herein provided, and for no other purpose whatever: and said' notes, scrip, or certificates of debt, when issued and delivered, shall be obligatory upon said city and the inhabitants thereof, according to the tenor and purport of the same.

The treasurer of said City of Hartford shall be trustee of the notes, scrip, or certificates of debt hereby authorized: to hold, dispose of and account for the same, subject to the orders and directions of the Court of Common Council and the provisions of the charter of said city.

SEC. 3. Neither the said board of water commissioners, nor the said common council, shall be authorized to take any action under this act until the same shall be approved in the manner herein prescribed. A special meeting of the legal voters of said city, shall be called by the mayor of said city in the manner provided by the ordinances of said city for calling special meetings thereof, for the purpose of approving or disapproving this act; the vote at said meeting shall be by ballot, and shall be cast by the freemen of said city, in their respective wards; the ballot boxes shall be opened at seven o'clock in the forenoon, and close at five o'clock in the afternoon of the day of said meeting; upon each ballot shall be written or printed the word, "Yes," or the word "No." If a majority of the ballots cast at said meeting, shall have the word "Yes," then this act shall be deemed approved.

Approved, June 25, 1874.

XIII.

SECTION 1. That the City of Hartford and the towns of Hartford, East Hartford, West Hartford, Glastonbury, Manchester, South Windsor, East Windsor, Vernon, Bolton, Andover, Hebron, Marlborough, Wethersfield, and other towns in Hartford and Tolland counties, any or all of them, are hereby authorized and empowered by a major vote of the inhabitants in city or town meeting legally warned and held specially for that purpose to raise by tax or loan, and if by loan may issue bonds therefor any sum of money not exceeding two per cent. of the assessment list of the city or towns last made and perfected for the purpose of uniting with the city and other towns in the purchase of the bridges, causeway, and road of the Hartford Bridge Company, for a free, public highway over the same. *City of Hartford and other towns may raise funds to purchase Hartford bridge, etc. S. A., vol. 6, p. 740.*

SEC. 2. That the City of Hartford, and any towns so raising money for that purpose may associate, enter into contract and agreement, and bind themselves to furnish the money voted in the city or towns as their proportions respectively, of one hundred and fifty thousand dollars, to effect the purchase of the bridge, causeway, and road, and provide a surplus or fund for repairing and keeping the same in repair. *City and towns may agree as to proportion.*

And the city and towns associating shall be liable in the proportions of their several subscriptions to one hundred and fifty thousand dollars for all damages to persons or property on said bridge, causeway, and road, as a public highway, through defect of the same, and shall be liable in the same proportions for all future repairs, and for rebuilding the *Liability for damages and repairs.*

bridges whenever the same shall be required and ordered by a majority of the association or of the Legislature.

SEC. 3. That the mayor and council of the City of Hartford, and the selectmen of the several towns, shall constitute a board for the management of the bridge and highway, under the name of the board of managers of the Hartford Bridge, and in that name may sue and be sued. The board

shall appoint a superintendent, who, under their directions shall have charge of the bridge and highway. They shall appoint a secretary and treasurer, and make annual reports to the city and towns of all receipts and expenditures, and of the condition of the bridges and highway.

SEC. 4. That the county commissioners are hereby instructed to lay out a public highway over the bridge, causeway, and road of the Hartford Bridge Company, when it shall be made to appear to them that the sum of one hundred and fifty thousand dollars shall have been raised, and the board of managers organized according to section third of this act, which road, when so laid out and in the possession of the board of managers, shall be a public highway under the statutes of this state.

SEC. 5. If the parties shall be unable to agree as to the compensation to be paid to said Hartford Bridge Company, for the appropriation of its property to public use as aforesaid, said board of managers may prefer their petition to the Superior Court for Hartford county, praying that such compensation may be ascertained and determined by said court, which petition shall be served upon said company, and proceeded with, in all respects, as if a petition in chancery. And said court may appoint three judicious and disinterested men, who, after being sworn, and after giving reasonable notice to the parties to be heard, shall examine the bridges, road, and property of said company, and assess the just value or compensation to be paid therefor, and make report of their doings, in writing, to said court.

SEC. 6. Upon the return of said report to said court, any person or persons interested therein, may object to the acceptance of the same for any irregularity or improper conduct, and the court may for such cause set aside such report, and order a rehearing before another committee, but if said court accept and establish the same it shall be final and conclusive in the matter. And whenever the amount of compensation so determined, shall have been paid to the Hartford Bridge Company, or deposited by said board of managers with the clerk of said court for the use of said bridge company, said board of managers may take possession of said bridge and road and throw the same open to free public travel.

Approved July 9, 1869.

XIV.

SECTION 1. The treasurer of every county, city, and borough, and the first selectman of every town shall, on the second Monday of October, 1880, and in every fourth year thereafter, make and return to the comptroller of public accounts, a clear and accurate statement, under oath, of all the items constituting the particulars of the total indebtedness of such county, city, borough, or town, on the first day of October next preceding such return, the purpose and object for, and the year in which such indebtedness was incurred, the form in which the same exists, and when payable, the amount actually raised by such corporation during the four years next preceding said first day of October, by taxation and by loan, and the amount actually expended during said period for interest, roads, paupers, salaries, schools, police and fire department, and the rate per centum of taxes laid during said period. Every such officer who shall fail to make and return such statement within one month after the time limited by this act, shall forfeit and pay to the treasurer of the state one hundred dollars, which may be sued for and recovered in the name of said treasurer.

SEC. 2. The comptroller shall, on or before the first day of September, 1880, and in every fourth year thereafter, furnish to said officers printed blanks, adapted to such returns, and shall without delay publish said returns, so as to exhibit the same by counties, and show their several aggregates, and send one copy thereof to the town clerk, the mayor, and chief burgess of every town, city and borough, which shall be kept on file in the office of such officer, and at all times open to public inspection.

Repeal. SEC. 3. Chapter thirty of the public acts passed in January session, A. D. 1877, is hereby repealed.

Approved, March 28, 1879.

HIGHWAYS AND PUBLIC WORKS.

I.

**Powers of Court of Common Council.
S. A., vol. 6, p. 314.** SECTION 1. The Court of Common Council of the City of Hartford shall have exclusive power to lay out,* make, and

---

* Powers granted de lay-out of highways, etc., constitutional. Nichols v. Bridgeport, 23 Conn., 189.

No obligation on the city to lay out, construct and repair highways, except as imposed by statute. Stonington v. States et al., 31 Conn., 213.

establish, within said city, new highways,[b] streets, public ^Highways.
parks, and walks,[c] whenever they deem it for the public good
to do so, or to alter the lines and location of those already
laid out, and discontinue the same and exchange highways
for highways, or sell highways for the purpose of purchasing
other highways, to establish building lines on the land of pro- ^Building lines.
prietors adjoining any street, highway, alley, park or walk,
within said city, between which and such street, highway,
alley, park, or walk, no building or part of a building, or
appurtenance thereof, shall be set up or erected. Also, to
order and establish openings between buildings, for the pur- ^Openings.
pose of free circulation of air for the benefit of the public
health; to cause low grounds where water at any time ^Low lands.
becomes stagnant, to be raised, filled up, or drained. Also, to
lay out, construct, and alter public sewers[d] through the high- ^Sewers.
ways, streets (including turnpike roads), alleys, and public
grounds within said city, and also through the private enclosures within the same; to order and construct and alter sidewalks, gutters, and crosswalks, in and upon all highways, ^Sidewalks, etc.
streets (including turnpike roads), alleys, and public grounds,
within said city, according to the grade and plan, of such
materials as shall be designated by said court. Also to estab-

---

Definition of phrase "laying out." Wolcott v. Pond *et al.*, 19 Conn., 597.
 Land once taken for public use cannot be taken for another. Evergreen Cemetery
Association v. New Haven, 43 Conn., 234; Bridgeport v. New York and New Haven
Railroad Company, 36 Conn., 255.
 Various points as to lay-out. Hawley v. Harrall, 19 Conn., 142; Townsend v.
Hoyle, 20 Conn., 1; Clark v. Middlebury, 47 Conn., 331; Ives v. East Haven, 48
Conn., 272; Parrott v. Bridgeport, 44 Conn., 180.

[b] Highways by dedication. Canday v. Lambert, 2 Root, 173; Sherwood v. Weston,
18 Conn., 32; Curtiss v. Hoyt, 19 Conn., 154; Noyes v. Ward, 19 Conn., 250; Green v.
Canaan, 29 Conn., 157; Riley v. Hammel, 38 Conn., 574; Williams v. New York and
New Haven Railroad Company, 39 Conn., 509; Hamlin v. Norwich, 40 Conn., 13;
Derby v. Alling, 40 Conn., 410; Hall v. Meriden, 48 Conn., 416.
 Giving a deed of land to city for a highway and acceptance of deed, does not
constitute the land a street. New York and New Haven Railroad Company v. New
Haven, 46 Conn., 257.
 A highway dedicated to city which it is its duty to repair, cannot be dedicated by
the city to the town. Guthrie v. New Haven, 31 Conn., 308.

[c] The inner railing of sidewalk is no part of the sidewalk, and without the jurisdiction of Common Council. Williams v. Brace, 5 Conn., 190.

[d] The City of Hartford has power under the general authority to make and maintain highways, to make common sewers under the highways. Cone v. Hartford, 28
Conn., 363.

Fire districts. lish and designate districts of said city, within which it shall not be lawful to erect, enlarge, or elevate, or into or within which it shall not be lawful to remove any wooden building, except by license of said court. Also, to cause to be made,

Repair of highways. and repaired,[e] and altered, highways, streets, parks, and public grounds within said city, and sidewalks, and crosswalks, upon said highways, streets, or public grounds; to assume for said city the duty of making and repairing any part of any

Taxes. turnpike company's road within said city. Also to lay taxes on the polls and ratable estate within said city, sufficient to defray all lawful expenses incurred by said city, according to the corporate powers hereby granted or recognized; and

Assessment for public works. whenever any public work (including dykes), shall have been lawfully laid out or altered by the Court of Common Council, said court may assess[f] the whole or any part of the expense

---

[e] For decisions *de* repairs and defects, see p. 10.

[f] Legislature has power to authorize municipal corporations to assess benefits for local improvements. Nichols v. Bridgeport, 23 Conn., 189.

Such assessments are not "taxes" within the meaning of our statutes. Bridgeport v. New York and New Haven Railroad Company, 36 Conn., 255.

Macadamizing street is a work of repairs, and not a public improvement for which benefits may be assessed. New Haven v. Whitney, 36 Conn., 373.

Under the charter of City of Hartford, the whole expense of a sewer may be assessed upon the parties especially benefited thereby. Clapp v. Hartford, 35 Conn., 66.

Under the charter of the City of Hartford, an ordinance requiring the whole expense of sewers to be assessed upon the parties especially benefited is valid, in all cases where the benefits equal the assessments. Park Ecclesiastical Society v. Hartford, 47 Conn., 89.

An assessment for the entire cost of a sewer is valid, where the benefits are equal to the assessments, although the sewer be larger than the present needs of the section require and it be intended to serve other incidental purposes of drainage. Hungerford v. Hartford, 39 Conn., 279.

If land dedicated to city is accepted and worked no formal lay-out is necessary as prerequisite to assessment. Meriden v. Camp, 46 Conn., 284.

The benefits and damages to be considered are those which are direct and immediate. Clark v. Saybrook, 21 Conn., 313; Hartford v. West Middle School District, 45 Conn., 462.

As to what must be considered in the assessment of benefits. Clapp v. Hartford, 35 Conn., 66.

As to measure of benefits. Clapp v. Hartford, 35 Conn., 66; Bowditch v. New Haven, 40 Conn., 503.

What property may be assessed: Horse railroad track; New Haven v. Fair Haven and Westville Railroad Company, 38 Conn., 422. Vacant lot in full; Clapp v. Hartford, 35 Conn., 66. Shallow lot; Terry v. Hartford, 39 Conn., 286. Lands not abutting; same. Railroad lands not permanently appropriated for railroad uses; New York, New Haven and Hartford Railroad Company v. New Britain, 49 Conn., 40. Land already sufficiently sewered and assessed therefor; Park Ecclesiastical Society v. Hartford, 47 Conn., 89.

of laying out, altering, and making such public work (including highways, streets, sidewalks, gutters, sewers, parks, public walks, openings between buildings, the establishment of building lines, sidewalks, and crosswalks, draining low grounds, or filling up the same), upon the persons whose property is, in the judgment of said Court of Common Council, specially benefited[a] thereby, and estimate the proportion of such expense which said persons shall respectively defray, and enforce the collection of the same, or may, if they deem proper, assess the expense of any such public *Assessments; how made and altered.* work directly upon land benefited thereby, describing said land in said assessments, by metes and bounds, and specifying the amounts assessed on each piece so described, respectively, which said land on default of payment of said assessment *Land sold for assessment.* within six months after public notice thereof shall have been given, shall be liable to be sold for the payment of the same; and said court shall prescribe by ordinance of [the] manner of giving notice of said assessment, and the time, manner, and place of sale of said land: *provided always*, that before *Agreement with owners as to damages.* taking any land or private property for any of the public uses aforesaid, said court shall agree with the owner or owners thereof as to the damage done thereby, or shall cause to be made, a fair appraisal of such damage, which shall be *Appraisal where disagreement.* the actual damage done to the property of such owner or owners,[b] by taking such land or private property, without deducting therefrom any benefits on account of such public *Measure of damage.* work, and shall pay to or deposit the same for the benefit of such owner or owners. *And provided further*, that it shall be *Ordinances de notice.* the duty of said court to enact ordinances, containing suit-

---

What property may not be assessed: School property used solely for school purposes cannot be assessed for highway; Hartford v. West Middle School District, 45 Conn., 462. Railroad depot cannot be assessed for paving highway leading thereto; New York and New Haven Railroad Company v. New Haven, 42 Conn., 279. Railroad tracks cannot be assessed for highway; Bridgeport v. New York and New Haven Railroad Company, 36 Conn., 255.

[a] Damages and benefits should be separately estimated; Terry v. Hartford, 39 Conn., 286. See in this connection Nicholson v. New York and New Haven Railroad Company, 22 Conn., 74; Nichols v. Bridgeport, 23 Conn., 189; Trinity College v. Hartford, 32 Conn., 452.

[b] The mortgagee is not the owner of property and is not entitled to compensation. Norwich v. Hubbard *et al.*, 22 Conn., 587; Whiting v. New Haven, 45 Conn., 303.

able provision for giving notice[1] to all persons interested in any property so taken, of the proceedings of said court in that behalf, and of the appraisal of damages.

Commissioners of relief; how appointed.

SEC. 2.   Said Court of Common Council shall appoint, by concurrent vote of both boards, commissioners of relief, one from each ward of said city, who shall be freeholders, and not members of said court, who shall severally hold office

Term of office, and duties of.

during the pleasure thereof, and shall be sworn to the faithful and impartial discharge of their official duty; and said

Appeals to, final.

commissioners shall hear and determine all appeals from appraisals of damages or assessments of benefits as hereinafter provided, and their jurisdiction of such appeal shall be final.[1]

Appeals, when allowed.

SEC. 3.   An appeal shall be allowed to any person aggrieved by any appraisal of damages or assessment of benefits to said commissioners of relief within thirty days after public notice shall be given of such appraisal or assessment, and said commissioners may reassess said damages or benefits.   And said

Commissioners' meetings; how ordered.

Court of Common Council shall prescribe by ordinance the times and place of the meetings of said commissioners, and the form and mode of service of said appeals.[1]

Reapportionment; how made.

SEC. 4.   If on any appeal from an assessment of benefits the assessment of the appellant is reduced, said commissioners of relief may, thereupon, if they think proper, proceed to reapportion the whole of said assessment appealed from, among the persons whose property is so specially benefited thereby, so that no portion of the expense of such public work shall, by reason of said appeal, be thrown upon said city.[1]

Section vii. of charter repealed.

SEC. 5.   Section seven of "An Act to alter the charter of the City of Hartford, and to combine sundry public statutes relating thereto," approved June 24, 1859, is hereby repealed.

Pending suits.

SEC. 6.   This act shall affect no suit now pending.

Approved, July 24, 1867.

---

[1] A party notified to appear before a board of assessment is bound to take notice of all subsequent proceedings in the matter.   Gilbert v. New Haven, 39 Conn., 467; Bridgeport v. Giddings *et al.*, 43 Conn., 304.

[1] Amended.   See xlv.

II.

Whenever a public highway or street is laid out, extended, Lay-out, change, or discontinuance of highway to be recorded. P. A., 1880, p. 540. straightened, widened, or discontinued, the Court of Common Council in cities, the warden and burgesses in boroughs, and the board of selectmen in towns and parts of towns not within the limits of any city or borough, shall cause to be made a written description of each piece or parcel of land taken from or annexed to the lands of adjoining proprietors, and shall cause the same to be recorded in the land records of the town or city in which the said highway or street is situated.

Approved, March 25, 1880.

III.

Section 1. Whenever it shall be necessary for the proper Diversion of streams not navigable. S. A., vol. 7, p. 178. construction of any bridge, sewer, culvert, highway, embankment, or other public work in the City of Hartford, or for the protection and security of any such public work already constructed, it shall be lawful for the Court of Common Council of said city to direct, and for the board of street commissioners of said city to cause any stream or watercourse, not navigable within the limits of said city, to be changed and diverted from its natural or present channel into a new or different channel.

Sec. 2. Before causing any stream or watercourse to be Compensation. diverted, as provided in the first section of this act, the said board of street commissioners shall agree with the owner or owners of any property or franchise, which may be required for the said purpose, as to the amount of compensation or damage to be paid to the said owner or owners for the same; and in case of disagreement between said board and any such owner or owners, as to the amount of such damage or compensation, then the same shall be appraised in the same manner as damages are now appraised for the laying out of highways in said city; and any person aggrieved by said appraisal, shall have the same right of appeal as is now had by parties aggrieved by the appraisal of damages in laying out highways in said city.

SEC. 3. This act shall not be so construed as to impose any new liability for damages upon the said city for any change in any watercourse, indirectly or necessarily, resulting from the legal lay-out and construction of any public work already built or hereafter to be built.

Approved, July 17, 1874.

IV.

Power over streams, dams, etc., for sewerage and health.
S. A., 1882, p. 419.

SECTION 1. The Court of Common Council of the City of Hartford are hereby authorized, whenever in their opinion the public health or the proper sewerage of said city shall require such action, to take, occupy, and appropriate, in such manner as they shall from time to time deem expedient, any stream or part of a stream, natural or artificial, running in or through said city, and to straighten, deepen, or lower the same, or lower, alter, or remove any or all walls, dams, flumes, or other obstruction to the free and healthy flow of such stream or part of a stream, or raise any of said dams or build and maintain other dams where the public health or convenience may require, or to cover any such stream or part thereof by arches, culverts, or other structures, or to divert the water from such stream or part thereof and cause it to flow through a sewer or other aqueduct built in and upon the bed of such stream, or laid in the earth in or near either bank thereof, or to remove or cause to be removed or altered any or all structures which at any season of the year cause the accumulation of stagnant water, or interrupt in any manner the free and healthy flow of any part of said stream.

Survey and estimates.

SEC. 2. Whenever said Court of Common Council shall take action under the foregoing power, the vote or resolution proposing said improvement shall be referred to the board of street commissioners of said city, who shall prepare a descriptive survey of the improvement proposed, with a careful estimate of the cost of completing the same, and agree if possible with the parties interested upon the damages and special benefits on account of such improvement. They shall give notice ten days prior to the time appointed in said notice Notices. for said hearing in two daily newspapers published in said city, of a time and place for meeting all parties interested in said improvement, and if at such meeting no agreement can Agreement as to damages. be made, said city may proceed in the manner provided in the next succeeding section. But if such agreement shall be made by said board and ratified by said Common Council, the sums agreed upon having been paid to the parties entitled thereto, or deposited to their credit in the city treasury, said city may proceed with and complete said improvement, and do all things necessary or convenient for that purpose without further liability.

Sec. 3. If said board of street commissioners shall be una- Condemnation and appraisal. ble to agree with the parties interested upon the damages or benefits to be paid on account of such improvement, the Superior Court for Hartford county may, on application of said city, after causing such notice to be given of the pendency of such application as said court shall order, appoint three judicious and disinterested freeholders of the county of Hartford to estimate the damages and benefits resulting from said improvement; and said committee having been duly sworn, and having given notice of the time and place of their meeting for the purpose aforesaid, by publishing the same not less than three times in two newspapers published daily in said city at least ten days prior to said meeting, shall meet at the time and place designated, and having heard all parties in interest who shall appear before them, shall determine what parties will be damaged by said improvement in excess of special benefits and the amount thereof; also what parties owning or interested in lands, easements, or franchises within a reasonable distance of said improvement will receive special benefit over all damage and the amount thereof; and also what parties will receive an equal amount of damage and benefit; and thereupon said committee shall report in writing to said court, which may confirm, correct, alter, or set aside said report, and decide all questions that may be raised in the proceedings. If said report shall be set aside, said committee, or a new one to be appointed by said court, shall proceed as before, and their report being finally accepted by such court shall be confirmed by the order or decree of said court; and said report and order or decree shall be recorded by the clerk of the Superior Court for Hartford county, and the award of damages and benefits therein contained shall be final between the parties, and said damages being paid or deposited as before provided, said city may proceed with and complete said public improvement, and do all acts necessary or convenient for that purpose without further liability.

Collection of benefits.

SEC. 4. All amounts due to said city as special benefits under the preceding sections, whether reached by agreement or assessment, may be collected by warrant under the hand of the mayor or acting mayor of said city, directed to the collector thereof, who shall enforce the same in the same manner as tax warrants are served and enforced. Every

Benefits a lien.

such amount shall also be and remain a lien upon the land or other property on account of which it was assessed, which said lien shall commence and attach to said land from the time the Common Council shall take action, laying out or ordering said improvement: *provided* that the same shall not

Lien recorded.

remain a lien thereon for a longer period than three months after the final completion of said work or improvement, unless the board of street commissioners shall within that time lodge with the town clerk of the town of Hartford, for record, a certificate signed by the clerk of said board, describing the premises, the amount assessed, and the improvement for which it was assessed.

Notice of payment of benefits.

SEC. 5. Upon the completion of said work or improvement, the said board of street commissioners shall give notice thereof, and that said benefits are due and payable, by publication twice in two daily newspapers published in said city, and all benefits assessed thereon shall be immediately due and payable. If the actual cost of the construction of such improvement or public work shall be less than the sum assessed upon the parties benefited, each of the parties so assessed shall be entitled to a proportionate deduction from his assessment.

Sec. 6. This act shall be a public act, and shall take effect from and after its passage.

Approved, March 22, 1882.

V.

Section 1. Persons authorized to construct or to repair highways may make or clear any watercourse or place for draining off the water therefrom into or through any person's land so far as necessary to drain off such water; and when it shall be necessary to make any drain upon or through any person's land for the purpose named in this act it shall be done in such a way as to do the least damage to such land: *provided* nothing in this act shall be so construed as to allow the drainage of water from such highways into or upon any door-yard in front of any dwelling-house or into or upon yards and inclosures used exclusively for the storage and sale of goods and merchandise. <small>Drainage of highways. P. A., 1881, p. 34.</small>

Sec. 2. Section sixteen of part one, title sixteen, chapter seven (page 233), of the general statutes is hereby repealed. <small>Repeal.</small>

Approved, April 5, 1881.

VI.

Section 1. Every railroad company or trustee operating any railroad which may locate and construct a railroad across any turnpike, highway, or public street, shall construct it so as to cross over or under the same; and may, under the direction of the railroad commissioners, raise or lower the same at said crossing, or change the location thereof; and shall make and maintain such bridges, abutments, tunnels, arches, excavations, embankments, and approaches as the railroad commissioners shall order, and the convenience and safety of the public travel upon said turnpike, highway, or street may require; but the railroad commissioners may, upon due notice to said company and to the selectmen of the town or mayor of the city in which said crossing is situated, direct such company or trustee to construct its railroad at such crossing upon a level with the turnpike, highway, or <small>Railroads to be constructed so as not to cross highways at grade. P. A., 1883, p. 284. Exceptions.</small>

street; but no such direction shall be given in any case except for special reasons which shall be recorded in the records of the railroad commissioners.

New highway crossing railroad, how constructed. SEC. 2. Whenever a new highway or a new portion of a highway shall hereafter be constructed across a railroad, such highway or portion of highway shall pass over or under the railroad, as the railroad commissioners shall direct. The company or trustee operating such railroad shall construct such crossing to the approval of the railroad commissioners, and may take land for the purposes of this section in the manner now provided by law for the taking of lands by railroad companies. One-half the expense of such crossing shall be borne by the company or trustee constructing the same and the other half thereof shall be paid to said company or trustee by the town, city, or borough which constructs said **Expense, how defrayed.** highway or portion of highway. If said highway shall cross over said railroad the structure necessary therefor shall be maintained and kept in repair by the party bound to maintain said highway; but if it shall cross under said railroad such structure shall be maintained and kept in repair by said company or trustee.

Alteration of highway crossed at grade. SEC. 3. The railroad commissioners may, when in their opinion public safety requires an alteration of any highway crossed at grade by a railroad, after such notice as they shall deem reasonable to the company owning or operating or the trustees operating said railroad, and to the selectmen of the town or the mayor of the city in which said highway is so crossed, and to the owners of the land adjoining said crossing, order said company or said trustees to make such alteration in such highway as said commissioners shall find is practicable and ought to be made, and shall determine by whom **Expense, how paid.** the expense of such alteration shall be paid; *provided,* that in no case shall more than one-half the expense be paid by the town or city aforesaid; *and provided further,* that such alterations as are made at the primary instance of the railroad commissioners, shall not be ordered at the rate of more than one a year on any one railroad, except in the case of railroads now having a double track throughout their entire length.

Railroad companies may take land for the purposes of this **Power to take land.** section in the manner now provided by law for the taking of lands by railroad companies.

SEC. 4. No lands shall be taken by any railroad company **Taking of land for the purpose.** or trustee operating a railroad for the purposes mentioned in this act, except such as are necessary, which necessity shall be certified by the railroad commissioners; but no such taking need be based upon any special finding that public necessity and convenience require such taking.

SEC. 5. Every railroad company or trustee operating a **Penalty for non-compliance.** railroad which shall fail to comply with any provision of this act shall forfeit to the state one hundred dollars for each and every month of such non-compliance, in each and every instance of such non-compliance. The railroad commissioners shall give notice of all such forfeitures to the state treasurer, who shall collect the same.

SEC. 7. Nothing contained in this act shall in any respect **Act of 1876 not repealed.** repeal or modify the provisions of chapter thirty-six of the public acts of 1876 (page 102).

Approved, May 3, 1883.

VII.

SECTION 1. The selectmen of any town within which a **Provision for safety of highway at railroad crossing. P. A., 1876, p. 102.** highway crosses or is crossed by a railroad, or the directors of any railroad company whose road crosses or is crossed by a highway, may bring their petition in writing to the railroad commissioners, therein alleging that public safety requires an alteration in such crossing, its approaches, the method of crossing, the location of the highway or railroad, or the removal of obstructions to the sight at such crossing, and praying that the same be ordered. Whereupon the railroad commissioners shall appoint a time and place for hearing the petition, and shall give such notice thereof as they judge reasonable to said selectmen, the railroad company, and to the owners of the land adjoining such crossing, and after such notice and hearing said commissioners shall determine what alterations or removals shall be made, by whom done, and at whose expense.

Assessment of damages.

SEC. 2. In case the party by whom the changes are to be made cannot agree with the owner of the land or other property to be removed or taken under the said decision of the railroad commissioners, the damage shall be assessed in the same manner as is provided in case of land taken by railroad companies. The expense of such assessment to be paid in the same manner as the expense of the alterations.

Appeal.

SEC. 3. The decision of the commissioners shall be communicated to the selectmen, to the railroad company, and to the owners of any property directed to be removed or taken, within twenty days after final hearing, and any person aggrieved by such decision may appeal therefrom in the same manner and with like effect as is provided in the case of appeals from any order of the railroad commissioners upon any proceeding relative to the location, abandonment, or changing of depots or stations.

Approved, June 19, 1876.

VIII.

Provision for safety of highway at railroad crossing. P. A., 1877, p. 152.

That all the provisions of chapter thirty-six, entitled "An Act in regard to railroad crossings," of the acts of 1876, applying to selectmen of towns, in regard to highways crossing or crossed by railroads, be, and the same are hereby extended to mayors and common councils of cities, and to the warden and burgesses of boroughs, in regard to streets crossing or crossed by railroads.

Approved, February 21, 1877.

IX.

Highway not to be laid out near railroad track. P. A., 1876, p. 345.

SECTION 1. No highway which does not cross a railroad track shall hereafter be laid out or opened to the public within one hundred yards of any railroad track unless the lay-out has been approved by a judge of the Superior Court, after notice to all parties in interest, and his written approval has been lodged in the office of the town clerk of the town in which the proposed highway is situated.

Power of judge of Superior Court.

SEC. 2. A judge of the Superior Court shall not approve the lay-out of any highway, which does not cross a railroad track, within one hundred yards of any railroad track, unless he finds that public convenience and necessity requires such highway to be within such distance; and he shall have power to require any town opening a highway to the public within such distance, to erect and maintain such a fence between such highway and the railroad track as, in his opinion, the safety of the public may require.

Approved, March 28, 1878.

X.

SECTION 1. That the Court of Common Council of the City of Hartford, by the board of street commissioners of said city, may assess a proportional sum of the expense of laying out, altering, and making any highway, street, sewer, or park, lawfully laid out or altered, upon any person or persons in the judgment of said board specially benefited thereby, whether the land of such person or persons abuts upon such highway, street, sewer, or park, or not. *Assessment for public improvements on land not abutting. S. A., vol. 7, p. 376.*

SEC. 2. This act shall not affect the right of appeal from the action of said board. *Right of appeal preserved.*

Approved, July 30, 1872.

XI.

When any assessment of damages or benefits, or both, for the lay-out or construction of any highway or other public work by any town, city, or borough, has been or shall be made upon or in respect of any land, or interest in land which has belonged to a deceased person, of whose estate no distribution has been recorded, it shall be sufficient if the report or schedule of such assessment describe the property assessed as land of the estate of such deceased person, or describe his estate as being assessed; and any lien or claim upon said property, resulting from said assessment, otherwise legal and formal, may be foreclosed or otherwise enforced against said property, or the amount of said assessment collected from any persons claiming said land under the title of such deceased person. *Land belonging to estate of deceased person may be assessed for damages and benefits, without naming the heirs. R. S., p. 91, § 5.*

XII.

Cost of improvement to be ascertained and assessed before lay-out. S. A., vol. 8, p. 111.

SECTION 1. Before any public work or improvement, for the cost of which the City of Hartford under its charter may assess benefits, shall be laid out or constructed, the cost of the same, including damages to be paid, shall be ascertained by the Court of Common Council of said city, and all benefits to be paid by the persons benefited thereby, shall be ascer-

Manner of assessment.

tained as follows: The vote or resolution proposing the laying out or construction of such work or improvement shall be, by said Court of Common Council, referred to the board of street commissioners of said city, who shall first estimate the cost of the construction of such work or improvement, and shall also appraise the damages to be paid to any person for land, or any interest therein, taken for such improvement, and shall also assess the said cost of construction, and the amount of said damages upon the persons benefited thereby in the manner now provided by the charter and ordinances of said city, and all appeals therefrom shall be taken, and all proceedings had thereon, as now by law provided. Upon the completion of such proceedings the board of street commissioners shall report the same to said Court of Common Council with their recommendations, and said Court of Common Council may thereupon direct the lay-out or construction of such work or improvement at its discretion.

Notice of payment of benefits.

SEC. 2. Upon the final lay-out or completion of the construction of any such public work, the board of street commissioners shall give notice thereof, and that said benefits are due and payable, by publication twice in two daily newspapers published in said city, and all benefits assessed therefor shall be immediately due and payable. If the actual cost of the construction of any public work shall be less than the sum estimated by the board of street commissioners and assessed upon the parties benefited, each of the parties so assessed shall be entitled to a proportionate deduction from his assessment. Said benefits shall be a lien upon the land on

Benefits a lien.

account of which they were assessed, which said lien shall commence and attach to said land from the time of the passage by the Court of Common Council of the vote laying out or ordering the construction of said work: *provided*, that the same shall not remain a lien thereon for a longer period than three months from the final lay-out, or completion of such work or improvement, unless the board of street commissioners shall within that time lodge with the town clerk of the town of Hartford for record, a certificate, signed by the clerk of said board, describing the premises, the amount assessed, and the improvement for which it was assessed.

Lien recorded.

Approved, March 19, 1877.

XIII.

Whenever any assessment has been or shall hereafter be laid by any town, city, borough, or other municipal corporation, upon private property benefited by any public work or improvement, for the expense of such public work or improvement, or for benefits accruing therefrom, and a certificate of lien upon such property has been or shall be lodged for record with the town clerk, neither the principal of such assessment nor any interest thereon shall be collectible by such municipality until such public work or improvement shall have been completed and the fact of such completion recorded on the record books of such municipality by order of the board or officers by whom such work or improvement was ordered.

Assessment lien nor interest thereon to be collectible until completion of work, etc.
P. A., 1883, p. 261.

Approved, April 26, 1883.

XIV.

· Section 1. All appeals hereafter taken from any appraisal of damages or assessment of benefits made by the board of street commissioners of the City of Hartford, shall be to the judge of the Court of Common Pleas for the county of Hartford.[a]

Appeals from appraisals and assessments; to whom made.
S. A., vol. 7, p. 527.

---

[a] The judge takes judicial notice of the charter and its provisions. Clapp v. Hartford, 35 Conn., 66. That he adopts a different rule of apportionment than that uniformly applied by the Common Council is no error unless the rule itself is unjust. Same.

If an undistinguishable part of an assessment for benefits be void the whole is void. Bridgeport v. New York and New Haven Railroad Company, 36 Conn., 255.

On an appeal from an assessment of benefits for altering highway the appellant

Joinder in appeal: all constitute one cause.

SEC. 2. As many of the parties interested as may choose to do so, may join in such appeal; and, when separate appeals are taken by different parties from one assessment and appraisal, all such appeals shall be heard and tried as one cause.[b]

Appeals; how taken.

SEC. 3. Appeals may be taken from the assessment of benefits only, but, if taken from the appraisal of damages, shall be from the said appraisal and also from the assessment of benefits made at the same time and for the same public

When taken.

work. Such appeals shall be taken within ten days after public notice shall be given of such appraisal or assessment, and shall be by a suitable petition in writing, setting forth the whole of said assessment or appraisal and assessment appealed from, and asking for a reappraisal and reassessment,

Citation.

or for a reassessment only, with a citation attached thereto, signed by any authority authorized to sign writs, and return-

Return day.

able before said judge at two o'clock in the afternoon on the day three weeks subsequent to the day on which public

Service.

notice of said appraisal shall have been given; and said citation shall be served upon the clerk of said city at least six days before the return day thereof.

Heard by judge or committee.

SEC. 4. Such appeals may be heard by said judge, but shall, upon the motion of any party thereto, or person interested therein, be referred to a committee for hearing.

Reapportionment.

SEC. 5. If, upon the hearing of any appeal, the judge or committee shall find cause to alter said appraisal and assessment, or assessment of benefits only, then said judge or committee shall proceed to reapportion the whole amount of the damages and benefits, or benefits only, upon the persons or land specially benefited.

---

cannot claim that the alteration was unnecessary and unreasonable. Gilbert v. New Haven, 39 Conn., 467. Evidence of previous assessments not admissable. Same. Evidence to show that assessments against others are unreasonable is inadmissable. Same.

Courts will not consider the motives of action on the part of city authorities, provided their proceedings are regular and the matter within their jurisdiction. Park Ecclesiastical Society v. Hartford, 47 Conn., 89.

Reasons of appeal must be specified with as much particularity as in bills of equity. Bowditch v. New Haven, 40 Conn., 503.

[b]If but one appeals, his assessment only is brought up for revision. Clapp v. Hartford, 35 Conn., 66.

SEC. 6. If the judge or committee hearing said appeal Notice to all interested in reapportionment, etc. shall be of opinion that persons other than those who appear upon the record are interested in the subject-matter of said appeal, said judge or committee shall cause the appellants to give notice of the pendency of the proceedings to such other persons; which notice shall be by publication in one or more newspapers published in said city, for such time and in such form as said judge or committee shall direct.

SEC. 7. Such judge shall have, for the purpose of disposing Powers of judge. of said appeal, all the power of the Superior Court, and may render judgment thereon, and may tax costs in favor of either party and issue execution for said costs, to be taxed as upon Costs. civil process in the Superior Court.

SEC. 8. Said judge shall, when the proceedings in any case Return of papers to city clerk. arising under this act are closed, return all the papers connected with the case to the clerk of said city, to be by him kept on file.

SEC. 9. This act shall take effect from its passage; and all Pending suits. acts and parts of acts inconsistent herewith are hereby repealed; but this act shall not affect any suit now pending.

Approved, July 1, 1873.

XV.

Any person aggrieved by the appraisal of damages in lay- Right of appeal. P. A., 1880, p. 496. ing out any highway, or in making any improvement or public work in any city (except Bridgeport and Hartford) or borough, or by the assessment of benefits therefor, may appeal from such appraisal or assessment, to any judge of the Superior Court, within thirty days after public notice shall be given of such appraisal or assessment, which appeal shall be a written petition for a reappraisal or reassessment, with a citation attached thereto, and returnable in not less than six, nor more than twenty days after its date, and shall be served at least six days before the return day, upon the clerk of such city or borough.

XVI.

All appeals now taken, or which may hereafter be taken Completion of pending appeals by successor of judge. S. A., vol. 7, p. 398. from any appraisal of damages, or assessment of benefits made by the board of street commissioners of the City of Hartford, and the City of New Britain, to the judge of the Court of Common Pleas for the county of Hartford, and which shall be pending at the time of the completion of the term of service of such judge, shall be heard and disposed of as fully and completely by the successor of such judge as said appeals might have been by the judge to whom they were originally taken.

Approved, June 18, 1875.

XVII.

Revising decision of a judge.
R. S., p. 450, § 17.

When jurisdiction, original or appellate, over any subject matter or proceeding, is or shall be vested in a judge of the Superior Court, any party to such proceeding, who is aggrieved by the decision of such judge, upon any question of law arising therein, may, within ten days after he or his attorney shall have been notified of the final decision or judgment of such judge, present to such judge a motion for a new trial, stating therein said questions of law, or a motion in error for questions arising on the record of such proceedings; and said judge, if he shall be of opinion that such motion is not intended for delay, and that the questions are such as to entitle the party to a revision thereof, shall reserve such motion for a new trial, for the opinion of the Supreme Court of Errors next to be holden in the district or county, where the parties, or any of them, reside, and shall allow such motion in error, and transmit such record to said Supreme Court of Errors, in the manner by law provided in the case of similar motions made in court; but in cases of appeal from the appraisal of damages in laying out any street, or in making any improvement or public work, in any city, village, or borough, upon paying to the person or persons entitled thereto damages appraised therefor, or upon depositing the same in the manner provided by law; and in cases where no damages shall be appraised, such city, village, or borough, may immediately proceed to lay out and open such street, or make and complete such improvement or public work, in the same manner as if no such motion had been made; and in proceedings

In appeals from appraisal of damages for public improvements.

on writs of *habeas corpus*, the judge may, at his discretion, Stay of execution. decline to order a stay of execution.

XVIII.

SECTION 1. That section seventeen, chapter fifteen, title Revising decision of a judge. nineteen, of the revised statutes, be and hereby is amended P. A., 1876, p. 107. by inserting after the words "Superior Court," at the end of the second line of said section, the following: "And whenever jurisdiction, original or appellate, over any subject matter or proceeding has been or shall be vested in any judge of the Court of Common Pleas or District Court."

Approved, June 22, 1876.

XIX.

In all cases of assessments of damages or benefits for the Correction of errors in assessments for lay-out or construction of public works, the Superior Court, public works. R. S., p. 91, § 6. or any other appellate or revising tribunal to which such cases may be removed, may, by reassessment or otherwise, correct any errors which may be shown to exist in the report or schedule of said assessments, provided reasonable notice be given to any person not before said court or tribunal, who may be injuriously affected by the correction of said errors, to appear and show cause why said correction should not be made; but said court or tribunal may, without special notice, correct manifest clerical errors and misdescriptions, when it is evident that no person interested has been misled thereby.

XX.

That in all cases where the Court of Common Council of Benefits set-off against damages. the City of Hartford shall have agreed upon with, or ap- P. A., 1870, p. 418. praised to any person or persons, damages for taking any land or private property for any public work in said city and shall also have assessed betterments on account of the same public work, upon the owner or owners of such land or private property or upon such land or private property, the amount of such assessment shall be an off-set against such damages, and the city treasurer may credit such owner or owners with the amount of such assessment, so assessed upon or payable by him or them, and the entry of such credit upon the books of said treasurer shall have the same effect as the payment to such owner or owners so credited in whole or part payment, as the case may be, of the sum appraised for such damages; but the Court of Common Council may in any individual case where they see fit pay the whole of such damages and collect the assessments of betterments as heretofore.

Approved, July 6, 1870.

Effect.

Common Council may direct concerning.

XXI.

Assessment for highways discontinued before opened, void. R. S., p. 240, § 52.

Actual damages recoverable.

When any highway, duly laid out, has been or shall be legally discontinued before being opened and worked, no action shall be brought to recover damages assessed therefor, but the owner of the lands over which it is laid out may recover of the town, city, or borough his actual damages from laying it out.[1]

XXII.

Damages and benefits by change of grade.
P. A., 1882, p. 158.

SECTION 1.　When the owner of land adjoining a public highway, or of any interest in such land shall sustain special damage or receive special benefits to his property by reason of any change in the grade of such highway by the town, city, or borough in which such highway may be situated, such town, city, or borough shall be liable to pay to him the amount of such special damage, and shall be entitled to receive from him the amount or value of such special benefits, to be ascertained in the manner provided for ascertaining damages and benefits occasioned by laying out or altering highways therein.　Whenever special benefits shall be finally assessed and established concerning any lands or interest therein, under the foregoing provisions, such town, city, or borough shall have a lien upon the lands concerning or upon which they are so assessed, to be established and enforced in the manner provided for establishing and enforcing liens for

Liens.

---

[1]See Kirtland v. Meriden, 39 Conn., 107; Carson v. Hartford, 48 Conn., 68.

benefits occasioned by public works in such towns, cities, and boroughs.[2]

Approved, April 6, 1882.

XXIII.

SECTION 1. The party bound to maintain any bridge or road shall erect and maintain a sufficient railing or fence on the side of such bridge, and of such parts of such road as are so made or raised above the adjoining ground as to be unsafe for travel; and whoever shall suffer damage in his person or property, by reason of the want of any such railing or fence, may recover damages from such party. *Railings to be erected on roads and bridges. R. S., p. 232, § 9.* *Liability for injuries.*

SEC. 2. Any person injured in person or property by means of a defective road or bridge may recover damages from the party bound to keep it in repair; but no action for any such injury shall be maintained against any town, city, corporation, or borough, unless written notice of such injury, and the nature and cause thereof, and of the time and place of its occurrence shall, within sixty days thereafter, or if such defect consist of snow or ice or both, within fifteen days thereafter, be given to a selectman of such town or to the clerk of such city, corporation, or borough; and when the injury is caused by a structure legally placed on such road by a railroad company, it, and not the party bound to keep the road in repair, shall be liable therefor. *Liability for injuries. P. A., 1883, p. 283.* *Notice.*

XXIV.

When any person shall place or keep building materials, or any obstacle, in any highway, either with or without a license therefor from the city, town, or borough, in which such highway may be situated, he shall pay to said city, town, or borough, all costs and damages which it shall sustain, or be compelled to pay, by reason thereof. *Liability of property owner for obstructions. R. S., p. 488, § 2.*

---

[2] See Fellowes v. New Haven, 44 Conn., 240.

XXV.

Coasting in cities,
boroughs, and
towns regulated.
P. A., 1881, p. 42.

SECTION 1. The mayor of any city, the warden of any borough, or the majority of the selectmen of any town, may limit or prohibit coasting in the public streets and highways of such city, borough, or town, and may issue an order stating such prohibition or the limit to be observed, and shall cause the same in case of cities to be published in a newspaper of said city, and in case of towns or boroughs to be printed or plainly written and posted in at least ten conspicuous places within the limits of such borough or town: *provided*, selectmen of towns having cities or boroughs within their limits shall not exercise such power within the limits of such cities or boroughs.

Penalty.

SEC. 2. Any person who shall disobey any order so issued and published or posted shall, on conviction, be fined not less than two nor more than seven dollars.

Approved, April 6, 1881.

XXVI.

Highway near
bridge in a city not
to be obstructed by
railroad trains.
P. A., 1881, p. 80.

SECTION 1. Where any railroad crosses a highway in any city at grade, within two hundred feet of a covered bridge on said highway, such highway shall not be obstructed by the making up of railroad trains, nor by allowing any train, car, or locomotive to stand on or across said highway, for more than three minutes at one time; and whenever such highway has been once so used or occupied, or whenever a locomotive or train has passed entirely over it, said highway shall not again be so used or occupied, or crossed by locomotive or cars, until a sufficient time has been allowed to enable all teams which are ready, and waiting for the purpose, to cross the tracks of said railroad.

Penalty.

SEC. 2. Any servant, agent, or employee of any railroad corporation, wilfully violating any provision of the preceding section, shall be deemed guilty of a misdemeanor, and on conviction thereof, on complaint of any grand juror of the town where the offense is committed, shall be punished by a

finc not exceeding seven dollars, or by imprisonment not
exceeding thirty days, or by both.

Approved, April 14, 1881.

XXVII.

SECTION 1. The railroad commissioners when requested
in writing by the selectmen of any town, the mayor and
common council of any city, or the warden and burgesses of
any borough, to order a gate or electric signal to be erected,
or a flagman to be stationed at any railroad crossing, shall visit
such place, first giving the authorities making such request
reasonable notice thereof, and if the public safety requires
it, shall order the company operating said railroad to maintain a gate, or electric signal, to keep a flagman at said place,
or to do any other act at said place needful for the protection of the public, and may specify when said gate shall be
opened and closed, or when flagmen shall be on duty, and
may change any such order when they deem it necessary,
first visiting the town, city, or borough in which said crossing is located, and there giving the authorities thereof an
opportunity to be heard thereon; and if any railroad company shall neglect to station flagmen, or maintain gates or
electric signals as ordered by said commissioners, or shall
neglect to comply with any order of said commissioners
provided for by this section, or any order heretofore issued
by said commissioners relating to the maintenance of gates,
electric signals, or flagmen, at any railroad crossing, it shall
forfeit to the state fifty dollars for each day of such neglect.

SEC. 2. When the railroad commissioners, on application
as aforesaid, shall make an order as provided herein, or
refuse to make the same, their decision shall be communicated to the parties in interest within thirty days from the
final hearing on the same, and either party aggrieved by
such decision may appeal therefrom to the Superior Court,
in the manner and with like effect as provided for appeals in
section fifty-two of article two, part nine, chapter two, title
seventeen, of the general statutes (page 327). But in all
cases where a flagman, gate, or electric signal shall be ordered

Gates, signals, or flagmen at railroad crossings.
P. A., 1881, p. 294.

Penalty.

Decision of commissioners, how communicated.

Appeals.

Expense.

by the Superior Court upon an appeal taken by the applicants therefor, such court may at its discretion order a portion of the expense of maintaining or erecting the same, but not exceeding one-half, to be borne by the town, city, or borough in which the crossing is situated; and the Superior

Amendment of order.

Court may at any time upon the application of either party, with due notice to adverse parties, annul or vary any order passed as aforesaid; *provided*, such court shall find there has been a change of circumstances surrounding such crossing.

Approved, May 1, 1883.

XXVIII.

Switching, etc., across highway, how forbidden. P. A., 1893, p. 269.

SECTION 1.   The railroad commissioners are empowered and authorized to order any railroad company not to use for switching purposes, nor for standing trains of any kind, such portion of its tracks which now are or hereafter may be placed upon or across any public street or highway as in their opinion the public convenience requires should not be so used.

Complaint.

SEC. 2.   Said commissioners, when requested in writing by the selectmen of any town, the mayor and common council of any city, or the warden and burgesses of any borough, to forbid the use for switching purposes of the tracks of any railroad company where the same cross any public street or highway within said town, city, or borough, shall visit such crossing, first giving reasonable notice to the authorities making said request, and if public convenience requires, shall

Order of railroad commissioners.

order the company operating said railroad not to use the same or such part thereof as may be specified in said order for switching purposes, and may make any order regulating such switching that they shall deem proper.   Said commissioners may change any such order when they deem it necessary, first visiting said town, city, or borough, and giving the authorities thereof an opportunity to be heard thereon.

Penalty.

SEC. 3.   Any railroad company neglecting or refusing to obey any order of the railroad commissioners provided for in this act shall forfeit to the state fifty dollars for each day of such neglect.

Sec. 4. When said commissioners, on application as afore- *Appeals.* said, shall make an order as provided herein, or refuse to make the same, their decision shall be communicated to the parties in interest within twenty days from the final hearing on the same, and either party aggrieved by such decision may appeal therefrom to the Superior Court in the manner and with the like effect as provided for appeals in section fifty-two of article two, part nine, chapter two, title seventeen of the general statutes (page 327); and the Superior Court may at any time, upon the application of either party, with due notice to adverse parties, amend or .change any order passed as aforesaid: *provided*, such court shall find that there has been a change of circumstances surrounding such crossing.

Approved, April 17, 1883.

XXIX.

Section 1. Whenever the selectmen of any town, the *Locomotive whis-* mayor and common council of any city, or the warden and *tling restricted.* *P. A., 1881, p. 21.* burgesses of any borough, shall bring their petition in writing to the railroad commissioners, representing that the interests of the public require that the blowing of the locomotive whistle upon a railroad at certain points within the limits of such town, city, or borough should be dispensed with, said commissioners shall appoint a time and place for hearing said petition, and shall give reasonable notice thereof to the petitioners and the railroad company in question; and if after such hearing they shall be of opinion that the sounding of the whistle can be dispensed with, without danger to the public, they shall direct said railroad company to omit the same, and require that the engine bell shall be rung in lieu thereof, at such points as they may specify.

Sec. 2. Whenever any railroad company shall receive such *Directions.* directions from the railroad commissioners, it shall thereafter omit the sounding of the whistle at the points named in said order.

Approved, March 22, 1881.

XXX.

SECTION 1. No person or corporation shall disturb the surface of any street or highway in the City of Hartford by digging or making excavation, or cause the same to be so disturbed, without first giving notice to the board of street commissioners of said city, and said board of street commissioners shall have the power to supervise and direct any such digging or excavating, and may prescribe the manner in which the same shall be done and the condition to which said street or highway shall be restored: *provided, however,* that no such person or corporation shall be compelled to do more than to restore said street or highway to its usual condition.

Streets not to be disturbed without notice to street commissioners. S. A., 1883, p. 762.

SEC. 2. If any person or corporation so disturbing or causing to be disturbed the surface of any street or highway as aforesaid, shall fail to comply with the directions of said board of street commissioners in restoring the same to its usual condition, said board may, after reasonable notice to such person or corporation if known, otherwise without notice, restore the same, and collect and recover from such person or corporation double the cost of such restoration.

Streets to be restored to their ordinary condition.

SEC. 3. Any person or corporation who shall neglect to comply with the provisions of section one of this act as to notice shall forfeit and pay to the City of Hartford, for the use of the city treasury, a penalty of not less than five and not more than twenty-five dollars, the same to be recovered in an action brought in the name of said city in the manner provided in the charter of said city for the recovery of fines and penalties.

Penalty.

SEC. 4. The board of water commissioners of said city shall be exempt from such of the provisions of this act as pertain to the notice required to be given to the board of street commissioners and the penalty prescribed therein.

Water commissioners not required to give notice.

Approved, April 4, 1883.

LIBRARIES.

SECTION 1. The city council of any city shall have power to establish and maintain* a public library and reading-room, together with such kindred apartments and facilities as said council shall approve, for the use and benefit of such city, and may levy a tax not to exceed one mill and one-half of a mill on the dollar annually, on all the taxable property of the city, such tax to be levied and collected in the same manner as other taxes of said city, and to be known as the "library fund." ^{Council may establish library and reading-room. P. A., 1881, p. 50.}

SEC. 2. When any city council shall have decided to establish and maintain a public library and reading-room, under this act, the mayor of such city shall, with the approval of the city council, appoint a board of nine directors for the same, chosen from the citizens at large, with reference to their fitness for such office; and not more than one member of the city council shall be a member of said board. ^{Directors, how chosen.}

SEC. 3. Said directors shall hold office, one-third for one year, one-third for two years, and one-third for three years from the first of July following their appointment, and at their first regular meeting shall cast lots for the respective terms; and annually thereafter the mayor shall before the first of July in each year appoint, as before, three directors, to take the place of the retiring directors, who shall hold office for three years, and until their successors are appointed. The mayor may, with the consent of the city council, remove any director for misconduct or neglect of duty. ^{Term of office.}

SEC. 4. Vacancies in the board of directors, occasioned by removal, resignation, or otherwise, shall be reported to the city council, and be filled in the same manner as original appointments. ^{Vacancies.}

SEC. 5. Said directors shall, immediately after their appointment, meet and organize by the election of one of their number as president, and by the election of such other ^{Powers and duties.}

---

* Concerning appropriations for libraries, see p. 38.

officers as they may deem necessary. They shall make and adopt such by-laws, rules, and regulations for their own guidance and for the government of the library and reading-room as may be expedient, not inconsistent with this act. They shall have the exclusive control of the expenditure of all moneys collected to the credit of the library fund, and of the construction of any library building, and of the supervision, care, and custody of the grounds, rooms, or buildings constructed, leased, given, or set apart for that purpose: *provided*, that all moneys collected and received for such purpose shall be placed in the treasury of said city, to the credit of the "library fund," and shall be kept separate from other moneys of the city, and shall be drawn upon by the proper officers of said city, upon the properly authenticated vouchers of said directors. Said board shall have power to purchase, lease, or accept grounds, to erect, lease, or occupy an appropriate building or buildings for the use of said library; to appoint a person of suitable learning, ability, and experience as librarian, and all necessary assistants, and fix their compensation, to remove such appointees; and shall in general carry out the spirit and intent of this act, in establishing and maintaining a public library and reading-room, together with such kindred apartments and facilities as said council shall approve.

Libraries to be free.   SEC. 6. Every library and reading-room established under this act shall be forever free to the use of the inhabitants of the city where located, always subject to such reasonable rules and regulations as the board of directors may adopt, in order to render the use of said library and reading-room of the greatest benefit to the greatest number; and said board may exclude from the use of said library and reading-room any and all persons who shall wilfully violate such rules. And said board may extend the privileges and use of such library and reading-room to persons residing outside of such city in this state, upon such terms and conditions as said board may from time to time prescribe.

Annual report.   SEC. 7. The said board of directors shall make on or before the second Monday in June an annual report to the city

council, stating the condition of their trust on the first day
of June of that year, the various sums of money received
from the library fund and from other sources, and how such
moneys have been expended, and for what purposes; the
number of books and periodicals on hand; the number added
by purchase, gift, or otherwise, during the year; the number
lost or missing; the number of visitors attending; the number of books loaned out, and the general character of such
books; with such other statistics, information, and sugges-
tions as they may deem of general interest. All such portions of said report as relate to the receipt and expenditure
of money, as well as the number of books on hand, books
lost or missing, and books purchased, shall be verified by
affidavit.

SEC. 8. The city council of said city shall have power to Penalties for abuse.
pass ordinances imposing suitable penalties for the punish-
ment of persons committing injury upon such library, or the
grounds or other property thereof, and for injury to, or failure to return, any book belonging to such library. It shall
be the duty of every librarian or board of directors, having
charge or control of such library or property, to post up in
one or more conspicuous places connected therewith a printed
copy of this section. And justices of the peace, or city or
police courts, in their respective counties, shall have jurisdiction to hear, try, and determine all prosecutions under this
section.

SEC. 9. Any person desiring to make donations of money, Directors may hold
personal property, or real estate for the benefit of such donations.
library, shall have the right to vest the title to such donation
in the board of directors created under this act, to be held
and controlled when accepted by such board according to the
terms of the deed, gift, devise, or bequest of such property;
and as to such property the said board shall be held to be
special trustees.

SEC. 10. When fifty legal voters of any town or borough Tax for support of
shall present a petition to the clerk of the town or borough, borough.
asking that an annual tax may be levied for the establishment and maintenance of a free public library and reading-

room in such town or borough, and shall specify in their petition a rate of taxation, not to exceed three mills on the dollar, such clerk shall, in the next legal notice of the regular annual election in such town or borough, give notice that at such election every elector may vote "for a —— mill tax for a free public library and reading-room," or "against a —— mill tax for a free public library and reading-room," specifying in such notice the rate of taxation mentioned in said petition; and if the majority of all the votes cast in such town or borough shall be "for the tax for a free public library and reading-room," the tax specified in such notice shall be levied and collected in the same manner as other general taxes of said town or borough, and shall be known as the "library fund," *provided*, that such tax may be lessened or increased within the three-mill limit, or made to cease, in case the legal voters of any such town or borough shall so determine by a majority vote at any annual election held therein; and the corporate authorities of such town or borough shall have and may exercise the same powers conferred upon the corporate authorities of cities under this act.

Directors.

SEC. 11. At the next regular election after any town or borough shall have voted to establish and maintain a free public library and reading-room, there shall be elected a library board of six directors, one-third for one year, one-third for two years, and one-third for three years; and annually thereafter there shall be elected two directors, who shall hold their office for three years and until their successors are elected and qualified; which board shall have the same powers as are by this act conferred upon the board of directors of free public libraries and reading-rooms in cities. No director of any free public library or reading-room established under the provisions of this act in any city, town, or borough shall receive any compensation for any services rendered as such director.

Public documents.

SEC. 12. The secretary of state is hereby authorized to send a copy of the annual laws of the state, together with the legislative documents and journals, to each free public library which shall desire them.

Approved, April 13, 1881.

LICENSES.

I. Auctioneers. | II. Exhibitions.

I.

SECTION 1. Every person not a resident of any town, city, or borough in which he shall expose for sale by auction any goods or articles, except provisions, charcoal, wood, and the products of a farm, and second-hand household furniture, without a license therefor from a majority of the selectmen of such town, or from the authorities of such city or borough, authorized by the charter or by-laws of such city or borough to issue such license, shall be fined not more than fifty dollars, nor less than twenty dollars, or imprisoned in the common gaol of the county in which said town, city, or borough is situated, not less than twenty days nor more than sixty days, or by such fine and imprisonment both.

Non-resident auctioneers to procure license.
P. A., 1877, p. 227.

SEC. 2. The majority of the selectmen of every town are hereby empowered to issue such licenses, and in case the charter or by-laws of any city or borough do not authorize any person or persons to issue such license, the mayor of such city and the warden of such borough are hereby empowered to issue the same, but no license shall be issued unless an application therefor in writing shall have been made and filed with one of the selectmen, or with the authority authorized by law to issue such license, at least three days before the issue of the same; and the authority issuing such license shall have power to revoke the same, if in the judgment of such authority it shall be for the public interest so to do.

License, how and by whom granted.

SEC. 3. Section twenty-two, of title twenty, of chapter nine, of the general statutes of this state, and all acts and parts of acts inconsistent herewith, are hereby repealed; but this repeal shall not affect any suit or prosecution now pending, or license already issued, and such suit or prosecution shall proceed the same in all respects as if this act had not been passed.

Repeal, and its effect.

Approved, March 21, 1877.

II.

Exhibitions, how
regulated.
R. S., p. 546, § 6. The mayor, aldermen, and common council of any city, the warden and burgesses of any borough, and the selectmen of any town, may license and regulate any exhibitions therein; but selectmen shall not license any such exhibition within the limits of any city or borough.

MISDEMEANORS.

Misdemeanors un-
der the city charter.
S. A., vol. 5, p. 481. SECTION 1. That the eighth section of the act to alter the charter of the City of Hartford, and to combine sundry public statutes relating thereto, approved June 24, 1859, be amended by the addition of the following clauses, to wit: The violation of any ordinance, or by-law of the City of Hartford, made or to be made, relative to the speed of animals, vehicles, and cars; for protecting and preserving trees and other ornaments of public places; for protecting the state-house yard in said city; for restraining cruelty to animals and inhuman sports; for prohibiting, restraining, licensing, and regulating all sports, exhibitions, public amusements, and performances, and billiard and bowling saloons; for regulating or prohibiting swimming or bathing in public or exposed places within said city; for preventing and punishing trespasses in gardens, cemeteries, and enclosures, and public buildings; for protecting said city from exposure to fire, regulating the mode of building or altering buildings within said city or any part thereof, and the mode of using any building therein; for prohibiting and regulating the bringing in, carrying out or through, or storing gunpowder; for regulating the location of stationary steam boilers, barns and out-houses, sinks and drains, in said city; for preventing illegal practices with dead bodies in medical institutions, or elsewhere, in said city, shall be a misdemeanor; and may be prosecuted as such before the City

Police Court, like other offences; which court may inflict ^{Police Court to have jurisdiction of same.} therefor the penalty named in such ordinance or by-law, and enforce the same in the same manner as other judgments of said City Police Court are enforced.

SEC. 2. This act shall take effect from its passage.

Approved, June 26, 1862.

MISFEASANCE IN OFFICE.

I.

Every officer or agent of the state, or of any city, town, borough, or public institution, and any person employed by either of them to procure any materials, or other articles, by purchase or contract, or to employ labor, who shall directly or indirectly, for himself or another, receive any allowance or reward from the person or persons making such contract, furnishing such materials, or other articles, or rendering such labor, and any person who shall give or offer any such allowance or reward, shall be fined not less than ten dollars, nor more than five hundred dollars, or imprisoned not more than one year. ^{Commissions to public agents. R. S., p. 521, § 52.}

II.

The auditor of any city, town, borough, or public corporation or institution, or any person authorized to approve demands for the price of articles furnished or services rendered for the same, may, before approving any such demand, require the claimant to make oath, that the whole of said articles have been furnished, or that the whole service has ^{Oath may be required of claimant under any contract, etc. R. S., p. 90, § 2.}

been performed, and that no commission, discount, bonus, reward or present of any kind has been received, or is promised or expected on account of the same.

III.

Penalty for public officer taking more than his legal compensation. P. A., 1877, p. 213

If any officer of the state, or of any district, city, county, town, or borough, whose salary or compensation is fixed by law, shall charge and receive, or shall retain, receive, or collect to his own use any sum or sums in excess of the legal salary or compensation, he shall, upon conviction thereof, be fined not exceeding one thousand dollars, or be imprisoned not exceeding one year, at the discretion of the court having cognizance of the offence.

Approved, March 16, 1877.

IV.

Misfeasance by public officers. R. S., p. 524, § 2.

Any magistrate, or officer or agent of any public community, who shall, with intent to prejudice it, appropriate its property to the use of any person, or make upon its books any false entry, or draw any order upon its treasurer; or present or aid in procuring to be allowed any fraudulent claim against such community, shall be fined not less than fifty dollars, nor more than five hundred dollars, or imprisoned not less than sixty days, nor more than one year, or both.

V.

Embezzlement defined, and how punished. P. A., 1878, p. 289.

SECTION 1. Every officer or agent of any public, municipal, or private corporation; every executor, administrator, guardian, conservator, or any trustee under a testamentary or any express trust, who shall wrongfully appropriate and convert to his own use the money, funds, or property of such corporation, estate, ward, trust, or other person, shall be guilty of embezzlement, and shall be punished by a fine not to exceed ten thousand dollars, or by imprisonment not to exceed ten years, or by such fine and imprisonment both.

Sec. 2. All acts and parts of acts inconsistent with this Repeal. act are hereby repealed.

Approved, March 29, 1878.

VI.

Section 1. The General Assembly in behalf of the state; the representatives of the towns in the several counties in behalf of their counties; every city, by its common council when so authorized by its charter, or by its freemen in legal meeting assembled; and every town, borough, or school district, by legal meeting of its qualified voters, may make appropriations of specific sums of money for any purpose authorized by law, and by the warnings of the meetings at which the appropriations are made. *General Assembly and public corporations may make specific appropriations. P. A., 1877, p. 218.*

Sec. 2. Whenever any specific appropriations of money may have been made by the General Assembly, the representatives of the several counties, or by any community or corporation named in the first section of this act, every agent, commissioner, or executive officer of the state, or of any county, city, borough, town, or school district, who shall wilfully authorize or contract for the expenditure of any money, or the creation of any debt for any purpose in excess of the amount specifically appropriated for such purpose by the General Assembly, the county representatives, or the community or corporation of which he is the agent, commissioner, or executive officer, unless such expenditure shall be made or debt contracted for the necessary repair of roads or bridges, or the necessary support of schools or paupers, in cases arising after the proper appropriation has been exhausted, shall be guilty of a misdemeanor, and upon conviction thereof, shall be punished by a fine not exceeding one thousand dollars, or by imprisonment in the county jail not exceeding one year, or by such fine and imprisonment both. *Expenditure beyond such appropriation not to be made by officer of the state or public corporation. Exceptions. Penalty.*

Approved, March 20, 1877.

OFFICES.

Mayor and members of Common Council prohibited from holding certain city offices.
S. A., vol. 7, p. 259.

That from and after the first Monday of April, A. D. 1873, neither the mayor nor any member of either branch of the Court of Common Council of the City of Hartford, shall be chosen or appointed to any other office by such Court of Common Council of said city, nor shall any member of either branch of said Court of Common Council be chosen or appointed to serve upon any of the several commissions, having charge of the various departments or public works of said city.

Approved, June 11, 1872.

* * *

OFFENCES AGAINST PUBLIC PROPERTY.

Injuries to public buildings or furniture, etc.
R. S., p. 500, §§ 3, 6, 7 and 8.

SECTION 1. Every person, who shall wilfully injure any public building, house of public worship, college or school-house, or who shall wilfully injure or carry away any stove, stove-pipe or furniture, in and belonging to any such building, shall be fined not more than twenty dollars, or imprisoned not more than ninety days, or both.

Injury to trees on public squares.

SEC. 2. Every person, who shall injure or destroy any tree growing on any public square or grounds, without the consent of the city, borough or town, where the same is situated, or shall wilfully injure the fences or herbage of any such public square or grounds, shall be fined not more than fifty dollars.

Wilful injury to public property in highways or parks.

SEC. 3. Every person, who shall wilfully injure any statue, monument, chair, or other seat, or any lamp, or lamp-post, constructed or being in any highway, public space, or park, or any railing, or fence erected for public use, or inclosing any such space, or park, or any walk, or crossing for foot passengers, or any sewer, curbing, or paved gutter, shall be fined not less than ten, nor more than fifty dollars, or imprisoned not less than seven, nor more than thirty days, or both.

SEC. 4. Every person, who shall wilfully tear down, remove or deface, any notice posted in compliance with law, shall be fined not more than seven dollars. _{Tearing down notices.}

ORDINANCES.

I.

SECTION 1. The Court of Common Council of the City of Hartford shall have power by a majority of the members of each branch present and absent, subject to the approval or disapproval of the mayor, to make, alter, and repeal ordinances for the following purposes: To require a suitable license fee from and grant licenses to all persons who desire to sell any kind of goods, wares, or merchandise, for a short space of time at holiday seasons, or at other times, and who only temporarily occupy storerooms, sidewalks, or street corners, for the purpose of such sales, also to require a suitable license fee from and grant licenses to peddlers and venders of goods, wares, and merchandise about the streets, and at the stores, houses, offices, and banks in said city, and to regulate all such traffic and vending, provided that such ordinances shall not hinder or interfere with the sale within said city of the produce of the farms and gardens of this state. *S. A., 1879, p. 240. Licenses for temporary business. Licenses to peddlers.*

SEC. 2. Said Court of Common Council shall also have power to make, alter, and repeal ordinances to suppress the playing of policy, so called, and all kinds of gaming or gambling, and to prevent idlers and persons without apparent *Gambling.*

employment from inveigling youth and unsuspecting persons into policy shops, gambling places, and places of ill-repute.

Penalty for violation of various ordinances. SEC. 3. Said Court of Common Council shall have power by ordinance to provide for the punishment in and by the Police Court of said city, by fine not exceeding fifty dollars, or imprisonment not exceeding thirty days, or both, of all violations of ordinances made under the authority of this act, and of all violations of ordinances relating to nuisances, and ordinances regulating public hacks or carriages, the charges of hackmen and public drivers, cartmen and truckmen, and ordinances requiring sidewalks to be kept clean and free from snow, ice, and other obstructions, and ordinances to prevent the running at large of cattle, sheep, swine and goats.

Mayor to furnish statement of municipal affairs. SEC. 4. It shall be the duty of the mayor of said city, from time to time, to furnish a statement to the Court of Common Council of the condition of municipal affairs, and to communicate such recommendations in relation thereto, as may seem to him proper.

When act takes effect. SEC. 5. This act shall take effect from its passage.

Approved, March 28, 1879.

II.

By-laws to suppress gambling. P. A., 1881, p. 43. The court of common council of any city, and the warden, burgesses, and freemen of any borough in this state, and the inhabitants of any town in legal town meeting assembled shall have power to make, alter, and repeal ordinances or by-laws to suppress and punish all kinds of gambling and gaming, pool selling, policy playing, lottery dealing, bucket-shop business, and the staking or deposit of money or collaterals for the same on margins or otherwise against a rise or fall in the markets of the price of stocks, bonds, or merchandise, and to prevent idlers and persons without apparent employment from enticing persons into places where gambling of any kind is carried on.

Approved, April 6, 1881.

III.

Section 1. That the ninth section of the act to alter the charter of the City of Hartford, and to combine sundry public statutes relating thereto, approved June 24, 1859, be so amended in the ninth section of said act as to read as follows:

"Sec. 9. No ordinance passed by the Court of Common Council shall take effect until ten days from the passage of said ordinance, nor until it has been published twice in two or more daily papers issued within the City of Hartford, and the clerk of said city shall cause every ordinance passed by said Court of Common Council to be published without unreasonable delay; and the certificate of the city clerk upon the record of such ordinance, that the same has been so published, shall be *prima facie* evidence thereof, in any suit or proceeding; and no ordinance shall be valid, if repugnant to the laws of the state." *Ordinances to be published. S. A., vol. 5, p. 340.*

Sec. 2. All parts of said ninth section, repugnant herewith, are hereby repealed. *Repeal.*

Sec. 3. This act shall take effect from its passage.

Approved, May 23, 1860.

IV.

That the Court of Common Council of the City of Hartford may, from time to time, revise the ordinances of said city, combining therein existing ordinances, and making such alteration as they may deem necessary, which revision so made shall be legal and valid without the publication now required to be made of new ordinances. *Publication of revised ordinances unnecessary. S. A., vol. 7, p. 276.*

Approved, June 26, 1872.

POLICE AND POLICE REGULATIONS.

I.

Authority of police. R. S., p. 33, § 1. Active members of any legally organized police force, in a city or borough, shall have the same authority to execute criminal process in their respective cities or boroughs, as constables have in their respective towns.

II.

Arrest without warrant. R. S., p. 34, § 2. Sheriffs, deputy sheriffs, constables, borough bailiffs, police officers, and railroad and steamboat police, in their respective precincts, shall arrest, without previous complaint and warrant, any person for any offence in their jurisdiction, when the offender shall be taken or apprehended in the act, or on the speedy information of others; and all persons so arrested shall be immediately presented before proper authority.

III.

When officers may break into houses. P. A., 1882, p. 148, § 5. Every officer who shall have a warrant for the arrest of any person charged with keeping a house of ill-fame, or with keeping a house reputed to be a house of ill-fame or a house of assignation, or with keeping a house where lewd, dissolute, or drunken persons resort, or where drinking, carousing, dancing, and fighting are permitted, to the disturbance of the neighbors, or with violating any law against gaming in the house or rooms occupied by him, or with resorting to any house for any of said purposes, or who shall have a warrant for the arrest of any person charged with keeping open on Sunday any room, place, enclosure or any building or struct-

ure of any kind or description in which it is reputed that
spirituous and intoxicating liquors are exposed for sale, or
with selling spirituous and intoxicating liquors in any place
on Sunday, or for the seizure of spirituous and intoxicating
liquors, may at any time, for the purpose of gaining admission to such house, room, place, enclosure, building, or structure, or for the purpose of arresting any of the persons
aforesaid, make violent entry into such house, room, place,
enclosure, building, or structure, or any part thereof, after
demanding admittance and giving notice that he is an officer
and has such warrant, and may arrest any person so charged
and take him before the proper authority. The county commissioners, sheriff of the county, and any deputy sheriff by
him specially authorized, the chief of police of any city, or
any policeman by him specially authorized, may at any time
enter upon the premises of any person licensed under this
act to ascertain the manner in which such person conducts
his business, and to preserve order.

IV.

SECTION 1. The mayor of any city, clerk of the board of
police commissioners in any city, or any justice of the peace,
may sign and issue process of *subpœna* to compel the attendance of witnesses before the board of police commissioners in
said city, at any lawful meeting of said board. Witnesses before board of police commissioners. P. A., 1880, p. 498.

SEC. 2. Such process of *subpœna* may be served in the
same manner as now by law provided as to witnesses in civil
causes, except that no fees shall be tendered to any witness
at the time of such service. Any person upon whom such
process has been legally served shall appear before said board
in obedience to such process, and testify as to any matters
lawfully pending before said board, and any wilful false
swearing in the premises shall be punished in the same
manner as perjury before courts of justice. Service of subpœna. False swearing.

SEC. 3. If any person upon whom such *subpœna* has been
duly served shall refuse to attend before said board, the clerk
of the board of police commissioners, by direction of said
board, may issue a *capias*, directed to some proper officer, to Refusal of witness to attend or to testify.

arrest such witness and bring him before said board to testify; and in case such person shall refuse to testify, said board shall have power to adjudge such person to be in contempt, and may issue a *mittimus*, signed by its clerk, and commit such person to jail for a period of not more than thirty days.

Fees.

SEC. 4. The same fees as provided by law for witnesses in civil causes shall be paid out of the city treasury to any witnesses, except policemen, who shall attend and testify under the provisions of this act, the amount of such fees to be certified by the mayor or clerk of said board to the proper auditing officers of the city.

SEC. 5. This act shall take effect from its passage.

Approved, February 25, 1880.

V.

Saloons to be closed on election days.
P. A., 1882, p. 187, § 5.

Every person who by himself, his servant or agent, between the hours of five o'clock in the morning and the hour of closing the polls of the day of any annual city, town, or electors' meetings, shall keep open any room, place, or enclosure, or any building or structure of any kind or description, in which spirituous and intoxicating liquors are sold to be drunk on the premises, shall be fined fifty dollars.

VI.

Discharge of firearms.
R. S., p. 509, § 121
and P. A., 1879, p. 448.

Every person, who shall discharge any firearm in any city, or borough, except on military occasions, without permission first obtained from the mayor of said city, or the warden of said borough, shall be fined not more than seven dollars, or imprisoned not more than thirty days; and the proprietor of any private military school, which has received or shall receive, by authority of the General Assembly, arms or accoutrements from the state, or the principal person having charge of such school, who shall fire, or cause any cannon to be fired, in the limits of any city or borough, without a permit from the mayor of such city, or warden of such borough, shall be fined not more than two hundred dollars; but in

other respects, such school may be conducted according to
the military rules established for its government.

Every person, who shall use firecrackers, except on the Using firecrackers.
R. S., p. 510. § 13.
fourth day of July, or other public holiday, under such regulations as the authorities of the town, city or borough in
which they are used shall prescribe, shall be fined five dollars.

VII.

SECTION 1.   Every tramp shall be punished by imprison- Tramps.
P. A., 1879, p. 393.
ment in the state prison not more than one year.

SEC. 2.   All transient persons who rove about from place Definition.
to place begging, and all vagrants living without labor, or
visible means of support, who stroll over the country without
lawful occasion, shall be held to be tramps within the meaning
of this act.

SEC. 3.   Any act of beggary or vagrancy by any person Evidence.
not a resident of this state, shall be *prima facie* evidence that
the person committing the same is a tramp within the meaning of this act.

SEC. 4.   Any tramp who shall wilfully and maliciously Aggravation of
offence.
injure any person, where such offence is not now punishable
by imprisonment in the state prison, or shall be found carrying any firearm or other dangerous weapon, shall be punished
by imprisonment in the state prison not more than three
years.

SEC. 5.   Any sheriff, deputy sheriff, constable, special con- Arrest.
stable, or policeman, upon view of any offence described in
this act, or on speedy information thereof, may without warrant apprehend the offender and take him before any competent authority for examination, and on his conviction shall
be entitled to a reward of five dollars therefor, to be paid by
the state.

SEC. 6.   All mayors, wardens, and selectmen are empowered Special constables.
and required to appoint special constables whose duty it shall
be to arrest and prosecute all tramps in their respective cities,
boroughs, and towns.

SEC. 7. This act shall not apply to any female or minor under the age of sixteen years, nor to any blind person, nor to any beggar roving within the limits of the town in which he resides.

SEC. 8. Upon the passage of this act, the secretary of state shall cause to be printed durable copies of this act to be sent to the several town clerks, who shall cause the same to be posted in at least twelve conspicuous places, six of which shall be in the public highway.

SEC. 9. This act shall take effect on the twenty-eighth day of April, 1879.

Approved, March 27, 1879.

VIII.

SECTION 1. Whenever any transient person shall apply to any individual residing in this state to give him food, lodging, clothing, or money, the individual to whom such application shall be made, may require the applicant to perform a reasonable amount of labor for such food, lodging, clothing, or money; and if the same be furnished, may detain him until such labor is performed, but not beyond the hour of eleven o'clock in the forenoon of the day succeeding his application;

and if such applicant shall neglect or refuse to perform such labor, being suited to his age, strength, and capacity, or shall wilfully injure the person or property of the individual requiring the labor, he shall be deemed a vagrant, and shall be committed to any town workhouse, or any county workhouse in the county where the offence shall have been committed; or in case there be no such workhouse in the town or county, then to the common jail in the county, for a period not less than thirty days, nor more than six months, and until the costs of prosecution against him be paid; and upon a second conviction of such transient person for a similar offence, he shall be committed to such workhouse or common jail, for a period not less than four months, nor more than one year, and until the costs of prosecution be paid. But such person may appeal from any such order or judgment to the Superior Court next to be holden in said county, as provided by law in other criminal prosecutions.

SEC. 2. Every sheriff and deputy sheriff in any county, every selectman, constable, and grand juror in any town, and every executive officer in any city or borough in this state, may, within their respective limits, without warrant, arrest any such transient person, and take him forthwith before any magistrate having criminal jurisdiction, and shall make a written complaint to such magistrate of the particular offence of which such person is suspected, and said magistrate shall proceed to hear said complaint, and on finding the allegations true, shall render judgment against the accused according to the provisions of the preceding section, and if no appeal be taken from said judgment, said magistrate shall issue a warrant, directed to any proper officer or indifferent person by name, authorizing such officer or indifferent person to convey said transient person to said workhouse or jail in accordance with said judgment.

SEC. 3. The selectmen of any town may appoint one or more special constables in each school district in such town to carry out and enforce the provisions of this act.

Approved, July 21, 1875.

IX.

SECTION 1. Each city and town may make regulations concerning habitual truants from school, and any children wandering about its streets or public places, having no lawful occupation, or business, nor attending school, and growing up in ignorance, between the ages of seven and sixteen years; and such by-laws, also, respecting such children, as shall conduce to their welfare and to public order, imposing suitable penalties, not exceeding twenty dollars for any one breach thereof; but no such town by-laws shall be valid, until approved by the Superior Court in any county.

SEC. 2. Every town, and the mayor and aldermen of every city, having such by-laws, shall annually appoint three or more persons, who alone shall be authorized to prosecute for violations thereof. All warrants issued upon such prosecutions shall be returnable before any justice of the peace, or judge of the City or Police Court, of the town or city; who shall receive such compensation as the city or town shall determine.

Arrest of truants without warrant.
P. A., 1877, p. 201.

SEC. 3. The police in any city, and bailiffs, constables, sheriffs and deputy sheriffs in their respective precincts, shall arrest all boys, between eight and sixteen years of age, who habitually wander or loiter about the streets or public places, or anywhere beyond the proper control of their parents or guardians, during the usual school hours of the school term; and may stop any boy under sixteen years of age, during such hours, and ascertain whether he be a truant from school; and if he be, shall send him to such school.

Prosecution.

SEC. 4. Any boy arrested a third time under the provisions of the preceding section, shall be taken, if not immediately returned to school, before the judge of the criminal or police court, or any justice of the peace in the city, borough or town where such arrest is made; and if it shall appear that such boy has no lawful occupation, or is not attending school, or is growing up in habits of idleness or immorality, or is an habitual truant, he may be committed to any institution of instruction or correction, or house of reformation in said city, borough, or town, or, with the approval of the selectmen, to the State Reform School, for not more than three years.

Warrant and hearing.
R. S., p. 128, § 12–14.

SEC. 5. In all cases arising under the provisions of the two preceding sections, a proper warrant shall be issued by the judge of the criminal court of the city, or by a justice of the peace in the borough or town, where such arrest is made; and the father, if living, or if not, the mother or guardian of such boy, shall be notified, if such parent or guardian can be found, of the day and time of hearing. The **Fees.** fees of the judge or justice shall be two dollars for such hearing; and all expenses shall be paid by the city, borough, or town in and for which he exercises such jurisdiction.

SEC. 6. After the hearing in any such case, such judge or justice of the peace may, at his discretion, indefinitely suspend the rendition of judgment.

Suspending judgment.

SEC. 7. Upon the request of the parent or guardian of any girl between eight and fifteen years of age, a warrant may be issued for her arrest in the same manner and on the same conditions as is provided in the preceding sections with respect to boys; and thereupon the same proceedings may be had, as are above provided, except that said girls may be committed to the Connecticut Industrial School for Girls.

Arrest of vagrant girls.

— — —

X.

It shall be the duty of sheriffs, constables and city police officers to assist the managers, trustees and directors of any inebriate asylum established by law, in enforcing the powers and duties now vested by law in such managers, trustees and directors.

Police to assist managers of inebriate asylums. P. A., 1879, p. 386.

Approved, March 27, 1879.

XI.

SECTION 1. Whenever any boy under the age of sixteen years shall be convicted of any crime or misdemeanor, punishable by fine or imprisonment other than imprisonment for life, the court or justice of the peace, as the case may be, may commit him to the reform school, to remain until he shall arrive at the age of twenty-one years, unless sooner discharged by the board of trustees. And the judges of the criminal and police courts of the state and justices of the peace shall have power to commit to the reform school: first, any boy under sixteen years of age, who may be liable to punishment by imprisonment under any existing law of the state, or any law that may be enacted and in force in the state; second, any boy under sixteen years of age, with the consent of his parent or guardian, against whom any charge of committing any crime or misdemeanor shall have been made, the punishment of which, on conviction, would be confinement in jail or prison; third, any boy under sixteen years

Commitment to Reform School. P. A., 1881, p. 65.

of age, who is destitute of a suitable home and adequate means of obtaining an honest living, or who is in danger of being brought up, or is brought up, to lead an idle or vicious life; fourth, any boy under sixteen years of age, who is incorrigible, or habitually disregards the commands of his father or mother or guardian, who leads a vagrant life, or resorts to immoral places or practices, or neglects or refuses to perform labor suitable to his years and condition, or to attend school.

To remain till twenty-one.
P. A., 1879, p. 478.

SEC. 2. That every boy sent to the reform school shall remain until he is twenty-one years of age, unless sooner discharged or bound as an apprentice; but no boy shall be retained after the superintendent shall have reported him fully reformed.

Notice to be given if accommodations insufficient.

SEC. 3. That whenever there shall be as large a number of boys in the school as can be properly accommodated, it shall be the duty of the president of the board of trustees to give notice to the criminal and police courts of the fact; whereupon no boys shall be sent to the school by the said courts until notice shall be given them by the president of the board that more can be received.

Arrest of boy escaping from said school.
P. A., 1881, p. 66.

SEC. 4. If any person shall entice or attempt to entice away from said school any boy legally committed to the same, or shall knowingly harbor, conceal, or aid in harboring or concealing any boy who shall have escaped from said school, such person shall, upon conviction thereof, be deemed guilty of a misdemeanor and shall pay a fine of not less than ten nor more than one hundred dollars, which shall be paid to the treasurer of the board of trustees; and every sheriff, deputy sheriff, constable, or officer of local police, and any officer or employee of said school shall have power, and it is hereby made his duty to arrest any boy, when in his power so to do, who shall have escaped from said school, and return him thereto.

XII.

SECTION 1. The parent or guardian of any girl between Commitment to Industrial School. R. S., p. 94, §§ 1-5. P. A., 1875, pp. 62, 64. P. A., 1876, p. 110. P. A., 1878, p. 337. the ages of eight and sixteen years, or a selectman or grand juror of the town where she may be found, may present a written complaint to the judge of the Court of Probate for the district in which such town is, or to the judge of the Police or City Court of any city, sitting in chambers, where she may be found, or to any justice of the peace of such town, alleging that she has committed any offence within the final jurisdiction of a justice of the peace, or belongs to the class specified in the third section of Chapter VI of Title XIV, or in the seventh and eighth sections of Chapter I of Title XI, or that she is leading an idle, vagrant, or vicious life, or is in manifest danger of falling into habits of vice, praying that she may be sent to the Connecticut Industrial School for Girls, and such judge or justice of the peace shall thereupon, after notice to her and such other notice as he may deem proper, inquire into said complaint, and on being satisfied of the truth of the allegations therein, may order her to be committed to the guardianship and control of such school, until she shall arrive at the age of twenty-one years, unless sooner lawfully discharged, and if he finds that she has committed an offence punishable by imprisonment other than imprisonment for life, she may be sentenced to the Connecticut Industrial School for Girls, or judgment may be suspended, on such terms, and for such time, as he may prescribe; and said authority may issue a warrant for the execution of such sentence.   *   *   *

SEC. 2. Any proper officer may arrest within his precincts Arrest. any girl whom he shall judge to be between the ages of eight and sixteen years, whom he shall find in any improper place or situation, and who is, in his judgment, liable to be arrested for any of the offences specified in the preceding section, and make complaint and proceed in the same manner as a parent could do under the provisions of the preceding section.

SEC. 3. Said authority shall tax the costs on such com- Costs. plaint and transmit a certified copy of the items of the same to the clerk of the Superior Court for the county in which the trial was had, within thirty days after the trial; and if approved by the state's attorney for such county, it shall be paid by said clerk, upon the order of such judge or justice.

SEC. 4. The authority committing any girl to said school, shall ascertain as nearly as possible, and endorse on the mittimus, her age, parentage, birth-place, offence, and such other facts relative to her as may aid in her proper care and instruction in the school; and the age thus ascertained shall be taken as the true age of said girl with reference to the term of her commitment.

Endorsement on mittimus.

XIII.

SECTION 1. The board of police commissioners, or other authority having charge of the police department of any city, may sell at public auction any and all articles found, or stolen articles recovered, and any and all articles which have hitherto, or hereafter may come into the possession of such department, in the performance of the duties of its members, and which have remained in the possession thereof for one year or more.

Sale of unclaimed articles in possession of police departments.
P. A., 1883, p. 244.

SEC. 2. Before such sale, such authority shall cause the time and place thereof, and a description of such of said articles as are of the appraised value of five dollars or more, to be advertised at least once a week, for four successive weeks, in some daily newspaper, published in said city, if any there be, otherwise in some weekly newspaper published therein.

Advertisement.

SEC. 3. The proceeds of such sale, after deducting the expenses thereof, shall be paid to the city treasurer, who shall keep the same as a separate fund to be used and applied for the relief of sick, injured, or disabled policemen, and which shall be expended under the sole direction of said commissioners or other authority in charge, and upon their orders only.

Disposition of avails.

Approved, March 21, 1883.

PUBLIC HEALTH AND SAFETY.

I.

SECTION 1. The mayor, aldermen and common council of *Fire marshal. R. S., p. 206, § 1-4,* each city, and the wardens and burgesses of each borough, may appoint a fire marshal, who shall hold his office for one year, and may inquire into the cause of any fire which may happen in the limits of the corporation for which he is appointed, on request of a proper officer of said corporation, or of any one interested in the property burned, at the expense of the applicant; and he may summon witnesses to appear before him at such times and places as he may designate, and examine said witnesses on oath touching said fire, and shall report the facts to the clerk of said city or borough.

SEC. 2. When a fire shall happen without the precincts of *Investigation by justice of the peace.* any fire marshal, any person interested in the property burned, may apply to any justice of the peace in the town where said fire has taken place, and said justice shall proceed in like manner as fire marshals, and file his report in the town clerk's office.

SEC. 3. The testimony of all witnesses examined before *Testimony to be put in writing.* any inquest, shall be reduced to writing, and subscribed by the witnesses.

SEC. 4. The fees of such fire marshal or justice of the *Fees.* peace, while engaged in investigating the cause of any fire, as aforesaid, shall be two dollars and fifty cents a day; and the fees for witnesses, subpoenas, and the service of subpoenas, shall be the same as are allowed in civil actions.

II.

Inspection of
buildings.
S. A., 1880, p. 65.

SECTION 1. That the Court of Common Council of the City of Hartford shall have power to make, alter, and repeal ordinances providing for the proper inspection and examination of all walls, buildings, and structures within its limits, with reference to their safety, and to regulate their construction or continuance, and shall have power to make, alter, and repeal ordinances to provide for the maintenance, repair, or removal of all such walls, buildings, or structures as upon examination and inspection shall be found to be unsafe or dangerous, and to regulate or prevent the use of heavy and dangerous machinery or the storage of goods, wares, and merchandise in any building or structure in a manner to render it dangerous or unsafe, and to regulate or prevent the exercise of any business in any building or upon any land in a manner to expose the same, or the adjoining or neighboring property to danger by fire or otherwise.

Penalties.

SEC. 2. Said Court of Common Council shall have power in and by said ordinances to provide for the punishment of any violation thereof in and by the Police Court of said city by fine or imprisonment, or both, or by forfeiture recoverable in the City Court of said city.

SEC. 3. This act shall take effect from and after its passage.

Approved, March 24, 1880.

III.

By-laws regulating
public halls, etc.
R. S., p. 261, § 25-28.

SECTION 1. In all cities the court of common council, in all boroughs the warden and burgesses, and in all towns and parts of towns not within the limits of any city or borough, the selectmen, shall require that all public halls for lectures, exhibitions, or amusements shall have ample facilities for entrance and exit, and be arranged so as to promote the comfort and safety of persons visiting them, and be closed till such requisitions are complied with; and any city, borough, or town may make suitable by-laws regarding the same.

Sec. 2. Every person who shall let or use any hall for **Penalty.** such purpose, after it shall have been ordered to be so closed, shall forfeit one hundred dollars to the city, borough, or town by the authorities of which such order was made.

Sec. 3. Any person aggrieved by any order closing such **Appeal by aggrieved party.** hall may appeal therefrom to a judge of the Superior Court, who shall, on notice, inquire into the facts by a committee or otherwise, and may make such order in the premises as to him may seem proper, and tax costs in favor of the prevailing party and issue execution therefor.

Sec. 4. The court of common council of each city shall **Cities may make ordinances to prevent the erection of unsafe buildings.** have power to make ordinances to prevent the erection of unsafe buildings therein; to provide for the examination of all plans and specifications of proposed buildings; to provide for the inspection of all buildings in process of erection; to make general rules regarding the materials to be used in building, and the strength and manner of using the same; to prohibit the erection of any building not in conformity with such rules, and the plans and specifications of which shall not have been examined and approved in accordance with such ordinances; and to provide for the appointment of an **Inspector of buildings.** inspector of buildings.

Section 5, The selectmen of any town, the court of **Powers of city or town authority as to buildings, with reference to safety. P. A., 1883, p. 271.** common council of any city, and the warden and burgesses of any borough, may, and on the written application of any of its inhabitants shall, examine any building or proposed building therein with reference to its safety, after reasonable notice to the owner or builder and occupant, and may make such written order relative to its construction, maintenance, protection, repairs, or removal, as they may deem proper; a true and attested copy of which shall be left by some proper officer with, or at the usual place of abode of, such occupant, and such owner or builder, if resident within this state.

Owner may appeal. SEC. 6. Such owner, builder, or occupant may appeal from such order to the Superior Court of the county in which said building is, or to any judge of said court in vacation, by a petition, to which shall be annexed a citation to the town, city, or borough, which shall be served within three days after the service of such order, and be returnable within three days after the service of such petition; and **Action on appeal.** upon such petition such court or judge shall appoint three disinterested freeholders to view the premises and report to such court or judge such an order as they may deem expedient in reference thereto, which being accepted shall become effectual between the parties to the appeal; and said court or judge may award costs at discretion.

Execution of final order. SEC. 7. If any final order shall not be executed within ten days after its service by copy, or, if made on appeal, after its acceptance by such court or judge, the selectmen, common council, or warden and burgesses shall execute it, and the person who failed to comply with it shall pay to the town, city, or borough, the expense of its execution, **Penalty.** and forfeit not more than one thousand dollars, half to said town, city, or borough, and half to any informer.

Approved, April 24, 1883.

IV.

Churches, school-houses, and public halls to be provided with facilities for safe and speedy exit. P. A., 1878, p. 303. In all cities the court of common council, in all boroughs, the warden and burgesses, and in all towns and parts of towns, not within the limits of any city or borough, the selectmen shall require that all churches, school-houses, and all public halls that are used for lectures, amusements, or assemblages of people, shall be provided with ample facilities for safe and speedy exit in case of necessity. And such court of common council, warden and burgesses, or selectmen, may cause such churches, school-houses, and public halls to be closed until such requisitions are complied with.

Approved, March 27, 1878.

V.

SECTION 1.   Every story above the second story, not in- Fire escapes to be provided for certain classes of buildings. P. A., 1883, p. 305.
cluding the basement, in any workshop, manufactory, hotel,
building occupied on such story as an assembly or lodge-room
by any literary, benevolent, or other society, boarding-house
accommodating more than twelve lodgers, or tenement-house
arranged for or occupied by more than five families, shall be
provided within six months from the passage of this act with
more than one way of egress, by stairways on the inside or
fire escapes on the outside of the building, and such stairways
and fire escapes shall be kept free from obstruction and shall
be accessible from each room in said story.

SEC. 2.   It shall be the duty of the first selectman of the Examination of buildings.
town, or the fire marshal of the city, or the warden of the
borough in which any such building is situated to examine
all buildings referred to in the first section of this act, and if
on examination he finds that such building is provided with
fire escapes or stairways, as required by said section, he shall
furnish the owner thereof with a certificate to that effect, in
which case such owner shall not be liable under this act.

SEC. 3.   Every owner of such building who shall violate Penalty.
the provisions of this act shall be fined fifty dollars.

Approved, May 3, 1883.

VI.

SECTION 1.   The standard measure for the sale of illumi- Standard of gas. R. S., p. 275, § 23-26.
nating gas by meter shall be the cubic foot, containing sixty-
two and three hundred and twenty-one one-thousandths
pounds avoirdupois weight of distilled or rain water, weighed
in air of the temperature of sixty-two degrees Fahrenheit,
the barometer being at twenty-nine and one-half inches; and
no such gas shall be merchantable unless a standard argand
burner consuming five cubic feet of it an hour shall give a
light as measured by the photometric apparatus in ordinary
use, of not less than twelve sperm candles, each consuming
one hundred and twenty grains an hour.

Inspectors of gas and gas meters.

SEC. 2.   The Governor shall, every third year, beginning in 1877, appoint a resident of Hartford or New Haven an inspector general of gas meters and illuminating gas, who shall hold his office three years; but the person appointed during the year 1874 shall hold his office until September 1, 1877; and the Governor may fill vacancies for the unexpired part of any term.   Said inspector general shall appoint a deputy in every town and city where gas works are established, when requested by the mayor of such city, the selectmen of such town, or the warden of any borough therein.

Their duties.

The inspector general or any of his deputies shall inspect and prove the accuracy of every gas meter in his town furnished to any person by a manufacturer of gas, at the request of any consumer or such manufacturer.   Such inspection shall be made for a temperature of sixty degrees Fahrenheit, and at the average pressure at which gas is supplied in such town, and he shall stamp or mark every such meter found not to vary more than two *per cent.* from the standard, with some suitable device, and his name, and the date of its inspection.

Fees of inspectors of gas meters.

SEC. 3.   One dollar for each meter so inspected, with the cost of moving and replacing it, not exceeding fifty cents, shall be paid to the officer inspecting it, if it be found correct, by the consumer if he requested such inspection, otherwise by the party furnishing the gas.

Gas to be inspected, etc.

SEC. 4.   The inspector general and his deputy shall inspect monthly the quality and purity of illuminating gas furnished in his town or any city or borough therein, if requested by the mayor of the city, warden of the borough or selectmen of the town, and report to them the result of such inspection, for which he shall be paid five dollars by the town, city or borough requesting it.   When any gas so furnished shall be found upon such inspection to be below the standard value, on the average for the quarter, the person furnishing it shall make a deduction in favor of the consumer from the price charged for gas of a legal standard, proportioned to the inferiority of the gas as reported by the inspector.

VII.

SECTION 1. Any town, city, or borough, having a gas Apparatus for testing gas and gas meters. P. A., 1877, p. 229. manufactory established within its limits, may appropriate a sum not exceeding three thousand dollars for the purchase of proper apparatus to test gas and gas meters, and which apparatus may be used by the inspector general of gas meters and gas, or by his deputies.

SEC. 2. Whenever any town, city, or borough shall have Meters to be sealed. purchased apparatus for the testing of gas as provided in section first, the inspector general of gas meters, or his deputies, shall seal every meter which shall be found not to vary more than two per cent. from the standard established by law, and if any party furnishing gas to consumers shall neglect or refuse to furnish such consumers, after request made in writing, with meters which have been sealed by the inspector general or one of his deputies, within thirty days after demand made by such consumer, such party shall forfeit the sum of ten dollars per month to any person who shall sue therefor, and shall not be entitled to recover by any action at law or equity for any gas furnished to such consumers through an unsealed meter.

SEC. 3. No illuminating gas shall be merchantable unless Standard of gas. a standard argand burner consuming five cubic feet of it an hour, shall give a light as measured by the photometric apparatus in ordinary use, of not less than fifteen standard sperm candles, each consuming one hundred and twenty grains an hour.

SEC. 4. All acts inconsistent with this act are hereby Repeal. repealed.

Approved, March 22, 1877.

VIII.

SECTION 1. The member of the board of railroad com- Supervisors of dams and reservoirs. P. A., 1876, p. 343. missioners who is a civil engineer, and one civil engineer residing in each congressional district in this state, to be appointed by him, shall constitute a board of civil engineers, and have the supervision of all dams and reservoirs now existing or hereafter constructed in any locality where by the breaking away of the same life or property may be in danger of destruction.

Term of office, oath and fees.

SEC. 2. The members of said board shall be sworn to faithfully and impartially perform the duties imposed upon them by this act, and shall continue in office for the term of two years and until others are appointed in their places and stead. They shall each receive ten dollars per day and all necessary and reasonable expenses while actually in the business of their office, to be paid as hereinafter provided.

Proceedings to call them out.

SEC. 3. The mayor and aldermen of any city, the warden and burgesses of any borough, the selectmen of any town or a majority of them, shall, upon the application of two or more persons or corporations who would suffer loss or damage by the breaking away of any dam or reservoir within said city, borough, or town, shall forthwith inspect the same, and if in their opinion said dam or reservoir is not sufficiently strong and substantial to withstand the action of water under any circumstances which may reasonably be expected to occur, they shall at once notify one or more of the board of civil engineers to inspect the said dam or reservoir with them, and if in the judgment of the said engineers said dam or reservoir is unsafe, they shall serve notice on the person or persons owning or having the care and control of the same, to place said dam or reservoir in a safe and permanent condition, under the supervision of one of the said board of civil engineers, and when such repairs are completed and accepted by said civil engineer, he shall issue a certificate to said owner or persons owning or controlling the same, and also cause to be recorded upon the records of the town in which said dam is located, his doings, with a copy of the certificate so issued; but if said engineer shall find said dam or reservoir to be secure and safe, then the expense of such inspection shall be paid by the town in which said dam or reservoir is located.

Approval of new constructions.

SEC. 4. Whenever any person or corporation purpose constructing a dam or reservoir in a locality where the life or property of any other person may be endangered through the insufficiency thereof, the plans and specifications for such dam or reservoir shall be submitted to any member of said board of civil engineers, who shall examine the ground where the dam or reservoir is to be built, and the plans and specifications therefor, and if he approve the same, he shall issue a certificate authorizing the construction of such dam or reservoir, and no such dam or reservoir shall be constructed without such approval and certificate.

SEC. 5. The engineer under whose authority any dam or reservoir is being constructed, shall cause the work upon the same to be inspected at least three several times before its completion, and if he shall be satisfied that such dam or reservoir has been built in a substantial and safe manner, and in accordance with the plans and specifications approved by him, and is strong and secure, he shall issue a certificate approving of the same, which certificate shall be recorded in the office of the town clerk of the town in which such dam or reservoir is located; and no such dam or reservoir shall be used until such certificate is obtained and recorded. *Inspection during progress of new work.*

SEC. 6. The compensation and expenses of the board of engineers, or any one of them, when acting under the provisions of sections three, four, and five of this act, shall be paid by the persons or corporation owning or constructing the dam or reservoir. *Expenses, by whom paid.*

SEC. 7. The Superior Court shall have jurisdiction in equity, and may make all judgments and decrees necessary to carry into effect the provisions of the preceding sections. *Power of Superior Court.*

SEC. 8. This act shall take effect upon its passage.

Approved, March 28, 1878.

IX.

Cities, boroughs, and towns may, at any legal meeting, duly warned for the purpose, appoint inspectors of illuminating oils and burning fluids, and make by-laws regulating the inspection of the same within their respective limits; and the inspectors so appointed shall make complaint to the *Inspectors of burning fluids. R. S., p. 261, § 24.*

proper authority for all infringements of the law regulating the mixture or sale of naphtha and illuminating oils.[1]

X.

Inspectors of leather, hides and skins.
R. S., p. 274, § 13.
Each city may make by-laws regulating the inspection of leather, hides, and skins, within its limits, but no penalty exceeding twenty dollars shall be imposed for any one violation of any such by-laws.

XI.

Common Council empowered to adopt sanitary measures.
S. A., Vol. 6, p. 107.
That the Court of Common Council of the City of Hartford be, and hereby is, empowered to adopt such sanitary measures as, in the judgment of said council, may be necessary to protect the health of said city. And for that purpose Removal from city limits of certain animals and trades. to cause to be removed from the limits of said city, or from any part thereof, such animals, trades, business, and occupations as are, or may become, injurious to the health of the residents of said city. And to pass such ordinances as may be necessary or proper to carry out the provisions of this Previous ordinances ratified. act. And all ordinances heretofore passed by said council, for protecting the health of said city, and all rules and regulations established by any sanitary board, or committee, in pursuance of such ordinances, and all acts done by such sanitary board or committee, in carrying out such rules and regulations, are hereby ratified and confirmed.

Approved, June 30, 1866.

XII.

Adulteration of food.
P. A., 1879, p. 456.
SECTION 1. The boards of health of the several cities, boroughs, and towns, in this state, may from time to time at their discretion, procure from any dealer in provisions, groceries, medicines, or other articles of consumption, samples of such articles, and cause the same to be analyzed by Analysis by board of health. one of the state chemists, and if on such analyzation it shall be found that the article analyzed is adulterated with any

---

[1] City not liable for negligence of an inspector legally appointed by it. Mead v. New Haven, 40 Conn., 72.

deleterious or foreign ingredient or ingredients, other than is represented verbally and in a conspicuous label by the seller, the chemist making the analysis shall issue his certificate setting forth the kind and quantity, as near as may be, of deleterious and foreign ingredients found in the article analyzed, and the board of health causing such analysis to be made shall cause said certificate to be published in some paper published in the city, borough, or town, or one nearest thereto, where the article analyzed was obtained, for such length of time as they may think proper, and the cost of analysis, together with the cost of the publication of the certificate, shall be paid by the person or firm from whom the article analyzed was obtained; and if such person or firm shall so elect, he or they may annex to said certificate his or their sworn affidavit setting forth from whom the article analyzed was purchased by him or them.

SEC. 2. In all cases where an analysis has been made according to the provisions of section one, of this act, and the article or articles analyzed shall have been found pure and free from foreign ingredients, the cost of the analysis shall be paid by the city, borough, or town, whose board of health, or any officer thereof, caused such analysis to be made.

Approved, March 28, 1879.

XIII.

SECTION 1. No person shall sell, offer, or expose for sale any milk from which the cream or any part thereof has been removed, without distinctly and durably affixing a label, tag, or mark of metal in a conspicuous place upon the outside, and not more than six inches from the top of every can, vessel, or package containing such milk, and such metal label, tag, or mark shall have the words "Skimmed Milk" stamped, printed, or indented thereon in letters not less than one inch in height, and such milk shall only be sold or retailed out of a can, vessel or package so marked.

SEC. 2. No person shall sell or offer for sale, or shall have in possession with intent to sell or offer for sale, any impure or adulterated milk.

Penalty.

SEC. 3. Every person who shall violate the provisions of sections three and four of this act shall be deemed guilty of a misdemeanor, and on conviction thereof shall be fined not more than seven dollars, or be imprisoned not more than thirty days, or both.

XIV.

By-laws concerning registration of births, etc.
R. S., p. 86, § 11.

Any town or city may enact by-laws, not contrary to law, more effectually to obtain a perfect registration of births, marriages and deaths; and the registrar of the town, in which such by-laws may be enacted, shall execute their provisions under the same oath and penalty as if they were the statute laws of the State.

XV.

Powers of health committee.
S. A., 1874, p. 58.

The health committee of the City of Hartford shall have and exercise within the territorial limits of said city, all the powers and duties now conferred by law upon the board of health of the town of Hartford; and said health committee shall hereafter exclusively have and exercise all the aforesaid powers and duties within said city, in addition to those now vested in them by the laws of this state, and the ordinances of said city.

Approved, July 7, 1874.

XVI.

Board of health.
R. S., p. 258,
§§ 1–5 and 7–19.

SECTION 1. The justices of the peace and selectmen in each town, and such reputable physicians resident in said town as shall be chosen for that purpose by said justices and selectmen, shall constitute a board of health, and have all

Powers of.

the power necessary and proper for preserving the public health and preventing the spread of malignant diseases therein, and may appoint its president and such health officers or health committees as it may deem expedient, and delegate to them any of its powers, and the members present at any meeting convened as the board shall direct, or as by statute provided, shall be a quorum for business; and may appoint a clerk, who shall be sworn and shall record the acts of such board.

SEC. 2. Such board, or such health officers, or health com- *Its duty to examine into nuisances, etc., and to remove them.* mittees shall examine into all nuisances and sources of filth injurious to the public health and cause to be removed all filth found within the town, which in their judgment shall endanger the health of the inhabitants; and all expenses for such removal shall be paid by the person who placed it there, if known, and if not known, by the town; and when any such filth or nuisances shall be found on private property, such board shall notify the owner or occupant of such property to remove the same at his expense, within such time as the board shall direct; and if he shall neglect to remove it, he shall be fined not less than twenty dollars nor exceeding *Expenses of removal.* one hundred dollars, and pay such expense and costs as the town shall incur by such removal; and after the expiration of such time, such board shall cause such filth or nuisance forthwith to be removed or abated; and such board, or such health officer or committee as it shall direct, may enter all *Entrance to places suspected of containing filth.* places, where such board shall have just cause to suspect any such nuisances or causes of filth to exist.

SEC. 3. It shall be sufficient notice to all persons of any *Notices.* regulation of such board, if it be published in a newspaper published in the town, or posted for three days on each sign-post in said town; and if any person shall wilfully violate such rules, after they have been so published or posted, or after actual notice thereof shall have been given to him, he shall be fined not less than fifteen dollars, nor exceeding one *Penalty.* hundred dollars.

SEC. 4. The board of health, in any town contiguous to *Quarantine.* navigable waters, may assign within the town, or the waters contiguous thereto, the port or place in any harbor, road, river or bay, where vessels coming into the limits of such town or into such contiguous waters, shall, if need be, per-form quarantine; and every vessel which shall, between the first day of June and the first day of November, come from any foreign port or place, or from any port or place in the

United States south of the capes of the Delaware, and come to anchor in any such harbor, road, bay, river or contiguous waters, if any place for quarantine shall have been assigned as aforesaid, shall come to anchor and lie at such place so assigned, and at no other place, until discharged in manner as is hereinafter provided; and the master of every vessel coming to anchor as aforesaid shall forthwith make signal for a health officer by hoisting colors in the shrouds, or, if need be, may send a person on shore, who shall notify the health officer of the port, or if there be no health officer, a member of the board of health, of the arrival of such vessel, and forthwith return on board; but the provisions of this section shall not apply to any such vessel which shall have entered any port or place in the United States north of said capes, where there are quarantine regulations, and been visited by a health officer, received a clean bill of health, and been permitted to go to the wharves and unload thereat; and such clean bill of health, or a certified copy thereof, shall be left with the collector of the port within twenty-four hours after the arrival of such vessel.

SEC. 5. When the board of health in any town shall deem it expedient that vessels arriving in its town or in the waters contiguous thereto, from any port or place in the United States, north of the capes of the Delaware, should perform quarantine, such board may by an order, published or posted as aforesaid, subject such vessels to quarantine in the same manner as if they arrived from a foreign port or place.

SEC. 6. On notice given to a health officer or member of the board of health of the arrival of any vessel as aforesaid, he shall visit it without delay, and may, on examination, give

a certificate of health, discharging it from quarantine, or cause it to continue subject to quarantine; and every vessel so subjected to quarantine shall perform quarantine under the regulations of such board of health.

SEC. 7. The board of health may establish the fees, not exceeding five dollars, which the health officer shall be entitled to receive for visiting a vessel as aforesaid, and the master or owner of such vessel shall pay the same to such health officer.

SEC. 8. No master of any vessel, liable to perform quarantine as aforesaid, shall fraudulently attempt to elude a quarantine by false declarations of the port or place from whence he came, or land, or suffer to be landed from his vessel any person or thing except in the manner hereinbefore provided, nor permit any person to board such vessel, before it shall have been visited as aforesaid. *Penalty for attempting to elude quarantine.*

SEC. 9. When a health officer or member of the board of health, shall, on visiting any vessel as aforesaid, think it necessary that it should be cleansed or purified, he shall direct its master to hoist a white flag on the head of the mainmast, there to be kept during the daytime; and shall apply without delay to the board of health to direct the time and manner in which the cargo on board such vessel shall be, in part or in whole, cleansed or purified; and such vessel, or such part thereof as may be infected, shall be cleansed in such method as such board shall direct. And when such vessel shall contain any person ill of a contagious or infectious disease, he shall be removed on shore to such place as said board may direct, and nursed and provided for, in the manner prescribed by law. And such board may also cause any passenger on board, and such of the mariners as the master shall not require to continue on board, to be removed on shore and secluded for fourteen days, in such place as the board shall direct; and if any person shall, without such permission, visit any person so confined, he shall be deemed to be contaminated with infection, and be liable to the same confinement and penalty as are imposed upon the person visited. *Health officers may order vessel to be cleansed, etc.* *Persons diseased to be removed and secluded.* *Penalty for escaping or associating with those who escape.*

SEC. 10. If the board of health shall find that any certificate of health granted by them was obtained by fraud or false representation, or be of opinion that any vessel, person, or cargo, should perform further quarantine for the purpose of being cleansed or purified, on notice thereof being given by the board to such person, or the owner, master, supercargo or consignee, of such vessel or cargo, as the case may *Certificates obtained by fraud or mistake, void.*

be, the same shall in all respects be liable to be proceeded with in the same manner as if no certificate of health had been given.

Board may interdict communication with infected places.

SEC. 11. The board of health of any town may interdict communication between it and any other town or place in which any contagious or malignant disease is prevalent.

Taverners to give notice of sick lodgers.

SEC. 12. Every taverner or lodging-house keeper, in whose house any lodger becomes sick of any malignant or contagious disease, between the first day of May and the first day of November, shall within twelve hours after such lodger becomes sick, report in writing to the board of health or health officer, the name of such person if known, and the nature of his disorder.

How board may enforce its orders.

SEC. 13. When any person shall refuse to obey any legal order given by a board of health, or shall endeavor to prevent it from being carried into effect, any justice of the peace, on the request of such board, may issue his warrant to any proper officer, or, if need be, to any indifferent person, therein stating such order, and requiring him to carry it into effect, and such officer or indifferent person shall execute the same.

Fines, how appropriated.

SEC. 14. All fines imposed for the violation of any provision of this Chapter relating to public health, or regulation of any board of health, shall be paid to the town in which the offence is committed, and constitute a fund in such town, subject only to the order of such board, to be by it applied to its contingent expenses, and to the relief of such poor persons in the town as may be ill with malignant or infectious disease, or to the prevention of such disease.

Persons sick of contagious disease may be confined.

SEC. 15. The board of health in any town may order any person, whom they may have reasonable ground to believe to be infected with any malignant, infectious, or contagious disease, into confinement in any place to be designated by said board, there to remain so long as said board shall judge necessary.

Rules for vaccination.

SEC. 16. Boards of health may adopt such measures for the general vaccination of the inhabitants of their respective towns as they shall deem proper and necessary to prevent the introduction or arrest the progress of small-pox, and the expenses in whole or in part of such general vaccination shall upon their order be paid out of the town treasury. .

SEC. 17. Every person who shall refuse to be vaccinated, Forfeiture for refusing to be vaccinated. or prevent any person under his care and control from being vaccinated, on application being made by any member of the board of health, or by a physician employed by the board of health for that purpose, unless, in the opinion of another physician, it would not be prudent on account of sickness, shall forfeit five dollars to the town where the offence shall be committed.

SEC. 18. Every person who shall violate any provision of General penalty. the preceding sections of this Chapter, or legal order of a board of health for which no other penalty is provided, shall be fined not exceeding five hundred dollars, or imprisoned not exceeding six months, or both.

RAILROADS.

I.

SECTION 1. No horse railroad company shall use steam for Steam power forbidden. motive power.

SEC. 2. The use of any improved motive power for drawing passenger cars on any horse railroad, other than that Other motive power permitted.
R. S., p. 339,
§§ 1-6 and 8-11. furnished by locomotives, dummies, or box engines used on steam railroads on the first day of January, 1875, may be permitted and regulated, in any city by the mayor and common council; in any borough, by the warden and burgesses; and in any part of a town not included in any city or borough, by the selectmen; subject to revocation by the authority granting the same, by a two-thirds vote of its members.

Rails, how laid, and their form.

SEC. 3. No such company shall lay down its rails upon any highway, except in the manner prescribed by the common council of the city, if the same be in any city, otherwise by the selectmen of the town in which such rails are laid; and such common council or selectmen may prescribe the form of rail to be used in the construction of such railroad, and the plan and form of the curves in its tracks or branch road for turning street corners; and may permit said company to change the form of rail prescribed in its charter; but if any such company shall be aggrieved by such action of the common council or selectmen, it may appeal by petition to the Superior Court in the county, which may confirm, annul, or modify such action.

Companies to keep the track in repair, etc.

SEC. 4. Every such company shall grade and keep in repair the railroad track and way, and the surface of the street adjoining the rails of its railroad, for a space not less than two feet in width on each side of each rail; and construct all crosswalks so that all vehicles can conveniently cross or turn off from such track; and in case of injury to any person, animal or vehicle, arising from any defect in the grading or repair of such railroad track, or way, or such part of the surface of such street, no action shall be maintained against such city or town therefor.

City or town not liable for defect in road occasioned by railroad track.

Neglect to repair track, etc., how remedied.

SEC. 5. If any such company shall neglect to repair any track, highway or crosswalk, as required in the preceding section, for thirty days after the common council or selectmen shall have ordered such repairs to be made, then such common council or selectmen may make such repairs, and the city or town, as the case may be, may collect the expense from said company.

Snow not to be removed from track in city highway.

SEC. 6. No such company, having a track in any highway which is under the control of the authorities of any city, shall remove the snow which shall fall upon said track, if it is of sufficient depth to allow vehicles to pass over the road on runners, without consent in writing, first obtained of the mayor of the city.

Snow not to be thrown on sidewalk, etc.

SEC. 7. No horse railroad company shall allow any snow so removed from its track to be placed upon any sidewalk or paved gutter, or where it obstructs or endangers public travel.

SEC. 8. No such company shall sprinkle any article of a decomposing nature on its tracks or rails, or wash them with brine or pickle, or allow it to be done, for the purpose of melting the snow thereon, without written permission from the first selectman of the town, or from the mayor of the city, where the city authorities have the control of highways, in which such track is located; and no officer of any such company shall knowingly permit the snow to be removed from its track, or the track or rails to be sprinkled or washed with any article of a decomposing nature. *Company may not sprinkle salt, etc., on track or rails.*

SEC. 9. Every person who shall wilfully hinder any such company, in the use of its roads or tracks, shall for every such offence be fined not exceeding fifty dollars, or imprisoned not exceeding three months, or both. *Penalty for obstructing track.*

SEC. 10. Every person who shall, without the consent of such company, use upon any horse railroad any vehicle with running gear fitted for the track of such road, and different from vehicles ordinarily used on other highways, for the purpose of conveying passengers for hire upon the track of such road, shall be fined not exceeding one hundred dollars, or imprisoned not exceeding three months, or both. *Penalty for using vehicles fitted to track without consent of company.*

II.

The board of aldermen of any city, and in cities where there is no board of aldermen, the common council, and the board of selectmen of any town, which has control of the highways therein, may abate in whole or in part any assessment laid upon any horse railroad company, or its property, or the person, persons or corporation owning or operating any such horse railroad, on account of such property, and may discharge in whole or in part any lien created by such assessment, or connected therewith; and such abatement and discharge shall be by resolution, specifying the particular assessment and lien, and a certified copy thereof shall be recorded in the records of such liens. *Abatement of assessment on horse railroad companies. R. S., p. 91, § 7.*

REWARDS.

Rewards.
S. A., vol. 8, p. 16.

SECTION 1. The Court of Common Council of the City of Hartford may offer suitable rewards for the apprehension and conviction of such person or persons as shall have committed or shall commit crimes within the limits of said city.

SEC. 2. This act shall take effect from its passage.

Approved, June 19, 1876.

TAXATION.

I.

City taxes.
S. A., vol. 5, p. 340.

That no city tax exceeding two cents on a dollar of the grand list computed according to the system heretofore in use in this state, shall be assessed or levied upon any land or lands within the area and territory annexed to and incorporated with the City of Hartford, by virtue of an act entitled "An act extending the limits of the City of Hartford," approved June 22, 1853, so long as said land is or shall be used exclusively for farming purposes, or is vacant and unoccupied land; and that all farming produce, and all stock used in farming, and all implements of husbandry belonging to persons residing on said territory so annexed, shall be exempt in the same manner and to the same extent, from such city taxation; and that the persons now and hereafter residing on

Farming lands exempt.

Personal property exempt.

said territory so added to said city, and the estate of such What property not liable for bonded debts. persons, both real and personal, shall not be liable by taxation, or in any other mode, for any bonded debt of said city, or for interest on the same, contracted in aid of any railroad company; *provided*, that this resolution shall not be so con- Property in business in city not exempt. strued as to exempt from liability any property invested in business in said city and now liable to taxation for said city debt.ª

Approved, June 15, 1860.

II.

That no city tax exceeding six-tenths of one mill on a Tax on farming lands in city limits, limited when. S. A., vol. 6, p. 316. dollar of the grand list shall be laid or levied upon any land or lands within the present limits of the City of Hartford so long as said land is or shall be exclusively used for farming purposes, and has a market value not exceeding six hundred dollars an acre; and no other land shall be so exempt by reason of any provisions of said charter.[1]

Approved, July 26, 1867.

III.

SECTION 1. All taxes laid by either the town or the City Town and city taxes, when payable. R. S., 1866, p. 728, § 87-99. of Hartford shall be payable and collectible on or before the fifteenth day of July next, after the same are laid, and if paid on or before said day, two per cent. discount shall be allowed thereon, and no discount shall be allowed thereafter. Discount. On all such taxes remaining due and unpaid after the first day of August next after the same are laid, one per cent. shall be added and made collectible, as a part of such tax, and Addition. a further sum of one per cent. shall be, in like manner, added and made collectible, on the first day of each succeeding month thereafter, until such tax is paid.

SEC. 2. The collector, or collectors of each of the aforesaid Notice. taxes, shall, on or before the fifth day of July in each year,

---

ªConcerning taxation of farming lands, see Gillette v. City of Hartford, 31 Conn., 351.

[1] For similar exemptions, see pp. 2, 39–42.

give written or printed notice to each tax-payer on his rate-bill, stating the amount of his tax, and that the same is due and payable at the office of such collector; and such notice shall also contain a copy of the preceding section of this act, or a full and plain abstract thereof, and they shall also further

Publication. publish, on or before said fifth day of July, and continue such publication daily, until the fifteenth day of said July, a like notice, except as to the amount of such tax, in at least two daily newspapers, published in said town or city.

Further notice. Sec. 3. Each collector aforesaid shall, on or before the tenth day of December, in each year, give further notice, written or printed, to each tax-payer on his rate bill, whose tax shall then remain due and unpaid, that unless the same is paid on or before the first day of January next succeeding, the same with all accrued and accruing additional percentage,

Warrant. will be immediately thereafter collected by warrant of distress, together with twenty-five cents fees for such notice, and fifty cents fees for such warrant, which additional percentages and fees, it shall be lawful to add and collect.

ufficient notice. Sec. 4. A written or printed notice, deposited in the post-office in said Hartford, addressed to the tax-payer at the post-office delivery within which he resides, where the same is known, or actual notice, written or printed, given in any other manner, shall be sufficient notice under this act; but no notice, other than that required to be publicly advertised, shall be held or construed to be an essential legal prerequisite for the enforced collection of any of said taxes.

Delayed city tax. Sec. 5. In case the laying of either the town or city annual tax, for the current year, and the appointment of a rate-maker shall be delayed from any cause beyond the first day of May, then the same, if it be the town tax and rate-maker, shall be laid and appointed, by the board of selectmen

Ratemaker. of said town, and if it be the city tax and rate-maker, shall be laid and appointed by the City Court of said city, on or before the tenth day of May, then next succeeding, and said board of selectmen and said City Court shall severally fill all vacancies, which may occur respectively in the office of rate-maker.

SEC. 6. The rate-makers shall, immediately after their appointment, proceed to make out their respective rate bills, and shall complete and deliver the same to their respective collectors, on or before the tenth day of June, next succeeding. *Duties of rate-makers.*

SEC. 7. The collectors of said town and city taxes shall hold their respective offices for the term of two years, and until their successors shall be duly chosen and qualified in their stead. *Terms of office of collectors.*

SEC. 8. Whenever a vacancy shall exist, by death, removal, resignation, or otherwise, in the office of either of said collectors, the remaining collector shall discharge all the duties of said vacant office for the unexpired portion of the term; and in case a vacancy shall exist as aforesaid, in both of said offices, the same shall be filled for the unexpired portion of said term, by a major vote of the selectmen of the said town, and the aldermen of said city, at a meeting specially called and warned by the mayor of the city for that purpose. *Vacancies, how discharged.* *How filled.*

SEC. 9. The first selectman of said town, and the mayor of said city, shall locate and provide a suitable office for the payment and collection of the respective town and city taxes, the expense of which shall be borne equally between said town and city; and said respective collectors shall keep said office open, and be therein in attendance, for the transaction of all business connected with their respective offices, at all reasonable times, between the hours of nine o'clock in the forenoon, and four o'clock in the afternoon, on all ordinary business days. *Collector's office.* *Business hours.*

SEC. 10. The said collectors shall be allowed annually in lieu of all other compensation for the collection of said taxes, the sum of three thousand dollars, payable quarterly, and the portion of said sum, payable to each collector, shall bear the same proportion to the whole sum, as the whole amount of his rate bills bears to the whole aggregate amount of the rate bills of both the town and city for the current year, to be computed and ascertained, by the clerk or clerks of said town and city, for the time being, within one month after such rate bills shall have been completed. *Compensation of collectors.*

SEC. 11. Whenever a complaint shall be made in writing *Complaints against collectors,*

by a majority of the selectmen of said town, against any collector of said town taxes, or by a majority of the aldermen
of said city, against any collector of said city taxes, to any
judge of the Superior Court for incapacity, neglect, fraud,

Removal. malfeasance in office, said judge, upon due order of notice,
may summon such collector to appear, and upon full hearing,
may remove such collector from his said office.

Bonds. SEC. 12. The collector of each of the taxes, in the town or
City of Hartford, shall give bonds, with sufficient surety in
the penal sum of twenty-five thousand dollars, for the faithful
discharge of the duties of his office, which bond shall be executed to the satisfaction of the board of selectmen of said
town, in case of the town tax collector, and to the satisfaction
of the mayor of said city, in case of the city tax collector.

Payments to treasurer. SEC. 13. Each of said collectors shall pay over to the
treasurer of said town or city, by whom his tax collections
are receivable, on the first Monday in each month, all moneys
by him collected on such taxes, up to the time of such payment.

IV.

**Collectors.
P. A., 1876, p. 316,
§§ 3 and 4.** SECTION 1. In the town of Hartford and City of Hartford
the term of office of the collectors, including the collector of
said town elected in October, 1877, shall commence on the first
Monday of May next succeeding their election, and continue

Terms of office. for two years, and the terms of all the other town officers of
Hartford, elected for one year, shall commence on the first
Monday of January next succeeding their election; and all

Other officers. town officers, and the collector of said city, shall hold their
offices until their successors shall be chosen and qualified.

Appointments of rate-makers. SEC. 2. The selectmen of the town of Hartford shall, from
time to time, appoint one or more persons to act as rate-
makers for said town; and the Common Council of the City
of Hartford shall annually appoint a rate-maker for said city,
who shall respectively discharge the duties appertaining to
their appointment, and shall be the proper authority to sign
the rate-bills by them made until others shall be appointed in
their stead.

Approved, March 28, 1878.

V.

SECTION 1. All town and city collectors whose compensa- *Authority of collectors. P. A., 1879, p. 396.* tion is fixed by a salary and not by a rate of commission, shall during their term of office have authority to collect all taxes due the towns and cities of which they are collectors, they having proper warrants therefor; and upon the expiration of their terms of office, the rate-bills not fully collected *Uncollected rate-bills.* shall be delivered to their immediate successors in said offices respectively, who, with warrants to them directed, shall have authority to collect the taxes remaining due thereon.

SEC. 2. This act shall take effect from its passage.

Approved, March 27, 1879.

VI.

SECTION 1. The first selectman of any town, the mayor of *Continuance of tax liens. P. A., 1879, p. 425.* any city, the warden of any borough, and the chairman of the committee of other communities may continue any tax lien upon any real estate by causing to be recorded in the land records of the town in which the real estate is situated, within the first year after the tax becomes due, his certificate describing the real estate, the amount of the tax and the time when it became due, and thereupon such tax, with the interest thereon at seven per cent. per annum, shall remain a lien upon such real estate for five years thereafter unless the tax and interest shall be sooner paid; and any tax lien so continued, when the tax has been paid, may be discharged *Discharge.* by a certificate of the collector of the tax recorded in such land records.

SEC. 2. All acts inconsistent herewith are hereby repealed; *Repeal.* but any tax lien continued by a certificate heretofore recorded as required by section sixteen, chapter two, title twelve of the general statutes, and the amendment thereto approved July 2, 1875, shall continue in force as therein provided.

Approved, March 28, 1879,

VII.

Foreclosure of tax liens.
P. A., 1879, p. 421.

Tax liens may be foreclosed in the manner provided by law for the foreclosure of mortgages of real estate; and the court having jurisdiction may limit a time for redemption, or order the sale of the property, or pass such other decree as it shall judge proper.

Approved, March 27, 1879.

VIII.

Foreclosure of tax liens.
P. A., 1881, p. 11.

SECTION 1. In all actions hereafter brought for the foreclosure of tax liens, all the municipal corporations which have such liens upon the property in question may join in one complaint to foreclose the same.

SEC. 2. This act shall take effect from its passage.

Approved, March 9, 1881.

IX.

Correction of tax assessments.
P. A., 1881, p. 54.

SECTION 1. Any clerical omission or mistake in the assessment of taxes may be, at any time, corrected according to the fact, by the assessors or board of relief, and the tax shall be levied and collected according to such corrected assessment.

Collection by suit.

SEC. 2. All taxes, properly assessed, shall become a debt due from the person, persons, or corporation against whom they are respectively assessed to the city, town, district, or community in whose favor they are assessed, and may be, in addition to the remedies now provided by law, recovered by any proper complaint or proceeding at law, in the name of the community in whose favor they are assessed, for the recovery of money due, as in other cases.

Approved, April 12, 1881.

X.

Form of tax warrant.
R. S., p. 164.

SEC. 21. Warrants for the collection of taxes may be in the following form:

To A. B., collector of taxes of the [*here insert the name of the community laying the tax*], in the county of ———, greeting:

By authority of the State of Connecticut, you are hereby commanded forthwith to collect of each person named in the annexed list, his proportion of the same, as therein stated, being a tax laid by [*name of community*], on the ——— day of ———, A. D. 18—, for the purpose of [*here state the purpose for which the tax was laid*]. And you are to pay the sums collected to the treasurer of said [*name of community*], on or before the ——— day of ———, A. D. 18—. And if any person fails to pay his proportion of said tax, you are to levy upon his goods and chattels, and dispose of the same as the law directs; and after satisfying said tax and the lawful charges, return the overplus, if any, to him; and for want of such goods and chattels you are to levy upon his real estate, and sell enough thereof to pay his tax and the costs of levy, and give to the purchaser a deed thereof, or take the body of said person and him commit unto the keeper of the jail of said county within the prison, who is hereby commanded to receive and safely keep him until he shall pay said sum, together with your fees.

Dated at ———, this ——— day of ———, A. D. 18—.

A. B., *Justice of the Peace.*

TELEGRAPH AND TELEPHONE.

I. Style of telegraph poles regulated.   III. Injury to fire alarm telegraph.
II. Style of telephone poles regulated.

I.

The warden and burgesses of any borough, and the common council of any city, may, upon giving reasonable notice to any telegraph company, compel it to furnish poles of such style and finish as they may determine, within their limits.

Telegraph poles.
R. S., p. 341, § 4.

II.

Telephone
companies.
P. A., 1879, p. 381. SECTION 1. That the statutes concerning telegraph companies, to wit, sections one, two, three, four, six, seven and eight of part ten, chapter II, title seventeen, and section thirty-four, chapter IV, title twenty, of the revised statutes of 1875, be amended by adding after the word "telegraph," wherever the same may occur in either of said sections, the words "or telephone."

SEC. 2. This act shall take effect from its passage.

Approved, March 26, 1879.

III.

Punishment of
injuries to fire
alarm telegraphs.
S A., vol. 6, p. 557. SECTION 1. The courts of common council of the cities of Hartford and New Haven, respectively, shall have power to pass ordinances providing for the punishment of all wilful or malicious injuries to the fire alarm telegraph, and fire apparatus, and property of said cities, and for the unlawful making, use, or possession of keys to the alarm-boxes conPenalty.nected with said telegraph; and the penalty for violating the provisions of any ordinance passed in pursuance of this act may be a fine not exceeding five hundred dollars, or imprisonment in the county jail not exceeding three months, or such fine and imprisonment both.

Jurisdiction. SEC. 2. The City Police Court shall have jurisdiction of all cases arising under this act, *provided*, an appeal shall be allowed to the Superior Court, as in other cases.

Approved, July 30, 1868.

WATER WORKS.

I.

That the board of water commissioners of the City of Hartford are hereby empowered to make such by-laws or regulations for the preservation, protection, and management of the water works of said city as may be deemed advisable and enforce the same by suitable penalties, and when said by-laws or regulations have been approved by the Court of Common Council and shall have been published ten days, at least, in two or more daily papers issued within said city, they be of binding validity; and said commissioners may bring in their own name, actions of debt on such by-laws, before the City Court for said city to recover any penalty for the breach of the same. *Powers of water commissioners. S. A., vol. 5, p. 456. By-laws. Publication. Suits.*

The City Police Court of said city shall also have jurisdiction over any breach of said by-laws or regulations, and may punish the offender by a fine not exceeding thirty dollars, or by imprisonment not exceeding thirty days, or by a fine and imprisonment both. *Jurisdiction of offences.*

The board of water commissioners shall have power to establish rates for the use of water, subject to the approval of the Court of Common Council; and whenever any water rent shall remain unpaid after the time prescribed and limited for payment, by the rules of said board, it shall be lawful for said board to charge and receive additional percentage for collecting the same; *provided*, the conditions of said percentage be published as aforesaid in the rules of said board. *Water rates. Additional percentage.*

Approved, July 3, 1861.

II.

Water mains
extended to state
prison, etc.
P. A., vol. 6, p. 713. That the board of water commissioners of the City of Hartford, with the consent of. the mayor and Common Council, be and they are hereby authorized to extend their water main from the Hartford and Wethersfield town line north of the bridge known as Folly bridge, over and across said bridge Wethersfield. through the highway in the town of Wethersfield to the Connecticut State Prison, and from thence to such points as may be agreed upon by said commissioners and the selectmen of said town of Wethersfield. The said water commissioners Control. to have control of said main and its connections the same as if laid in the town of Hartford.

Approved, July 8, 1869.

III.

Trout brook water.
S. A., vol. 5, p. 539. WHEREAS, Doubts have arisen in regard to the manner of calling and holding city meetings in said city, for purposes other than for the election of officers; *and whereas*, doubts have also arisen whether, under and by virtue of said act, the board of water commissioners thereby constituted have the power to take and convey for and in behalf of said city, a supply of water from Trout Brook (so called), in the town of West Hartford, or from any other source than the Connecticut river; therefore,

Resolved by this Assembly:

City meetings. SECTION 1. All meetings of said city, whether for the choice of officers, or for any other purpose whatever, shall be warned and held in the respective wards of said city, and the votes shall be taken by ballot; and said meetings, and all the incidents of voting therein, and of the proceedings in relation Votes. to said votes, shall be subject to the same regulations as are provided in case of meetings for the election of city officers; Voting list. except, that the official list of the names of persons entitled to vote in either of said wards last prepared for any annual meeting for the choice of officers, shall be and remain the official list for all subsequent meetings, until the next annual meeting for the choice of officers.

SEC. 2. The said act, which this is an addition to and in Construction.
explanation of, shall be construed in the same manner as if
the said Trout Brook, or any other source of water supply
within the towns of West Hartford or Hartford had been
expressly named therein, but the said board of water commissioners shall not be authorized under this section to take
and convey water from said Trout Brook, until further
authorized thereto by a major vote of a city meeting especially warned by the mayor, and held for such purpose in the Limitation.
several wards of said city, on the seventh day of July, A. D.,
1863, at which meeting all ballots cast, inscribed with the
words "For *Trout Brook*," shall be counted as authorizing
and approving a supply of water from said Trout Brook;
and all ballots cast, inscribed with the words "For *Connecticut* Ballots.
River," shall be counted as approving a supply of water from
Connecticut River.

Approved, July 1, 1863.

IV.

WHEREAS, Doubts have arisen whether the charter of said Trout Brook water.
city confers upon the board of water commissioners therein S. A., vol. 5, p. 769.
constituted, the power to take and convey for and in behalf
of said city a supply of water from any other source than the
Connecticut river; therefore,

Resolved by this Assembly:

SECTION 1. That said charter shall be construed in the Trout Brook.
same manner, and said board of water commissioners shall
have the same powers as if the stream in West Hartford,
called "Trout Brook," or any other stream, or water source
within the towns of West Hartford or Hartford had been
expressly named therein, and any land or water right, title,
privilege, or franchise which may be required, taken or impaired for the purpose of supplying said city or said towns
with water under said charter, shall be compensated for, and
the damages ascertained, liquidated and paid in the same Damages.
manner as is provided in the twenty-fourth section of said
charter.

SEC. 2. If said city shall approve this resolution in the manner hereinafter provided, and said board of water commissioners shall introduce water into said city from said Trout Brook, or other water source as aforesaid, it shall be lawful, and shall be the duty of said board of water commissioners to supply said water to the inhabitants of the aforesaid towns living within a reasonable distance from the line of main pipes at the same rate of water rents and upon the same terms and conditions, that the inhabitants of said city are or may be from time to time supplied, and the said water rents shall constitute a lien on lots, houses, and tenements within said towns, and be collected and enforced in the same manner that water rents are, or may be collected and enforced in said City of Hartford.

Water supplies.

Liens.

SEC. 3. Said board of water commissioners shall not be authorized under this resolution to take and convey water from said Trout Brook or other water source as aforesaid, within the towns of West Hartford or Hartford, until this resolution shall be approved in the manner herein prescribed. A special meeting of said city shall be called by the mayor of said city, in the manner provided by the ordinances of said city for calling special meetings thereof, for the purpose of approving or disapproving this resolution. The vote at said meeting shall be by ballot, and shall be cast by the freemen of said city, in their respective wards. The ballot boxes shall be opened at seven o'clock in the forenoon, and close at five o'clock in the afternoon of the day of said meeting. Upon each ballot shall be written or printed the words "Trout Brook," or the words "Connecticut River." If three-fifths of the ballots cast at said meeting shall have upon them the words "Trout Brook," then this resolution shall be deemed approved.

Approval.

Manner.

Ballots.

Approved, July 21, 1865.

V.

Water supplies.
S. A., 1875, p. 10.

The board of water commissioners of the City of Hartford, for the purpose of improving and increasing the water supply of said city, are hereby authorized and empowered, in behalf of said city, to take and hold any stream or water source, and any land necessary or convenient for constructing aqueducts and reservoirs within the limits of the towns of Avon, Farmington and Bloomfield, and any land or water right, title, privilege, or franchise which may be required, taken or impaired for the purpose aforesaid, shall be compensated for, and the damages therefor ascertained, liquidated and paid in the same manner provided in the twenty-fourth section of the charter of said city. *Avon, Farmington and Bloomfield.*

Approved, June 2, 1875.

VI.

That the act passed by the General Assembly at the present May Session, A. D. 1875, entitled an act to extend the powers of the board of water commissioners of the City of Hartford, shall be so construed as to allow said board to use (subject to the order and direction of the Court of Common Council of said city) for the purpose of acquiring and utilizing the lands, water rights, privileges and franchises mentioned in said act, any unexpended balance of the "water works improvement fund of the City of Hartford;" but shall not be so construed as to authorize the expenditure of any further sum, or the incurring of any other liabilities for such purposes. *Powers of water commissioners. S. A., 1875, p. 55.* *Limitation.*

Approved, June 24, 1875.

VII.

The care and control of the public hydrants in the City of Hartford shall hereafter be vested in the board of fire commissioners of said city, reserving to the board of water commissioners of said city the right to use and grant to others the use of the same for purposes not inconsistent with the use thereof by the fire department of said city. *Control of hydrants. S. A., 1874, p. 52.*

Approved, June 24, 1874.

VIII.

Land owned or taken by any municipal corporation, for the purpose of creating or furnishing a supply of water for its use or benefit, shall be liable to taxation, and shall be set *Taxation of water board lands. P. A., 1879, p. 429.*

in the list in the town where such land is situated, to the
corporation owning or controlling such water supply, at a
valuation which would be fair for said land if used for agri-
cultural purposes; *provided, however*, that no such land shall
be liable to taxation, or set in any list as aforesaid, wherever
the inhabitants of the town in which the said land is situated
have the right to the use of such water supply upon the same
terms and conditions as the inhabitants of such municipal
corporation, and when such town actually uses the same.[*]

Approved, March 28, 1879.

IX.

Petition to court to prevent defilement of water.
P. A., 1883, p. 243.

SECTION 1. Whenever any land or building is so used,
occupied, or suffered to remain, that it is a source of injury
to the water stored in any reservoir used for supplying any
town, city, or borough with water, or to any source of supply
to any such reservoir, the authorities of such town, city, or
borough having charge of said water, may bring their petition to the Superior Court in and for the county in which
said town, city, or borough is located, for relief.

Power of court.

SEC. 2. Said court upon said petition shall have full power
to order the removal of any building, to enjoin any use or
occupation of any land or building, which is detrimental to
said water, or make any other order, temporary or permanent, which in its judgment may be necessary to preserve
the purity of said water.

Compensation to party injured.

SEC. 3. In cases where the law requires compensation to
be made to any person whose rights, interests or property
are injuriously affected by said orders, such court shall appoint
a committee of three disinterested freeholders of the county
who shall determine and award the amount to be paid by
such authorities before such order is carried into effect.

Decree of court, how enforced.

SEC. 4. For the purposes of this act said court is vested
with all the powers of a court of equity, and may enforce its
decrees in any lawful manner.

Approved, March 21, 1883.

---

[*] See West Hartford v. Board of Water Commissioners, 44 Conn., 360.

CORPORATIONS.

I.

HARTFORD CITY GAS LIGHT COMPANY.

That Solomon Porter, Harvey Seymour, Ezra Clark, Jr., Thomas Belknap, William B. Ely, and Richard D. Hubbard, with such other persons as shall associate with them for that purpose, are constituted a body politic and corporate, by the name of "The Hartford City Gas Light Company," and by that name are empowered to sue and be sued, plead and be impleaded in any court in this state; to make and have a common seal, and the same to break, alter, or renew at pleasure; and the said company is hereby vested with all the powers, privileges, and immunities which are or may be necessary to carry into effect the purposes and objects of this act, as hereinafter set forth; and said company is hereby authorized and empowered to manufacture, make, and sell gas, to be made from rosin, coal, oil, and any other material or materials, and to furnish such quantities of gas as may be required in the City of Hartford, for lighting streets, stores, and buildings, or other purposes; and to enter into and execute contracts, agreements or covenants in relation to the objects of said company, and to enforce the same. And said company shall be capable of purchasing, taking and holding, and of granting, selling, and conveying any estate, real or personal, necessary to give effect to the specified purposes of this company, and for the accommodation of their business and concerns.

SEC. 2. That said company shall be empowered to lay down their gas pipes, and to erect gas posts, burners and reflectors in the streets, alleys, lanes, avenues, or public grounds of the said City of Hartford, and to do all things necessary to light the said city, and the dwellings, stores, and

Streets to be left uninjured. other places situated therein; *provided*, that the streets, side and crosswalks, public grounds, lanes and avenues shall not be injured, but all be left in as good and perfect condition as before the laying of said pipes or the erection of said posts.

Injury to property of company prohibited. Sec. 8. If any person shall wilfully and maliciously do or cause to be done any act or acts whatever, whereby any building, construction, or works of said company, or any gas pipe, gas post, burner or reflector, or any matter or thing appertaining to the same, shall be stopped, obstructed, injured, or destroyed, the person or persons so offending shall be deemed guilty of a misdemeanor, and being thereof convicted, **Penalty.** shall be punished by a fine, not exceeding one hundred dollars, or imprisonment in the county jail, not exceeding six months, or by such fine and imprisonment both, at the discretion of the court having cognizance of such offence: **Prosecution no bar to civil suit.** *provided, however*, that such criminal prosecutions shall not in any way impair the right of action for damages by a civil suit, hereby authorized to be brought for any such injury as aforesaid, by and in the name of the said corporation, in any court in this state having cognizance of the same.

II.

THE HARTFORD HOSPITAL.

Corporators. S. A., vol. 3, p. 369. SECTION 1. That David Watkinson, Ebenezer Flower, A. S. Beckwith, S. S. Ward, A. W. Butler, A. M. Collins, Wm. T. Lee, Job Allyn, Samuel Colt, James B. Crosby, Albert Day, Chester Adams, James G. Bolles, George Beach, Thos. Smith, Jonathan Goodwin, A. W. Birge, Lucius Barber, and Charles T. Hillyer, and all such persons as are, from time to time, associated with them, for the purpose of establishing and maintaining a hospital in the City of Hartford, and their successors be, and they hereby are, incorporated for said purpose, and made a body corporate and politic, by the name of **Corporate name.** the Hartford Hospital, and by that name shall be capable of suing and being sued, pleading and being impleaded, and may purchase, take, receive, hold, sell, and convey estate, real _{May sue and hold property.} and personal, to such an amount as may be necessary for the purposes of said corporation; may have a common seal, and _{Seal.} the same may alter and change at pleasure, and may make and execute such by-laws and regulations, not contrary to _{May make by-laws.} the laws of this state, or of the United States, as shall be deemed necessary for the well ordering and conducting the concerns of said corporation.

SEC. 2. That said corporation shall be governed by the _{How governed.} following articles:

Article 1. This corporation shall be called the Hartford _{Members, etc.} Hospital. Persons contributing for the use of the corporation, at any one time, the sum of fifty dollars, shall be members for life. Persons contributing the sum of five hundred dollars shall be vice-presidents for life, and also directors for life; those contributing two hundred dollars shall be directors for life; those twenty-five dollars shall be members for five years; and those ten dollars shall be members for one year.

Art. 2. In order the better to carry into effect the objects of said corporation, the members thereof shall, at an annual meeting, to be held at such time and place as the by-laws of the said corporation shall direct and appoint, elect from their own members by ballot, and by a majority of the votes given at such election, twelve persons as directors of the said cor- _{Twelve members and mayor to be directors.} poration; and the persons so elected, together with the mayor of the City of Hartford for the time being, shall constitute a board of directors. The directors so elected shall hold their offices for one year and until others are elected in their _{Term of office.} places. In case of any vacancy in the board, the remainder _{Vacancy.} of the directors shall have power to fill such vacancy until the next election.

Art. 3. The board of directors shall annually, as soon as _{Directors to elect officers.} may be convenient after the said annual election, elect by ballot, from among their own numbers, a president, a vice-president, and shall also elect a secretary and a treasurer, who shall hold their offices for one year, and until others are elected in their stead. But as many directors may be chosen as there may be directors by subscription.

Directors;
powers of.

Art. 4. The said board of directors shall have power to manage and conduct all the business and concerns of the corporation, and to make such laws as may be necessary for the management and disposition of the estate and concerns of the corporation, and to appoint such officers and servants

Medical officers.

as they may deem necessary. The medical officers, including all attending and consulting physicians and surgeons, shall

Vacancies.

be appointed annually. Vacancies occurring before the expiration of a year from the time of any appointment, shall be filled by the directors as soon as the same can conveniently be done.

First meeting; how called.

Art. 5. A majority of the corporators shall call the first meeting for the election of officers, at such time and place in the City of Hartford as they shall appoint, giving three days' notice thereof, by publishing the same in the daily papers of

Annual meeting.

the city, and the annual meeting of said corporation shall be held at such time and place, and on such notice, as shall be fixed by the by-laws of said corporation.

Sec. 3. This act may be altered, amended, or repealed, by the General Assembly.

Passed, 1854.

III.

HARTFORD AND WETHERSFIELD HORSE RAILWAY COMPANY.

Corporators.
S. A., vol. 5, p. 308.

Section 1. That S. W. Robbins, Henry C. Dwight, Nathan M. Waterman, Edward Wadsworth, George W. Moore and James Bolter, with such other persons as shall associate with them for the purposes hereof, be and they hereby are constituted a body politic and corporate, by the name of the Hartford and Wethersfield Horse Railway Company, and by that

Powers.

name they shall have and enjoy all the powers usually granted to railroad corporations in this state. And said company is hereby authorized and empowered to locate, construct, and finally complete a single or double railway, from a point in the highway, at or near the brick Congregational church, in the town of Wethersfield, over and along said highway, to the City of Hartford; and thence to such point on Main strcct, in said city, as the directors of said company shall designate.

Provided, however, that such railway shall not be con- _{Consent of council for construction over city highways necessary.} structed over said highways, or any part thereof, without the consent of the towns or Common Council of the city having charge of such highways. And said corporation is hereby authorized and empowered to transport, take and carry persons and property upon and over said road; *provided, however,* _{Steam not to be used as a motive power.} that steam shall not be used as a motive power in operating said road. And the said company is hereby vested with all the powers and privileges, and is made subject to all the duties, conditions and requirements of the Act relating to Railroad Companies, passed May session, 1849, and all other acts in addition or in alteration thereof.

IV.

SECTION 1. That section sixth of the resolve incorporating _{H. & W. H. R. R. Co. Certain sections repealed. S. A., vol. 5, p. 492, § 1, 2, 7, 9 and 10.} the Hartford and Wethersfield Horse Railway Company, and so much of the first section of said resolve as provides that said company shall be subject to the duties, conditions and requirements of the act of 1849, relating to railroad companies, and the other acts in addition to and in alteration thereof, be and the same are hereby repealed.

SEC. 2. Upon the completion of the railway specified in its _{May operate over other highways than specified in original charter.} original charter, said corporation is hereby authorized and empowered to build, construct, and operate over any of the other highways in the City of Hartford, such other railways, branches, or extensions, as public convenience may require; *provided, however,* that no such railways, branches, or exten- _{Consent of council necessary.} sions shall in any case be constructed, built, or operated without the consent of the Common Council of said city first had and obtained; *and provided, also,* that the grades and location of such railways, branches and extensions shall in all cases be subject to the direction and approval of said Common Council.

SEC. 7. Said corporation may establish and collect a toll _{Tolls.} upon all passengers and property transported by them over said railway, at such reasonable rates as may be determined from time to time by the directors, and approved by said Common Council; and said directors shall have power to make and prescribe such by-laws, rules, and regulations in relation to the stock, property and business of said corporation, as may from time to time be found necessary.

Sec. 9. Said corporation shall, in all cases in which their railway is located in the traveled part of the highway, keep and maintain all that part of the highway, over which their railway is laid, together with a space two feet on each side of their track, in good and sufficient repair, without expense to the city or town having charge of such highways. Said company shall also make good all damage to any highways in said town of Wethersfield, over which their road or way shall pass, caused by the construction of such road or way; and all such highways shall be restored to, and left, on completion of said railway, in as good condition as they were when the same was located thereon, subject to the approval of the selectmen of said town of Wethersfield.

Sec. 10. No such railway shall be constructed over any highway, or any part thereof, without the consent of the selectmen of the towns, or the Common Council of the city having charge of such highways; and so much of the first section of the original charter as provides that no such railway shall be constructed over any highway, without the consent of the towns having charge of such highways, is hereby repealed.

Approved, July 1, 1862.

V.

SECTION 1. That the rate of fare to be charged by the Hartford and Wethersfield Horse Railway Company for transporting one person to or from the town of Wethersfield over the main line or route of said road from or to any point within the limits of the City of Hartford, shall not exceed fifteen cents; and that the rate of fare for transporting one

Side notes:
Tolls to be approved by Common Council.

By-laws.

Repair of track.

Highways to be left in good condition.

Consent of city authorities necessary to construction.

Repeal.

H. & W. H. R. R. Co. Rates of fare. S. A., vol. 6, p. 836.

Within city limits.

person over said main line, between any two points within the present limits of said city, shall not exceed seven cents; and that the rate of fare for transporting one person over any On branch lines. branch of said main line between any points within the present limits of said city, shall not exceed seven cents; and that all parts of the charter of said company and of the Former acts repealed. amendments thereto which are inconsistent herewith, are hereby repealed.

Sec. 2. Said railway company shall at all times keep for Place of sale and price of tickets sale at the office of the secretary of said company, and at least regulated. at three other convenient places in said city, tickets to the number of sixteen for the sum of one dollar, each of which tickets shall transport one person over said main line, or over any branch of said main line between any two points within the limits of said city; and said railroad company shall at all times keep for sale, at the places aforesaid, tickets to the number of eight for one dollar, each of which tickets last mentioned shall transport one person to or from the town of Wethersfield, over the main line or route of said road, from or to any point within the limits of the City of Hartford.

Sec. 3. This act may be altered, amended, or repealed at the pleasure of the General Assembly.

Approved, July 1, 1870.

VI.

HARTFORD HOME.

Section 1. That the Court of Common Council of the Common Council authorized to establish the City of Hartford shall have power and authority to make Hartford Home. S. A., vol. 5, p. 535. ordinances for the establishment, support, and maintenance of an institution to be located within the county of Hartford, and known and called by the name of the Hartford Home, for the reception, restraint, support, government, and moral, Objects. intellectual, and physical education and culture of all such minor children, residing within the limits of said city, as shall be voluntarily surrendered to the trustees of said institution by their parents or lawful guardians, or shall be committed to the care of such trustees by competent

How supported. authority; and said Court of Common Council may, for such purpose, lay taxes and provide for the collection thereof, in the same manner that taxes may now or hereafter be laid and collected for ordinary city purposes: *provided*, that such insti-

Location. tution shall not be located in any town except the town of Hartford, without the assent in writing of a majority of the

Legal settlement of child. selectmen of such town; *and provided further*, that no child shall gain a legal settlement in any town except the town of Hartford, while under the legal care and custody of the trustees aforesaid.

Management. SEC. 2. The government and general management of said

Trustees. Hartford Home shall be vested in five trustees, residents of said City of Hartford, who shall be appointed by the board of police commissioners of said city, and who shall hold their

Term of office. offices respectively for the term of five years (except as here-inafter provided,) and until their successors shall be duly appointed and qualified in their stead. Immediately after the passage of this act, the said board of police commissioners, at a meeting specially warned for the purpose, shall appoint one

Trustees, manner of appointment. trustee of said Hartford Home, for the term of one year, one for two years, one for three years, one for four years, and one for five years, from the fourth day of July, 1863; and annually thereafter in the month of June, said board shall appoint one trustee for the term of five years as aforesaid; and each of said trustees so appointed for the term of five years, shall enter upon the duties of his office, in place of his predecessor, on the fourth day of July next succeeding his appointment; and said board of police commissioners may, at any time, fill

Vacancy. any vacancy for the unexpired term of any trustee, which may occur by death, resignation, non-residence in said city, or otherwise; and in case said board of police commissioners

Chief Justice shall appoint trustees, when. shall, from any cause, fail to appoint said trustees, as afore-said, the appointment thereof shall then devolve upon the chief justice of the Supreme Court of this state, for the time being.

Duties of trustees. SEC. 3. It shall be the duty of said trustees to take charge of the general interests of said Hartford Home; to provide for its sustenance and support, and to exercise a careful and vigilant supervision over all its affairs; to guard, as far as possible, against any harsh or arbitrary exercise of authority over the children under their care; and also against any undue exercise of sectarian or political influence over the minds of such children; to appoint a superintendent, and all such subordinate officers, assistants, and agents, as they may deem necessary, and to fix the amount of their compensation, and define their duties; to make by-laws for the government, support, and management of said Hartford Home, not inconsistent with law and the ordinances of said City of Hartford; to cause the proper registration of the names, ages, sex, place of birth and parentage, so far as can be ascertained, of all the children committed to their charge; to keep full and accurate accounts of all expenditures, receipts, and donations, on account of said Hartford Home, and to make an annual report in the month of January in each year to the board of police commissioners, giving a full and concise history of the financial and general operations and transactions of said Hartford Home, for the year preceding, which report shall be laid by said police commissioners before the honorable Court of Common Council for approval. *Superintendent. Compensation of officers. Registration of names, etc. Trustees to keep accounts. Annual report. Approval by Common Council.*

SEC. 4. All moneys raised by taxation for the support and maintenance of said Hartford Home shall be paid into the hands of the treasurer of said city, and shall be applied to the purposes for which it was so raised, and for no other purpose whatever. *Moneys.*

SEC. 5. If any person residing in said city, who has had relief or supplies from said town of Hartford, shall suffer his children to misspend their time and live in idleness, and shall neglect to bring them up and employ them in some honest calling; or if any family in said city cannot or does not provide competently for their children, whereby they are exposed to want; or if any poor children residing in said city, live idly or are exposed to want and distress, and there are none to take care of them; or if any heads of families residing in said city shall neglect the education of the children under their charge, after due admonition by the judge *Judge of Police Court may bind out minor children to Hartford Home by approval of mayor, when.*

of the Police Court of said city, whereby such children grow up rude, stubborn, and unruly, or if there be found residing in said city any minor children, over whom there is exercised no proper parental or moral restraint, and who, from such neglect and exposure, have fallen, or are in manifest danger of falling into habits of vice and immorality, it shall be the duty of the said judge of the Police Court to cause such minor children to be brought before him, upon his proper warrant duly issued for such purpose; and said judge shall cause proper notice to be given to the parents or guardians of such children, if any there be residing in said city, and upon such notice and a full hearing, said judge may, with the approval of the mayor of said city, bind out all such minor children to the trustees of said Hartford Home; males till twenty-one, and females till eighteen years of age, that they may be properly educated and brought up to some lawful calling and employment; and said trustees shall have all the rights and shall discharge all the duties in relation to the children committed to their custody, pertaining to the parental relation, and may re-indenture and apprentice such children to proper masters during their minority as aforesaid; males till twenty-one and females till eighteen years of age; to be properly educated and brought up to some lawful calling and employment; said trustees may also receive all such minor children as shall be voluntarily surrendered to them by the parents or guardians having the legal custody and control of such children, and shall have the same powers and discharge the same duties in relation to the children so surrendered, as are herein provided for children bound to them by the judge of the Police Court as aforesaid. And said trustees shall have and exercise all the rights and powers to inquire into the treatment by their masters of the children by them indentured, and to cause such indentures to be canceled, that parents, guardians, or selectmen now by law have in relation to children by them indentured.

Notice.

Powers and duties of trustees de children.

Trustees may apprentice during minority.

Trustees may receive minor children otherwise, when.

Trustees may cancel indentures.

Visits of trustees. SEC. 6. It shall be the duty of one or more of said trustees to visit said Hartford Home as often, at least, as once in

each month, and inspect every apartment, and the accounts
and register of the institution, to see that the by-laws, rules,
regulations, and orders of the trustees are properly observed
and obeyed; to see that no abuse or mismanagement is prac-
ticed; and in general to exercise a vigilant and scrupulous
supervision over every department of such institution and
the management of all its affairs, and it shall also be the duty
of one or more of the police commissioners aforesaid to visit *Visits of police commissioners.*
said institution as often, at least, as once in each quarter, for
the like purpose of inspecting its condition, and the management of all its affairs.

SEC. 7. Said trustees may receive for the benefit of said *Trustees may receive property for the home.*
Hartford Home, donations, gifts, bequests, deeds, and grants
of money, choses in action, lands, rents, incomes or other
property, from any person, association or incorporation; and
when so directed by the parties making such donations,
bequest, deeds, and grants as aforesaid in writing, may hold
or dispose of the same in their own name as such trustees,
and apply the avails thereof, according to such directions;
and all such donations, bequests, deeds, and grants, when not
otherwise ordered, in writing, by the donors, shall vest in the *Property donated to vest in the city, when.*
City of Hartford, and the avails thereof shall be paid into
the city treasury, and applied for the use and benefit of said
Hartford Home, and for no other purpose whatever. And
said trustees may form an alliance, as auxiliary to them, *Trustees may form alliance.*
with any other association incorporated for the same general
purposes contemplated by this act; and may admit to a share
and participation with themselves, in the government, support, management, and control of said Hartford Home, so
many trustees, to be appointed by such auxiliary incorpora- *Auxiliary trustees.*
tion or incorporations, not at any one time exceeding four, as
shall be mutually agreed upon; and said auxiliary trustees
shall, when so admitted, have and exercise all the powers,
rights, and privileges conferred upon the trustees appointed
under this act.

Provided, That no such alliance shall be formed, nor auxil- *Approval of alliance.*
iary trustees admitted, except under a covenant or agreement

in writing, duly executed by the parties thereto, and approved by the Court of Common Council of said City of Hartford.

Police commissioners may annul indentures upon notice, when.   Sec. 8. The board of police commissioners may, at any time, upon giving proper notice to the said trustees, cancel and annul any indentures made to said trustees by the said judge of the Police Court, whenever they shall find upon a full hearing of the parties interested, that such cancellation, in their judgment, will be an act of justice to the said parties.

Common Council may pass ordinances to carry out provisions of this act.   Sec. 9. The Court of Common Council of said city shall have and exercise all the powers necessary and proper to carry into full effect all the purposes contemplated by this *act*, and may make ordinances prescribing the form and manner in which all the accounts of said Hartford Home shall be kept, audited, liquidated, and paid; the bonds and oaths of the trustees, officers, and agents thereof; and the manner in which all the affairs of said Hartford Home shall be managed and conducted: *provided*, said ordinances shall not be inconsistent with the provisions of this act.

Approved, June 24, 1863.

VII.

THE HARTFORD STEAM COMPANY.

Powers in streets. S. A., 1879, p. 106, § 3.   Said corporation is hereby authorized and empowered to manufacture, use, and sell steam within the city or town of Hartford, for any purpose, and may heat any public or private building within said territory, by means of steam or hot water conducted in pipes through the streets and public grounds of said city or town, and may make and enter into contracts to furnish such quantities of steam or hot water as may be required for heating any buildings, or for other purposes, in said city or town, and enforce the same. Said corporation is also empowered to erect buildings or other works necessary to carry on the business of said corporation, and shall have general power to do all things necessary to the successful prosecution of the business of said corporation. But before using any of the streets or public grounds of said city for the purpose of this act, the consent of the Common Council of said city shall be obtained, and said consent having been obtained, said corporation shall be empowered to lay down their steam and hot water pipes and radiators, or other apparatus necessary to carry on said business, in the streets, alleys, lanes, avenues, or public grounds of said city or town of Hartford; and, in the location of their works, and in laying their pipes or other conductors of heat, said corporation shall be subject to the orders and general direction of the Court of Common Council of said city; and the streets, side and crosswalks, public grounds, alleys, lanes, and avenues shall not be injured, but shall be left in as good condition as before the laying of any pipe or other apparatus in the same by said corporation, and said corporation shall repair all defects or injuries to said streets, side and crosswalks, public grounds, alleys, lanes, and avenues, caused by its use of the same for the purposes of this act, to the satisfaction of the board of street commissioners of said city. Said corporation shall be liable for any injury done to any public or private property in the construction of their works, or the laying of any pipes or other apparatus used for carrying on the business authorized by this act.

Consent of Common Council required for use of streets.

Streets not to be injured.

Liability for injuries.

Approved, March 25, 1879.

VIII.

HARTFORD ELECTRIC LIGHT COMPANY.

Said corporation is hereby empowered and authorized to manufacture and sell electric light and electricity within the city and town of Hartford, for any purposes whatever, and may light any public or private buildings or grounds, streets, avenues, lanes, parks, and squares within said territory, by means of electricity conducted by wires through, over, or along, or across the streets and public grounds of said city or town, and may make and enter into contracts to furnish

Powers in streets. S. A., 1881, p. 212, § 3.

such quantities of electricity as may be required for lighting any streets or buildings or other places, or for other purposes in said city or town, and may enforce the same. Said corporation is also authorized to erect such buildings, poles, posts, fixtures, or other works or structures necessary to carry on the business of said corporation, and to buy, own, sell, and deal in all patent rights and other property necessary or convenient for the purposes of said corporation, and generally shall have power to do all things necessary to the proper management of its business: *provided*, that before said corporation shall erect any structures, or suspend any wires upon or over the streets or public grounds of said city, the consent of the Common Council of said city shall first be obtained, and all such structures shall be erected and maintained subject to the approval of the board of street commissioners of said city.

Consent of Common Council.

Approved, April 12, 1881.

Amended powers.
S. A., 1883, p. 82.

SECTION 1. The Hartford Electric Light Company is hereby empowered and authorized to construct and maintain a line of wires for the purpose of conducting electric currents, between some convenient point in the City of Hartford and some convenient point without said city and in either of the towns of Windsor Locks, Manchester, Simsbury, or Windsor, where the works of said company may hereafter be located. Said wires are to be laid in the ground or suspended upon poles along any public highway between said points, in the manner, and subject to all the provisions of the general statutes relating to the construction of lines by telegraph and telephone companies.

May lay wires under ground.

SEC. 2. Said company may, within the limits of the City of Hartford, lay down, construct, and maintain beneath the surface of the ground and in the public streets of said city, lines of wires enclosed in pipes or otherwise insulated and protected, or other apparatus for conducting electric currents about said city, and may use said lines of wires or conductors for the purposes of said company's business as provided in its charter, and may license other companies organized for telegraph and telephone purposes to use the same for any lawful purpose within the scope of their corporate powers, and particularly for transmitting messages by telegraph and telephone. Whenever any of said streets and highways shall *Highways not to be injured.* be dug up and excavated for any of the purposes expressed in this resolution, it shall be the duty of said company to restore them to as good condition as they were in before making such excavation; and all such excavations and restorations shall be made only with the consent and approval, and under the supervision, of the town and city authorities having charge of said streets and highways.

Approved, April 24, 1883.

ORDINANCES.

.

ORDINANCES

OF THE

CITY OF HARTFORD.

Revision of 1883.

CHAPTER I.

CITY AND COUNCIL MEETINGS.

*Be it ordained by the Court of Common Council of the City of
Hartford.*

SECTION 1. Annual ward meetings for the election of city
and ward officers, shall hereafter be held in the several wards
of said city, simultaneously in all the wards on the first
Monday of April in each year, and shall be warned in the
manner hereinafter provided, without any previous order
of the Court of Common Council.

Annual ward meetings, when and where held.

SEC. 2. The annual city meeting for the election of city
and ward officers, and all other city and ward meetings shall
be held at such places, in the respective wards, as the mayor,
or other officer acting in place of the mayor, shall, in his

City and ward meetings to be held in such places as mayor shall designate.

warrant warning the same, designate, and the polls shall be opened at six o'clock in the forenoon, and remain open until five o'clock in the afternoon of said day, and no longer, at each of said meetings; and the Court of Common Council shall cause to be provided, at the expense of the city, suitable ballot-boxes, and books of record for each of said wards, and when not required for use at said meetings, the same shall be placed in the custody of the clerk of said city.

SEC. 3.   It shall be the duty of the alderman of each ward, who was chosen at the last annual election, to preside[a] at all meetings of the freemen of the ward where he was elected to office, (except when otherwise provided by the statutes of this state,) and he shall have full power and authority to preserve order and decorum therein, to repress all riotous, tumultuous, and disorderly conduct, and for that purpose he may call to his aid any police officer, and may
also command the assistance of any citizen or citizens who may be present; and any citizen neglecting or refusing to afford such aid when so required, shall forfeit and pay to the treasurer of said city the sum of five dollars for each and every offence.

And said presiding officer shall also have power and authority to cause any person or persons who may be guilty of any riotous, tumultuous, or disorderly conduct, at such meetings, to be taken into custody and restrained until the adjournment of said meeting, and the said person so guilty of disorderly conduct, notwithstanding such restraint, shall be liable to be prosecuted and punished in the same manner as if such arrest and restraint had not been made.

If any person or persons shall, by noise, tumult, quarreling, or any disorderly conduct whatever, disturb any such ward
meeting, or shall villify, abuse, or interrupt the presiding officer of such meeting, he shall forfeit and pay to the City of Hartford, for the use of the city treasurer, the sum of not less than one dollar nor more than five dollars, for each and every offence.[b]

---

[a] See p. 74, I, and p. 75, § 24.
[b] See R. S., 1875, p. 510, § 15.

SEC. 4. That in case the alderman mentioned in the pre- *Mayor may appoint presiding officer, when.* ceding section shall be absent at any meeting of the freemen of the ward whenever it shall be his duty to preside thereat, the mayor shall appoint some suitable person to preside at such meeting; and the presiding officer of any such meeting in each ward shall appoint a clerk for such ward, whose duty *Ward clerk.* it shall be to make a fair and true record, and keep an exact journal of all the acts and votes of the freemen at their several ward meetings, and to deliver over to the city clerk, for safe keeping, all such records, journals, documents, and *City clerk to have custody of votes and records.* other papers, as may be held by him in his said capacity, within twenty-four hours after adjournment of, each ward meeting, which said records and documents shall, at all times, be open, and subject to the inspection of all the citizens of said City of Hartford.

SEC. 5. That all the freemen of said City of Hartford, who *City electors may vote, where.* are legally qualified to vote in city meetings, shall be voters in the ward in which they respectively reside and have their home; and the residence or home of each voter shall be in the ward where he has his place of lodging, and no person shall have a right to vote in any ward until he has resided in said ward at least sixty days next preceding the time of said voting: *provided,* that no one shall lose his right to vote in the ward of his last previous residence in less than sixty days *When change of residence, where to vote.* from his removal if he still resides in the city. And if any person not a legally qualified voter shall vote at any city or ward election, or if any legal voter shall vote in more than *Penalty for illegal or double voting.* one ward, or give in more than one ballot at any such election, such person so voting, or such legal voter, so voting in more than one ward, or depositing more than one ballot, shall forfeit and pay to the City of Hartford, for the use of the city treasury the sum of seventeen dollars for each offence.

SEC. 6. At the annual ward meetings, as aforesaid, there *City officers chosen at annual meetings.* shall be chosen for said city, by the freemen thereof, by ballot, a mayor and a city collector, if the official term of the mayor and city collector shall then expire, a city clerk, a treasurer, an auditor of city accounts, and a city marshal; and there shall be also chosen for each ward, by the freemen

Ward officers
chosen.
thereof, an alderman, and four common councilmen, who shall
be residents of the ward where chosen, and shall all be voted
for at one ballot, and whose names shall be either written or
printed on one piece of paper, with the office for which each
person is intended designated thereon; and the persons hav-
Plurality vote
elects,
ing the greatest number of votes for each of said city offices,
and for alderman, and the four persons in each ward having
the greatest number of votes for common councilmen, shall
be duly elected to such offices, respectively, for the full term
thereof, and until their successors are duly chosen, and shall
be so declared and returned.

Ballot boxes in care
of presiding officer.
SEC. 7.   The ballot-box in each ward shall, during the time
the polls remain open at any ward meeting, and until the
votes are duly counted, be under the special care of such officer, or other person, as the presiding officer of such meeting
shall appoint[a] (except when otherwise provided by the stat-
Ballots, how voted. utes of this State); and all ballots shall be laid on the lid of
the ballot-box, and the name of each person shall be checked
upon the ward list, and being so checked, his ballot shall then
be put into the ballot-box by the officer or person in charge
of said ballot-box, or the voter shall be permitted to deposit
the same, and said presiding officer shall see that the names
are so checked, and for that purpose may call to his aid such
person or persons as he may think proper;[b] and such presid-
Presiding officer
decides as to
legality of votes.
ing officer, at any city or ward meeting, before receiving any
vote there offered, may examine the person offering to vote,
and other witnesses, under oath, concerning the qualifications
of such person as an elector of said city, and decide concerning the same.[c]

Tellers, how
appointed.
SEC. 8.   The presiding officer, in each ward, shall appoint
not more than eight tellers, to receive and count all votes
given in their respective wards, immediately after the closing of the polls, in open meeting[d] (except when otherwise
provided by the statutes of this state); and all the votes so
given shall be declared by the presiding officer, and recorded
at large in open meeting by the clerk; and in making such

---

a See p. 75, § 25.   c See P. A., 1877, p. 241, § 27.
b See P. A., 1877, p. 241, § 28.   d See p. 76, § 33.

declaration and record, the whole number of votes given in shall be distinctly stated, together with the names of every person voted for, the number of votes given for each person for any office, respectively, and the name of each and every person there found to be elected as alderman, or common councilman, for such ward;* and at the close, and within twenty-four hours after the adjournment of such meeting, the clerk of such ward shall deliver to the clerk of the city a transcript of the record of such votes, duly signed and certified by the presiding officer and clerk of such ward; and the said city clerk shall forthwith record such transcript, or a plain and intelligent abstract thereof, upon the city records, or upon some book to be kept for that purpose; and any presiding officer, or ward or city clerk, who shall make, certify, or record, any false or illegal return or abstract of such votes, shall forfeit and pay to the treasurer of the City of Hartford, for the use of said city, the sum of thirty dollars for each and every such offence.

Votes, how counted.

Ward clerk shall deliver to city clerk copy of votes recorded within twenty-four hours.

City clerk shall record same on city records.

False returns, how punished.

SEC. 9. The clerk of each ward shall also, within twenty-four hours after the close of any ward meeting, deliver to each person found and declared by the presiding officer of the ward to have been elected as alderman or common councilman of such ward, or shall leave at his usual place of abode, a certificate of such election signed by such clerk, which certificate shall be presumptive evidence of such election, and shall entitle such person to a seat in the Court of Common Council: *provided, however*, that the Court of Common Council shall have authority to decide ultimately upon all questions relative to the qualifications, elections, and returns of its members, but no member shall vote upon any question relative to his own right to a seat in the council.

Notice of ward election to be given to person elected within twenty-four hours.

Qualifications of members of Common Council, how determined.

SEC. 10. The mayor, aldermen, and common councilmen, last chosen, shall constitute a board of canvassers of all city or ward elections, and a majority of the members of said board shall constitute a quorum, and the mayor shall be the presiding officer, or in his absence a presiding officer shall be chosen by the board, and said board shall meet together

Board of canvassers.

* See p. 76, § 33.

Canvassers shall meet within two days after election.

within two days after any such election, and compare all the returns of votes, and ascertain what officers, whether city or ward, are duly elected, and shall furnish to each and every

Certificate of election to be furnished.

person so found to be duly elected to any office, a certificate of his election, certified by the clerk of said city; and the mayor, or other presiding officer of the said board of canvassers, shall thereupon, upon the order of said board, issue

Proclamation of mayor.

to the public his proclamation of the election of such persons.

Meeting, when and how called in case of no election.

And in case said board shall find that no person has been duly elected to any or either of said offices, whether ward or city, the mayor, or other presiding officer of the said board of canvassers, shall also make the public proclamation thereof, and shall issue his warrant for a special election in each of said wards, or either, or so many of said wards as may be necessary to fill such vacancy or vacancies so found, on the Monday next succeeding such last city or ward meeting, and at any special city or ward meeting the same rules and proceedings, in all respects, shall be observed as are provided for annual city or ward meetings. And the mayor

Special meetings to fill vacancies, when to be called.

may call special city or ward meetings, by warrant, as aforesaid, at any time when so ordered by said Court of Common Council, to fill any vacancy which may happen in any city or ward office by death, resignation, or otherwise.

Pay of election officers.

SEC. 11.   There shall be allowed and paid from the treasury of the city to the presiding officer of each ward, ten dollars; to the clerk of each ward, three dollars; to the person having charge of the ballot box, five dollars; to an assistant box tender, three dollars; to each of two persons who may be appointed by the presiding officer of any ward to check the electors' lists, five dollars; and to the deputy registrar, five dollars for each day such officers or persons shall severally be engaged in their respective duties at any city or ward election, which allowances shall be approved and certified by one of the deputy registrars of each ward where such services were rendered, and by one of the registrars, and no other expenses of any kind shall be incurred at any such election to be paid for by the city.

SEC. 12. The city clerk shall be the clerk of all joint conventions of the Court of Common Council, and also of the board of canvassers, and in his absence a clerk *pro tempore* shall be chosen; and the city clerk shall have the custody and care of all the records and papers of the common council board, after final action thereon has been taken by said board; and it shall be the duty of the clerk of said board to deliver the same to said city clerk, who shall give true and attested copies thereof whenever required so to do.

City clerk, clerk of joint conventions of Common Council, and board of canvassers.

Records of Common Council to be delivered to city clerk.

SEC. 13. The mayor, or in case of his absence or disability, the acting president of the board of aldermen, or in the absence of the mayor and of said president, the senior alderman present in the city may, at any time, and when thereunto instructed by order of the Court of Common Council, shall call a city meeting; and may, at any time, and upon the request in writing of any two members of the board of aldermen, and four members of the common council board shall, without unreasonable delay, call a meeting of the Court of Common Council, by issuing a warrant to the marshal or any deputy marshal of the city, requiring him to notify the electors of the city, or the members of the Court of Common Council, as the case may be, that such meeting will be holden at the time and place in such warrant designated, which warrant, in the case of a city meeting shall specify the objects thereof, and shall be issued and served at least two days before the day when such meeting is to be holden, and service of said warrant shall be made by causing a true and attested copy thereof to be published in at least two daily newspapers issued in the City of Hartford, and by fixing a true and attested copy thereof on the public signpost in said city. The Court of Common Council, whenever, in their judgment, an emergency requires a city meeting to be called on shorter notice, may, by a suitable vote, prescribe the manner of warning the same. Warrants for city meetings shall be returned before the meeting to the city clerk, with a suitable endorsement of service. All warrants for meetings of the Court of Common Council shall be served by leaving a copy thereof with each member of said court,

City meetings, how called.

Common Council meetings, how called.

What notice to be given for city and Common Council meetings.

Common Council may prescribe shorter notice, when.

Service and return of warrants.

or at his usual place of abode, and shall be returned, with a
proper endorsement of service, before said meeting, to the
clerk of the board of aldermen; and a certified copy thereof,
and of said endorsement shall, before said meeting, be left
with the clerk of the common council board.

CHAPTER II.

ELECTION AND DUTIES OF CERTAIN CITY OFFICERS.

Joint Convention of Common Council, when held.
Other officers, when and how chosen; and terms of office.
Vacancies, how filled.
President of Council may vote, when.
Duties of city clerk.
Journals of Court of Common Council.

City weigher, and duties.
Inspector of fire wood, and duties.
Deputies of.
Sealer of weights and measures, and duties.
Inspection of milk.
Port warden, and duties.
Jurors of City Court, how appointed.

*Be it ordained by the Court of Common Council of the City of
Hartford.*

Joint convention, when held for election of officers. SECTION 1. A meeting of the entire Court of Common
Council shall be holden yearly upon the second Monday after
the annual city election, for the choice of such officers as are
to be chosen by said court in joint convention. If any
vacancy shall occur in any of the offices filled by this board
Vacancies, how filled. in joint convention, said vacancy may be filled at a meeting
of the same especially warned for that purpose, and the
person chosen to fill such vacancy shall hold his office until
the next annual meeting of said board, and until another be
chosen in his place, and sworn.

Officers chosen annually by concurrent vote. SEC. 2. A meeting of the Court of Common Council shall
be holden annually within fifteen days after the annual city
election, for the choice of such other officers as may be
required, to be chosen annually by the Court of Common
Council; all of which shall hold their office for one year, and
until a successor shall be appointed and qualified. If any
vacancy shall occur in any of the offices so filled said

vacancy may be filled at a meeting of the Court of Common Vacancies, how filled. Council specially warned for that purpose, and the person chosen to fill a vacancy in any office under the charter or ordinances of the city shall, when qualified according to law, be vested with all the powers and functions pertaining thereto, for the full unexpired portion of the term in which Appointee of, entitled to part salary. the vacancy shall have occurred, and shall be entitled to such part of the salary and emoluments of his office as shall be justly proportioned to the time for which he shall hold the same.

SEC. 3. There shall be chosen, annually, at the first sepa- Officers of common council board, when chosen. rate meeting of the common council board after the annual city meeting, a president, vice-president, clerk, and messenger, who shall hold office until their successors are chosen and qualified. The president and vice-president shall be members of said board. The presiding officer of said board Presiding officer may vote, when. shall not vote in any meeting except when the action of said board shall result in a tie, or when by voting in the negative his vote shall make a tie, in which latter case such question shall be lost.

SEC. 4. The clerk of each board shall attend the meetings Duties of clerks of board of aldermen and common council. thereof, and duly record the orders and proceedings thereof, and deliver true and attested copies of his records as often as required. The clerk of each board shall note on every vote, resolution, or ordinance of such board, a brief statement of the action of such board thereon; and whenever such proceedings are had thereon as make the action of the other board proper, he shall cause the same to be transmitted as soon as may be to said other board; and whenever the board, of which he is clerk, shall have concurred with the other branch of the Court of Common Council in passing any vote, ordinance, or resolution, he shall cause the same to be transmitted as soon as may be to the mayor for his approval.

SEC. 5. The clerks of each branch of the Court of Com- Journals of the Court of Common Council. mon Council of said city, shall keep a journal of the doings and proceedings thereof, and after each meeting shall cause the same to be printed in sufficient numbers, and distributed to each member of said Court of Common Council, and to such other officers of said city as they judge best, and within four weeks after the last meeting of said Court of Common Council for the year, they shall cause two hundred copies of such journal, properly indexed, to be printed and distributed, one to each member of the Court of Common Council for the year during which said journal was kept, and one to each officer of said City of Hartford, and shall deposit the remainder in the office of the city clerk of said city, one of which said clerk shall certify under his hand, to be a true record of the doings and proceedings of said Court of Common Council, and which shall be the official journal thereof.

City clerk the custodian of records, etc.

SEC. 6.   The city clerk shall be the stated custodian of all votes, resolutions and ordinances which shall have been made or passed by the Court of Common Council, and shall keep all bills, claims, and vouchers, which shall have been allowed by said court, until the same shall have been delivered to the auditor; and shall take prompt possession of all documents and vouchers, as soon as the same shall have been finally acted upon by said court, and shall immediately make an orderly arrangement of all city papers, which are to be kept on file in his office.   He shall keep an office at such place as he may select, with the approval of the mayor and auditing committee, or at such place as the Court of Common Council shall provide.   He may employ a messenger at a salary not exceeding sixty dollars a year.

City weighers, how appointed.

SEC. 7.   Said Court of Common Council shall appoint city weighers, each one of whom shall give bond with surety in the sum of one hundred dollars, payable to the city, and all anthracite or bituminous coal brought to and sold in this city shall be weighed by one of said weighers, who shall give a certificate of the weight of the same, signed by him, which shall be delivered to the purchaser at the time of sale.

Short weight, how made good.

Whenever any coal shall fall short of the weight specified in the certificate, such deficiency shall be paid for by the weigher who gave the same, to the purchaser on demand,

Penalty for.

and said weigher shall forfeit and pay to the treasurer of the City of Hartford for the use of the city, for each and every offence, the sum of ten dollars.   The fees of said weigher shall be six cents for each load of coal weighed by Fees of weigher. him to be paid by the seller.

Every person who shall sell any anthracite or bituminous Penalty for selling coal unweighed, etc. coal without having the same weighed as aforesaid, or shall sell the same without delivering a certificate of the weight thereof as aforesaid to the purchaser at the time of such sale, shall forfeit and pay a fine to said city not exceeding ten dollars, for each offence.

Sec. 8. An inspector of fire wood shall be appointed an- Inspector of fire wood, how appointed. nually by said court, who shall give a bond with surety in the sum of five hundred dollars, payable to the city. All fire wood brought to and sold in this city shall be measured by Fire wood, how measured. the inspector or deputy inspector by him appointed, who shall give a certificate of the measure of the same in square or solid feet, signed by him, which shall be delivered to the purchaser at the time of sale. There shall also be provided by the city and kept under his superintendance, as many sealed Sealed baskets for charcoal. baskets as he shall think necessary for the measuring of charcoal, each of which, even full, shall hold three bushels.

Sec. 9. Whenever any fire wood shall fall short of the Short measure, how made good. measure specified in the certificate, such deficiency shall be paid for by the principal inspector to the purchaser on demand; and after such demand the same may be recovered in any proper action, or by a suit upon his bond. The fees of the inspector shall be twelve cents for each load of wood Fees of inspector. brought by land; six cents for each cord brought by boat, one-half of which shall be paid by the purchaser, and the other half by the seller.

Sec. 10. Every person who shall sell or purchase any fire Non-compliance with ordinance, how punished. wood without having the same measured as aforesaid, or shall sell any fire wood without delivering a certificate of the measurement thereof to the purchaser at the time of such sale, or shall sell any charcoal except the same shall have been measured in the baskets furnished by the city, or who shall pack any wood, measured or sold in this city, so as to decrease in the measurement of the same, shall forfeit and pay a fine not exceeding twenty dollars.

Pressed hay, how weighed.

SEC. 11. All pressed hay, brought to and sold in this city, shall be weighed by the inspector of fire wood, or his deputy, who shall give a certificate of the weight of the same, signed by him, which shall be delivered to the purchaser of such hay at the time of sale.

Deputy inspectors, how appointed, powers and duties of.

SEC. 12. The inspector of fire wood may appoint any number of deputies not exceeding twelve, who shall each qualify in the same manner, and have the same powers, for the weighing of coal, or hay, and measuring of wood, and certifying thereto as the inspector has, and be liable therefor in the same manner and to the same extent, and the appointment of every such deputy shall be in writing, specifying the term of his appointment, a copy of which shall be lodged on file in the city clerk's office. Whenever any pressed hay

Short weight, how made good.

shall fall short of the weight specified in the certificate of the weight of the same, such deficiency shall be paid for to the purchaser by the inspector who gives the certificate, on demand, and after such demand, the value of said deficiency, if not paid, may be recovered by such purchaser of said inspector in any proper action, or by suit upon his official

Fees of inspector.

bond. The fees of the inspector shall be six cents for each bale of hay weighed by him, to be paid by the seller.

Inspector to prescribe weight of material used in binding hay.

SEC. 13. The inspector of fire wood shall establish and announce a rule fixing the weight which may be allowed to the materials used in binding up pressed hay, and the weight of said materials so fixed by him shall be deducted from the gross weight of all pressed hay. Every person who shall

Non-compliance with ordinance, penalty for.

sell any pressed hay which is bound up with materials whose weight shall exceed the weight allowed by the rule established by the inspector of fire wood, or who shall sell any pressed hay containing any substance other than hay, except said materials, or who shall sell any pressed hay without having the same weighed as aforesaid, or who shall sell any pressed hay without delivering a certificate of the weight thereof to the purchaser at the time of such sale, shall forfeit and pay a fine of not exceeding five dollars for each and every offence, and the sale of each bale of pressed hay sold contrary to or in violation of any one of the foregoing provisions, shall constitute a separate offence.

SEC. 14. There shall be provided, at the expense of the city, and kept by the inspector of fire wood and under his superintendance, a sufficient number of tubs, each of which shall contain three bushels, when even full, of coal measure, and all the anthracite or bituminous coal brought into this city and sold shall, if required, be measured in said tubs under the inspection of the said inspector or one of his deputies. Any person who shall sell any anthracite or bituminous coal brought into this city as aforesaid contrary to the provisions of this ordinance shall forfeit and pay a fine of not less than one nor more than five dollars for each and every offence.

Coal tubs to be kept by inspector.

Penalty for violation of ordinance.

SEC. 15. Said Court of Common Council shall appoint annually a sealer of weights and measures, who shall devote his whole time to the duties of said office, and whose duty it shall be to annually inspect, prove, correct and seal all measures, balances, scales, steelyards, weights, or any instrument, machine or article used for weighing or measuring, by any person, in doing business within said city, according to the standards of the City of Hartford.

Sealer of weights and measures, how appointed, powers and duties.

All such measures, balances, scales, steelyards, weights, instruments, machines or articles as are formed or made to correspond in degree with said standard shall be marked or sealed with the letters H. S. In addition to such annual inspection, said sealer of weights and measures shall, from time to time, as he shall deem necessary, visit all places where measures, balances, scales, steelyards or weights are used for weighing or measuring by any person, in doing business in said city, and inspect such measures, balances, scales, steelyards or weights, as have not been inspected within one year, and if found correct shall mark or seal the same, and shall when requested by any person try and test by said standards the measures, balances, scales, steelyards, weights or other instruments, machines or articles for measuring or weighing used by any person in doing business in this city.

SEC. 16. Any person who shall within the limits of said
city use any weight, scale or measure, to ascertain the
weight, length or quantity of any article by him sold, which
weight, scale or measure has not been marked or sealed by
said sealer of weights and measures in the manner provided
in the foregoing section; or who shall knowingly and with
intent to defraud, sell any article as of a greater weight,
measure or quantity than such article does in fact weigh or
measure according to said standards shall pay to the City of
Hartford a penalty of not less than two nor more than
twenty dollars.

SEC. 17. The owner of the several measures, balances,
scales, steelyards, and weights, shall pay said sealer of
weights and measures for each inspection made by him, as
required by the ordinances of the city, as follows: For
testing each weight, measure, box, or basket, three cents; for
each scale, steelyard, or balance, excepting platform balances,
ten cents; for each platform balance made for weighing less
than five thousand pounds, fifty cents; and for each platform
balance made for weighing five thousand pounds or over, one
dollar.

In addition to the foregoing fees, the owner shall also pay
said sealer of weights and measures a reasonable compensation for all repairs, alterations, and adjustments, which it is
necessary for him to make.

SEC. 18. Whenever the sealer of weights and measures,
upon inspection of any balance, scale, steelyard, or weight,
shall find that it is incorrect. and cannot be adjusted by him,
he shall forbid its further use until it is made to conform to
the authorized standard, and shall fix thereon a written or
printed notice, stating the facts so found by him and forbidding its use, and any person who shall remove such notice,
without the consent of said sealer of weights and measures,
shall forfeit and pay to the City of Hartford a penalty of
twenty-five dollars. Whenever said sealer of weights and
measures, upon inspection, shall find any measure or vessel,
used for measuring any goods sold in said city, to be below
the standard of correct measurement, he shall, with a brand,

dic, or other proper instrument, affix or impress to or upon it, the word "condemned."

Every person who shall use any measure or vessel con- *Penalty for use of condemned measures, etc.* demned and branded, or stamped, as aforesaid, or who shall use any balance, scale, steelyard, or weight, the use of which has been forbidden as aforesaid, for the purpose of ascertaining the weight or quantity of any goods by him sold, shall forfeit and pay to the City of Hartford a penalty of not less than twenty-five and not more than one hundred dollars.

Every person who shall hinder or obstruct said sealer of *Penalty for obstructing sealer in the performance of his duties.* weights and measures, in the discharge of his duty, shall forfeit and pay to the City of Hartford, for each offence, a penalty of ten dollars.

SEC. 19. It shall be the duty of the sealer of weights and *Sealer may enter building and may inspect weights and measures of itinerant vender.* measures, and it shall be lawful for him, to enter any store, house, or other building, or any yard, in said city, where weights or measures are used by any person, in doing business, at any reasonable hour, to inspect any measures, balances, scales, steelyards, or weights contained therein; and it shall be lawful for him to inspect any measures, balances, scales, steelyards, or weights of any itinerant vender of fruits, vegetables, or other articles of merchandise in said city.

SEC. 20. Said sealer of weights and measures shall inquire *Inspection of milk.* into and investigate the quality of milk which may be sold or kept, offered or exposed for sale within said city, and shall make such examinations and inspections thereof as may be necessary to ascertain whether adulterated or impure milk is sold or kept, offered or exposed for sale within said city, contrary to statutes of the State of Connecticut, and shall report all violations of said statutes relating to the sale and adulteration of milk to the city prosecuting attorney for prosecution forthwith.

SEC. 21. Said sealer of weights and measures shall, for the *Powers under preceding section.* purposes of the foregoing section, have the power to enter any store, house, building, or yard, and upon any premises within said city where milk is sold or kept, offered or exposed for sale, or where it is believed to be sold or kept, offered or exposed for sale, at any reasonable time, to make an examination and inspection as provided in the preceding section, and it shall be lawful for him, for the purposes of inspection and examination, to stop and detain any team, wagon or vehicle within said city which is used in the sale of milk, or for the -transportation of milk which is to be sold or kept, offered or exposed for sale, or to be delivered on sale, and to stop and detain any person carrying milk which is to be sold or kept, offered or exposed for sale, or to be delivered on sale.

Police to assist sealer and report violations of the ordinance.

SEC. 22.   It shall be the duty of every policeman to assist the sealer of weights and measures when required, and to report to him any violation of the ordinances relating to the inspection of measures, balances, scales, steelyards, or weights, or of the statutes of the state relative to the inspection of milk, within his knowledge; and the sealer of weights and measures shall report the same to the prosecuting attorney of the city for prosecution forthwith.

Violations to be reported to prosecuting attorney.

Port warden, how and when appointed.

SEC. 23.   The Court of Common Council shall annually appoint a suitable person to be warden of the port, whose duty it shall be to take the charge and superintendence of the public landings; to direct the persons having the care or charge of any vessel, raft, boat, or other water-craft, where they may place or move, lade and unlade the same, and when to remove such boats, or other water-craft from such landing place or places; to see that said landing places are not unnecessarily obstructed, and to do all such matters and things relative to said public landings as will best secure the public in the full enjoyment of the same.

Duties of port warden.

Port warden shall direct location of vessels.

SEC. 24.   Under the direction of the warden of the port, any steamboat, vessel, boat, raft, or other water-craft, may be moored at or opposite any of the public landing places of said city, and the same shall be chargeable with dockage or wharfage at the following rates, that is to say; all steamboats which are constructed for the navigation of Long Island Sound, which may be moored at or opposite either of the public landing places as aforesaid, so as to occupy or lie at, or opposite said landings, or any part thereof, shall be chargeable and pay at the rate of fifty cents per day; and all other steamboats, in like manner, shall pay at the rate of twenty-five cents per day; and all sailing vessels of suitable construction for navigating Long Island sound, or boats of any kind for the sale of fish, which may be moored as aforesaid, shall be chargeable and pay at the rate of one cent per ton per day for the first inside or shore berth, two-thirds of one cent per ton per day for the second berth, and one-third of one cent per ton per day for any berths outside of the second berth, and no such vessel of whatever tonnage, shall pay less than twelve and a half cents per day, for any inside or shore berth. And the port warden of said city is hereby empowered and directed to collect and pay over to the city treasurer, the rates of dockage and wharfage accruing as aforesaid, deducting therefrom twenty-five per centum for his fees for collecting the same, and taking the charge and regulation of said vessels and public landings.

What wharfage dues vessels shall pay.

Port warden shall collect wharfage and pay over to city treasurer.

Fees of port warden.

SEC. 25. That no person or persons shall unlade, discharge, or place at, in or opposite any of the public landing places in said city, or within one hundred feet of low water mark, in Connecticut river, opposite said city, any ballast, rubbish, clam or oyster shells, or any other substance which may tend to obstruct or fill up landing places, or the channel of said river; or leave or place any putrid fish, clams, or oysters, or the offals or dressings of fish, or any animal or vegetable substance likely and liable to putrify, in or upon any wharf, shore, creek, land, or street of said city, or in the waters of said city, if within one hundred feet of the shores thereof, under a penalty of not less than one dollar nor more than ten dollars for each and every offence. And it shall be the duty of the port warden to report to the city attorney, for prosecution, all breaches of this ordinance that shall come to his knowledge.

Depositing rubbish, etc., in Connecticut river, prohibited.

Penalty for violation of.

Port warden shall report violations of ordinances to city attorney.

SEC. 26. If any vessel, boat, raft, or water-craft of any description, or any stone, plaster of Paris, lumber, wood, timber, or goods of any kind, shall be, or lie at any of the public landing places aforesaid, either afloat or on the shore, contrary to the orders of the port warden of said city, the person having the care or charge of said vessel, raft, boat, or water-craft, or any articles above specified, shall forfeit and

Non-compliance with orders of port warden, how punished.

pay to the treasurer of said city, for the use of said city, the
sum of fifty cents per hour for every hour such vessel, raft,
boat, or other water-craft, or any other article above specified,
shall continue to lie in or upon the said landing places, after
notice of such order, and for any penalty incurred under this

section, the master or owner of the vessel, raft, boat, or any
other water-craft, shall be responsible in the same manner as
the person who shall have the charge or custody of the same:
provided however, that nothing in this ordinance shall in any
way impair or affect the rights of the public or individuals to
the free use of the ferry place for the purpose of a ferry.

SEC. 27.   The board of aldermen shall be warned by the
mayor, in the manner provided by law for warning meetings
of the Court of Common Council, to meet on the fourth

Monday of April, in each year, for the choice of jurors of the
City Court; and said board shall, at such meeting, select not
less than seventy nor more than one hundred and fifty free-

holders of said city to serve as such jurors, for the year
ensuing, whose names shall be immediately returned by the
clerk of the board to the clerk of the City Court, who shall
write each of said names upon a separate piece of paper,
which, after being rolled up, shall be placed in a suitable box;

whenever a jury warrant shall be issued by the clerk of said
court to the city marshal, or his deputy, the officer serving
the same shall, in the presence of the clerk and the recorder

of said court draw from said box such number of names as
his warrant requires, and no more, without knowing in any
manner any name so drawn, before drawing the same; and
shall then summon the persons whose names shall have been
thus drawn, according to the mandate of such warrant.   If,

for any reason, more jurors shall be required to complete the
panel, the officer attending the court shall supply the
deficiency, by drawing the names of other persons from said
box, in the manner aforesaid, and summoning them to attend

and serve.   The names of such jurors as do not attend, or
are excused for the whole term from serving, shall be immediately returned to said box, and the names of such as do
attend and serve shall be placed by the clerk in another box

or receptacle, to be drawn after those remaining in the first mentioned box shall have been exhausted. Any juror who shall have been duly summoned, who shall refuse to attend or serve, shall pay a penalty of five dollars for the use of the city, recoverable upon this ordinance. Refusal of juror to serve, how punished.

· Taxable fees in the City Court, and of the clerk of the City Court, shall be the same as are provided in the general statutes. Taxable fees of City Court.

CHAPTER III.

FINANCE AND CONVEYANCES.

Money, how drawn from city treasury.
Orders of city auditor, how drawn.
Auditor *pro tempore*, how appointed.
Auditing committee, how appointed, and duties.
Money due the city, how paid.
Duties of treasurer.
Duties of clerks of City and Police Courts.
City attorney, duties of.
May employ additional counsel and shall keep register of legal proceedings.

Committee of ways and means to examine accounts of treasurer and condition of the sinking fund.
Committee on ways and means to examine accounts of collector.
Conveyance of real estate, how made.
Conveyance of personal property, and evidences of debt, how executed.

Be it ordained by the Court of Common Council of the City of Hartford:

SECTION 1. No money, except for the payment of notes of the city payable at bank, or of interest on city notes, scrip, or certificates of debt, shall be paid from the city treasury, except upon the written order of the auditor of city accounts, specifying the nature of the claim for which such order is drawn; and any payment made without such order, except in the above-excepted cases, shall be without authority and not obligatory upon the city. No order shall be drawn by such auditor, or be valid, without a previous vote of the Court of Common Council authorizing the same, and the only evidence of such authority shall be a certified copy of such order, which it shall be the duty of the city clerk to deliver Payments from city treasury, how made. Orders of auditor, when valid.

as soon as may be to said auditor. In case of the temporary illness, absence, or disability of the auditor, the Court of Common Council may appoint a deputy auditor for the time being, whose acts, in conformity with the votes of said court, shall be valid and obligatory. The auditor shall render his account to the Court of Common Council at least two weeks before the annual election of city officers, and shall keep the same in such a mode of classification as to show the receipts and expenses of each department of the city government and business, including the receipts and expenses of each of the courts of said city, and the various sources and objects of the expenditure made on account of said courts.

He shall receive from the city clerk, and file and safely keep in his office all bills, claims, accounts, and vouchers allowed by the Court of Common Council, and the certified copies of all resolutions appropriating money. He shall be *ex-officio* chairman of an auditing committee, consisting of two members besides such auditor, one of whom shall be appointed by the board of aldermen from their own number, and one by the common council board from their own number, to hold office during the pleasure of the board appointing them; to which committee every bill, account, or claim against the city shall be referred by the Court of Common Council, for their approval or disapproval, before the same shall be approved by said court, unless both branches of said court concur in dispensing with such reference. And it shall be the duty of such auditing committee faithfully to examine all accounts, bills or claims so referred to them, and all monthly accounts of water rents received and expended by the water commissioners, and faithfully to report any informality or improper charge, by them detected, to the Court of Common Council; and also to note their approval of any such account upon the same. And it shall be the duty of the auditor to provide himself with such lists of officers or stated employees of the city, in the various departments of its business, as will enable him to examine thoroughly all claims, accounts, or exhibits presented to the Court of Common Council on their behalf.

Marginal notes:

Deputy auditor may be appointed, when.

Auditor shall render account, when, and how.

Shall preserve claims, vouchers, etc.

Auditor *ex-officio* chairman auditing committee.

Auditing committee, how composed.

Duties of auditing committee.

Duty of auditor.

Sec. 2. All moneys accruing to the use or benefit of the city shall be paid into the city treasury, and duplicate receipts or certificates shall be made by the treasurer for all moneys by him received as such, one of which he shall forthwith deliver to the auditor of city accounts, and the other, if required, to the party from which such money is received. He shall keep a faithful and true account of all his receipts and disbursements in such a mode of classification as to correspond to the classification required in the foregoing section from the auditor, and shall render his account to the Court of Common Council at least two weeks before the annual city meeting. The treasurer shall apply any avails of the water rents by him received to the payment of interest on the water debt or scrip, without special order of the Court of Common Council; and if there be any excess of such avails he shall so report to the said court, who shall thereupon direct whether the same shall be applied to the extinguishment of the principal of the water debt or otherwise.

Moneys, how paid into the city treasury.

Duties of city treasurer.

Water rents, how appropriated.

Excess to be reported to common council, when.

Sec. 3. The clerks of the City Court and City Police Court shall supervise and defray all contingent expenditures in behalf of their respective courts, and shall be entitled to be reimbursed for the same, after being allowed and certified by the judge of such court, out of the fees, fines, penalties, costs, or moneys accruing to the city treasury from said courts. And all such fees, fines, penalties, costs, or moneys shall be paid to the clerk of the court, on account of which they shall accrue. The clerk of the City Police Court shall pay over quarterly to the city treasurer all such fines, fees, costs, penalties or moneys as shall be in his hands, and shall annually on the first day of July account with the city auditor for all the receipts and expenditures of said City Police Court for the preceding year. The clerk of the City Court shall account for all the receipts and expenditures of his court with the auditor of city accounts at least three weeks before the annual city meeting, and immediately thereafter shall pay over all the receipts in his hands to the city treasurer, who shall execute duplicate receipts therefor in the manner aforesaid. And each of said clerks shall keep

Contingent expenses of City and Police courts, how defrayed.

Clerks shall account for receipts to city auditor, when.

Clerks shall keep accounts, how.

a faithful and detailed account of all sums accruing to and due to the city treasury on account of his said court, distributing the items thereof according to the various kinds of sources of expenditure or income.

City attorney, and duties of.

SEC. 4.   The city attorney shall bring all necessary suits for the recovery of penalties and forfeitures accruing to the city treasury for violations of city ordinances, before the City

Shall bring and prosecute suits.

Court; shall prosecute and defend, as the attorney and counsel of the city, all suits or actions brought by or against the city; shall, when requested by the chief of police, appear and prosecute any cause pending before the Police Court; shall draft

Shall draw all instruments for city.

all instruments, process, or forms of proceeding required of him by the officers of said city, or the Court of Common Council, or any committee thereof; and shall pay into the city treasury, as often as once in three months, all sums received or collected by him, and at the same time deliver an

Shall render accounts, when, and how.

account thereof to the auditor of city accounts, deducting from the amounts thereof any necessary disbursements which he shall have made on account of the city. He shall also transmit to the Court of Common Council, at its meeting next succeeding the making by him of any payment into the city treasury, a statement of his charges for his official ser-

Compensation of, how made.

vices, and such compensation shall be made therefor as said court shall allow.   This last account, for the current year, shall be by him delivered to the city auditor at least three weeks before the annual city election.   He may employ such

May employ additional counsel, when.

additional counsel to aid in the trial or preparation of any cause, wherein the city is interested, as shall be approved by the mayor and auditing committee.

Shall keep register of writs and make report to Court of Common Council annually.

SEC. 5.   The city attorney shall keep a register of all writs and legal proceedings to which the city is a party or in which the city shall have assumed the defence; and at the expiration of each year, or sooner if required, make a full report to the Court of Common Council of all suits or other legal proceedings, in which the city is interested, whether finished or pending, the names of the parties and the progress or results of the suits.

SEC. 6. It shall be the duty of the committee on ways and means to examine at least twice in each year, to wit: on the last business days of March and September, the accounts of the city treasurer relating both to receipts and disbursements and the vouchers for the same, also to examine the bonds, cash, and trust and other funds in the hands of said treasurer, and to examine the condition of the sinking fund, and to report the results of such examinations in detail to the Court of Common Council. *Examination of accounts of city treasurer.* *Examination of sinking fund.*

SEC. 7. Said committee of ways and means shall at least twice in each year, to wit: on the last business days of April and October, examine and audit the accounts of the city collector, and report the result of such examination to the Court of Common Council. *Examination of accounts of city collector.*

SEC. 8. All grants, leases and conveyances of any real estate belonging to said city, executed by the mayor of the city, sealed with the city seal, approved by the Court of Common Council in a legal meeting, and recorded in the town where the lands conveyed lie, shall be effectual to convey such estate. *Grants, leases and conveyances of city, how made.*

SEC. 9. All conveyances of personal property belonging to the city, of greater value than one hundred dollars, and all evidences of debt issued by the city, shall, when specially authorized by the Court of Common Council, be executed by the city treasurer, sealed with the city seal, and certified by the mayor. *Personal property and evidences of debt exceeding $100, how executed.*

CHAPTER IV.

FIRE DEPARTMENT.

Be it ordained by the Court of Common Council of the City of Hartford:

Board of fire commissioners, how constituted, and terms of office.

SECTION 1. There shall be a board of fire commissioners[1] of the City of Hartford consisting of six electors of said city, and each commissioner shall hold his office for three years and until his successor is appointed and qualified.

Shall have management of fire department, subject to ordinances.

SEC. 2. Said board of fire commissioners shall have the general management and control of the fire department of said city in the manner, hereinafter provided, subject however to the ordinances of the city and to the orders of the Court of Common Council.

Powers of the board.

SEC. 3. The fire commissioners shall have power to appoint the requisite number of persons to perform the duties of their several positions as set forth in this ordinance, the

May appoint and remove members of department.

fire marshal excepted, who shall hold their places during good behavior, and until removed for cause. But no person shall be appointed to any office without the assent of at least four of said commissioners. Said commissioners shall have

May expel members or disband and reorganize company.

power to suspend or expel any member of any company, and to disband or reorganize any company; and they shall also adopt a suitable uniform to be worn by the officers and men; and generally said fire commissioners shall adopt such rules

---

[1] For appointment of fire commissioners, see page 53.

and regulations for their own government, and of the fire department, as they shall deem expedient for the interest of said department; *provided*, such rules and regulations are not inconsistent with the laws of this state or the ordinances of the city of Hartford. They shall keep a record of all their proceedings, subject to the inspection of the mayor and members of the Court of Common Council.

Shall keep record of proceedings.

SEC. 4. The fire department shall consist of a chief engineer, three assistant engineers, one fire marshal, one superintendent of fire alarms, who shall be appointed and paid pursuant to existing ordinances, and shall perform the duties prescribed therein: six steam fire engine companies, to consist as follows: each company in charge of a self-propelling engine, of one foreman, one engineer, one second engineer, one tillerman, one driver of hose carriage, and nine extra men; the remaining companies of one foreman, one engineer, one fireman, one engine driver, one driver of hose carriage, and eight extra men; one hose company, to consist of one foreman, one driver, one assistant driver and four hosemen; one hook and ladder company, to consist of one foreman, one driver, one tillerman and eighteen extra men; one permanent substitute.

Fire department, how constituted.

SEC. 5. The steam engine companies shall each have one steam engine, one hose reel, and necessary horses, hose and apparatus.

Steam engine companies.

SEC. 6. The hook and ladder company shall have one truck, and necessary horses and apparatus. The hose company shall have one hose carriage, and necessary horses and apparatus.

Hook and ladder company. *Hose company.*

SEC. 7. The salaries of the officers and men comprising this department shall consist of the following sums per annum, payable monthly: Chief engineer two thousand dollars; each assistant engineer two hundred and fifty dollars; the fire marshal four hundred dollars; the superintendent of fire alarms nine hundred dollars; the foreman of each company two hundred dollars; the engineer of each steamer one thousand dollars; the second engineer of each steamer eight hundred dollars; each fireman one hundred and seventy-five dollars; each driver or tillerman of steamer eight hundred

Salaries of members.

dollars; each driver of hose carriage seven hundred and fifty dollars; each assistant driver of hose carriage six hundred and fifty dollars; tillerman of hook and ladder truck seven hundred and fifty dollars; the driver of the hook and ladder truck eight hundred dollars; each extra man, known as bunker, one hundred and seventy-five dollars; each extra man, known as hoseman or ladderman, one hundred and fifty dollars; the permanent substitute seven hundred and fifty dollars.

Engineer of steamer must be a practical machinist.

Chief engineer must give undivided attention to duties.

SEC. 8. No person shall hereafter be appointed to the position of engineer of any steamer unless he shall be a practical machinist, and the chief engineer shall give his undivided attention to the duties of his office.

Engines, where located.

SEC. 9. The steam fire engine, hose, and hook and ladder companies shall be located at such points as the commissioners shall designate.

Fire commissioners chargeable for good order.

SEC. 10. The fire commissioners shall be responsible for the discipline, good order, and proper conduct of the whole department, both officers and men, and for the care of the horses, engines, hose reels, and other furniture and apparatus thereto belonging; they shall have superintendence and control of all the engine and other houses used for the purposes of the fire department, and all the furniture and apparatus thereto belonging.

Duties of chief engineer and assistants.

SEC. 11. It shall be the duty of the chief engineer and his assistants, whenever a fire shall break out in the city, to immediately repair to the place of the fire, and to take proper measures that the several engines and other apparatus be arranged in the most advantageous situations.

Chief engineer to command at fires.

SEC. 12. The chief engineer shall have the sole command at fires over all other officers, all members of the fire department, and all other persons who may be present at fires, and shall take all proper measures for the extinguishment of fires and for the protection of property, preservation of order, and observance of the laws of the state, ordinances of the city, and regulations of the fire commissioners respecting fires;

Duties of engineer. and it shall be the duty of said engineer to examine into the condition of the engines and all other fire apparatus, and of the engine and other houses belonging to the city used for the purposes of the fire department and the companies attached, as often as circumstances may render it expedient, or whenever directed to do so by the Court of Common Council or fire commissioners, and annually to report the same to said court; and whenever the engines or other fire apparatus, engine, or other houses used by the fire department, require alterations, additions, or repairs, the chief engineer shall report the same to the fire commissioners, and on their order, such alterations, additions, or repairs shall be made, provided however, that when the cost of making such alterations, additions, or repairs will exceed the sum of five hundred dollars, said fire commissioners shall first submit the estimates of the same to the Court of Common Council, and shall not order the same until the Court of Common Council shall by vote have given their approval thereto. And it shall be moreover the duty of said chief engineer to receive and transmit to the said fire commissioners, for the use of the Court of Common Council, all the returns of the officers, members, and fire apparatus made by the respective companies, and all other communications relating to the affairs of the fire department; to keep proper and exact rolls of the respective companies, specifying the time of admission and discharge, and age of each member, which he shall report in writing to said fire commissioners, who shall safely file and preserve such reports. *Shall make report annually.* *Alterations or repairs, how made when exceeding five hundred dollars.* *Chief engineer shall submit what returns.*

SEC. 13. In case of the absence of the chief engineer at any fire, the senior assistant engineer present shall have the power and perform the duties of chief engineer. *Senior assistant engineer shall act, when.*

SEC. 14. It shall be the duty of the fire commissioners to prepare rules and regulations for the government of the fire companies and the members thereof, and to furnish each member of the fire department with a copy of said rules, and to have said rules posted conspicuously in and about the several engine houses belonging to the department, and to give notice that they are prepared to receive application for membership in the city fire department, whenever vacancies shall occur therein. *Commissioners shall make rules and regulations.* *Rules to be posted in engine houses.*

SEC. 15. It shall be the duty of the fire commissioners to purchase for the city such apparatus and other property, both real and personal, as may be necessary for the wants of the department, and also to sell or exchange in the manner provided by the ordinances of the city, when they shall deem best, any of the real and personal property of the city in use by the fire department, *provided* such purchase or sale shall be first approved by a resolution of the Court of Common Council.

SEC. 16. The auditor is hereby authorized and directed to draw his order on the city treasurer in favor of the persons entitled thereto, for such amounts of money as may be necessary for the payment of the salaries of the officers and men appointed by virtue of the charter and ordinances of the city to serve in the fire department. And in no case except the fire marshal shall such order be drawn unless a proper voucher, indorsed "correct" by at least two of the fire commissioners, be first filed with said auditor.

SEC. 17. If any person or persons not a member of the city fire department shall use the uniform determined upon by the fire commissioners, or any part thereof, such person or persons shall each forfeit and pay to the City of Hartford a fine of not less than five dollars, nor more than twenty dollars for each and every offence.

SEC. 18. If any person or persons shall injure, deface, or in any manner destroy any city fire apparatus, or if any person or persons shall hinder or obstruct any city fire company, hose, or hook and ladder company, or any member thereof, from freely passing along the streets of the city to or from a fire, or in any manner hinder or prevent any of said fire companies or any member of the same from operating at any fire, each and every person or persons so hindering, obstructing, or preventing shall forfeit and pay to the City of Hartford a penalty of not less than five dollars nor more than twenty dollars for each and every offence.

SEC. 19. The chief engineer and his assistants are hereby authorized to exercise the powers of police officers in going to, while at, and returning from any fire that may occur, or

Fire commissioners shall purchase and sell property, when.

Provided.

Auditor shall draw order for salaries, when.

Vouchers to be indorsed.

Fire uniform to be used only by department.

Penalty for violation.

Injuring fire apparatus or obstructing firemen, how punished.

Chief engineer and assistants shall have police powers, when.

any fire alarm; and they shall have the use and control of any and all the hydrants and reservoirs belonging to the city during the continuance of fires.

SEC. 20. No pay shall be allowed either of said fire commissioners for any services rendered by him in the discharge of his duties as such commissioner; but his necessary expenses and disbursements in the execution of the duties of his office shall be paid from the city treasury.

No pay allowed commissioners.

SEC. 21. The chief engineer shall designate the assistant engineers as first, second, and third assistant engineers; and the seniority of said assistant engineers shall be determined by the number which said assistant engineer bears.

Assistant engineers, how designated.

SEC. 22. If in the opinion of the chief engineer, or in case of his absence, of the senior assistant engineer present, the safety of the hose, or other apparatus belonging to the fire department of said city, or the facilities for the performance of any other duties required of the firemen by the laws of said city, at any time require that the traveling or passing of any wagon, carriage, or other vehicle, be interrupted and stopped in or upon or excluded from any highway, or portion of any highway or highways in said city, during the performance of said duty, or any part thereof, the engineer, or, in his absence the senior assistant engineer present, is, and they, each of them, are hereby authorized and empowered to order and cause the traveling or passing on said highway, or part of highway, to cease during the performance of said duty; and also, to put and place in, upon, or across said highway, or part of highway, as he shall direct, suitable iron chain or chains, rope, or other obstructions, there to remain until said fire duty is performed, and no longer; and also to order and command any owner, driver of any and all vehicles, of any description whatever, to remove the same from any portion of said highway, and not to drive on, to, or across the same during the performance of said duty; and if any person shall willfully remove or assist in removing any chain, rope, or other things thus placed in, upon, or across any highway in this city, as aforesaid, or, if any owner or driver of any vehicle shall neglect or refuse to obey any order

Travel on highway and streets may be stopped during a fire.

Vehicles may be removed.

or command made upon him, or given to him, as aforesaid, every person so offending shall forfeit and pay to the City of Hartford a penalty of five dollars.

SEC. 23. Whenever it shall be necessary to demolish any building in said city, in order to stop the progress of fire, the chief engineer may cause the same to be done, having first obtained the consent of the mayor thereto, or, in the absence of the mayor, the consent of any fire commissioner.

SEC. 24. If any person shall knowingly give a false alarm of fire in said city, or shall knowingly proclaim that any fire is extinguished or out when it is not, such person shall forfeit and pay to the City of Hartford a penalty of twenty dollars.

SEC. 25. If any person shall carry into any barn or hay loft, any lighted candle or lamp not enclosed in a lantern, or any lighted cigar or pipe, such person shall forfeit and pay to the City of Hartford a penalty of five dollars.

SEC. 26. All forfeitures and penalties incurred under the ordinances, relating to the fire department, except when otherwise provided, shall be recoverable by the attorney of the city before the City Court, in an action brought in the name of said city, for the use of the city treasury; and when any minor shall be guilty of any breach of this ordinance, the parent, guardian, or master of such minor shall be liable to pay the penalty therefor; and the same shall be recoverable of such parent, guardian, or master, by action brought against them in the manner aforesaid.

SEC. 27. At the annual meeting of the Court of Common Council, for the choice of city officers, there shall be chosen by concurrent vote a fire marshal, who shall hold his office for one year, and until his successor shall be chosen and qualified.

SEC. 28. It shall be the duty of the fire marshal, from time to time during the year, as occasion may require, to examine, throughout said city, the fire-places, chimneys, heating and cooking apparatus and pipes connected therewith, of all houses, out-houses, and buildings in said city, also all places where ashes are kept, and upon finding any of them defective or dangerous, shall order such to be cleaned, altered, or amended, as may seem to him the occasion requires. And in case any heating or cooking apparatus, or the pipes connected therewith, are erected or set up in such places as to unreasonably endanger said city to the perils of fire, and the same cannot be altered so as to be rendered *May order removal of, when.* reasonably safe, said fire marshal shall order all such apparatus to be removed; and all orders, in respect to any of the particulars in this section mentioned, shall be given in the manner following, viz.: The fire marshal shall specify in *Orders to be in writing, and how served.* writing the thing to be done, and a reasonable time within which the order must be complied with, and shall leave a true copy of said order, signed by him, in the hands of the person upon whom said order is made; or if he or she be absent, at his or her place of abode.

SEC. 29. In all cases in which said fire marshal shall judge *Fire marshal may order scuttle, when.* it necessary for the safety of said city from fire, that a scuttle should be made to a dwelling-house, or any other building in said city, he shall give an order in writing, in the manner *Orders, how given.* specified in the twenty-eighth section of this ordinance, to the proprietor or 'proprietors of said dwelling-house or building, directing that a scuttle, with proper steps or stairs leading to the same, be made within such time as shall be limited in said order.

SEC. 30. In all cases in which shavings, straw, or other *Shavings, straw, etc., may be removed, when.* combustible material shall be suffered to be or remain in or near any buildings in said city, in such manner as to expose said city to danger from fire, it shall be the duty of the fire marshal to give a written order, in the manner specified in *Order, how made.* the twenty-eighth section of this ordinance, to the person or persons occupying or owning the place where such shavings, straw, or combustible materials may be, to remove the same within such time as shall be specified in said order.

SEC. 31. The fire marshal shall have power, at all reasona- *Shall have power to examine buildings and other places.* ble times, and it shall be his duty, to enter into and examine all buildings and lots where lumber and other combustible materials are stored, in said city, to inspect places where fire is used, to direct in what manner ashes and matches shall be kept, and it shall be his duty to examine into any and all

violations of any ordinance within the scope of his duty, and
report the same to the city attorney for prosecution.

No person shall erect
or place stove, fur-
nace, or other cook-
ing or heating appa-
ratus in certain
houses, except by
consent of fire mar-
shal or common
council.
SEC. 32.   Every person who shall erect or place within any
building within the limits of the City of Hartford, except
such as have their outer walls composed wholly of iron,
brick, stone, or mortar, any chimney, stove, fire-place, furnace, or other apparatus, for heating or cooking, without the
consent of the fire marshal, or contrary to the direction of
the Court of Common Council, shall forfeit and pay a fine of
Penalty.
not more than thirty dollars, for the use of the city treasury,
for every month that the same shall remain, either without
the consent of the said fire marshal, or contrary to the direction of the Court of Common Council, and said fire marshal,
before giving his consent, shall see that such cooking or
Consent not to be
given till apparatus
be safely arranged.
heating apparatus be safely placed, and that the pipes thereof
to conduct the heat and the smoke be set and run in a secure
manner so as not to endanger the building in which the same
is placed, or any building or buildings adjoining or adjacent
thereto.

Consent of council
necessary for the
erection of
buildings.
SEC. 33.   Every person who shall erect, add to, move or
place any dwelling house, shop, store, barn, or other building,
except privies, in this city, without the consent of the Court
of Common Council, as to the mode of said erection or addi-
Erection of building
without consent of
council, how
punished.
tion, or materials used or without the consent of said Court
of Common Council to such removal, or in any manner contrary to the ordinances of said city, or the allowance or
direction of the Court of Common Council, shall forfeit and
pay the sum of fifty dollars to the City of Hartford for the
use of the city treasury, and the further sum of not more
Penalty if building
remain without
permission.
than fifty dollars for every week that such building shall
remain without such permission; and it is hereby provided
that the continuance of any such building without such permission, shall for each week after such act be deemed a
separate and single offence.

What petitions to
build shall specify.
SEC. 34.   All petitions to the Court of Common Council,
relating to buildings, shall specify the material of which the
outer walls and the outer covering of the roof of said building are to be composed, the street upon which, and the dis-

tance from the street at which the said building is to be placed, and all such petitions shall be referred to the committee of the fire department, who shall enquire into the matters asked for in said petitions, and make their report to the Court of Common Council, who may grant such petitions under such restrictions as they may think proper.

Shall be referred to fire department committee.

SEC. 35. It shall be the duty of the fire marshal to attend at every fire occurring in said city; and when he shall have any reason to believe that any fire may have been incendiary in its origin, it shall be his duty to inquire into the cause of said fire, in behalf of said city, and to proceed in said inquiry in the manner provided by the statutes of this state in such case provided. No fee shall be paid said fire marshal for his said inquiry and investigation on behalf of said city into the cause of any such fire, but his salary shall be in lieu thereof, and in lieu of any other services devolved upon him by virtue of this ordinance, or any other ordinance, imposing duties upon him. All witness fees, service of subpœnas, and cash advances arising out of the investigation into the cause of any fire, shall be paid from the treasury of said city; and it shall be the duty of said fire marshal to forward the amount of the same to the Court of Common Council for payment, accompanied by his certificate that said expenses were justly incurred in the prosecution of said investigation.

Duty of fire marshal in case of incendiary fires, and how to proceed.

No fees to be paid fire marshal.

Cash advances to be paid from city treasury.

Same, how paid.

SEC. 36. It shall be the duty of every person to fulfill all and every written order of the fire marshal, issued by him in conformity with any ordinance now existing or which shall hereafter be enacted.

The duty of every person to obey written orders of fire marshal.

SEC. 37. If any person or persons shall, contrary to the ordinances of the city, neglect or refuse to comply with any such order of the fire marshal, or shall hinder or obstruct the fire marshal in the discharge of any of his duties, such person or persons shall be punished by a fine not exceeding fifty dollars for each offence, and the same shall be deemed a misdemeanor and may be prosecuted as such before the Police Court like other offences.

Penalty on failure.

SEC. 38. It shall be the duty of the fire marshal to keep a record book, wherein he shall record all orders by him made,

Fire marshal shall keep record.

Shall make annual report.

and all written complaints made to him under this ordinance, and all examinations made by him pursuant to the provisions hereof, and to make an annual report to the Court of Common Council of the services performed by him during the year as said fire marshal.

CHAPTER V.

BONDS OF CITY OFFICERS.

Be it ordained by the Court of Common Council of the City of Hartford:

Bonds of city officers, how payable and how executed.

SECTION 1. All bonds of city officers shall be payable to the City of Hartford, and shall be executed by the principal and two sufficient sureties to the approbation of the mayor. Such bonds shall be conditioned on the faithful performance by the principal of all his official duties due to the City of Hartford by virtue of his appointment, and upon his saving

Conditions of bond.

the city from all loss, cost, or damage, by reason of his mis- feasance in office, and upon his rendering a true account of all his money dealings for, in behalf of, and with said city, and upon his just and true payment to the city treasurer of all moneys in his hands at any time as an officer or agent of

On re-election no new bond required.

the city, for and during the entire period for which he shall remain in his office by appointment or reëlection. Such

Bonds, when executed.

bonds shall be given before any such officer shall enter upon his official duties or continuance longer in the exercise thereof.

Penalties of bonds.

SEC. 2. The penalties of the bonds required of the several city officers shall be respectively as follows: Of the city treasurer, twenty thousand dollars; of the president of the board of water commissioners, ten thousand dollars; of the auditor of city accounts, three thousand dollars; of the president of the board of street commissioners, three thousand dollars; of the city marshal, three thousand dollars; of the clerk of the Police Court, two thousand dollars; of the clerk of the City Court, one thousand dollars; of the city attorney, one thousand dollars. Bond of president of water commissioners, auditor, president board of street commissioners, and city marshal.

Bond of clerk of Police Court, clerk of City Court, and city attorney.

SEC. 3. Every other officer[1] or committee, in whose hands money may be placed for disbursements, shall give bonds to the city for the faithful disbursement of the same in such sums as the mayor shall require. Other officers to give bonds in whose hands money is placed.

.

CHAPTER VI.

OATHS OF CITY OFFICERS.

Oaths to be administered to Mayor.— Aldermen.— Common councilmen.— City clerk.— Clerk of council board.— Marshal, and deputy marshal.— Clerk of City Court.— Clerk of Police Court.— Police commissioners.— Park commissioners.— Fire commissioners.— Police officers.— Policemen.— Street commissioners.—Water commissioners.—Treasurer.—Auditor.—Recorder, and judges of City Court.— Police judge.— City jurors.— City attorney.— Collector.— City surveyor.—Inspector of fire wood. —Sealer of weights and measures. Certificate of such oaths to be lodged with city clerk.

Be it ordained by the Court of Common Council of the City of Hartford:

SECTION 1. Before any mayor, alderman, common councilman, clerk of the city, clerk of the common council board, marshal or deputy marshal, clerk of the City Court, clerk of the City Police Court, police commissioner, police officers, policemen, treasurer, auditor, city attorney, street commissioner, water commissioner, fire commissioner, park commissioner, collector, city surveyor, inspector, sealer of weights City officers to be sworn before qualified for duty.

---

[1] For bond of city collector, see section 12, page 170.

and measures, or any other officer of the city (except judges and jurors of the City Court), required by law or by ordinance to be sworn, shall be qualified to enter upon the duties of his office, he shall receive from some person qualified to administer oaths, a form of oath or affirmation specifying the office, and requiring the said officer faithfully and uprightly to perform all the duties and obligations thereof, according to the best of his ability, during the full term for which he shall hold or continue in such office by election or reëlection; and shall also receive from the person administering such oath or affirmation a certificate that the same has been administered in due and legal form, and shall lodge said certificate with the city clerk, to be by him kept on file: *provided,* that when any such oath shall be administered by the mayor or by any other qualified person at any meeting of the Court of Common Council in joint convention, or of either board of said court, a record of the fact by the clerk of such board or convention, as a part of the proceedings of such meeting, naming the person or persons present and sworn, shall be sufficient without a certificate; *provided, however,* that whenever any such officer shall continue in his office by reëlection or reappointment, no new oath shall be required.

SEC. 2. The recorder of the City Court and the judge and associate judge of the Police Court shall, before being qualified to enter upon the duties of their offices, take the oath by law prescribed for judicial officers of the state. Appraisers of damages or betterments shall be sworn justly and truly to estimate and appraise all the damages or betterments by them to be appraised during their continuance in office, according to their best and honest judgment; and certificates or a record of such oath shall be made according to the requirements of the first section of this ordinance.

SEC. 3. Jurors of the City Court shall take the oath prescribed by law for jurors in civil actions.

(margin notes)
What oath shall specify and require.
Certificates to be given by person administering oath.
Certificate of oath to be lodged with city clerk.
Except in certain cases,
No new oath required in case of re-election.
Oath of judge of City and Police Court,
Oath of appraisers.
Oaths of jurors of City Court,

CHAPTER VII.

AMUSEMENTS.

Public exhibitions prohibited without license of common council or its committee.

Penalty for exhibiting without license. Amusement committee, power and duty of.

Be it ordained by the Court of Common Council of the City of Hartford:

SECTION 1. Any person or persons who shall, without first obtaining a license from the Court of Common Council, or from the committee appointed by them for that purpose, make a public display of any sport, amusement, performance, concert, opera, or other public exhibition, within the limits of the City of Hartford, shall forfeit and pay a penalty of not less than five dollars, nor more than one hundred dollars, for each offence, to the City of Hartford, for the use of the city treasury; and each separate exhibition shall be a separate offence within the meaning of this act.

Public exhibitions prohibited except by license of amusement committee.

Penalty.

SEC. 2. The committee on amusements of the Court of Common Council shall have power, unless otherwise directed by the council, to grant a license to any person who shall apply for the same, for the exhibition of any such sport, public amusement, performance, concert, opera, or other exhibition, as they the said committee, shall consider proper to be licensed, for such time as they shall deem fit, which license may, at any time, be revoked by the said committee, or by the Court of Common Council.

Powers of amusement committee to grant licenses.

SEC. 3. Such person, so applying, as aforesaid, shall pay to said committee, for the use of the said city, such license fee as the said committee shall deem proper to fix; and said decision shall be subject to revision by the Court of Common Council, who may lessen or increase the same.

Fees to be paid for license.

SEC. 4. It shall be the duty of the said committee to report all violations of this ordinance to the city attorney, for the collection of the penalties mentioned herein.

Committee to report violations of this ordinance.

CHAPTER VIII.

GUNPOWDER.

All water craft carrying gunpowder prohibited from coming to anchor within the jurisdiction of the City of Hartford above Hockanum river.
Handling of powder, how conducted.
How conveyed and kept within the city.
License to keep, required when.
Licenses to be recorded.
Gunpowder may be seized and forfeited, when.

Penalty for rescue or attempt to rescue gunpowder.
Duty and powers of fire marshal.
Damages for injuries by, how collected.
Penalties for violation of this ordinance.
Sale of toy pistols regulated.
Licenses, how printed.

Be it ordained by the Court of Common Council of the City of Hartford :

Vessels carrying gunpowder prohibited from coming to anchor or lying at wharves within city, except where.

SECTION 1. That no vessel, boat, or other water-craft, on board of which gunpowder shall be laden, shall come to or lie at any wharf, slip, or landing place, within the City of Hartford, or come to anchor, or otherwise make fast on Connecticut river within the town of Hartford or within the jurisdiction of said city, except as is hereinafter provided.

Vessels may receive gunpowder below Hockanum river.

SEC. 2. Any vessel, boat, or other water-craft, of suitable construction with regard to safety, may be allowed to receive gunpowder on board, from any wharf on the Connecticut or great river opposite the City or town of Hartford below the mouth of the Hockanum river and remain a reasonable and proper time for such lading, which time shall not exceed one day for undecked vessels, and three days for decked vessels:

Vessels, how conducted.

provided, there be kept or allowed no fire, in any manner whatever, on board such vessel, boat, or other water-craft during the receiving such gunpowder, nor while the same may remain within the jurisdiction of said city. And said powder, when laden on board any vessel, shall immediately, and as each cask or package is received on board, be stowed

Powder, how stored on vessels.

away under deck; or if received on board of an open boat, or other water-craft, shall be immediately, and as each cask or package is received on board, covered over with canvas, or other suitable covering. *And provided further,* that whenever any gunpowder shall be received on said vessel, boat, or craft, said vessel, boat, or craft, shall, within the time hereinbefore Vessels laden shall depart, when. mentioned in which said powder shall be so received, remove without the jurisdiction of said city, and shall not be returned while said powder, or any part thereof, is on board.

SEC. 3. Whenever any gunpowder shall be brought into Conveyance of gunpowder through the city. said city for the purpose of transit, or delivery at stores or other buildings, it shall be conveyed in a suitable carriage which shall be lined on the bottom and sides with canvas or leather, so as to prevent the escape of any particle of powder, and such carriage, and the powder on the same, shall be en- Powder, how protected. tirely covered with canvas or leather, to prevent the possibility of any fire or sparks communicating with said powder, and said carriage shall be marked on either side with capital Powder carriage, how marked. letters, "approved powder carriage;" such carriage having first been approved by the fire marshal of said city, whose duty it shall be to attend to the provisions of this ordinance. And in no case shall powder so conveyed, be suffered to re- How removed in certain quantities. main in any such vehicle for any longer time than is necessary for its removal; excepting, however, that no more than two quarter-casks of twenty-five pounds each, may be removed from one place to another in the city, in any other prudent manner, the same being in tight casks, each of which shall be put into a strong leather bag, and closely tied, on which shall be legibly marked the word "gunpowder." And the same shall remain within said bags, while being so removed.

SEC. 4. No person or persons shall keep, or have for sale, No gunpowder exceeding one pound to be kept except by license. or any other purpose, in any house, store, or other building, or in or upon any vessel, boat, or other water craft, within the limits of said city or the jurisdiction thereof, any quantity of gunpowder exceeding one pound in weight, without special license from the Court of Common Council; and every person so licensed shall give notice thereof, by a sign erected Notice of license, how given. in a conspicuous place, in front of the building where gunpowder is or may be deposited: *provided*, that nothing contained in this ordinance shall be construed to prohibit vessels Passage of vessels with, allowed. or boats, loaded wholly or in part with powder, from passing up or down the river.

SEC. 5. Every person or firm licensed to sell gunpowder, as is provided in the preceding section, shall have a sign painted in capital letters, with the words "licensed to keep and sell gunpowder," and placed as therein directed; and shall also have and keep a suitable copper, tin, or zinc chest, marked in front with the word "gunpowder," which chest shall be approved by the fire marshal aforesaid, and the same shall be made with two strong handles, with a tight lid or cover, with hinges, and secured with a padlock and key, which key shall be of copper or brass. Said chest shall always be kept locked, except when open to put in or take out powder, which shall be done as speedily as may be consistent with proper care; shall be placed on the lower floor, at the right side of, and within six feet of the principal door or entrance from the street, over which the sign before mentioned is placed; and shall not be kept in any other part of the building, unless by permission of the Court of Common Council, which permission shall be expressed in the license; and no gunpowder shall be sold or exhibited for sale except by daylight.

SEC. 6. Every person or firm who may be licensed and provided, as aforesaid, may be allowed to keep a quantity of gunpowder, not exceeding three quarter-casks of twenty-five pounds each, which shall be deposited in the chest described in section fifth; each cask shall be kept in a leather bag, closely tied, as is provided in section third, and such person or firm may be allowed to keep such additional quantities as may be required for retailing, not exceeding at any one time, twenty-five pounds, and the same shall be kept in tin or copper canisters, and these kept in the chest with the above named quarter-casks.

SEC. 7. The city clerk shall keep a record of all licenses granted, and renewals thereof, and of the place designated in each license. for keeping and selling gunpowder, which place shall not be altered or changed without the consent of the Court of Common Council, expressed in such license, and the city clerk at the time of recording the same shall call the attention of each dealer licensed to this ordinance, that all persons concerned may be duly informed thereof.

SEC. 8.   All gunpowder, which shall be kept. had. or pos- sessed within the City of Hartford, or brought into, or transported through the same, contrary to the provisions of this ordinance, shall be forfeited, and may be seized and taken into custody by the fire marshal of said city, and it shall be his duty to seize the same, and the same shall be libelled within ten days next after the seizure thereof, by filing in the office of the clerk of the City Court of the City of Hartford. a libel, stating the time, place, and cause of such seizure, and the estimated value of said property, a copy of which libel, together with a summons to the person or persons therein named, to appear before the court having cognizance of the offence. which summons may be signed by any justice of the peace in the county of Hartford, and shall be served on the person or persons in whose custody or possession such gun- powder may be seized, if such person be an inhabitant of the State of Connecticut, or with the occupant of the premises where the seizure is made, or the person in charge of such powder, if seized on any vehicle, by delivering a copy thereof to such person or persons, or by leaving a copy at his, her, or their usual place of abode, at least twelve days before the sitting of the court to which the same is made returnable. that such person or persons may appear and show cause why said gunpowder, so seized and taken, shall not be adjudged forfeited.   And in case the said court shall find the allega- tions of the libel true, they shall adjudge that so much of the powder as does not exceed the value of fifty dollars, shall be forfeited to the city, and shall cause the same to be sold, and the avails to be paid into the hands of the treasurer of the city, for the use and benefit of said city, deducting therefrom the costs of prosecution, if the same are not otherwise collectible.   And the court shall have power, at their discretion, to render judgment for costs against any or all of the parties cited to appear, or appearing in said cause.   And such libel or summons, and also such writ of execution for costs, may be served and executed by any officer competent to execute civil process in like cases.

SEC. 9. And in case the fire marshal making such seizure shall, at the time of filing said libel, insert therein an allegation, that he is ignorant of the name and residence of the person or persons in whose custody or possession, or upon whose premises, such powder was found, or the person to whom said powder belongs, then the citation shall be directed "to all persons whom it may concern," and shall be published at least two several times in a newspaper printed in the City of Hartford, the last publication to be at least six days previous to the session of the court at which the same is to be heard, or to which it may be returnable, which publication shall be sufficient notice to bring the case to trial, and any person shall have a right to appear and be made a party to the proceedings.

SEC. 10. Any person or persons, who shall rescue, or attempt to rescue, any gunpowder seized as aforesaid, or shall aid or assist therein, or who shall counsel or advise, or procure the same to be done, or who shall molest, hinder, or obstruct the fire marshal in such seizure, or in conveying gunpowder so seized to a place of safety, shall forfeit and pay a fine, for each offence, of not less than five dollars, and not exceeding fifty dollars, to the City of Hartford, for the use of

the city treasury. And it is hereby made the duty of all persons to aid and assist such fire marshal in executing the duties hereby required.

SEC. 11. That the fire marshal, at all suitable times, may enter any store or place of any person or persons licensed to sell gunpowder, to ascertain if the laws and regulations thereof are strictly observed, and on an alarm of fire in the vicinity, may cause the gunpowder there deposited to be removed to a place of safety, or to be destroyed by water, or otherwise, as the case may require, and it shall be the duty of

said fire-marshal to report to the city attorney all violations of this ordinance which may come within his knowledge.

SEC. 12. Any person who may suffer injury of person or property, by the explosion of gunpowder, had, kept or transported within the City of Hartford, or the jurisdiction thereof, contrary to the provisions of this ordinance, may have an action on the case, in any court proper to try the same, against the owner or owners of such gunpowder, at the time of the explosion thereof, to recover reasonable damages for the injury thus sustained.

SEC. 13. Any person or persons who shall violate any of the provisions of this ordinance, or who shall suffer any gunpowder to be or remain on the premises owned or occupied by him or them, contrary to the provisions of the same, in addition to the forfeiture of the gunpowder, as aforesaid, shall forfeit and pay to the City of Hartford a fine of not less than twenty-five cents, nor more than one dollar, for each pound of gunpowder over the amount of twenty-five pounds, so kept, transported, received or suffered to remain. *Violations of this ordinance, how punished.*

SEC. 14. No person shall sell to any child under the age of sixteen years, without the consent of the parent or guardian of such child, any cartridge or fixed ammunition, of which any fulminate is a component part, or any gun, pistol, or other mechanical contrivance arranged for the explosion of such cartridge or of any fulminate. *Sale of toy pistols, etc., regulated.*

SEC. 15. Any person who shall violate any of the provisions of the foregoing section shall forfeit and pay a penalty to the City of Hartford, for the use of the city, of not exceeding fifty dollars for each offence. *Penalty.*

SEC. 16. Every license hereafter granted for the sale of gunpowder shall conform to the foregoing provisions, and contain or have printed thereon the last two foregoing sections or the substance thereof. *License to conform to foregoing provisions.*

CHAPTER IX.

PUBLIC PARKS.

Board of park commissioners, how con-stituted.	Rules, how made public.
Terms of office.	May make repairs.
Commissioners, duty of.	Accounts, how kept.
Park improvements, how authorized.	Expenses, how paid.

Be it ordained by the Court of Common Council of the City of Hartford:

Board of park commissioners, how composed, and terms of office. SECTION 1. There shall continue to be a board of park commissioners[1] of the City of Hartford, consisting of five electors of said city, and each commissioner shall hold his office for five years, and until his successor is appointed and qualified, and upon the expiration of the present term of office of each of said commissioners his successor shall be appointed for the full term of five years next succeeding, and until his successor is appointed and qualified.

Powers and duties of board. SEC. 2. Said board shall have the care and management of all matters relating to any of the public parks of said city, and to the improvement and adornment of the same, and may **May make rules and regulations.** make such rules and regulations for the management thereof, and the government of all persons visiting the same, not inconsistent with the laws of the state or ordinances of the city, as they shall think proper, and every person who shall **Penalty.** violate any of the rules or regulations made by the commissioners for the purpose aforesaid shall forfeit and pay for the use of the city treasury a fine not exceeding thirty-five dollars.

Regulations shall be made public, how. SEC. 3. It shall be the duty of the park commissioners to cause all rules or regulations so made by them relating to the government of the persons visiting any of said parks, to be plainly printed with the penalties attached thereto, and to be kept conspicuously posted up in proper places on the parks to which they relate, while the same shall continue in force or relate thereto.

---

[1] For appointment of park commissioners see page 53.

Sec. 4. Whenever the park commissioners of said city shall think it desirable or expedient to make any alteration or improvement in any of the public parks of the city, it shall be their duty to submit to the Court of Common Council a plan or written description of such improvement or alteration, accompanied by an estimate of the cost of the same. If the Court of Common Council shall approve of the alteration or improvement submitted as aforesaid, and shall appropriate the amount of money necessary for the completion of the same, said park commissioners shall then be authorized to proceed and make such alteration or improvement by contract, or otherwise, as to them shall seem most expedient. *Plans of improvements to be submitted to the common council for approval.* *Commissioners may proceed, when.*

Sec. 5. Nothing in the foregoing section shall be so construed as to prevent said park commissioners from making, at any time, any and all necessary repairs of the walks, drives, or mechanical structures connected with any of the public parks of said city. *Commissioners may make necessary repairs.*

Sec. 6. The park commissioners shall keep an account of all expenditures made in their department, which shall be open at all times to the inspection of any member of the Court of Common Council, and shall make a report to said court of such expenditures, at least once a month, unless excused therefrom by said court. *Shall keep accounts.* *Shall make monthly report to Court of Common Council.*

Sec. 7. No pay shall be allowed either of said commissioners for any services rendered by him, but his necessary expenses and disbursements shall be paid from the city treasury. *Necessary expenses to be paid by city.*

CHAPTER X.

NUISANCES RELATING TO HIGHWAYS.

Be it ordained by the Court of Common Council of the City of Hartford:

Executive and police officers to keep streets and public places free of obstructions.

SECTION 1. Any executive or police officer of the city shall have authority to keep open and free from obstruction the streets and public places of said city, and to require all persons unlawfully obstructing such streets and public places to desist therefrom whenever the act of obstruction is done in view of such officer.

Nuisances of the first class.

SEC. 2. The following acts are declared to be acts of nuisance of the first class; the keeping or maintaining, or

Privy, when a nuisance.

using, any privy within the distance of fifty feet from any street or building line in said city in such a manner as to be unwholesome or offensive to any person, or injurious to

Removal of buildings.

health, or offensive to the public; the removal of any building through any street or highway of the city, or the permitting of any building in process of removal to remain in any such street or highway without license from the Court of

Opening of streets or alleys.

Common Council; the opening or keeping open of any street or highway, blind alley, or thoroughfare, within said city

Depositing materials in highway.

without such license; the placing or continuing the deposit of any building materials on any street or highway of said city without license of the Court of Common Council; the

Opening of vaults or cellars.

opening or continuing of any vault or cellar-way in or upon any street or highway of the city without license of the

Opening of drains.

board of street commissioners; the opening or continuance of any drain in such a manner that the same is discharged upon any street or highway of the city or other public place therein, or the use of any such drain; the excavation of any Excavation of streets. part of any street, highway, or public place of said city, or digging below the surface thereof without authority or license of the board of street commissioners, and without also protecting the public against danger therefrom by means of fences, lights, and any other precautions expedient or neces- sary for such protection; racing or trying the speed of horses Racing of horses. through or upon any street or highway of said city, or other public place therein; resisting, molesting, disobeying or Resistance to execu- tive or police officers. interfering with any executive or police officer, or the board of street commissioners of said city, while engaged in the duty of keeping the streets, or highways, or public places of said city, free from obstruction and convenient for public use; injuring any tree or shrubbery placed or kept as an ornament Injuries to trees and shrubs. to any of the streets, highways, or public places of the city; the erection or location of any building, or part of a building, or the continuance of any building so erected or located upon any street, highway, or public place of said city; the erection or location or continuance of any structure, building, or part Encroachment upon building line. of a building, or any appurtenance thereof, or obscuring the prospect, between any building-line lawfully established, upon any street or highway and the line of such street or highway.

SEC. 3. The following acts are declared to be acts of Nuisances of second class. nuisance of the second class; the carrying on of any trade or Carrying on of trade or business on sidewalks. business upon the sidewalks, or streets, or highways of said city, without license of the board of street commissioners; the defacing or injuring of any fence, rail, chain, lamp or post, Defacing any fence, etc., in street or public place. within any street, highway, or public place of said city; driv- ing or riding in or through any street, highway, or public Driving at greater rate than six miles per hour. place of said city, at a greater rate of speed than six miles an hour; drawing or using any sled or any wheel vehicle, pro- pelled by hand or otherwise, or the drawing or propelling of Drawing of fire apparatus on sidewalk. any engine, or fire apparatus, along any sidewalk of said city; the depositing or placing of any rubbish or other thing Depositing of rub- bish on highway. (excepting articles of merchandise, or wares, or boxes, or cases for containing the same) upon any street or highway of said city, in such a manner, or to such an extent as to impede

Injuring grass or ornamental herbage in public places. or cause inconvenience to public travel; injuring any grass or ornamental herbage within any public place of said city; **Brawling or fighting.** brawling or fighting within any street, highway, or public **Laying sidewalk without license of street commissioners.** place of said city; laying any sidewalk or gutter-stone without the license of the board of street commissioners.

Nuisances of the third class. SEC. 4. The following acts are declared to be acts of nuisance of the third class; the placing or continuing any **Placing of merchandise on sidewalks.** articles of traffic or merchandise, or of any wares, or any case or box for containing the same, or of any packing boxes upon any sidewalk, or street, or highway of said city, except for purposes of transit or delivery, and for such time and in such manner as shall be reasonably necessary for such pur- **Placing of post or other obstruction on highway.** poses; the placing or continuing of any post, rail, fence, or other obstruction, upon any street, highway, or public place of the city, without authority of the board of street commis- **Placing business sign within highway.** sioners; the placing of any business sign within the limits of any street of the city otherwise than parallel to and against, or as near as is convenient to the face of the building, wall, or fence, whereunto the same shall be attached; the setting out **Setting tree within line of sidewalk.** of any tree within the lines of any sidewalk in the city, without license of the board of street commissioners; the break- **Breaking of sidewalk with intent or negligence.** ing of any sidewalk or curb-stone, with mischievous intent, **Permitting animal to go at large or leaving horse unhitched.** or by negligence; permitting any animal to go at large, or leaving any horse unhitched, or permitting any animal to stand upon or over any crosswalk by the person having control at the time of such horse or animal, within any street or thoroughfare of said city; or the permitting by any person of **Blocking up of street by vehicle.** the blocking up or obstruction of any street or thoroughfare of said city, by any horse, animal or vehicle, under his charge **Driving drove animals through Main street or upon Sunday between sunrise and sunset.** or control; the driving of any drove of animals through Main street at any time without license of the board of street commissioners, or through any other street or highway of said city upon Sunday between sunrise and sunset; the firing or exploding of any fireworks, cannon, small arms, toy cannon, firecrackers, torpedoes or other explosive substances, or making or keeping up any bonfire in any street, highway, or public place in said city, without permission from the mayor.

SEC. 5. The following acts are declared to be acts of

nuisance of the fourth class: the continued keeping of any rubbish or other thing which does not impede or cause inconvenience to public travel, and which is not placed or deposited for purpose of transit or delivery, in or upon any street, high- way, or public place, after notice to remove the same, has been given by the proper city authority to the person placing or keeping the same therein, for the removal of such rubbish or other thing; the playing of ball, or kite-flying, in any such streets or highways; the driving with any sled, sledge, or sleigh, in or through any such street or highway, without bells attached thereto or to the horse drawing the same; the driving of any goat or dog in harness in or through any such street or highway; the riding or driving of any bicycle in or through any such street or highway; the posting of bills, pla- cards, or notices, without legal right, upon any building, wall, fence, or post, within or adjoining any such street or thoroughfare; the drawing or use of any hand-cart, or hand-sled, or wheelbarrow upon any sidewalk within said city; the permitting of any snow to remain on the roof of any building by the occupant or person in legal possession thereof in such condition that the same may slide therefrom upon any street or highway of the city.

SEC. 6. Any person who shall commit, or aid, advise, abet, or encourage the committing of any of the aforesaid acts of nuisance, shall pay to the City of Hartford for the use of the city a penalty or forfeiture of twenty-five dollars, if such act be of the first class; of fifteen dollars, if such act be of the second class; of five dollars, if such act be of the third class; and of one dollar, if such act be of the fourth class; and any such act shall be deemed malicious if repeated or continued after the person committing the same has been forbidden to repeat or continue the same. The continuance of any ob- struction or encroachment upon any street, highway, or building-line, for a day of twenty-four hours after the day of the commencement thereof, shall be deemed a separate and single offence.

Any building erected or located in violation of the second section of this ordinance shall be assessed at four-fold its taxable value in the last list prepared or next to be prepared, according to law for the purpose of laying city taxes thereon.

Whenever anything unlawfully placed, or kept on any street or highway, or any public place of said city, shall be removed by the board of street commissioners, the expense of such removal to any amount not exceeding fifty dollars shall be a debt or forfeiture against the person liable for such act of nuisance, provided that the board of street commissioners shall have first given such person notice and reasonable time to remove the same; and provided that the amount so recoverable, together with the fine or penalty for such act of nuisance shall not exceed the sum of fifty dollars. If any tree, fence, or other private property be injured by any of the aforesaid acts, the City of Hartford shall pay one-half of the penalty recovered therefor to the owner of such property.

When persons liable to expense of removing obstruction.

Penalty for fast driving.

Part penalty, to whom paid.

Depositing ashes or rubbish on public highway prohibited.

SEC. 7. No ashes, store sweepings, or rubbish, shall be put in any public street or highway in the City of Hartford, but shall be put in suitable vessels or places, and shall be removed in the manner provided in the succeeding section.

Ashes and rubbish, where deposited.

Street commissioner to remove ashes, etc.

SEC. 8. It shall be the duty of the board of street commissioners to remove said ashes, store sweepings, and rubbish so put and deposited, free of expense to parties so depositing them, whenever it shall be necessary and proper for the same to be removed.

Policemen to report violations of this ordinance.

SEC. 9. It shall be the duty of any policeman in the city to report any violation of the seventh section of this ordinance to the city attorney, and it shall be the duty of said attorney to prosecute any persons violating the same.

Penalty.

SEC. 10. Any person violating the seventh section of this ordinance, shall be fined in a sum not exceeding ten dollars, together with costs of suit; and every day's continuance of a violation thereof shall be considered a distinct offence.

What parties shall clean sidewalks from ice and snow.

SEC. 11. The owner or owners, occupant or occupants, private corporation, or any person having the care of any building or lot of land bordering on any street, square, or public place within the city where there is a sidewalk graded or graded and paved, shall cause to be removed therefrom any and all snow, sleet, and ice, within two hours after the

Shall remove same within two hours after falling.

same shall have fallen, been deposited or found, or within three hours after sunrise, when the same shall have fallen in the night season.

Sec. 12. Whenever the sidewalk, or any part thereof, adjoining or fronting any building or lot of land, or any street, square, or public place, shall be covered with ice, it shall be the duty of the owner or owners, occupant or occupants, private corporation or any person having the care of such building or lot, to cause such sidewalk to be made safe and convenient by removing the ice therefrom, or by covering the same with sand or some other suitable substance, and in case such owner or owners, or other person shall neglect so to do, for the space of one hour, during the day-time, the person or persons whose legal duty it shall be to so clear said walk, and so neglecting shall be liable to the penalty named in the succeeding section.

Icy sidewalks to be cleaned or covered with ashes.

Penalty.

Sec. 13. The owner or owners, occupant or occupants, private corporation, or any person having · the care of any building or lot of land, and whose duty it is to clear the same, who shall violate any of the provisions of the eleventh or twelfth sections of this ordinance, or refuse or neglect to comply with the same, shall pay a penalty of two dollars for every twelve hours such person, owner or owners, occupant or occupants, shall neglect to comply with said provisions, or any of them, after notice from any policeman of said city.

Penalty for violation of the eleventh and twelfth sections.

Sec. 14. It shall be the duty of the police force, under the direction of the chief of police, to have sections eleven and twelve of this ordinance strictly enforced, and to forthwith collect all penalties incurred under the same, upon a written or printed order of the chief of police, and if any person shall neglect to pay upon demand the penalty upon such order, the chief of police shall report the case to the city attorney, who shall, if he deem proper, immediately prosecute the person or private corporation so offending.

Police shall enforce sections eleven and twelve.

On neglect to pay penalty, how to proceed.

Sec. 15. The chief of police shall cause an abstract of sections eleven, twelve, and thirteen of this ordinance, to be published in two or more Hartford daily papers once a week during the month of December, in each year, and he shall

Chief of police shall cause abstract of sections twelve and thirteen to be published.

also publish, in one or more Hartford daily papers, at the commencement of each winter season, such regulations relative to the enforcement of sections eleven and twelve of this ordinance not inconsistent with the laws of the state, or ordinances of the city, as he shall deem proper.

City sidewalks to be cleaned by board of street commissioners.

SEC. 16. It shall be the duty of the board of street commissioners to cause to be cleared in accordance with the provisions of sections eleven and twelve of this ordinance all sidewalks properly belonging to the City of Hartford, and not adjoining the land of private individuals or private corporations, except such sidewalks as are in special charge of other *City officials shall clean walks of which they have charge.* city officials, and it shall be the duty of all city officers to cause to be cleared in accordance with the provisions of said sections, all sidewalks fronting on land under their official charge, and said board of street commissioners, and other city *Official liable to same penalties as other persons.* officials, shall be personally liable to the same penalties for any neglect in relation to the walks so under their official charge, that private persons are for a like offence.

When sidewalk may be cleaned by order of chief of police.

SEC. 17. If any sidewalk shall remain encumbered with snow, ice, or sleet, for twenty-four hours after the same has fallen, or been deposited, the chief of police shall notify the owner or person having the charge or care of the lot or building bordering on such sidewalk, and legally liable to clear the same, and if such sidewalk is not thoroughly cleared or properly covered with sand or some other suitable substance within twenty-four hours after such notice shall have been given, the chief of police shall cause the same to be *When expense of cleaning may be collected of owner.* cleared or properly covered and collect the expense thereof of such owner, or other persons, and the city attorney shall, at the request of the chief of police, collect by suit such expense as a debt due the city.

Authority under licenses.

SEC. 18. All licenses of the Court of Common Council, or board of street commissioners, to do any act whereby public travel may be incommoded or endangered, shall authorize the party licensed to do such acts in no other than a prudent and careful manner; and such licenses shall be subject, in all *Party liable to damages for injuries.* cases, to the conditions, that the person to whom the same is granted shall be liable to any party who shall receive actionable injury by the doing of such act, for such injury, and shall also be liable to indemnify and reimburse the city by reason of the doing of such act; and such condition shall be obligatory without other notice than that to be implied from this ordinance upon any person who shall receive such license.

SEC. 19. Any occupant of any house or building who shall permit any number of persons to assemble therein, and by indecent or disorderly conduct, or by quarreling or fighting, or by excessive or undue noise of any kind whereby the peace and quiet of his or her neighbors shall be disturbed, shall forfeit and pay a fine of not exceeding twenty-five dollars.

Disorderly conduct, quarreling, etc., how punished.

SEC. 20. Any person who shall wantonly deface or injure any public building in said city, or other inclosure of the same, or commit any trespass in any garden, cemetery, or inclosure therein, shall forfeit and pay a fine of not exceeding fifty dollars.

Injury to public building, etc., how punished.

CHAPTER XI.

NUISANCES INJURIOUS TO HEALTH.

Be it ordained by the Court of Common Council of the City of Hartford:

SECTION 1. The Court of Common Council shall, annually, appoint not exceeding ten persons, to be denominated the health committee, whose duty it shall be, at the expense of the city, to cause all matters and things which are or shall be, by any ordinance of this city, relating to health, and declared

Health committee, how constituted and appointed.

to be nuisances or prohibited, to be removed or suppressed, and from time to time report all violations thereof to the city attorney, that the same may be prevented or abated; and *Duties of committee.* said committee shall cause the public streets and all wharves and landing places to be frequently and carefully inspected and purified from filth and animal and vegetable putrefaction, at the expense of the city; and it shall be the duty of said *Any two or more members may order removal of filth.* committee, and any two of them are hereby empowered to inspect, as often as they shall deem necessary, all slaughter houses, tanneries, tallow chandleries, soap boilers, curriers' shops or works, and all other places in said city, and if they shall find filth or putrefaction in any shop or place by them visited, which in their opinion may prove detrimental to the health of the inhabitants of this city, said committee or any two of them, if they shall be a majority of the committee *Orders of, how given.* present, shall give orders to the person or persons owning or *What order may direct.* occupying said shop or place in which said filth or putrefaction shall be found, for the removing or burying of said filth or putrefaction, or for cleansing or purifying said shop or place in such other way or manner as such committee or such two of them, as aforesaid, there present, may deem advisable; and the said committee or such two of them, as aforesaid, are hereby empowered to give orders to the person or persons owning or occupying said shops or places, in relation to the ways and means to be by them used for keeping the same continually cleansed and purified from filth and putrefaction, and all orders and directions which shall be *Orders of committee to be in writing.* given by said committee or such two of them, as aforesaid, shall be in writing, under their hands, a duplicate of which *Duplicate of order to be lodged with clerk of City Court.* the said committee, or the members who shall sign the same, shall, immediately after delivery of said orders and directions to such person or persons, lodge with the clerk of the City Court; and every such person who shall neglect to obey and conform to any of the orders or directions, or any part *Penalty for non-compliance with order.* thereof, so given by said committee, or any two of them, in conformity to any ordinance of this city, shall forfeit and pay a fine not exceeding ten dollars for every day that such person shall neglect or refuse to comply therewith.

SEC. 2. Any person who shall, without permission of the Certain buildings and manufactures prohibited except by license of common council. Court of Common Council, build or set up, within the limits of this city, any kiln or furnace for burning or baking any stone or earthenware, or other pottery, brick or tile, or any distillery, or shall build or assist in building any fire in any such kiln or furnace, or distillery, or shall engage in the Brick kilns. manufacture or refining of kerosene or other oil, or set up or Distilleries. use any gas house or gas manufactory, or erect or use any Refining oils. building for making or boiling varnish, or blacksmith shop, Gas house. potter's shop, tallow chandler's shop, or for boiling soap, or Tallow chandlers. for rendering tallow, or for tanning leather or skins, or for Tannery. receiving or storing green hides or skins, or for any similar purpose, or keep or suffer to be kept in any building or place in this city, any guano, or other land fertilizer, or shall use Guano. any building or lot of ground for a vinegar yard, or set up or Vinegar yard. carry on either of said kinds of business in said city, or shall engage in any business which shall be prejudicial to public Any business prejudicial to health prohibited. health, without such permission, shall forfeit and pay a fine of not exceeding fifty dollars, and a further fine of not exceed- Penalty. ing twenty dollars for every week the same shall be so used or continued.

SEC. 3. The keeping of swine in any stye or pen, or other Keeping of swine, when prohibited. place in this city in such a manner as to become unwholesome or offensive to any person; the casting of filth of any kind in or upon any street, sidewalk, highway, private way, Filth in highway. green or park in this city; the carrying of any pail or vessel of swill on or along any sidewalk, in said city; any dung, filth, manure, offal, wash, dirty water, or brine, or any rub- Filth, offal, etc. bish accumulated in any building, yard, out-house, or enclosure, so as to be offensive; any privy now set up, or that Privies, how set up and arranged. shall hereafter be set up, without having a vault under it made and sunk in the earth to the depth of six feet, and of the length and width of said privy, or such tight boxes as shall be approved by at least two members of the health commit- To be approved by at least two members of health committee. tee, or without having the contents of said privy carried off by such suitable drains as shall be approved by at least two members of the health committee; the dressing or cleaning Dressing of fish. fish in any public place in this city, except on the margin of Connecticut river, at the foot of Ferry street, or below low water mark upon Connecticut or Mill rivers; bathing naked at any public place in said city, outside of any building, not designated by the mayor; the permitting wash or dirty water to pass from yards or houses into the streets, or the permitting the same to be thrown into the streets; the obstructing or altering the course of any stream or run of water therein; and each and every one of said acts shall be deemed a nuisance; and every person who shall do the same, or aid and assist therein, shall forfeit and pay a fine of not exceeding thirty dollars for each offence.

Bathing naked in public prohibited.

Penalty.

Erection of out-door privy, on land fronting a street having a sewer.

SEC. 4. Any person who shall erect any out-door privy upon land fronting upon any street in this city containing a sewer, without first obtaining the consent and permission of the health committee, shall forfeit and pay the sum of ten dollars to the City of Hartford, for the use of the city treasury; and the further sum of not more than ten dollars for every week that such building shall remain without such permission. And it is hereby provided that the continuance of any such building without such permission shall, for each week after such act, be deemed a separate and single offence.

Slaughter houses may be occupied by permission, when.

SEC. 5. Any person who shall, without permission of the Court of Common Council, occupy or use any building or other place in the city as a slaughter house, or place to slaughter animals; or who shall neglect to wash and thoroughly cleanse such slaughter house once each and every day the same shall be so occupied, shall forfeit and pay a fine of five dollars for each day said building or place shall be so used or remain uncleaned.

Penalty.

Contents of privies not to be removed except by permission.

SEC. 6. Any person who shall remove or cause to be removed, without permission of at least two members of the health committee, the contents of any privy vault or box, except in the night season, and in a tight box, between the hours of eleven o'clock in the evening and five o'clock in the morning, and between the first days of November and the first days of April, or shall deposit the contents of any privy vault or box, within the limits of this city, or shall cause or allow any night-soil cart to be within the limits of said city,

When removal to be made, and how.

except during the times and seasons mentioned in this section for the removal of night soil, shall forfeit and pay a fine of *Penalty.* ten dollars.

SEC. 7. When any grounds in this city shall be so situated *Stagnant water, how drained.* that water shall become stagnant thereon, thereby endangering the public health, the same shall be deemed a nuisance, and may be abated by draining or filling up; and the Court *Court of Common Council may order drained, upon notice.* of Common Council may order the same to be done within such time as they shall think proper, notice of which shall be given to the owner or owners, occupant or occupants, by the *Notice, how given.* health committee, causing a copy of such order to be left forthwith with such owner or owners, occupant or occupants, or at his or their place of abode. In case said order shall not be complied with within the time specified in said notice, said *Penalty for neglect to comply with order.* party or parties so neglecting shall forfeit and pay a fine of not exceeding thirty dollars, and a further fine of two dollars for each day thereafter, until such nuisance shall have been abated. And the health committee, or any two of them, may *Any two members of health committee may abate same.* cause said nuisance to be abated, and the cost of the same shall, by said court, be assessed upon the person or persons so neglecting to comply with said order, and may be collected of said person or persons as is provided in section eleven of this chapter. *Provided*, that if the Court of Common Council *Council may order part of expense to be paid from city treasury.* shall deem it just and proper, they may order any portion of said expense to be paid out of the city treasury.

SEC. 8. The keeping or allowing any heap or quantity of *Manure within thirty feet of highway or dwelling house a nuisance.* manure or compost, within thirty feet of any street, highway, walk, or dwelling house, shall be deemed a nuisance; and the owner or occupant of any stable, or other building or place, violating this section, shall forfeit and pay a fine of ten *Penalty.* dollars, and after conviction thereof, a further fine of two dollars for each day's neglect to remove the same.

SEC. 9. Any proprietor or occupant of any premises in *Neglect to remove nuisances upon order, how punished.* this city who shall neglect or refuse to remove therefrom anything which, in the opinion of any two members of the health committee, expressed in a written notice, shall be considered a nuisance injurious to health, within the time and in the manner specified in such notice given to said proprietor or occupant by said committee, or any two of them, as provided in section first of this ordinance, shall pay a fine of two dollars for each and every day that said proprietor or occupant shall neglect to comply with said notice.

Disobedience of orders of health committee, how punished. SEC. 10. Whenever any member of the health committee shall have given the occupant of any dwelling house or tenement in said city, written or printed notice, that no person residing or employed in said dwelling house or tenement shall throw any water or filth, or any animal or vegetable matter, liable to become a nuisance injurious to health, into or upon any premises or place within this city, and said order shall be violated by any person residing or employed in such tenement or dwelling house, such occupant shall forfeit and pay a fine of three dollars for each and every time the same shall be violated.

Any two members of health committee may abate nuisance, on neglect to obey orders. SEC. 11. If any person or persons, upon whom an order shall be made for removing a nuisance, or for cleaning and purifying the land, building or place where such nuisance shall be found, shall neglect to obey such order, in the manner and time appointed by the health committee, or any two of them, as aforesaid, said committee, or any two of them, may cause such nuisance to be removed, or abated, and such land, building, or place to be cleansed and purified, and the Court **Expenses to be paid by party offending.** of Common Council may adjust, liquidate, and pay the expense thereof, and the same may be collected of such person or persons by action of debt, in the name of the city.

Owners of building to provide privy accommodations. SEC. 12. That the owner of every building situated in the City of Hartford, occupied for dwellings or for any mechanical or manufacturing purposes, or for stores, offices, or lodging rooms, who shall neglect or refuse, while said building is so occupied, to provide suitable and convenient privy accom- **Penalty.** modations for the occupants of the same, shall forfeit and pay to the City of Hartford a fine of thirty dollars; and a further fine of ten dollars for every week that said owner shall neglect or refuse to provide the same.

Park river; no deposits to be thrown therein. SEC. 13. That no person or persons shall, within the limits of said city, discharge, deposit, or place, in Park or Mill river, any rubbish, stone, clam or oyster shells, bones, refuse iron, or any other substance which may tend to obstruct or fill up the channel of said river; or leave or place any putrid fish, clams, or oysters, or any animal or vegetable substance likely or liable to putrefy, in or upon the shore or margin of said river, or in the waters thereof; or discharge or place in said river any acid or other noxious substance likely to kill fish; or drown any dog, cat, or other animal therein, under a penalty of not less than one dollar nor more than thirty dollars for each and every offence. And it shall be the duty of the port warden and health committee to report to the city attorney, for prosecution, all breaches of this ordinance that shall come to their knowledge. *Nor on the river banks.*

Drowning animals therein prohibited.

Penalty.

Port warden to report violations to city attorney.

SEC. 14. The selling, keeping, offering or exposing for sale, as an article of food in any form, by any person within the limits of the City of Hartford, of any meat of any calf which shall have been killed before it has reached the age of five weeks, shall be deemed a nuisance; and any person who shall hereafter so sell, keep, offer or expose for sale, as an article of food in any form, any such meat. within the limits of the city, shall be guilty of a misdemeanor, and upon conviction shall pay a fine of not exceeding fifty dollars for each offence. *Sale of veal regulated.*

Penalty.

CHAPTER XII.

WATER DEPARTMENT.

Be it ordained by the Court of Common Council of the City of Hartford:

SECTION 1. The board of water commissioners, a majority of whom shall constitute a quorum, shall be trustees of the notes, scrip, or certificates of debt, issued by the City of Hartford, as its water fund (except where a trustee thereof is designated in the act, or acts, authorizing such issue), and under the direction of the Court of Common Council, may sell such scrip at par, or any higher rate, or pledge the same for loans, not usurious, to meet all lawful appropriations on account of the city water works; and shall keep a duplicate record of all transactions relative to such scrip, and deliver one copy thereof to the city treasurer. And all moneys received or held by said commissioners, from the avails of the sale or pledge of such scrip, shall be deposited in a bank or banks in said city, subject to be drawn out only upon the written order of the city treasurer.

SEC. 2. Said board shall elect a president, subject to approval by the Court of Common Council, who shall devote his whole time and attention to the construction, extension, supervision, care and management of the water works, under the general advice and direction of the commissioners, and to such other duties connected with said water works, or with other business of the city, as shall be assigned to him by the Court of Common Council; and no salary or fee shall be allowed to any other member of the board for services as commissioner, except as a remuneration for actual expenditures.

SEC. 3. Said board of commissioners may make contracts for labor and materials for the construction of water works, which, when ratified by the Court of Common Council, shall be valid and binding on said city; and all contracts for such labor or materials shall be in writing and executed in triplicate, one of which triplicates shall be kept by the commissioners, one shall be delivered to the city clerk, and one to the contractor; and no commissioner shall have any pecuniary interest, direct or indirect, in any such contract; and no such contract shall be executed unless good and satisfactory security for the faithful performance of the same shall be given by the contractor and approved by the commissioners. Said commissioners, when not otherwise specially authorized by the Court of Common Council, shall advertise in one or more newspapers in this city for sealed proposals for all such contracts, specifying the time and place when and where the same shall be received; and such proposals, in order to be received and acted upon, shall set forth a specified sum or price to be paid for all such labor and materials, or for either, without condition, limitation, or alteration, and shall be accompanied with a bond, satisfactory to the commissioners, conditioned for the faithful execution of the proposal, if the same shall be accepted; and no contract shall be assigned or transferred without the written assent of the commissioners. Nothing in this section contained shall be applicable to ordinary extensions of street mains, or repairs of the water works.

May make contracts.

Same to be ratified by council.

Contracts to be in writing, when.

Commissioners shall have no interest in contracts.

Security for execution of contract to be taken.

Shall advertise for sealed proposals, when.

Proposals, how made.

Bond to accompany proposal.

Contract, how assigned.

Extension of mains and repairs excluded.

SEC. 4. The commissioners shall superintend all constructions connected with the water works, and keep a record of their official proceedings in the matter; and report to the Court of Common Council, annually, and at such other intermediate times as said court may require, a general exhibit of the state of the works, including an estimate of needful expenditures for new and additional works in progress and all such other matters of information as they shall deem of importance to the public, or as said Court of Common Council may require. And the commissioners shall keep regular books of account, and all claims against the commissioners or the city, on account of the construction of the water works,

Duty of commissioners.

Shall make report to common council, when.

What report shall exhibit.

Shall keep books of account.

Claims against commissioners, how presented.

other than those for ordinary extensions, expenses, and repairs, shall be presented to said commissioners; and when
How approved, allowed, and paid. approved by them shall be laid before the Court of Common Council; who may allow the same, and direct the auditor of city accounts to draw his order on the city treasurer for the amount of any such claim.

Board shall regulate use of water. SEC. 5.   The board shall regulate the distribution and use
Shall establish rates subject to approval of council. of the water throughout the city; and shall establish, subject to the approval of the Court of Common Council, scales of prices, terms, or rates upon which the water shall be fur-
Shall collect water rents. nished to consumers; shall regulate the time of payment, and
May collect additional rents, when. collect all water rents; and may collect additional rents for the use of water, whenever extra quantities shall be used exceeding the quantities estimated for the same class of buildings or purposes, in the tariff of rates by them adopted.   But
No contracts for use of water to be for more than three years. no contract shall be made by said commissioners for the use of water, at any fixed rate, for a longer time than three years.

Shall keep a register of contractors and price paid. SEC. 6.   The commissioners shall keep a register of the names of all persons contracting for the use of water, the location where the same is used, and the price payable there-
Shall account semi-annually to common council. for; they shall faithfully account, semi-annually, to the Court of Common Council for the avails of all water rents, and other income of the water department received by them;
Shall use avails in payment of expenses. shall pay such parts of said avails or income as may be neces-sary in payment of the expenses of repairs, ordinary exten-sions, salaries of officers, hire of labor, and agents, rents, fuel,
Shall hold surplus subject to order of city treasurer. and all other ordinary and current expenses; and the surplus, if any shall remain in their hands, not required for such pur-pose, shall be held in trust by said commissioners, subject at all times to the order of the city treasurer.

When avails insufficient. SEC. 7.   Whenever the resources from water rents in any year shall be inadequate to meet the ordinary necessary extensions, repairs, and current expenses of the water works
Deficiency may be supplied by tax. and the interest on the water fund scrip, the deficiency shall be supplied by a tax on the grand list of all persons liable to
Same, how collected. city taxation for such purpose, and such tax shall be collected in the same manner as other city taxes, and any claim or
Use of water a lien. debt due for the use of the water shall be and constitute a

lien upon the land, building, tenement, or premises upon or in connection with which said water was used, against the owner of the same, his heirs and assigns, until such claim or debt is fully paid; but the same shall not remain a lien for a longer period than three months after the same becomes due, unless a certificate shall be lodged by the president of the board of water commissioners, with the town clerk of the town of Hartford, and signed by said president, describing the premises and the amount claimed under said lien. And said lien may be foreclosed in the name of the board of water commissioners, at any time after said debt or claim is due and payable, before the City Court of said city, in the same manner as a mortgage is foreclosed, or may be collected of the person or persons liable therefor in an action before the City Court.

Not to remain a lien unless certificate be filed within three months.

Lien, how foreclosed.

CHAPTER XIII.

POLICE DEPARTMENT.

Be it ordained by the Court of Common Council of the City of Hartford:

SECTION 1. There shall continue to be a police force for the City of Hartford, which shall be styled "the Police Department of the City of Hartford."

Police department.

SEC. 2. There shall continue to be a board of police commissioners of the City of Hartford, which shall consist of six

Board of police commissioners, how constituted and term of office of,

electors of said city, and each commissioner shall hold his
office for three years and until his successor is appointed and
qualified, and on the expiration of the terms of office of each
of the present commissioners his successor shall be appointed
for the full term of three years next succeeding and until his
successor shall be appointed and qualified.

Powers of board of commissioners.

SEC. 3.   Said commissioners shall have the general management of the police department of said city, and make all
May make regula- tions subject to ordi- nances and orders of common council. needful rules and regulations for the government thereof not
conflicting with the laws of the state, or ordinances of the
city, and further subject to the orders of the Court of Com-
May prescribe penalties. mon Council, and said board may prescribe suitable penalties
including suspension or removal from office for the infringe-
ment of its rules.

Mayor presiding officer.

SEC. 4.   The mayor of the city shall, *ex-officio*, be the presiding officer of the board of police commissioners, and shall
have the casting vote in all cases where there shall be a tie
May vote, when. vote of said board; *provided*. that he shall have no vote in the
appointment of any member of the police force.

Board may appoint secretary.

SEC. 5.   The board of police commissioners shall appoint
some person to act as secretary of said board, who shall keep
Duties of. the records thereof; and said person, so appointed as secretary, may be selected by said board from their own number,
if said board shall so direct.

Department, how constituted.
Number of police- men.

SEC. 6.   The police department shall consist of one chief of
police, one captain, one lieutenant, and not less than twenty
nor more than forty policemen, and not less than ten nor
more than thirty supernumerary policemen.

Appointments, how made.

SEC. 7.   All members of the police department named in
section six, shall be appointed by the board of police commis-
Shall hold office during good behavior. sioners, and shall hold their office during good behavior, and
until removed for cause.   But no person shall be appointed
to any office in the department without the assent of at least
four members of said board.   And no member of said depart-
Removals, how made. ment shall be removed unless upon a complaint in writing (a
copy of which shall be furnished to him), and after he shall
Notice, how given. have had a reasonable time, not less than six days, to prepare
a defence thereto; such complaint shall be made to the board

of commissioners, and may be made by any person whomsoever: *provided*, that any four members of said board may remove or suspend for cause any member of said department without charges being preferred. The chief of police, the captain of police, the mayor of the city, and the police judge, or any member of the board of police commissioners shall have power to suspend policemen from office for cause; but such suspension shall not continue for more than twenty-four hours thereafter, unless the person ordering such suspension, shall within that time notify the said board in writing of such suspension, the ground of such suspension, and the names of witnesses to sustain such charges. After notice shall have been given to the accused, the said board, or a committee of their own number, to be appointed by them, shall hear and examine witnesses under oath or affirmation, upon the charges and in defence; and said board may continue the suspension, remove the accused from office, or restore him to duty. In all cases in which the suspension is continued, the party suspended shall be deprived of his pay from the date of his suspension, but he shall not be exempt from performance of duty unless the officer making such suspension shall so expressly order. The violation of any law of the state, of any ordinance of the city, or of any rule or regulation of the police department, or incompetency, shall, if proved, be punished by suspension or dismissal from the force.

SEC. 8. No pay shall be allowed to members of the board of police commissioners for any services rendered by them, but the actual expenses and disbursements of said board incurred in the performance of its duties shall be paid from the city treasury when allowed by the common council.

SEC. 9. The pay of the chief of police shall be two thousand dollars per annum, the pay of the captain of police shall be fifteen hundred dollars per annum, the pay of the lieutenant of police shall be twelve hundred dollars per annum; and the pay of each policeman shall be one thousand dollars per annum; and the pay of the supernumerary policemen shall be at the same rate as the pay of the regular policemen, when acting in the place, or performing the duties of regular policemen, and when employed only for portions of the day, the pay of such supernumeraries shall be at the rate of two dollars and seventy cents for each day of twenty-four hours, and no allowance shall be made for any extra time or services during the same day of twenty-four hours.

Members of police must reside in city.

SEC. 10.   The office of any member of the police force shall become vacant whenever said member ceases to reside within the limits of said city.

Members of force not to engage in any other occupation.

SEC. 11.   No person while employed as a regular member of the police force, or as an officer of the same, shall engage, directly or indirectly, in any other occupation for pay, hire, reward, or compensation of any kind whatsoever, and no officer, policeman, or supernumerary policeman, shall demand,

To receive no rewards.

accept, or receive any compensation, present, or reward, for services rendered or to be rendered, except as hereinafter provided.

Service outside of city, when permitted and how regulated.

SEC. 12.   Whenever the services of any member or members of the police force may be required by parties, other than the City of Hartford (and citizens of the same where the crime has been committed within the limits of the city), the chief of police may, if in his judgment the interests of the city will not suffer thereby, detail such member or members of the force as he shall judge expedient, and shall charge

Charges for such service, how established.

such parties for said services so rendered, such sums as may be established by the board of police commissioners, and which sums shall not be less than three dollars a day for each policeman so employed, in addition to the necessary expenses.

Chief of police shall keep account of service, etc.

The chief of police shall keep, in a book kept expressly for that purpose, a true and correct account of all such services performed, the names of the parties for whom, and the names of the policemen by whom performed, the time spent, and expenses incurred, the sums charged, the amount and dates of payment, together with such other memoranda as in his opinion may be proper.

Penalty for receiving presents or reward.

SEC. 13.   No member of the police force shall perform any services as above specified except by order of the chief, captain, or lieutenant of police, and any officer or member of the force, who shall demand, accept, or receive, directly or indi-

rectly, any money, presents, or valuable articles for services
so rendered, or to be rendered, except the legal charges as
fixed by the police commissioners, or who shall neglect for
more than twenty-four hours after the performance of such
service to report the same in writing to the chief of police, *Shall make report of service to chief, when.*
with his legal charges and expenses, or who shall neglect, for
more than twenty-four hours after receiving such payments,
to pay over the full amount so received to the secretary of
the board of police commissioners, shall be dismissed from
the force. And it shall be the duty of the secretary of the *Penalty on failure.*
board of police commissioners to deposit on the first day of
each month, with the city treasurer, all moneys received by *Certain moneys received, how deposited.*
the police force, in accordance with this ordinance, and to
take from the city treasurer a receipt therefor.

SEC. 14. The city auditor shall draw his order on the city *Salaries, to be paid monthly.*
treasurer, monthly, for the pay of each member of the police
force, and the certificate of the chief of police, countersigned
by a member of the board of police commissioners, shall be
his sufficient voucher therefor, except in the case of the chief *What sufficient voucher.*
of police, when the certificate of a member of the board shall
be sufficient. No fees or compensation, other than is herein
provided, shall be charged or received by any member of the
police department ; but each member of said department shall, *What member shall do before being qualified.*
before being qualified for the discharge of the duties of his
office, execute, in writing, a transfer and assignment of all his
interest in any fees which may be taxed in his favor, in said
Police Court, to the treasurer of the city, for the benefit of
said city; and no member of the department shall be entitled
to receive any salary, for any services rendered by him, until
such transfer and assignment shall have been executed by
him to the satisfaction of the board of commissioners, and
lodged on file in the office of the city treasurer.

SEC. 15. Each officer and member of the police force shall *Policemen to have the powers of constables in city.*
have, within the city, the same powers as to the service of
criminal process and the arrest of offenders that constables of
towns have within their respective towns.

SEC. 16. It shall be the duty of the chief of police, under *Duties of chief of police.*
the direction of the police commissioners, to superintend the

police department; and it shall be his duty, once in three months, or oftener if necessary, to report to the common council, through the board of commissioners, the state of the department. The common council shall provide him with an office, wherein he shall keep all the records of the police department (except the records of the board of police commissioners), and shall also keep a roster of all the officers and members of the police force, and all reports shall be made to him at said office, which shall be the headquarters of the department. He shall receive from any subordinate member of the police force, and from every other person, all complaints of violations of any law of the state, or ordinance of the city, and shall see that the same be prosecuted according to law. He shall also have the general care and responsibility of the said police force; and all other members of said force shall be subject to his orders. He shall, from time to time, designate the officers to attend the Police Court, and to collect assessments, and to serve notices; and in case of the absence of any regular policeman from duty, shall appoint a supernumerary policeman to take his place. The captain of police, in case of the absence or disability of the chief of police, shall discharge the duties of said chief. He shall also, at all times, under the direction of said chief, have the management and control of said police force. He shall be on duty at such times and places as shall be ordered by the board of police commissioners, and shall receive and execute all orders received from them through the chief of police, when said chief of police shall be on duty. He shall, in connection with the lieutenant, have charge of the station house, and all persons who shall be committed to, or confined in said station house shall be in his custody and control, by whomsoever arrested; and it shall be his duty to inquire into the charges made against any person so committed; and shall cause them to be legally brought before the Police Court for trial, and see that the witnesses against them are duly summoned.

SEC. 17. No person shall be committed to or detained in the station house, or discharged therefrom, without the knowledge and consent of the chief of police, or captain, or

(marginal notes)
Shall make quarterly report.

Office records, where kept.

Chief shall receive complaints and cause the same to be prosecuted.

Shall designate officers to attend Police Court and collect assessments.

Captain shall act in absence of chief.

Duties of captain.

Duties of lieutenant.

Shall have charge of station house.

Commitments to and discharges from station house.

the lieutenant, when acting in his place, and then only as
provided by law.

Sec. 18. Either the captain or lieutenant shall be at the *Station house, who shall attend upon.*
station house, except when both are necessarily absent, in
which case a policeman shall be deputed by the chief of
police to take charge of the same; and while so taking
charge, he shall have the same authority over and discharge
the same duties in relation to the station house as the captain
when on duty. The lieutenant of police shall, in the absence *Duties of lieutenant.*
or disability of the captain of police, discharge all the duties
incumbent on said captain, and also such special duties as
shall be required of him by the board of police commissioners,
the chief of police, or captain of police, and shall also discharge the ordinary duties of a policeman when not otherwise employed.

Sec. 19. It shall be the duty of policemen to obey such *Duty of policemen.*
lawful orders and directions as they shall receive, from time
to time, from their superior officers respecting their duty;
and it shall be their duty to guard the city day and night; to
report to the chief of police, through the captain, all viola- *Shall report all violations of city ordinances.*
tions of city ordinances, all suspicious persons, all houses of
ill-fame, all pawnbroker shops, and shops for the purchase
and sale of second-hand articles, all gaming houses, and all
disorderly and suspicious places of resort. They shall pre-
serve the public peace, and render all possible assistance to *Shall preserve the public peace. Shall direct strangers.*
the ministers of the law. They shall direct strangers the
nearest way to their places of destination, and when necessary shall see that they are accompanied by a member of the
force. They shall, when necessary, attend the Police Court,
and shall serve the process of said court, and shall be subject
to the orders and directions of said court. They shall
especially attend to keeping the streets and sidewalks of the *Keep streets clear of obstructions.*
city clear of all unlawful obstructions, and shall report to the
chief of police, through the captain, all unlawful obstructions
thereof, who shall take immediate steps to remove the same.
They shall collect all assessments for betterments and con- *Shall collect assessments.*
struction laid by the board of street commissioners, and the
mayor shall issue his warrant to collect said assessments,

directed to said policemen, who shall serve the same; they

Shall serve notices. shall also serve all notices that shall be ordered to be served by the common council, and they shall receive no compensation for such collections or services. They shall also, without

Shall serve all process issued by the coroner. compensation, serve all process which may be issued by the coroner, and attend upon the inquests taken by him when directed by the chief.

Shall attend at fires and protect property. SEC. 20. All policemen not otherwise specially employed shall, on the breaking out of a fire, immediately repair to the vicinity thereof, and use their best endeavors to save and secure property.

Qualifications of policemen. SEC. 21. Every person appointed to an office in the police department shall be, at the time of his appointment, a citizen of the United States, and a qualified voter of the city, and capable of speaking, reading, and writing the English language; and shall, before exercising any functions of his

Shall make oath, how. office, make oath or affirmation, before some competent authority, that he will support the Constitution of the United States, and the State of Connecticut, and that he will faithfully discharge the duties of the office to which he shall have been appointed; and shall cause a certificate of such oath or affirmation to be lodged in the office of the board of police commissioners.

Visiting tippling or bawdy house while on duty, how punished. SEC. 22. Every member of the force who shall, while on duty, enter any tippling, or bawdy, or otherwise disorderly house, unless to suppress disturbance, or upon the order of his superior officer, or shall interfere in any caucus or primary election, or shall attempt, either directly or indirectly, to influence any elector in the exercise of his right of voting,

How punished for interference in elections. or shall attend to any poll or voting place unless so directed by his superior officer, shall be removed from his place in said department, and be ineligible to reappointment for the term of one year.

Mayor the chief executive magistrate. SEC. 23. The mayor shall be the chief executive magistrate and conservator of the peace of the city; and it shall be his duty to be vigilant and active in causing the laws and ordinances to be executed and enforced. He and the chief of police shall each have authority, with force and strong hand when necessary, to suppress all tumults, riots, routs, and *Shall have power to suppress riots.* unlawful assemblies, and to arrest without warrant and commit to prison for any time not exceeding twenty-four hours, any person or persons who shall be detected in reveling, quarreling, brawling, or otherwise behaving in a disorderly manner, to the disturbance or annoyance of the peaceable inhabitants of the city; each of them shall have power to enter any house or building which he has reasonable cause to *May enter houses of ill-fame to disperse parties, when.* suspect to be inhabited by persons of ill-fame, or to which persons of dissolute, idle, or disorderly character are suspected to resort; and if any dissolute, disorderly, or vagrant persons are found assembled in any such house or building he shall command all such persons immediately to disperse, if in his opinion the good order of any portion of the city require it; and in case of neglect or refusal to obey such command, he is hereby authorized and empowered to commit, without *May commit without warrant, when.* warrant, any person or persons so disobeying, to prison, for a term not exceeding twenty-four hours; and each of them shall have and exercise, within the limits of the city, all the powers given to sheriffs or other officers by Title XX., Chap- *Shall have within city same powers as sheriffs.* ter 6, Section 2 of the Revised Statutes, and may at all times, if necessary, require the aid of any city or deputy marshal, constable, policeman, or any and all of them, or any other person or persons; and whenever the mayor shall have reason to believe that great opposition will be made to the execution of his authority, he shall have power to call out all, any, or either of the military companies of the city, and *Mayor may call upon the military force, when.* may exert all the force necessary to enable him to execute the laws within the limits of the city.

SEC. 24. Every officer and soldier when called into service *Disobedience of commands of mayor, how punished.* by the mayor of the city in the manner aforesaid, who shall disobey the commands of the mayor, shall forfeit and pay a fine to the city not exceeding fifty dollars.

SEC. 25. Every person who shall hinder, obstruct, resist, *Resistance to officers, how punished.* or abuse the mayor, or any city or deputy marshal, or constable, police officer, or policeman, in the execution of his office, or, when commanded to assist him therein, shall refuse or unreasonably neglect to do so, shall forfeit and pay a fine not exceeding fifty dollars.

Crowds of three or more persons upon the sidewalks, parks, etc., prohibited.

SEC. 26. It shall not be lawful for persons to assemble idly and remain in crowds upon the sidewalks, crosswalks, or walks upon the public parks, or before churches, or before or within the cemeteries within the city, and all persons, to the

On refusing to disperse on command, how proceeded with.

number of three or more, so assembling and refusing to disperse when commanded by the mayor, or by any city or deputy marshal, police officer or policeman, special constable, or by any sheriff, deputy sheriff, constable, or justice of the peace, may be arrested and forthwith brought before the Police Court, or if it be on Sunday, or in the night season,

Penalty.

such person or persons may be confined in the station house until the next day upon which said Police Court shall be holden; and every such person shall be punished by a fine not exceeding thirty dollars.

CHAPTER XIV.

HIGHWAY DEPARTMENT.

Be it ordained by the Court of Common Council of the City of Hartford:

SECTION 1. Whenever any vote or resolution shall be offered in either board of the Court of Common Council, proposing to lay out, construct, or establish, any new highway, street, public park, dyke, or walk; or to discontinue, or to alter the location, grade, or width of any existing highway, street, public park, dyke, or walk; or to exchange or sell one highway for another; or to establish a building line or lines, or an opening between buildings; or to raise, fill up, or drain low grounds; or to lay out, construct, or alter a public sewer; or to order, construct, or alter, a sidewalk and gutters, under any of the provisions of the city charter, or amendments thereto, such vote shall not be passed by either board of said Court of Common Council, until said court has caused said proposed vote or resolution and a certificate that the same is pending in said court, attested by the city clerk, to be pub-

How published.

lished twice, at least, in two daily newspapers published in the City of Hartford, with a notice appended to such published vote or resolution to all persons to file a written state-

Objections to proposed Improvement, how made.

ment of their objections, if any they have, with the board of street commissioners within ten days inclusive from the day of the first publication of said notice. Nothing in this section, however, shall apply to mere repairing or reconstructing any existing public work or improvement once complete.

What vote shall state.

SEC. 2. Every such proposed vote or resolution shall briefly and intelligibly state the general character and descripton of the proposed improvements, but need not contain definite measurements, courses, or termini. It may embrace one or more of the several kinds of local improvement specified in the first section of this ordinance, and in case of a new street, or alteration of an established street, shall designate the building lines on said street.

Vote before passage shall be referred to board of street commissioners.

SEC. 3. The Court of Common Council shall, before further proceeding to pass or carry out said vote or resolution, refer the same to the board of street commissioners for their investigation, and said board shall forthwith inquire into the same,

Board shall report thereon, how.

and make report thereon to the Court of Common Council, either recommending or disapproving the passage of said vote or resolution with their reasons therefor.

After ten days, council may proceed how.

SEC. 4. At any time after the expiration of said ten days, and after the report of the commissioners thereon shall have been made and accepted, said Court of Common Council may proceed to carry said vote or resolution into effect in manner as hereinafter provided, or otherwise act upon the same.

Expense of land for improvement, how assessed.

And whenever said court shall order any of said proposed improvements, the entire expense of carrying out said improvements shall be assessed as betterments upon the persons or land specially benefited thereby as hereinafter provided.

Street commissioners to make appraisals, assessments, etc.

SEC. 5. Said vote or resolution shall be referred to said board of street commissioners, who shall estimate the costs of said proposed public work or improvement, and shall also appraise the damages to be paid to any person for land or any interest therein taken for such work or improvement, and shall also assess said cost of construction and the amount of said damages upon the persons or land specially benefited thereby, as hereinafter provided.

SEC. 6. The board of street commissioners, in all cases, *Notice before appraisal or assessment.* when called upon to appraise damages for land or any interest therein taken for any of said improvements, or special damages resulting to land or interest therein from change of grade of any highway, or to assess betterments on any party for taking said land for said improvements, or for special benefits resulting from such change of grade, shall, before making such appraisals or assessments, cause public notice to be given for two days, at least, in two or more daily newspapers published in the City of Hartford, and at least four days before the time of hearing, of a time and place where all parties in interest may appear before said commissioners, and be heard with witnesses relative to the *Commissioners shall examine parties under oath.* amount of damages or betterments, or both, to be appraised or assessed to them respectively, and said commissioners shall examine said parties and witnesses under oath.

SEC. 7. Whenever any vote or resolution described in the *Proceedings when land to be taken.* first section of this ordinance has been legally published, and it shall be necessary to take any land or any interest therein belonging to private owners or corporations for said contemplated improvement, the Court of Common Council, before otherwise carrying said vote or resolution into effect, unless they obtain such land or interest by voluntary dedication from the owners thereof, or unless in case of change of grade of any highway, they shall obtain releases of all special damages resulting to land or any interest therein from said change of grade, shall refer the subject matter of the con- *Reference to street commissioners.* templated improvement to the board of street commissioners, and said board shall thereupon proceed in behalf of said Court of Common Council, as follows: Said board shall obtain *Board shall proceed, how.* from the city surveyor a map, drawing, or written descrip- *Map.* tion, clearly explaining the contemplated improvement, and showing the adjoining land and owners thereof, and shall then agree, if possible, with the owners of the land required for said improvement, upon the compensation to be made therefor, including the damages for establishing a building line, or lines, in case of opening a now street, and with those whose land or interest therein will be specially damaged by change of grade of highway, and with those who will be specially benefited by said improvement or change of grade, as to the payment of the entire amount to be assessed as betterments for said improvement, and the respective amounts,

or proportions thereof, which each person so benefited will pay; and secure from each such owner, or person, proper written evidence of such agreement.

Sec. 8. If said board of street commissioners fail to agree with any owner of said land or interest therein, or with any of the parties who in their opinion should be assessed for any benefits on account of said proposed improvement, not includ-

ing cost of construction, they shall, after the requisite notice given as hereinbefore provided, proceed to appraise all damages therefor to the persons entitled to such damages and to assess upon the parties or land specially benefited by said improvement, betterments or benefits for said improvement, not including the cost of construction, in proportion to the damages and benefits to each respectively, and shall furnish a proper certificate thereof signed by a majority of said board to the city clerk, who shall forthwith cause the same

to be published at least twice in two or more of the daily newspapers published in the City of Hartford, at least four days before the same shall be acted on by said court, and the

original certificate shall be lodged on file in the city clerk's office; and the same shall be binding and conclusive upon all parties if said court order said improvement, unless appealed from and changed upon said appeal as by law provided, and when any appeal shall be taken, said board shall instruct and

aid the city attorney in the matter of said appeal, until the same shall be determined.

Sec. 9. Whenever all persons who are entitled to compensation for damages, or liable for betterments on account of any of said improvements, shall agree upon the respective amounts to be received or paid by them therefor; or when they shall deliver a written waiver of their right of appeal to said board at any time within the limit allowed by law for an appeal, said board shall immediately thereafter make their report to said Court of Common Council, and in cases where an appeal or appeals are taken as aforesaid, as soon as practicable after such proceedings are determined.

SEC. 10. Their report shall set forth the amount of damages agreed upon with each of said owners of land, and the amount of benefits agreed to be paid by the respective parties benefited by said improvement in cases of agreement with all parties; or in case of assessment by said board, of the amount of damages appraised or betterments assessed upon each of the parties entitled to such damages or liable for such betterments, or upon an appeal the amount fixed by the court or judge hearing the same, so that all damages thus ascertained may become a part of the expense to be assessed, and all betterments may be thus assessed upon the persons or property specially benefited thereby. And said board shall also embrace in their report a written descriptive survey of the proposed improvement concerning which said proceedings have been had, and such a vote, resolution, or ordinance as in their judgment ought to be passed in order to establish and carry out said improvement, fully describing therein the width, curve, boundaries, grade, and building lines, and such other particulars of said improvement as the case may require, and including an order for the payment, or deposit at some place named therein, of the amount of damages appraised to the respective owners of any land or interest therein required for said improvement, and an order to the mayor to issue his warrant forthwith to collect all said assessments for said betterments assessed as aforesaid.

Said court may alter said proposed vote, if it see cause, provided no change be made in the lines or location of the improvement which will require taking more or a greater interest in any land for said improvement than shown by said survey and report, and provided that no change of grade of highway be made that shall occasion greater damage than the grade shown by said survey and report, and shall there-

[marginal notes:]
What report shall contain.

Report shall contain a description and survey of improvement.

Shall include order for payment or deposit of damages, and order of issue of warrant for collection of betterments.

Common council may alter vote, when.

upon adopt such vote or resolution, with or without such alteration, or reject the same.

Land appraised may be taken for public use, when. SEC. 11. Whenever any vote establishing any public improvement has been passed as aforesaid, and the proper compensation has been paid to or deposited for the owners of any land taken for such improvement, then said land shall be immediately open and subject to the public use on such conditions as said court may impose, and shall be, to all intents, appropriated therefor, unless the public work or improvement require the previous sanction of a city meeting, under the sixth section of the city charter, in which case such appropriation shall not take effect until such sanction has been obtained.

Damages, how deposited in case of certain parties. SEC. 12. If any owner of said land, or interest therein, is not a resident of the City of Hartford, or upon due inquiry cannot be found therein, or is a lunatic, or idiot, or minor without a guardian, or in any way incapacitated to receive said compensation, or is unknown, or is entitled only to a contingent or uncertain interest, said court may prescribe in such particular case how and where the compensation due such owner shall be placed or deposited subject to the lawful call of said owner or his duly authorized agent or representative.

Assessments for construction to be made separately. SEC. 13. Before the final passage of the vote or resolution laying out any public work the expense of construction of which may be assessed as betterments upon the persons or land specially benefited thereby, the assessment of such betterments shall be made separately from the assessment of benefits for land taken, and shall be made as follows: When said vote or resolution shall have been published as required in the first section of this ordinance, the same shall be by the said court referred to the board of street commissioners for **Board of street commissioners shall assess a proportional part upon parties specially benefited.** assessment, and said board shall thereupon proceed to estimate the expense of construction, and shall assess the just proportion of such expense, which any person or persons, private or corporate, including railroad corporations[1] occupying streets with their tracks, or any piece of land specially

---

[1] City of Bridgeport v. N. Y. & N. H. R. R. Co., 36 Conn., 255.

benefited by said improvement, should respectively defray and make a proper written certificate of said assessment so made, with names and amounts assessed upon the respective parties or lands, and describing by metes and bounds, or otherwise, the land on account of which said assessments are made, and signed by a majority of said board, and cause the same to be published for four days at least in two or more daily newspapers published within said city, with a notice affixed to said certificate that any person aggrieved may, within ten days after the day of first publication of said notice, lodge with the clerk of said board a written statement of his objections to said assessment. After the expiration of said ten days, said board shall revise said assessment with reference to said objections, at which time said parties interested may appear and be heard thereon, and said board shall thereupon report their doings and final assessment, duly signed by a majority of said board, to the Court of Common Council, and said court shall then accept said report and assessments and order the same to be published twice at least in two or more daily papers published in the City of Hartford. After expiration of the time limited for appeal, if no appeal be taken; or after all proceedings on appeals have been concluded, the board of street commissioners shall report the facts to said court, with their recommendations thereon accompanied, in case the assessments have been changed or modified upon appeal, by a schedule of the assessments as finally determined, and said court shall thereupon proceed to pass or reject said vote or resolution, whereupon, if passed, said assessments shall be final and conclusive upon all parties in interest.

SEC. 14. Upon the final layout or completion of the construction of any such public work, the board of street commissioners shall give notice thereof, and that said benefits are due and payable, by publication twice in two daily newspapers published in said city, and all benefits assessed therefor shall be immediately due and payable.

SEC. 15. If the actual cost of the construction of any public work shall be less than the sum estimated by the board

Marginal notes: Certificate of doings, how made. Certificate, how signed. How published. What notice affixed to certificate shall state. After ten days said board shall revise the assessment. Shall make report to council. Council shall order assessments published, how. Final action. Benefits, when payable. What deduction allowed.

of street commissioners and assessed upon the parties benefited, each of the parties so assessed shall be entitled to a proportionate deduction from his assessment.

Deduction to be made from assessment, when.

SEC. 16. If any person upon whom any assessment of betterments has been made as herein provided shall pay the
same within five days after the first publication provided for
in section fourteen of this ordinance, he shall be entitled to a
deduction or repayment of four per cent. on the amount of

When liable to collection in full.

his assessment to be deducted therefrom. At the end of said
five days he shall be liable to pay the same in full.

Duty of mayor to issue his warrant for collection of assessment, how and when.

SEC. 17. As soon as any assessment of betterments made
in accordance with this ordinance becomes due and payable,
it shall be the duty of the mayor of said city to issue his
warrant directed to any officer or member of the police
requiring him to proceed to collect the same in the same
manner as collectors of public taxes are by law empowered
to proceed in the collection of taxes, and it shall be the duty
of said person to execute said warrant and pay over to the

Assessments collected to be paid to city treasurer.

city treasurer the assessments by him collected, and he shall
collect and pay over the same fees as sheriffs are by law

What fees allowed and how paid.

allowed upon collection by execution and levying of execution
whenever he shall levy upon property for said assessments.

Assessments for betterments a lien upon land benefited.

SEC. 18. All assessments of betterments for any of said
public improvements shall be made therefor on account of the
land or property liable to assessment and specially benefited
thereby. Every assessment of betterments for any of the
public improvements embraced in this ordinance shall be a

Lien expires unless certificate is filed, when and how.

lien on the land on account of which said assessment is made
until the same is fully paid, which said lien shall commence
and attach to said land from the time of the passage by the
Court of Common Council of the vote laying out or ordering
the construction of said work: *provided*, that the same shall
not remain a lien thereon for a longer period than three
months from the final layout or completion of such work or
improvement, unless the board of street commissioners shall
within that time lodge with the town clerk of the town of
Hartford, for record, a certificate, signed by the clerk of said

board, describing the premises, the amount assessed, and the improvement for which it was assessed.

SEC. 19. Such recorded liens shall be foreclosed in the name and behalf of the city by the city attorney before the City Court of said city in the same manner that a mortgage may be foreclosed, as soon as the same can be done, unless said assessment is paid or said Court of Common Council shall otherwise order. *Liens, how foreclosed.*

SEC. 20. In case of said assessments being made by said board directly upon any land, said land shall be liable to be sold to pay the same unless said assessments shall be paid within six months after public notice thereof has been given, and said court shall give fifteen days public notice in two or more daily newspapers published in the City of Hartford of the amount of said assessment, and the time and place where such sale will be made, and at the time and place named, any police officer to whom the warrant of the mayor is directed and delivered to collect such assessment, may sell said land, or so much thereof as may be necessary to pay said assessment and expenses of said sale, and give a title thereto to the purchaser, as in case of a sale of land for taxes, and the balance of the purchase money, if any, pay over to the owner of said land. *Land assessed may be sold for assessment, when. What notice to be given. Who may sell. Surplus to be paid to owner.*

SEC. 21. The vote or ordinance establishing or discontinuing any highway or street in the City of Hartford, and every survey of any new highway or street approved by the board of street commissioners and Court of Common Council, shall be recorded in a city highway record book kept for that purpose by the city clerk. *Vote establishing or discontinuing highway; and new highway to be recorded, how.*

SEC. 22. Turnpike roads within the City of Hartford shall be subject to the control of the Court of Common Council for purposes of city improvement to the same extent as other highways. *Turnpike roads in city subject to control of Court of Common Council.*

SEC. 23. Whenever the owner or occupant of any land fronting upon any street or highway in this city shall neglect to make or pave any sidewalk or gutter within the time and in the manner ordered by the Court of Common Council, or shall neglect or refuse to keep his sidewalk in good repair, it *Street commissioners may make or repair sidewalk, when.*

Cost of such making or repair to be a lien on premises liable therefor. shall be the duty of the board of street commissioners to make or repair the same, and the cost of making, or of repairs, and interest thereon, shall be and remain a lien in favor of the city upon the adjoining premises which are liable to be assessed therefor, but a certificate thereof shall be

Lien expires unless recorded, when and how. recorded, as is provided in case of assessments for betterments in section eighteen of this ordinance, and said lien may be

Lien, how foreclosed or collected. foreclosed in the same manner that a mortgage may be foreclosed, or said city may recover the same of the party or parties liable therefor by an action before the City Court of said city.

Duties of board of street commissioners. SEC. 24. Said board shall in executing public works conform to the votes or orders of the Court of Common Council, and to all general rules which said court may adopt relative to the locality, measurements, materials, and management of

Shall manage public works according to order of common council. all public works. Said board shall keep an account of all expenditures made in its department, which shall be open at all times to the inspection of any member of the Court of

Shall make report of expenditures monthly. Common Council, and shall make report to said court of such expenditure, at least once a month, unless excused therefrom.

Shall make provisional contracts subject to orders of common council. It shall make provisional contracts, subject to the approval of said court, for such public works connected with highways, streets, or thoroughfares, and the erection or lighting of street

Shall superintend lamps. lamps and repairs of the same, as ought to be, in the judgment of said board, let out to contractors, and shall keep a

Keep record of complaints. record of complaints, and faithfully enter therein all complaints made to it concerning streets, highways, lamps, and public places, and the breach of city ordinances relating thereto; and shall be diligent in ascertaining the facts in such matters of complaint, and in taking just and necessary action

Shall conform to plans of city surveyor. relative thereto. Said board shall consult and conform to the plans of the city surveyor in constructing public works unless otherwise ordered by the Court of Common Council, and shall have power to do all things which shall be necessary to be done in order to enforce such portions of any city ordinance as shall be within the scope of its official duties.

City surveyor, how and when appointed and term of office. SEC. 25. A city surveyor shall be annually appointed by a concurrent vote of the Court of Common Council, and shall hold his office for one year and until his successor is appointed and qualified. He shall have the custody of all the maps and plans of the public works of the city not expressly entrusted to other officers or persons; shall make and prepare, under Duties of. the direction of the Court of Common Council, or by request of the board of street commissioners, all surveys, maps, profiles, calculations, drawings, estimates, and specifications, required for the use of the city or its departments, and perform all such services in the surveying or engineering department, as may be required of him by said court or commissioners.

SEC. 26. No street, highway or alley in the City of Hart- No street or alley shall be opened less than forty feet wide, nor then without license of Court of Common Council. ford less than forty feet wide shall hereafter be opened to the public by dedication or otherwise, by any person or private corporation, nor in any case except by license of the Court of Common Council first obtained.

SEC. 27. If any person shall without authority from the Extinguishing public lights, how punished. board of street commissioners wilfully extinguish the lights in any public lamps in the City of Hartford, such person shall forfeit and pay to the city a fine of not less than one nor more than five dollars for each offence.

CHAPTER XV.

GOATS AND CATTLE.

<table><tr><td>Pasturing of goats in highway prohibited.</td><td>Goats, cattle, etc., may be impounded, when.</td></tr><tr><td>Pasturing or running at large of cattle, etc., prohibited.</td><td>Poundage, fees of.</td></tr><tr><td></td><td>Unless reclaimed, how sold.</td></tr><tr><td>Penalty for violation of ordinance.</td><td>Penalty for pound-breach.</td></tr></table>

Be it ordained by the Court of Common Council of the City of Hartford:

SECTION 1. Every person who shall pasture any goat in Pasturing of goats in highway prohibited. any public street, highway, or place, within the limits of the City of Hartford, and every person who shall cause or suffer any goat owned or kept by him or her to run at large or to be pastured in any public highway or place within the limits of said city, shall forfeit and pay a fine of not less than one dollar nor more than ten dollars for each offence.

SEC. 2. Every person who shall pasture any cow, calf, ox, or horse, within the limits of any public street, highway, or place, within the limits of the City of Hartford, shall forfeit and pay a fine of not less than one dollar nor more than five dollars for each offence.

SEC. 3. Every person who shall cause or allow any cow, calf, ox, or horse, belonging to him or her to run at large within the limits of any public street, highway, or place, within the limits of said city, shall forfeit and pay a fine of not less than one dollar nor more than ten dollars for each offence.

SEC. 4. It shall be the duty of the city attorney to collect the fines imposed in the three preceding sections whenever complaint shall be made to him, supported by satisfactory evidence that such offence has been committed.

SEC. 5. Any person finding any horses, sheep, goats, swine, geese, or neat cattle, going at large within the City of Hartford, or being pastured within any public street, highway, or place, in said city, may impound such animal in any pound within said city, and it shall be the duty of the pound keeper to receive the same, and the owner, keeper, or other person claiming the animal so impounded, shall pay the

pound-keeper before he shall be entitled to take such animal, twenty-five cents for every goose, and one dollar for every other animal, together with the expenses of keeping such animal, not exceeding fifty cents a day; of which the person impounding said animal shall receive twelve and a half cents for every goose and fifty cents for every other animal by him impounded. If said animal is not claimed by any person rightfully entitled so to do within five days after the same shall have been impounded, the pound-master may advertise the same for public sale in at least two newspapers published

in the City of Hartford, reasonably describing such animal, and stating the time and place of the sale, three days before the time fixed therein for such sale; at which time and place said pound-master may make public sale of said animal, and after applying the proceeds of said sale to his own fees and expenses on account of such animal, shall pay the balance thereof to the city treasury, where the said balance shall remain for the benefit of the lawful owner of said animal, and payable to him, without interest, upon satisfactory proof of such ownership. The pound-master shall keep a record of his doings and report the same to the Court of Common Council once in six months at least.

SEC. 6. The penalty for pound-breach, or for any rescue or any attempt at rescue from a pound-master, shall be a forfeiture of twenty dollars, recoverable for the use of the city upon this ordinance. Nothing herein contained shall in any manner affect the remedy of replevin, as the same is applied in ordinary cases where beasts are impounded. *Penalty for pound breach.*

CHAPTER XVI.

SALARIES AND FEES.

Salaries of—

Mayor, City Treasurer, Auditor; City Clerk, Clerk of Common Council Board, Recorder, Judge of Police Court, Clerk of Police Court, Messenger of Police Court, Prosecuting Attorney, City Surveyor.

Chairman and Assistant Chairman of Health Committee.

President of Board of Water Commissioners.

Superintendent of Streets.

Clerk of Board of Street Commissioners.

Clerk of the Board of Fire Commissioners.

Clerk of the Board of Police Commissioners.

Fire Marshal.

Messenger of Board of Aldermen.

Messenger of Common Council Board.

Port Warden.

Board of Street Commissioners.

Sealer of Weights and Measures.

Registrars of Voters.

Associate Judge of Police Court.

Salaries, when paid.

Fees of City Marshal.

Fees of Messenger of City Court.

Fees of City Attorney.

Fees of City Jurors.

Payment of office rent regulated.

City officers not to contract indebtedness.

Be it ordained by the Court of Common Council of the City of Hartford:

Salaries of city officers.

SECTION 1. That the following sums shall be paid as salaries and fees to the several city officers herein named : to the Mayor, fifteen hundred dollars a year.

Mayor.

City Treasurer.
City Treasurer, one thousand dollars a year.

City Auditor.
City Auditor, one thousand dollars a year.

City Clerk.
City Clerk, eight hundred and fifty dollars a year.

Clerk of Common Council Board.
Clerk of the Common Council Board, four hundred dollars a year.

Recorder of City Court.
Recorder of the City Court, twelve hundred dollars a year.

Judge of Police Court.
Judge of the Police Court, one thousand dollars a year.

Clerk of Police Court.
Clerk of the Police Court, eight hundred dollars a year.

Messenger of Police Court.
Messenger of the Police Court, three hundred dollars a year.

Prosecuting Attorney.
Prosecuting Attorney, one thousand dollars a year.

City Surveyor.
City Surveyor, two thousand dollars a year.

Chairman Health Committee.
Chairman of the Health Committee, six hundred dollars a year.

Assistant Chairman Health Committee.
Assistant Chairman of the Health Committee, four hundred dollars a year.

President Board of Water Commissioners.
President of the Board of Water Commissioners, two thousand dollars a year.

Superintendent of Streets, two thousand dollars a year and
four hundred dollars for hire of horse and carriage. ·
Superintendent of Streets.

Clerk of the Board of Street Commissioners, fifteen hundred dollars a year.
Clerk Board Street Commissioners.

Clerk of the Board of Fire Commissioners, two hundred
and fifty dollars a year.
Clerk Board Fire Commissioners.

Clerk of the Board of Police Commissioners, two hundred
and fifty dollars a year.
Clerk Board Police Commissioners.

Fire Marshal, four hundred dollars a year.
Fire Marshal.

Messenger of the Board of Aldermen, one hundred dollars
a year.
Messenger Board of Aldermen.

Messenger of the Common Council Board, one hundred
dollars a year.
Messenger Common Council Board.

Port Warden, twenty-five dollars a year.
Port Warden.

SEC. 2. The President of the Board of Street Commissioners shall be paid two thousand dollars a year, for the salaries
of said commissioners, said sum to be divided between the
members of said Board in such manner as they shall appoint.
Salary of Board of Street Commissioners.

The Scaler of Weights and Measures shall be paid five
hundred dollars a year in addition to the fees established by
ordinance.
Scaler Weights and Measures.

The Registrars of Voters shall receive annually, as compensation for the discharge of the duties of their office, so far
as city elections are concerned, the sum of seven hundred
dollars each, the same to be paid in equal installments on the
second Mondays of January and April of each year. Said
compensation to said registrars shall be in full payment for
the discharge of said duties and of any and all expenses
which shall be incurred by said registrars in relation to said
city election, except the printing of the lists of voters, the
expense of which shall be paid by the city.
Registrars of Voters.

There shall be paid to the Associate Judge of the Police
Court three dollars and thirty-four cents per day for every
day that he shall serve in the place of the judge thereof.
Associate Judge of the Police Court.

SEC. 3. The salaries established by the two preceding sections shall be in full for the performance of all official duties
unless otherwise provided by the laws of the state or ordinances of the city; and the city auditor shall draw his order
Salary to be in full for the performance of all duties.

Orders for salaries, when and how drawn. monthly on the city treasurer for the payment of the same (except in case of registrars of voters); and when any office is vacated during or before the end of any month, then for the proper proportional part thereof.

SEC. 4.   There shall be paid,

Fees of City Marshal. To the City Marshal—

> For each day's attendance on the City Court, two dollars and fifty cents;
>
> For summoning a jury, or serving legal process, the same fees allowed to sheriffs for like services;
>
> For warning a city meeting, three dollars;
>
> For warning a meeting of the Court of Common Council, five dollars.

Fees of Messenger of City Court. To the Messenger of the City Court—

> For each day's attendance, two dollars and fifty cents.

Fees of City Attorney. To the City Attorney—

> For each fine collected without suit, fifty cents;
>
> For all moneys collected for debts and paid into the city treasury, two and a half per cent.;
>
> For all fines amounting to or exceeding twenty-five dollars collected by suit, six dollars, in addition to the bill of costs collected;
>
> For all fines less than that sum, four dollars, provided that the amount paid shall not exceed the amount collected;
>
> For appearing by request of the chief of police in a case before the Police Court, the same fees allowed the state's attorney in the Superior Court;
>
> For complaint and attendance before the Police Court the same fees as allowed grand jurors for like services.

Fees of Jurors. To jurors in the City Court, one dollar and fifty cents per day, and travel as allowed jurors in the Superior Court.

No office rent to be paid. SEC. 5.   No sum shall be paid by any city officer for rent of office, unless such office shall have been hired by the direction of the Court of Common Council.

Officer not to contract indebtedness against the city for clerk hire. SEC. 6.   No officer of the city who has a stated salary for his services shall contract any indebtedness against the city for extra services of any kind or for clerk hire or shall have power to make the city liable for any such services or clerk hire without previous authority or direction from the Court of Common Council.

CHAPTER XVII.

MISFEASANCE IN OFFICE.

Members of council and city officers prohibited from certain acts. Inquiry, how instituted.

Citizen may make charges. Hearing, how proceeded with.

Be it ordained by the Court of Common Council of the City of Hartford:

SECTION 1. Any member of either branch of the Court of Common Council who shall bargain for, exact, or receive from any person, or corporation, any fee, compensation, or reward of any kind, for drawing any petition, or remonstrance to the Court of Common Council, or any committee thereof, or for acting as counsel, attorney, or agent, for such person or corporation, in the Court of Common Council, or before any committee thereof; or for any advice given, services rendered, or acts done, in connection with any petition, vote, resolution, or ordinance, or any other business coming before said court, or who shall be guilty of any other misfeasance in office, or any corruption, shall be expelled from office. *Members of the common council prohibited to do certain acts.* *Shall on conviction be expelled from office.*

SEC. 2. Any other officer of the city who shall bargain for, exact, or receive any fee, compensation, or reward of any kind, for any official act, or for refraining from any official act, or who shall be guilty of any other misdemeanor in office, or corruption, shall be removed from office. *City officers guilty of any misdemeanor to be removed from office.*

SEC. 3. Whenever either branch of the Court of Common Council shall receive a statement from any member thereof, or a written communication, verified by oath, from any citizen, charging any member of such branch with corruption or *Charges of corruption, or misfeasance, how made.*

misfeasance in office, the matter shall be immediately referred

Communication, how proceeded with.

to a committee of three members of said branch, and such committee shall immediately investigate the truth of the

Expulsion from office.

charge, and report the facts, and if said charge shall be found to be true, said branch shall proceed forthwith, by vote, to expel the offending member from office.

Charges may be preferred by any citizen.

SEC. 4.   Any citizen may prefer a charge against any city officer for corruption or misfeasance in office; such charge shall be in writing over the signature of the person making

Charge, how made and to whom directed.

the same, and verified by oath, and shall be directed to the recorder of the City Court, and served as civil process of said court.   Said judge may hear such witnesses as shall be produced by the complainant and respondent, and may hear

Judge may hear and give judgment thereon.

counsel, and give judgment according to the facts, and certify such judgment to the mayor.   The mayor, upon receiving

Mayor shall remove offender from office, when.

from the judge of the City Court a certificate that any city officer has been guilty of corruption or misfeasance in office, shall forthwith issue his order removing such officer from office, and such officer shall thereby be removed from office.

What exempted from ordinance.

SEC. 5.   Nothing in this ordinance shall prevent any officer from receiving such compensation from the city as is provided by law, or either branch of the Court of Common Council from expelling any member of such branch for such cause as they may deem just.

CHAPTER XVIII.

PUBLIC CARRIAGES.

Be it ordained by the Court of Common Council of the City of Hartford :

SECTION 1. Every hack, omnibus, cab, chariot, coach, barouche, express or baggage wagon, or any other vehicle, whether on wheels or runners (except horse cars), and drawn or propelled by animal power, which shall be used in the City of Hartford for the conveyance of persons or baggage for hire from place to place within said city, shall be deemed a public carriage within the meaning of this ordinance, and no vehicle as aforesaid shall carry or transport passengers or baggage for hire as aforesaid, nor shall any person or persons solicit or receive passengers or baggage to be carried or transported as aforesaid, unless duly licensed according to the provisions of this ordinance. *What shall be deemed public carriages.* *Soliciting or carrying passengers or baggage in city prohibited unless by license.*

SEC. 2. The mayor of the city shall, upon due application, issue a license in writing to the owner of any suitable vehicle, or such suitable driver as such owner may elect, to use the same in the transportation and carriage of passengers or baggage, or passengers and baggage from place to place within said city for hire, classifying such vehicle and designating its use in such license. And all licenses issued under the provisions of this chapter shall expire on the first day of June next succeeding their date, and may be sooner revoked by *Mayor may issue licenses.* *What license shall specify.*

the mayor or suspended for such time as he may think proper in his discretion for any improper conduct of the licensee acting thereunder, or any violation by him of the provisions of this chapter.

Every license so granted shall, before it becomes of any effect, be recorded by the city clerk in a book to be kept by him for such purpose, and the clerk shall receive from the

applicant twenty-five cents for recording the same, and every revocation or suspension by the mayor of any license granted shall be by the city clerk, upon notice to be given by the mayor, entered against the record of such license.

The mayor may, when requested, grant licenses auxiliary to each license so granted to suitable persons to act as substitutes in case such driver or person licensed shall be absent or unable to act, which shall be recorded as aforesaid, and such

persons so licensed as substitutes, when so acting, shall have the same rights and perform the same duties, and be subject to the same provisions and penalties as the principal.

SEC. 3. The mayor shall have the power of granting licenses for a shorter period of time, to be designated in such license, to owners or drivers of vehicles as aforesaid for the purpose of using said vehicles for the conveyance of passengers while some public occasion may require an unusual amount of travel, which shall be subject to the same provisions and penalties as apply to regular licenses, and every person not a resident of this city who shall be licensed as

aforesaid, shall pay therefor the sum of ten dollars for each ordinary hack, coach, carriage, or vehicle, and the sum of twenty dollars for each omnibus or other vehicle designed for and capable of carrying more than eight persons.

If such hack, omnibus, or other vehicle shall be owned by any person or persons not resident of this city, then the sum named in this section shall be paid for such license, though the person licensed be a resident of said city.

SEC. 4. Every person so licensed when soliciting passengers or baggage shall wear upon his hat or cap a distinctive badge indicating the number of his license, and also a corresponding number shall be placed in some conspicuous place upon the carriage which he drives. Vehicle, how numbered.

SEC. 5. It shall be the duty of every person so licensed to carry either passengers or baggage or both, to obtain proper cards, on each of which shall be plainly printed the name of the person to whom the license was issued, the number of the license and the fare or prices for carrying passengers or baggage, or both, according to such license as established by this ordinance, and it shall be the duty of every such driver whenever he shall accept or contract to accept any person or persons as passengers to be transported for hire within this city, to furnish and deliver to each of such persons so accepted or contracted with, one of said cards bearing his number so printed, and whenever any driver or person licensed to carry baggage for hire shall accept, receive, or bargain to receive any trunk, valise, or other article of baggage to be by him transported within said city, he shall furnish and deliver to such person so contracted with, a card as aforesaid, and each driver of baggage shall, at the time of delivering such card, write plainly and legibly thereon the article or articles which he has so received, and every driver or person so licensed who shall neglect to so deliver such card, or to endorse such article or articles so received thereon, shall forfeit and pay a fine of not less than five nor more than fifteen dollars to the City of Hartford for the use of the city treasury for each and every offence.

Every driver licensed and acting shall obtain card. Cards, how printed. Driver shall deliver one to each passenger on contracting to receive him. Baggage driver shall also deliver card so printed. Driver shall also write thereon articles received. Penalty.

SEC. 6. Every driver of passengers or passengers and baggage so licensed shall be held at all reasonable times to accommodate those who may apply to him for carriage, and no vehicle so licensed shall, while engaged so as to be unable to receive and transport passengers, remain standing upon any of the public stands established by this ordinance, or at any railroad or steamboat depot in this city, and no driver so licensed shall refuse or neglect to receive and transport, or neglect or refuse to contract to receive and transport any person, or neglect or refuse, to go to any point or place within the city, and there receive and transport, with ordinary baggage, any person from such point or place to any other point

Driver shall accommodate persons applying for carriage at all times. Vehicle when engaged prohibited from standing on public stand, or at railroad or steamboat depot. Driver shall receive passengers applying when on public stand or at railroad or steamboat depot.

or place within the city when so standing and applied to as aforesaid.

SEC. 7.　No public carriages for the conveyance of passengers shall stand at any place in said city waiting for employment except west of the west gate on the north side of the state house yard, and north of the gate on the west side of

the state house yard, the north side of the south park, so called, and on the south side of Main street near the corner of Ann street, and in such order and manner as the chief of police may prescribe.

No truck, wagon, dray, or vehicle which shall be used in the city for the conveyance of baggage, goods, wares, merchandise, produce, wood, or any thing whatever for hire or

for the sale thereof, shall stand for such purpose in any place on Main and State streets, around and near said state house yard, except on the south side thereof, and in such order and manner as the chief of police shall direct and prescribe.

SEC. 8.　No driver so licensed, while at a public stand or at any railroad station or steamboat wharf waiting to be employed or soliciting passengers, or while any public carriage is in his charge at any public place, shall use any profane, abusive, boisterous, or indecorous language, or utter loud cries or calls, or scuffle, or crowd about, or interfere with any other driver or porter with whom any passenger may be negotiating for the transportation of himself or baggage, nor

violate any of the rules and regulations made by any of the railroad or steamboat companies occupying stations or

wharves in this city; and all baggage delivered or taken away therefrom shall be delivered and taken in such manner as shall be designated by such steamboat or railroad company.

SEC. 9.　Within the following limits, viz: beginning at Connecticut river and running thence westerly on a line with the north line of Pavilion street to the west line of Garden street, thence southerly down Garden street, to the north line of Collins street, thence westerly along Collins street to the west line of Sigourney street, thence southerly down Sigourney street to Summit street, thence through Summit street to the south line of Jefferson street, thence easterly through Jefferson and Wyllys streets to Connecticut river, and including both sides of all said streets, the prices or rates of fare to be taken by and paid to persons licensed to carry passengers and baggage shall be as follows, viz:

For conveying one person to or from any place within said limits to or from any other place in said limits, twenty-five cents, and for each trunk conveyed with one passenger only, within said limits, fifteen cents.

For conveying one person, with ordinary baggage, to or from any point or place within the aforesaid limits to or from any point or place beyond said limits, and within the limits of the city, fifty cents.

For conveying two persons, with ordinary baggage, both going from one place to one other place within the limits of the city, fifty cents; three persons, seventy-five cents, and four persons, one dollar.

Children under four years of age, when carried in company with an adult person, free; and between the ages of four and twelve years, half price.

Between the hours of twelve o'clock at night and six o'clock in the morning, twice the above rates may be charged.

For the use of a public carriage by the hour, one dollar and fifty cents may be charged for the first hour, one dollar for each succeeding hour, and at the same rate for fractions of an hour.

For weddings and parties, three dollars. For funerals, two dollars and fifty cents.

SEC. 10. The charges for the carrying of baggage shall be: *Charges for carrying baggage.* For carrying one trunk from any place in said city to any railroad or steamboat depot or any stage station therein, or from any such railroad or steamboat depot or stage station to any other place therein, twenty-five cents; for any greater number carried at the same time from any one place to the same place, fifteen cents for each extra trunk so carried; for any valise, carpet-bag, band-box, hat-box, bundle or other similar parcel when carried with any trunk from any one place to any other place, five cents; when carried without any trunk or other piece of baggage, or to a different place, fifteen cents; for every extra similar package when carried to the same place, five cents.

Form of card for passengers. SEC. 11. Said cards specified in section five of this ordinance for passengers and baggage shall be in the form following:

PASSENGER & BAGGAGE LICENSE, No.   , C. D., LICENSEE.

LEGAL PASSENGER FARE.

1 passenger to or from any place within the following limits, viz: beginning at Connecticut river and running thence westerly on a line with the north line of Pavilion street to the west line of Garden street, thence southerly down Garden street to the north line of Collins street, thence westerly along Collins street to the west line of Sigourney street, thence southerly down Sigourney street to Summit street, thence through Summit street to the south line of Jefferson street, thence easterly through Jefferson and Wyllys streets to Connecticut river, and including both sides of all said streets, to or from any other place within said limits, ... $ .25

Each trunk carried with one passenger only within said limits, .15
1 passenger with ordinary baggage to or from any place within said limits to or from any place beyond said limits, . . .50
2 persons with ordinary baggage both going from one place to one other place within the limits of the city, ...50
3 persons ditto, ...75
4 persons ditto, ... 1.00

Children under four years of age, in company with an adult, free; and between the ages of four and twelve years, half price.

Fare between 12 o'clock at night and 6 o'clock in the morning, twice the above rates.

Public carriage, first hour, ... 1.50
"   "   each succeeding hour, or fractions thereof, . 1.00
Weddings and parties, ... 3.00
Funerals, ... 2.50

Form of card for baggage. SEC. 12. The form for cards for baggage as specified in section five of this ordinance shall be:

BAGGAGE LICENSE No.   , C. D., LICENSEE.

LEGAL RATES FOR BAGGAGE.

1 trunk from any railroad or steamboat depot or stage station
to any place in city, ...25 cts.
Each extra trunk from same place to same place,   .   .   .15 cts.
Each valise or similar package carried with trunk or other
piece of baggage from any one place to one other place,   . 5 cts.
Carried without trunk or other piece of baggage, or to a different place, ...15 cts.

SEC. 13.   Every person so licensed who shall violate any of the rules or regulations made and published by any of the railroad or steamboat companies in this city, or neglect or refuse to receive and transport, or refuse to contract to receive and transport any person applying to be carried while his vehicle shall be standing on any public stand or at any railroad or steamboat depot in this city, or neglect to transport any person contracted by him to be transported, or shall suffer his vehicle to remain standing on any public stand or at any railroad or steamboat depot while engaged so as to be unable to take or receive persons for carriage, or neglect to wear a badge as aforesaid upon his cap or hat while soliciting passengers or baggage, or neglect to keep a number corresponding to his license on the carriage which he drives, or shall charge or receive any greater rates for the carrying of baggage than established herein, or shall use, or deliver to any person received or contracted to be received for carriage, or for baggage, any different form of card than herein provided, shall forfeit and pay a fine of not less than five nor more than fifteen dollars for each offence, and in addition to the penalties herein prescribed for each and every violation of any provision of this chapter, the license issued to the offender may be revoked, and any conviction had for any violation of the provisions of this ordinance shall be deemed a sufficient cause for the revocation of such license.

SEC. 14.   Every person who shall, contrary to the provisions of this ordinance, solicit passengers or baggage to be transported for hire within said city, or engage in carrying or transporting passengers or baggage for hire therein, without

[margin notes:]
Violation of rules made by railroad or steamboat companies, how punished.

Refusal to transport passenger, how punished.

Penalty for suffering vehicle to remain on stand or at stations when engaged.

Various penalties.

License may be revoked in addition.

What a ground for peremptory revocation of license.

Penalty for driving or soliciting passengers or baggage without license.

having first obtained a license therefor as prescribed in this ordinance, shall forfeit and pay to the City of Hartford not less than five nor more than twenty-five dollars for each offence; and every day's continuance to so solicit passengers or baggage, or to drive any vehicle carrying passengers or baggage for hire therein after notice to desist therefrom by any member of the police force of the city, shall be deemed a separate and single offence.

Regulating the transportation of dead bodies in hacks.

SEC. 15. No hack or public carriage, owned or kept for hire, shall be used for transporting the body of any person who shall have died of disease. The owner or keeper of any such hack or carriage, who shall suffer the same to be used for the purpose aforesaid, shall be fined five dollars for each offence.

Chief of police shall report all violations to city attorney.

SEC. 16. It shall be the duty of every policeman to report all violations of this ordinance to the chief of police, and it shall be the duty of the chief to inquire into any and all violations of this chapter that shall come to his knowledge, and report the same to the city attorney for prosecution.

CHAPTER XIX.

MISDEMEANORS.

Committing or aiding acts of nuisance.	Violations of ordinances *de* running at large of cattle, etc.
Violations of ordinances *de* snow and ice.	Violations of hack ordinance.

Be it ordained by the Court of Common Council of the City of Hartford:

Committing or aiding nuisances.

SECTION 1. Any person who shall commit or aid, advise, abet or encourage the committing of any of the acts of nuisances enumerated in the ordinances of the city, shall be deemed guilty of a misdemeanor, and may be prosecuted therefor in the city Police Court, and if such act be a nuisance

of the first class may be fined not exceeding twenty-five dol- Penalty.
lars, if it be of the second class not exceeding fifteen dollars,
if it be of the third class not exceeding five dollars, if it be of
the fourth class one dollar.

SEC. 2.   Any person who shall violate or neglect to comply Violation of snow and ice ordinances.
with the ordinances of the City of Hartford, requiring the
sidewalks to be made safe and convenient by removing snow,
ice and sleet, or by covering the ice with sand or other suitable substance, shall be deemed guilty of a misdemeanor, and
may be prosecuted therefor in the city Police Court, and may
be fined not less than two nor more than twenty dollars for Penalty.
each offence.

SEC. 3.   Any person who shall violate any ordinance of the Violation of ordinance preventing cattle, etc., running at large.
City of Hartford made to prevent the running at large of
cattle, sheep, swine and goats, shall be deemed guilty of a
misdemeanor, and may be prosecuted therefor in the city
Police Court and fined not less than two nor more than Penalty.
twenty dollars.

SEC. 4.   Any person who shall violate any ordinance of the Violation of hack ordinance.
City of Hartford regulating public hacks or carriages, the
charges of hackmen and public drivers, cartmen and truckmen, shall be deemed guilty of a misdemeanor, and may be
prosecuted in the city Police Court and fined not less than Penalty.
two nor more than twenty dollars.

CHAPTER XX.

TAXES.

Be it ordained by the Court of Common Council of the City of Hartford:

Assessors of town *ez-officio* assessors of city.

SECTION 1. The assessors of the town of Hartford for the time being shall be *ex-officio* the assessors of the City of Hartford, and may prepare, annually, within such time as shall be

Assessment list of city, when and how made.

necessary for the use of said city, a city assessment list of the polls and ratable estate within the limits of the city, or may in some suitable manner distinguish or set apart such polls and ratable estate upon the town assessment lists by them prepared, for which service they shall receive such reasonable

Compensation of assessors.

compensation as the Court of Common Council shall allow;

Tax, how laid in case of neglect of town assessors to make list

and the list of city assessments thus prepared or distinguished, or in case of the neglect of the town assessors to perform the above described duty, the assessment list last completed, or next to be completed, by the assessors and board of relief of the town of Hartford, shall be the list according to which the taxes of the City of Hartford shall be laid after the first day of October, A. D. 1870.

Council may appoint a rate maker.

SEC. 2. The Court of Common Council may, at any regular meeting, held on or before the first day of May in each year, appoint, by concurrent vote, a city rate maker,[1] who shall hold his office for the term of one year, and who shall make

Duties.

out and certify a rate bill, setting forth the proportion which each taxable person shall pay according to law, for which

Compensation.

service he shall receive such reasonable compensation as the Court of Common Council shall allow; and the collector of the city, in collecting any tax laid by the Court of Common

---

[1] In case of neglect to appoint rate-maker, see sec. 5, p. 168.

Council, shall have the powers and conform to the regulations *Powers of city collector.* conferred upon and prescribed for the collection of town taxes by the public statutes of the state, after having received from the mayor a warrant[1] for the collection of any such tax, *Mayor may issue tax warrant.* which warrant the mayor is empowered to issue upon application of the collector. And the collector shall be accountable to the mayor in the same manner as collectors of town *Collector accountable to mayor.* taxes, are to the selectmen; and the mayor may also issue his warrant to and thereby require and empower the city mar-*Warrant, how framed and proceeded with.* shal to collect from any negligent collector the sums due from such collector to the city treasury; which warrant may be against the lands, chattels, and body of such collector; and said warrant shall be proceeded with like executions in civil actions.

SEC. 3. The Court of Common Council, at any regular *Council to lay annual taxes at any regular meeting before May first.* meeting thereof, held on or before the first day of May in each year, may lay a tax[2] upon the polls and ratable estate within the city, as the annual tax for the current year, for the purpose of defraying any lawful expense, or paying the principal or interest upon any lawful debt, or discharging any lawful liability of the City of Hartford; and it shall be its duty to lay such taxes annually, at least, upon the proper list, *Duty of council to lay annual tax.* *provided* that taxes authorized by law for any specific purpose, and other than the ordinary annual tax of the city, may be laid at any regular meeting of the Court of Common Council.

---

[1] For form of warrant, see p. 172.
[2] In case of failure to lay an annual tax, see sec. 5, p. 168.

CHAPTER XXI.

REGISTRATION OF BIRTHS AND DEATHS.

Sale of coffins prohibited unless certificate of death is furnished.	Penalty for neglect.
Form of certificate.	Compensation of registrars, and how paid.
Coffin dealers shall make return to registrars weekly.	Registrars shall make return of births to city clerk.
Duties of registrars.	

Be it ordained by the Court of Common Council of the City of Hartford:

Sale of coffins prohibited unless certificate of death be furnished by purchaser.

SECTION 1. No person shall sell and deliver or suffer to be taken from the place of sale or from his custody, any coffin, burial case, or casket, to be used for the burial of any one deceased within the city limits, unless he shall be furnished by the person applying for such coffin with a certificate of death signed by the attending physician of such deceased person, or (in case there was no attending physician) by some other physician or substantial inhabitant residing in said city, and of the form following, viz:

Form of certificate.

I certify, from the best information I can obtain, that   died at No.   street, in the   ward of the City of Hartford, on the   day of   , A. D. 18   , aged   years,   months, and   days. Condition (single, married, or widowed)   ; born in   ; residence at time of death,   ; disease or cause of death,   ; occupation,   ; color,   .

Dated at Hartford this   day of   , A. D. 18   .

Registrar shall furnish blank forms.

And it shall be the duty of the registrar of births, marriages and deaths of the town of Hartford to provide blank forms of such certificate at the expense of the city, and to distribute them, free of cost, to persons wishing to use the same.

Physician refusing to sign certificate, how punished.

SEC. 2. Any physician, or substantial inhabitant, residing in said city, cognizant of the death of any person dying within the city limits who shall refuse, on application, forthwith to fill and sign the certificate of death, prescribed in the foregoing section, shall forfeit and pay a fine of ten dollars.

SEC. 3. Each coffin vender shall return to the said regis- Coffin dealers shall make return to town registrar each week.
trar, on Saturday of each week, all certificates of death that
shall have come into his hands in conformity with the requirements of section one from and including the Saturday of the
preceding week.

SEC. 4. Any coffin vender who violates or neglects to com- Penalty.
ply with any provision of this ordinance, shall forfeit and pay
a fine of ten dollars for each offence, and every person who
shall sell, or furnish for use any coffin, burial case, or casket,
shall be deemed to be a coffin vender within the meaning of
this ordinance.

SEC. 5. Said registrar shall, on the first Wednesday of each Duty of registrar de reports and returns.
month, prepare and file with the city clerk a report of the
deaths occurring during the preceding month, which report
shall exhibit, in a tabular form, for the city, and for its
several wards, the age, sex, color, occupation, civil condition,
and nativity of the deceased; shall embrace in distinct classes
those under one year of age, those from one to five, those
from five to ten, those from ten to twenty, and so on for each
decennial period, shall show the rate per cent. of mortality by
wards, as well as for the whole city, and contain a summary
of the causes of death. On the second Wednesday of January in each year, said registrar shall prepare and file with the
city clerk a report of the deaths which have taken place in
the city and its several wards during the previous year,
showing the age, sex, color, civil condition, occupation, and
nativity of the deceased, the causes of death, and rate per
cent. of mortality, classified in tabular form as above required.
If said registrar shall neglect to file with the city clerk such Penalty in case of neglect of registrar to file report.
monthly report for three days, or such annual report for one
week after the time required to file the same, he shall forfeit and pay a fine of ten dollars for each offence, and if he
shall neglect to file such monthly report for more than three
days, or such annual report for more than one week after the
time required to file the same, he shall forfeit and pay, in
addition to the fine of ten dollars, a fine of three dollars for

Compensation of registrar, and how paid.

each day of such continued neglect. Said registrar shall receive from the city treasury the sum of five dollars for each such monthly, and the sum of ten dollars for each such annual report, and it shall be the duty of the city auditor to draw his order on the city treasurer for such amount, when he shall receive a certificate from the city clerk that such report has been filed.

Registrar shall make and file report of births with city clerk.

SEC. 6. Said registrar shall, on the second Wednesday of January in each year, prepare and file with the city clerk a report of the births which have taken place within the city, and within its several wards during the preceding year, which report shall exhibit in tabular form the rate per cent. of births, both in the city and in the several wards, the number of each sex born during the year, and during each month of the year, the number still-born, the color of all in each class, and the nativity of the parents. Said registrar shall receive for such report the sum of ten dollars, to be paid in the manner provided in the preceding section.

[Revision Adopted.]

AN ORDINANCE

TO CARRY INTO EFFECT THE REVISED ORDINANCES.

Be it ordained by the Court of Common Council of the City of Hartford:

Section 1. The Revised Ordinances reported to this court, January 28, 1884, by the committee of revision, together with this ordinance, shall constitute the General Ordinances of the City of Hartford, and. shall be and become operative on the first day of April, 1884, and shall then, on the first day of April, 1884, together with any ordinances that may be approved between said 28th day of January and 1st day of April be the ordinances of the city, and all other ordinances in force on said 28th day of January shall be thereafter repealed.

Sec. 2. The said repeal shall not impair or affect any rights, privileges, immunities, or offices vested in the City of Hartford, or in any of its officers, or in any person or body corporate, and all matters civil or criminal commenced by virtue of the ordinances repealed as aforesaid, and pending unfinished, may be prosecuted to final effect in the same manner as if this ordinance had not been passed, and no ordinance which has been heretofore repealed shall be revived by the repeal mentioned in this ordinance.

Sec. 3. No offence committed, and no penalty or forfeiture incurred under any of the ordinances hereby repealed, before the time when said repeal shall take effect, shall be affected by said repeal, except that when any penalty, punishment, or forfeiture, shall have been mitigated by the provisions of the revision, such provisions shall be extended to any judgment to be pronounced under said repeal.

SEC. 4. The rules of construction set out in sections 8 and 9, title XXII. of the General Statutes of Connecticut, are hereby made binding upon this revision.

By concurrent action of the Court of Common Council January 28, 1884, the foregoing ordinance was adopted.

Approved, January 29, 1884.

Attest,

JOHN E. HIGGINS,
City Clerk.

APPENDIX.

APPENDIX

APPENDIX.

Votes and Resolutions in force Feb. 1, 1884.

WRITS.

Voted, That all copies of writs served upon the city clerk in suits wherein the city is garnishee, shall be at once shown by him to the city attorney, if the same are lodged when this court is not in session, and the city attorney is authorized to appear for the city, in such suits, whenever he shall deem it necessary.

Passed, October 8, 1855.

CROSSWALKS.

Voted, That the board of street commissioners be and are hereby authorized to lay crosswalks other than those at the intersection of streets, whenever parties interested therein shall furnish material for the same.

Passed, July 23, 1860.

BILLS.

Resolved, That all bills presented to the Court of Common Council for its approval shall be so far itemized as to state in brief what each is for.

- Passed, April 18, 1881.

HORSE RAILWAY COMPANY.

Resolved, That the consent of this Court of Common Council is hereby given to the Hartford and Wethersfield Horse Railway Company, to construct a single or double horse railway from the southern limits of the city of Hartford on the Wethersfield avenue, over and along said avenue

and over and along Main street, in said city, to the north
line of the city, provided that the location of said railroad,
and the mode and manner of its construction, shall be subject to the approval of the highway committee.

Passed, June 28, 1861.

HORSE RAILWAY COMPANY.

Voted, That the Hartford and Wethersfield Horse Railway Company be, and they are hereby authorized and
licensed to lay down a single track of railway, with the
necessary turnouts, from the steamboat dock at the foot of
State street, through State and Asylum streets, Asylum
avenue, Woodland street, Farmington avenue, to its intersection with Asylum street; also through Sigourney street
between Asylum and Farmington avenues; provided, that
said railway company agree to extend and do extend and
lay their track as far west on Asylum avenue as Woodland
street, on or before July 1, 1863, and that the same be laid
under the supervision and to the satisfaction of the highway
committee.

Passed, October 27, 1863.

HARTFORD AND WETHERSFIELD HORSE RAILWAY COMPANY—
RESOLUTION OF LOCATION.

Whereas, By a vote of this court, passed August 10, 1863, the
license previously granted to Hartford and Wethersfield
Horse Railway Company, to lay a single track with necessary turnouts, from the steamboat dock at the foot of State
street, through State and Asylum streets, Asylum avenue,
Woodland street, Farmington avenue, to its intersection
with Asylum street, and also through Sigourney street,
between Asylum and Farmington avenues, was declared
forfeited by reason of the non-fulfillment by said company,
of the condition annexed to said license:

And Whereas, said company, without admitting a legal forfeiture of the prior license, or waiving any vested right
they may have under the same, have agreed to accept cer-

tain terms and conditions in consideration that this court will renew and confirm said license;

Resolved, That the permission and license given to the Hartford and Wethersfield Horse Railway Company, to lay a single track, with the necessary turnouts, from the steamboat dock at the foot of State street through State and Asylum streets, Asylum avenue, Woodland street, Farmington avenue from Woodland street at its intersection with Asylum street, and also through Sigourney street, between Asylum and Farmington avenues be, and the same is hereby renewed and confirmed.

The right to lay down this additional track is under the express proviso and condition to the renewal and confirmation of the location, that the whole work of laying down the track granted by this resolution, shall be done under the direction and to the satisfaction of the highway committee.

This renewal and confirmation is granted under the further express proviso and condition, that the said Hartford and Wethersfield Horse Railway Company agree to lay and extend, and do lay and extend their track from Main street through State street, to the steamboat dock at the foot of State street, and in the construction of said track, pave with stone the roadway for from twelve to eighteen inches, from and outside of each rail, during the present fall.

Also under the further express proviso and condition that the said Hartford and Wethersfield Horse Railway Company, agree to lay, and lay a stone pavement similar to the one to be laid in State street for from twelve to eighteen inches from and outside of each rail of their track in Asylum street, and Asylum avenue, from Main street to the top of Asylum Hill, commencing to lay said pavements the first of August next, and completing the same as soon as practicable and before the first of December, 1864. *Provided*, that during the first week of July next, the mayor and the two senior aldermen for the time being, or a majority of them shall notify said company that in their opinion said pavement has proved so far superior to McAdam's that the public interests require the same to be laid as aforesaid in Asylum street and avenue.

Also, under the further express proviso and condition that
whenever the Court of Common Council shall order any
street in which any track of the Hartford and Wethersfield
Horse Railway Company is or shall be located, to be paved
or repaved, the said company shall at their own expense, and
under the direction and to the satisfaction of the highway
committee, pave that portion of the street so ordered to be
paved or repaved, lying between the rails of their track, and
also that portion of the street lying outside of the rails and
adjacent thereto and extending two feet from and outside of
each rail.

Also, under the further express proviso and condition, that
the said Hartford and Wethersfield Horse Railway Company
shall not hereafter construct or begin to construct any turnout within the limits of the city, without first obtaining
from the highway committee permission and license so to do.

Also, under the further express proviso and condition, that
whenever there shall occur a fall of snow, of sufficient depth
to allow vehicles to pass over the snow on runners, no snow
plow shall be allowed to pass over the several tracks of the
Hartford and Wethersfield Horse Railroad Company, within
the limits of the city, nor shall the said company cause or
allow snow to be removed from their several tracks, without
consent being first obtained of the street commissioner. The
consent for the removal of the snow, for the opening of the
tracks, being refused, the said company, in such cases, is
authorized to use a sufficient number of sleighs to convey
passengers requiring transit over their roads, day by day,
until the cars can be used upon the tracks.

Also, that said company shall not sprinkle salt or any
article of a decomposing nature on their tracks or rails, or
cause or allow the same to be done by any of their agents,
for the purpose of melting the snow; or wash or cause to
be washed, by any of their agents, the said tracks and rails
with brine or pickle, for a like purpose, unless a permit be
granted by said commissioner allowing the same to be done,
and said permit shall only be granted when the use of said

articles shall not be detrimental to vehicles crossing the tracks and rails.

Also, under the further express proviso and condition, that the said Hartford and Wethersfield Horse Railway Company shall keep the whole of their track and the surface of the street within their track, and for two feet adjoining thereto, in good order and complete repair, and that, if upon written notice from the street commissioner, designating any place or places where said track is not in good order and complete repair, and requesting the said company to put the same in good order and complete repair, the said company shall not comply with the request within thirty days from the reception thereof, then the street commissioner shall proceed to put the designated place or places in good order and complete repair at the expense of said company.

Also, under the further express proviso and condition, that said Hartford and Wethersfield Horse Railway Company shall accept this resolution of location, and agree to its several provisions and conditions within ten days from the date of its passage, otherwise it shall be null and void.

Approved, September 15, 1863.

COPY.

At a meeting of the directors of the Hartford and Wethersfield Horse Railway Company, held September 21st, it was

Voted, That the license passed September 14th, 1863, by the Court of Common Council, with its conditions and provisions, be and is hereby accepted by this company.

   Attest, E. L. ELDREDGE, *Secretary.*

Hartford, September 21, 1863.
    To LEVI WOODHOUSE, Esq'r.
      Clerk of Court of Common Council.
Received September 22, 1863.
   Attest, LEVI WOODHOUSE, *City Clerk.*

ASYLUM STREET TURNOUT.

Resolved, That the turnout on Asylum street, west of Ford street, be allowed to remain. *Provided*, that said Hartford and Wethersfield Horse Railway Company shall, as soon as practicable, pave with Belgium or other similar pavement, approved by the highway committee, the whole space between the rails of said turnout and so much of said main track as is parallel to the same; also, a space two feet in width outside of the rails of said turnout and main track; also, the space between said turnout and main track; *and further provided*, that at no time shall more than one car be allowed to stand on said main track or turnout between Ford street and the track of the Hartford and New Haven Railroad Company, unless the same shall be unavoidable.

Passed, October 26, 1863.

RETREAT AVENUE AND PARK STREET LINES.

Resolved, That permission is hereby given to the Hartford and Wethersfield Horse Railway Company to lay a single track, with necessary turnouts, in the following streets, viz: Either from Main street present track of petitioners at Wyllys street, through Wyllys street, westerly across Main street and Retreat avenue to Retreat avenue, or from Main street present track of petitioners near Park street, in Main street on the west side of South Park to Retreat avenue, in Retreat avenue from Maple avenue to Washington street, across Washington street west from Retreat avenue to Vernon street, in Vernon street, in Broad street, in Park street, in Lafayette street, in Washington street from Lafayette street to Capital avenue, in Capital avenue, in Trinity street, in Ford street, in Pearl street, across Main street, in Central Row to present track on State street, the same to be at such grades and in such parts of said several streets as shall be approved by the street commissioners, and under the supervision of the board; *Provided*, That said tracks be laid, and said railway line be constructed and put in running order from Wyllys street to Broad street, and from State street through Central Row, Pearl, Ford, Trinity and Lafayette streets to Park street, within two years from July 1, 1881; *and further provided*, That the permission granted to lay the tracks through the streets named is, with the agreement on the part of the Hartford and Wethersfield Horse Railway Company, that the provisions of the license granted September 14, 1863, and accepted September 21, 1863, are hereby made a part of, and a condition to, the grants herein made; and also, that said Hartford and Wethersfield Horse Railway Company agree, that in case the Court of Common Council shall hereafter direct and order a change of grade in any of the streets or highways in which the tracks of said company are located, to re-lay said tracks, at their own expense, so as to conform to the grade ordered, under the direction and to the satisfaction of the board of street commissioners.

Passed, June 18, 1881.

ALBANY AVENUE LINE.

Resolved, That permission is hereby granted to the Hartford and Wethersfield Horse Railway Company to lay a single track in Main street and Albany avenue, beginning at a point in Main street within the existing track, near the intersection of the line of Albany avenue produced to said track, thence to Albany avenue, and in Albany avenue from its eastern terminus as far as the line of intersection of the Blue Hills road, so called; the said track to be laid at such grades, and in such parts (laterally) of said streets, and with such necessary turnouts as shall be approved by the board of street commissioners, all of which work shall be under the supervision of said board; *Provided*, That said track shall be laid and said railway be constructed and in running order as far as Vine street on or before July 1, 1885; *Provided also*, That in case a change of grade shall hereafter be made in either the street or avenue above named, the said railway company agree that they will relay their track at their own expense so as to conform to the grade ordered, under and according to the direction and supervision of the board of street commissioners; *and provided further*, That if upon written notice from the board of street commissioners designating any place or places where the said track or the street surface, or a crosswalk, which the said railway company are bound by law to keep in repair, is not in good order and complete repair, and requesting the said company to put the same in good order and complete repair, the said company shall not comply with the request within thirty days from the reception thereof, then the board of street commissioners shall proceed to put the designated place or places in good order and complete repair at the expense of said company.

Passed, May 28, 1883.

HORSE RAILWAY STONE.

Resolved, That the street commissioner be authorized and requested to comply, as far as he can without detriment to public interest, with applications from the Hartford and Wethersfield Horse Railway Company, for the purchase of stone for the purpose of keeping the tracks of said company within the city limits in repair.

Passed, September 14, 1863.

RULES, REGULATIONS AND WATER RATES

MADE BY THE

BOARD OF WATER COMMISSIONERS

OF THE

CITY OF HARTFORD,

In force February 1, 1884.

RULE 1. The regular water rents shall be due and payable at the office of the board of water commissioners semi-annually, on the first day of May and November in each year; and to all rents remaining unpaid ten days after due, there will be added five per cent. for collection, and a further sum of one per cent. will be added on the first day of each month thereafter until paid. *(margin: Water rents, when due and payable. Addition, when made.)*

RULE 2. No abatement of water rent will be allowed by reason of disuse, or diminished use, or vacant premises, unless notice thereof shall have been given at the office of the board at least thirty days before such rent shall be due and payable. *(margin: No abatement of rent unless notice is given.)*

RULE 3. All applications for service-pipe, or for the use of water, must be made in writing at the office by the owner of the premises in the form prescribed, and must state fully and fairly all and several of the various uses to which the water is to be applied. And whenever thereafter any other or further use of the water or additional service-pipe, or plumbing, or fixtures is required, a further application must be made as aforesaid. *Provided*, that the commissioners at their discretion may supply service pipes or water upon the *(margin: Application for service pipe, how made.)*

application of parties other than the owner of the premises, when the expenses of water rents are *paid in advance* or secured to the satisfaction of said commissioners. And

every person who shall use the water without such application, and statement as aforesaid, shall be liable to pay therefor at such extra rates as the commissioners shall fix and determine at their discretion, not exceeding three-fold the regular rates.

RULE 4. No service-pipe will be allowed for premises where the annual water rent therefrom shall be less than five dollars.

RULE 5. Service-pipes will be laid as soon as practicable, upon application; and the commissioners reserve the right in all cases to lay the service-pipe from the street main to the street line, but will charge the applicant for that portion only laid between the sidewalk line and the street line.

RULE 6. All persons supplied with the water will be required to keep the service-pipes, stop-cocks, and all fixtures connected therewith upon their premises, in good repair, and protected from frost, and so arranged and provided with stop and waste-cocks as to allow the pipes to be emptied and kept free of water during all periods of dangerous exposure to the action of frost, whether by night or by day; and must keep the same shut off and free from water whenever the safety of such pipes requires it.

RULE 7. No continuous flow to guard against frost or for any other purposes, will be allowed, except in special cases, by special agreement, as to conditions and rates.

RULE 8. Water used for building purposes will in all cases be chargeable to the respective owners of the buildings. Every builder is required to render at the office of the commissioners, on or before the 10th day of January in each year, a full and true account of all the water used by him for building purposes during the preceding year, with the time, place and quantity for each separate building; and it shall be the duty of such builder to pay for the same; and if so rendered and paid to the satisfaction of the commissioners, such payment shall be a full discharge to the owner of such building.

RULE 9. The regular water rents for the use of private *Rates for certain uses, how determined.* fountains, or jets in hotels, eating-houses, conservatories, or other buildings, will be based upon such use for a period equivalent to four hours each day, during four months in each year, and no greater use will be allowed except in cases, and at rates specially agreed upon with the commissioners. And the commissioners reserve in all cases the right to suspend or discontinue the use of water for all such fountains and jets, whenever the public interest requires it.

RULE 10. The regular water rents for street, sidewalk or *Rates for sprinkling, how determined.* garden sprinkling, will be based upon such use, only for dust laying or sprinkling purposes, fairly applied; and any excessive or unreasonable use thereof for these or other purposes, is prohibited.

RULE 11. Whenever two or more several parties or fami- *When supply may be withheld.* lies are supplied with water from the same service-pipe, the failure of any one of said parties to pay the water rent when due, or to comply with the published rules or regulations of the commissioners, shall authorize the commissioners to withhold all supply from such a service-pipe, without liability in damages to either of the other parties.

RULE 12. All supplies of water will be furnished, subject *Supply subject to rules of the board.* to the rules and regulations of the board, and it shall be the duty of every person supplied to prevent all unnecessary waste, and to answer at all reasonable times all proper inquiries made by the commissioners or their agents, relative to the quantity, purposes and manner in which the water is used upon their premises. And the commissioners and their agents shall have right, at all reasonable times, to enter into any dwelling-house or other premises where the water is supplied, to make such personal examinations of all fixtures, and inquiries as to the use of said water, as they shall deem necessary to a faithful supervision of the same.

RULE 13. The commissioners reserve the right at all *Reserved rights of commissioners.* times to shut off the water for necessary repairs, extensions, or other necessary purposes of the work, for non-payment of water rents, or for neglect or refusal to comply with the rules and regulations of the board. They also reserve the right, in all cases, to test the quantity of water actually supplied to any person or premises, by the application of a meter; and to revise and adjust all contracts made for the use of water, upon the basis of such actual quantity as the application of such test shall disclose.

Arrears of rent and expense of shutting off, etc., to be paid, before water is again turned on. RULE 14. Whenever the water is shut off from any service-pipe for non-payment of rent, or non-compliance with the rules and regulations of the board, the same will not be allowed to flow until the delinquent shall have paid all arrears of rent (if any) and the expense of shutting off and letting on the water as aforesaid.

Water not to be used except on the premises. RULE 15. If any owner, or lessee under him, shall suffer any water to be taken from the premises, for the use of any person or family, not belonging to such premises, without the *special* consent of the commissioners, every such owner shall be liable to pay such sum as the commissioners may assess therefor, at their discretion, not exceeding three-fold the regular rates.

Private hydrants subject to approval. RULE 16. The construction and location of private hydrants and fountains will be subject to the approval of the commissioners, and whenever the waste therefrom becomes a nuisance to adjacent property, the supply will be cut off, until the evil is satisfactorily corrected.

Injuries to pipes, how recovered. RULE 17. All injuries to service-pipes or street mains caused by careless undermining, or by negligent repacking or filling up, of excavations for private drains, sewers, or for other purposes, shall be chargeable to the person so causing such injury, and the expense of repairing the same may be recovered of such person, by the commissioners, in an action of debt, brought upon this section.

Duty of plumbers. RULE. 18. It shall be the duty of each and every plumber to return in writing, to the office of the commissioners, during the first week of each month, all connections or extensions of service-pipe made by him not before returned, giving the location of the premises, the name of the owner or occupant, the character of the work, the number of hydrants, baths, water closets, fountains, hose fixtures, or other fixtures, connected with such works; and on failure thereof every such plumber shall forfeit and pay to said board of water commissioners, for the use of the water department, the sum of five dollars. *Penalty.*

RULE 19. Every person who shall, without special author- *Penalty for connecting with main pipe, without consent.* ity from the commissioners, tap or make any connection with any street main, or service or other distributing pipe connected with the water works, shall upon conviction thereof by the Police Court of said city, be subject to a fine not exceeding thirty dollars, or imprisonment not exceeding thirty days, or such fine and imprisonment both, at the discretion of said court.

RULE 20. If any person except firemen, for the uses of *Penalty for unauthorized use or obstruction of public hydrant.* the Fire Department, shall open any public hydrant, or stopcock, without the consent of the commissioners, or if any person shall place any building material, or other articles or rubbish, in such manner as to hinder or obstruct the free access to any such hydrant or stop-cock, every person so offending shall, upon conviction thereof by the Police Court, be subject to a fine not exceeding thirty dollars, or by imprisonment not exceeding thirty days, or both, at the discretion of said Police Court.

RULE 21. If any person shall disturb or meddle with, or *Penalty for meddling with or corrupting water, or injuring water works.* fish in the waters of the reservoirs, or the water of the Connecticut river, near the inlet of the pumping engine, or shall cast any substance, filth, or impurities therein, or shall trespass upon the embankments of the reservoir, or travel over the same, or any part of the public grounds connected therewith, except upon the graveled or paved walks, or shall wilfully injure any pipe or fixtures connected with the water works, every person so offending shall, upon conviction thereof by the Police Court, be subject to a fine not exceeding thirty dollars, or imprisonment not exceeding thirty days, or to such fine and imprisonment both, at the discretion of said court.

RULE 22. It shall be the duty of the police of the City of *Duties of police de water works.* Hartford to exercise a vigilant supervision over the use of the water, to prevent all unnecessary profusion of flow and waste; and for this purpose they shall have the right of free access, at all proper times, to any premises where the water is used, and shall report all cases of waste and of profuse and excessive use, which shall come to their knowledge, to the Commissioners. They shall also report to the Police Court, for prosecution, all violations of the regulations and laws of the board, or of the city, relating to the water works of this city, which comes within the jurisdiction of said Police Court.

RATES.

The annual rates for the use of water after the first day of May, 1862, shall be as follows, viz:

FAMILIES.

1. For each tenement with inside fixtures, occupied by one family not exceeding five persons, . . $5 00

   For each additional person, ... 1 00

2. For each tenement occupied by two families or any number of separate occupants, not exceeding five persons, ... 7 00

   Exceeding five and not exceeding eight persons, . 8 00

   For each additional person, ... 1 00

3. For each tenement occupied by three families or any number of separate occupants, not exceeding ten persons, ... 10 00

   For any greater number of families or separate occupants, such rate as may be fixed by the commissioners.

4. Families not exceeding eight persons, supplied from outside hydrants, ... 5 00

   For each additional person, ... 50

   Or less at the discretion of the commissioners.

BOARDING HOUSES.

5. Minimum rate, ... $6 00
and a greater rate according to size and occupancy.

HOTELS.

6. Minimum rate, ... 25 00
and a greater rate according to size and occupancy.

STORES.

7. For stores and offices, from . . $1 00 to 10 00

RESTAURANTS.

8. For restaurants, etc., . . . 5 00 to 30 00

MARKETS.

9. For markets, ... 5 00 to 15 00

WATER CLOSETS.

10. For each family not exceeding eight persons, . 3 00
For every four additional persons, . . . 1 00
For each additional water closet, . . . 1 00
For hotels, stores, and all other buildings,
from . . . . $1 00 to 8 00

BATHING TUBS.

11. For each family not exceeding eight persons, . 1 00
For hotels, barber shops, and all other
buildings, from . . . . . $1 00 to 6 00

URINALS.

12. For each used by one family, . . . 1 00
For hotels, stores, and all other buildings,
from . . . . . $1 00 to 6 00

FOUNTAINS AND JETS.

13. For each 100 gallons discharged, . . 3 cents

HOSE.

14. For street, sidewalk, or garden sprinkling, such
rate as shall be determined by the commissioners, not less than . . . $3 00

LIVERY AND PRIVATE STABLES.

15. For each horse, including water for washing carriages, ... $2 00

    For each cow, ... 1 00

    Truckmen's stables, for each horse, . . . 1 50

BAKERIES.

16. Not exceeding 500 barrels of flour per annum, . 5 00

    For each additional barrel used, . . . 1 cent

BUILDING PURPOS .

17. For each 1,000 brick, ... 4 cents

    For each perch of stone, . . . $1\frac{1}{2}$ cents

    For each 100 yards of plastering, . 20 cents

STEAM ENGINES.

18. Working not over 12 hours per day, for each horse-power used, ... $6 00

19. For any manufacturing, mechanical, chemical, or other purpose, not specified in the foregoing tariff, such rate as shall be determined by the commissioners, but in no case less, for each 100 gallons, than . . . . . . 1 cent

20. The rates of water for each 100 gallons, where the actual quantity is determined by meter, shall be as follows:

    For any quantity not exceeding 500 gallons per day, per each 100 gallons, . . . 3 cents

    For any quantity exceeding 500 gallons, and not exceeding 1,000 gallons per day, per each 100 gallons, ... $2\frac{1}{2}$ cents

    For any quantity exceeding 1,000 gallons, and not exceeding 2,000 gallons per day, per each 100 gallons, ... 2 cents

    For quantities greater, such rates—not less than 1 cent for each 100 gallons—as shall be fixed by the commissioners.

21. In all cases where water is required for purposes not specified in the foregoing tariff, the rate shall be fixed by the board of water commissioners.

Approved by concurrent vote in Court of Common Council, April 14, 1862.

Attest,

LEVI WOODHOUSE,
City Clerk.

SUPPLEMENTARY RATES.

OFFICES.

Offices supplied from faucet inside the same,	$5 00 to $10 00
Offices supplied from faucet outside the same,	1 00 to 5 00

BARBER SHOPS.

For barber shops with two chairs or less, . . .	5 00
For barber shops with more than two chairs the rate for each chair, ...	2 00

PHOTOGRAPHERS.

For photographers, according to quantity of water used, ...	$10 00 to 50 00

MANUFACTORIES, WORKSHOPS, ETC.

For manufactories or workshops employing not more than ten persons, water for drinking and washing purposes, supplied from faucet inside the same, .	5 00
For each additional person employed, ...	50
For manufactories or workshops employing not more than ten persons, water for drinking and washing purposes supplied from faucet outside the same, .	3 00
For each additional person employed, . . .	30

GREENHOUSES AND GRAPERIES.

Minimum rate, ... $5 00

And a greater rate, according to size and quantity of
water used.

BARS AND BEER SALOONS.

According to size and quantity of water used, $5 00 to 30 00

Additional for hydrostatic beer pumps,   .   5 00 to 15 00

SODA FOUNTAINS.

According to quantity of water used, .   . $3 00 to 10 00

SLOP SINKS.

For families or other buildings, each,   .   .   1 00

STEAM-HEATING APPARATUS.

For dwellings and other buildings rate according to
quantity of water used.

PASTURE HYDRANTS.

Rated according to quantity of water used and wasted,
not less than, ...   5 00

ADDENDA.

AN ACT

CONCERNING COMMON PLEAS AND DISTRICT COURTS.

When any judge of the Court of Common Pleas or District Court shall be unable to hold any term of the court, he or the clerk of the court shall notify the chief justice, or, in case of his inability, the senior judge of the Supreme Court of Errors, who shall thereupon assign and direct any judge of the Court of Common Pleas, or District Court, or any judge, assistant judge, or recorder of any city court or police court, of the County, to hold it. The judge of any police court may hold a court of common pleas in the same manner as a judge of a city court is authorized so to do by Section 18, Chapter II, Title IV, of the General Statutes.

Judge unable to hold term, substitute, how designated. P. A., 1877. p. 224.

Judge of Police Court may hold Court of Common Pleas.

ORDINANCES.

CONCERNING TELEGRAPH AND TELEPHONE POLES.

Be it ordained by the Court of Common Council of the City of Hartford:

SECTION 1. All telegraph and telephone companies owning, erecting, maintaining, or using poles located in the highways and public places of the city, shall, on and after May 1, 1884,

Signs to be placed on telegraph and telephone poles.

cause to be placed and kept on each pole owned, erected, maintained, or used by them, a legible and durable sign, which shall state thereon the name of the company owning, erecting, maintaining, or using said pole, and which shall also bear thereon, in letters plainly visible, the words, "Post no Bills."

Penalty.

SEC. 2. Any company which shall neglect to comply with the provisions of the foregoing section, shall forfeit and pay to the City of Hartford a penalty of five dollars for each day of such neglect.

Penalty.

SEC. 3. Any person who shall wilfully injure, deface, or remove such sign from any telegraph or telephone pole, shall be deemed guilty of a misdemeanor, and upon conviction thereof, shall pay a fine of five dollars for each offence.

Approved, January 29, 1884.

CONCERNING THE AUDITING OF THE ACCOUNTS OF THE CITY COLLECTOR.

Be it ordained by the Court of Common Council of the City of Hartford:

That Section 7 of Chapter III, of the Revised Ordinances of the city, adopted January 28, 1884, be and the same hereby is amended by striking out the word "last" before "business" in the second line thereof, and substituting therefor the word "first," so that said section as amended shall read as follows:

Accounts of City Collector, when audited.

SECTION 7. Said committee of ways and means shall, at least twice in each year, to-wit: on the first business days of April and October, examine and audit the accounts of the city collector, and report the result of such examination to the Court of Common Council.

Approved, February 26, 1884.

CONCERNING THE CLERK OF THE POLICE COURT.

Be it ordained by the Court of Common Council of the City of Hartford:

SECTION 1. The clerk of the Police Court shall hereafter quarterly, on the tenth days of January, April, July and October in each year, render a detailed account to the ways and means committee of the Court of Common Council, of all the receipts and expenditures of said Police Court for the quarter ending on the first of said months, and thereupon pay over to the city treasurer such sum as may be due from him to the city upon said account. The ways and means committee shall audit said account, comparing the same with the books and papers of said clerk, and submit said account with the result of their audit endorsed thereon to the Court of Common Council.

SEC. 2. The provisions of existing ordinances, and of the revision adopted January 28, 1884, which provide that said clerk shall annually, on the first day of July, account with the city auditor for said receipts and expenditures, are hereby repealed.

Approved, February 26, 1884.

CONCERNING THE BURIAL OF DEAD ANIMALS.

Be it ordained by the Court of Common Council of the City of Hartford:

Any person owning, keeping or having the care or custody of any animal, who shall suffer or allow its body to lie exposed or unburied in any place in the City of Hartford, for a longer period than twelve hours after its death, shall be deemed guilty of a misdemeanor, and may be punished by a fine of not less than five dollars nor more than ten dollars.

Approved, February 26, 1884.

INDEX.

INDEX.

c